Christian Jacq is one of France's leading Egyptologists. He is the author of the internationally bestselling *Ramses* series, which has been translated into twenty-four languages and sold more than six million copies worldwide. He is also the author of the stand-alone novel *The Black Pharaoh*.

Also by Christian Jacq:

Ramses: The Son of the Light
Ramses: The Temple of a Million Years
Ramses: The Battle of Kadesh
Ramses: The Lady of Abu Simbel
Ramses: Under the Western Acacia
The Black Pharaoh
The Stone of Light: Nefer the Silent
The Living Wisdom of Ancient Egypt

About the translator

Sue Dyson is a prolific author of both fiction and non-fiction, including over thirty novels, both contemporary and historical. She has also translated a wide variety of French fiction.

The Stone of Light

The Wise Woman

Christian Jacq

Translated by Sue Dyson

SIMON & SCHUSTER
A VIACOM COMPANY

First published in France by XO Editions under the title *La Femme Sage*, 2000
First published in Great Britain by Simon & Schuster UK Ltd, 2000
A Viacom company

1 3 5 7 9 10 8 6 4 2

Simon & Schuster UK Ltd
Africa House
64-78 Kingsway
London WC2B 6AH

Simon & Schuster Australia
Sydney

A CIP catalogue record for this book is available
from the British Library

HB ISBN 0-684-86629-3
TPB ISBN 0-684-86630-7

Typeset in Times by SX Composing DTP, Rayleigh, Essex
Printed and bound in Great Britain by the Bath Press, Bath

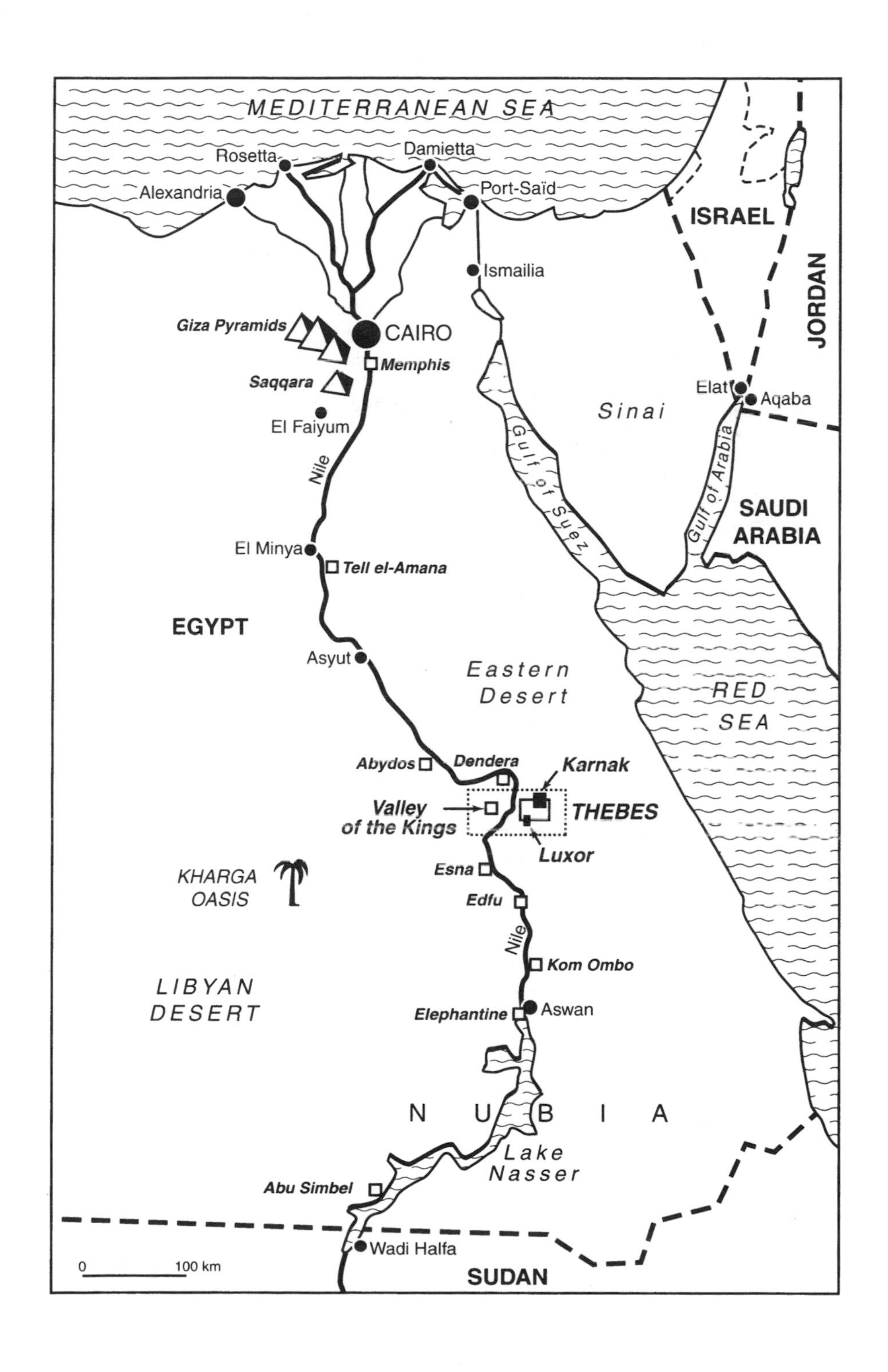

MEDITERRANEAN SEA
Rosetta
Damietta
Alexandria
Port-Saïd
ISRAEL
JORDAN
Ismailia
Giza Pyramids
CAIRO
Memphis
Saqqara
Elat
Aqaba
Sinai
El Faiyum
Gulf of Suez
Gulf of Arabia
Nile
SAUDI ARABIA
El Minya
Tell el-Amana
EGYPT
Asyut
Eastern Desert
RED SEA
Abydos
Dendera
Karnak
Valley of the Kings
THEBES
Luxor
KHARGA OASIS
Esna
Edfu
Nile
Kom Ombo
LIBYAN DESERT
Elephantine
Aswan
N U B I A
Lake Nasser
Abu Simbel
Wadi Halfa
0
100 km
SUDAN

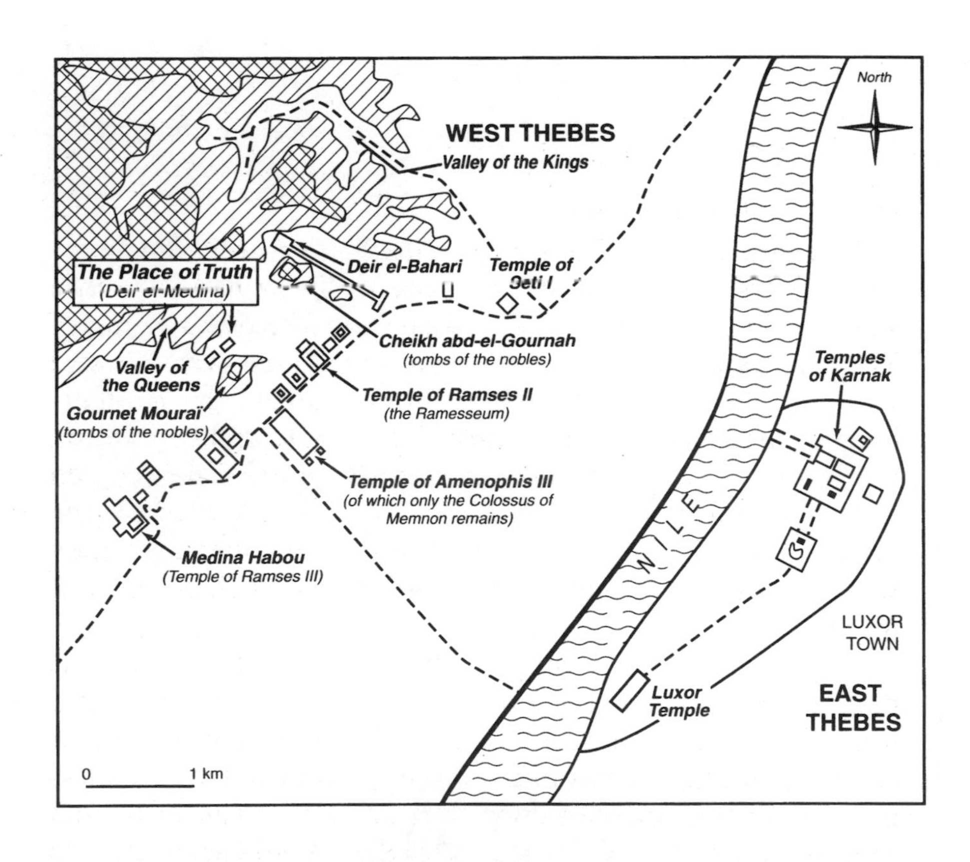

North
WEST THEBES
Valley of the Kings
Deir el-Bahari
Temple of Seti I
The Place of Truth
(Deir el-Medina)
Cheikh abd-el-Gournah
(tombs of the nobles)
Valley of
the Queens
Temples
of Karnak
Temple of Ramses II
(the Ramesseum)
Gournet Mouraï
(tombs of the nobles)
Temple of Amenophis III
(of which only the Colossus of
Memnon remains)
NILE
Medina Habou
(Temple of Ramses III)
LUXOR
TOWN
Luxor
Temple
EAST
THEBES
0
1 km

1

Danger stalked the land.

Since the death of Ramses the Great, after a reign of sixty-seven years, the people of the Place of Truth had been in a state of high anxiety. Their village on the west bank of Thebes was a place of secrets, and no outsider was allowed within its high walls. Its thirty-two craftsmen, the Brotherhood of the Place of Truth, worked devotedly at their calling, which was to construct and decorate royal tombs; the women were both housewives and priestesses of Hathor. Now the villagers wondered what fate had in store for them, for they were entirely dependent on the pharaoh and his first minister, the tjaty.

The seventy days during which the deceased pharaoh was mummified were nearly over. What would the new king, Ramses' son Meneptah, do? Ramses had been both protector and generous benefactor of the Place of Truth and of its craftsmen, allowing them their own courts of law, and ensuring that food and water were delivered every day. Would Meneptah do the same? If not, what would become of them? Nor was that their only worry. The new pharaoh was sixty-five and was said to be authoritarian, stern and just; but would he have the skill to handle the inevitable intrigues and rid himself of those plotters who sought to occupy the Throne of the Living and seize the Two Lands of Upper and Lower Egypt?

The craftsmen were not the only ones worried about the village's safety: Commander Sobek had been losing sleep over it. The Commander was a tall, athletic Nubian whose face was marked by a scar under the left eye. He and his men were responsible for guarding the village – though even he was forbidden to enter it – and now they had to be more vigilant than ever, for the craftsmen's work was vital to Egypt's spiritual survival.

Armed with sword, spear and bow, several times a day Sobek patrolled the area around the village, checking that all was well. To reach the village, an enemy would first have to get past the Five Walls, the small forts along the road to the village. If he succeeded, and reached the village, he would be confronted by high, strong walls and by the keeper of the great gate. There were two keepers, of whom one was on duty from four in the morning until four in the afternoon, the other from four in the afternoon until four in the morning. Sturdy fellows, adept at wielding their heavy cudgels, they prevented outsiders from entering the Place of Truth.

But these ordinary measures were not enough for Sobek. If there were serious riots, a mob might well try to attack the Place of Truth, for it was rumoured that the craftsmen could produce fabulous wealth and even transform barley into gold. He had ordered his men to keep permanent watch on the surrounding hills, the path leading to Ramses the Great's Temple of a Million Years, and the paths to the Valleys of the Kings and the Queens.

Even if Sobek was the village's last defender left alive, he would never desert his post and he would fight to the end. He had come to like the people he protected. Although he was an outsider and did not know the craftsmen's secrets, he nevertheless felt that he was part of their enterprise, and he could no longer imagine living anywhere else. He had failed them once: he would not do so again.

The thought of that failure tormented him. Some time ago,

one of his men had been murdered, and Sobek had received an anonymous letter accusing a member of the Brotherhood, Nefer the Silent, of being the killer. At Nefer's trial his innocence had been proved beyond doubt and he was reinstated in the Brotherhood; indeed, he had just become its new Master.

Sobek had been unable to discover either the real murderer or the author of the letter. As far as the letter was concerned, Sobek did have one trail to follow. He suspected Abry, governor of the west bank of Thebes, of being part of a plot to destroy the Place of Truth – he only hoped Ramses' death wouldn't throw everything into such chaos that he'd be unable to investigate properly. But all his efforts to identify the murderer had led nowhere, and he was haunted by the fear that the killer might be hiding in the heart of the Place of Truth. Perhaps it was one of Nefer's fellow craftsmen, someone who hated and envied him? As he continued his patrol, Sobek considered that possibility for the thousandth time.

The Brotherhood of the Place of Truth were divided into 'port crew' and 'starboard crew' as on a ship; in fact, the village was often compared to a ship. As overseer of the starboard crew, Nefer's duty was to 'create that which radiates light in the place of Light', to draw up plans and to assign work according to each man's skills. His responsibilities had become still heavier since the recent death of Kaha, leader of the port crew. Kaha had been succeeded by his spiritual son, Hay, a less experienced man who was a great admirer of Nefer. Sobek knew that all the craftsmen treated Nefer with great respect. Even crusty old Kenhir, Scribe of the Tomb and the tjaty's representative – Kenhir was responsible for the running of the Brotherhood, which bore the symbolic name of the Great and Noble Tomb of a Million Years to the West of Thebes – had recognized in Nefer someone exceptional, a man of great artistic gifts and incontestable authority.

But, wondered Sobek, could Nefer the Silent fight the forces of darkness that menaced the Place of Truth? Nefer set great store by carrying out his task in accordance with the rule of seclusion followed by his predecessors, and he might have forgotten how cruel and greedy the outside world could be. Would he realize just how grave the danger was and be able to counter it? Would his personal magic be enough to drive away misfortune?

Sobek halted before a recess in the village wall. Within it was a delicate statue of Ma'at, divine ruler of the village, wearing as headdress the magic feather that enabled birds to find their way through the skies. The goddess embodied the Brotherhood's ideal, its aspiration to harmony and rectitude, essential elements of artistic creation. It was said among them that 'to accomplish Ma'at is to do that which God loves'.

Sobek found he was panting. It was hot, and the air was becoming more and more oppressive: the danger was getting closer. To calm himself, he raised his eyes to the pyramid-shaped Peak of the West, the highest of the mountains around Thebes. According to legend, the Brotherhood's first stone-cutters had given the Peak that shape as a Southern echo of the Northern pyramids.

Like everyone else, Sobek knew the sacred peak housed a fearsome female cobra, 'She Who Loves Silence', and that an impenetrable barrier prevented unbelievers from disturbing her tranquillity. The pharaohs had placed their houses of eternity under her protection, and the villagers hoped she would protect them, too.

The towering peak was at the very centre of the temples built by the pharaohs to make shine forth their *ka*, the inexhaustible energy spread throughout the universe. The temples formed a fan-shape round the peak and offered up eternal homage to it. At sunset, when dusk covered the desert, the fields and the Nile, the peak was still in the light, as if the darkness had no hold upon it.

Sobek's musings were suddenly interrupted by a shout. He swung round. One of his men was yelling to him, while another pointed urgently at the nearest of the Five Walls: outside the fort all was commotion.

Sobek raced over to the fort, where he found several guards encircling ten or so terrified donkey-drivers and beating them with sticks. The donkey-drivers had their hands over their heads to protect them from the guards' blows, heedless of the fact that their animals were scattering in all directions.

'Stop!' ordered Sobek. 'These are lay workers for the village.'

At once, the guards stopped laying about them.

'We thought they were suspicious characters, sir,' one of them explained, 'who'd try to force their way through to the village.'

Sobek scowled. His men should have realized that these 'suspicious characters' were simply peasants bringing, today as every day, the water, fish, fresh vegetables, oil and other provisions the Place of Truth needed. The hardiest donkey-drivers were recapturing their donkeys, while the others moaned in pain or voiced their protests. Commander Sobek would have to write a lengthy report to explain the incident and justify his men's actions.

'Take care of the wounded,' he said curtly, 'and have the donkeys unloaded.'

When the procession arrived outside the village, the main gate opened a little way and the craftsmen's wives and children came out to collect the provisions. Before Ramses' death, this had been a time to chatter, to call out, to laugh over nothing and at least give the appearance of haggling over the best meat, fruit or cheese. Now, though, everyone, even the children, was silent. The women took their supplies without a word, then went back into the village to continue their daily work of kneading dough to make bread and beer. In each woman's mind was the question: how much longer would they be able to carry out these simple tasks, the prelude to the happiness of a family meal?

The water-carriers, meanwhile, had taken their loads to the Place of Truth's two reservoirs, one to the north of the village, the other to the south. They emptied the pure water into the reservoirs; the villagers would draw water later and use it to fill the enormous earthenware jars, all made with a pale yellow or dark red glaze, that stood in the narrow streets, sheltered in recesses to keep the precious contents cool. Some were inscribed with the name of Amenhotep I, of Tuthmosis III or of the queen-pharaoh Hatshepsut, and they were a reminder that Egypt's rulers cared about the villagers' wellbeing.

The reservoirs were not the Place of Truth's only source of water. Within the walls, some sixty paces to the north-east of the Temple of Hathor, there was a deep well. It was a true masterpiece, with its vertical walls, hewn at right-angles to each other, its limestone tiles and its superb stairs, which allowed the ritualists to go down and draw water for the ceremonies. But it could not provide enough water for washing, cooking, and cleaning – and cleanliness was central to the craftsmen's lives – so the water deliveries were awaited impatiently each day. Not that there had ever, since the Brotherhood was created, been a shortage; indeed, there had always been enough and more than enough, which was vital for the survival of the little desert community.

A young policeman ran towards Sobek. 'Sir, sir! There's another lot coming!'

'More lay workers?'

'No, sir, soldiers with bows and spears.'

2

In a reception hall in a sumptuous house in Thebes, a man was pacing back and forth. He was powerfully built, with a round face, black hair plastered to his head, dark hazel eyes, thick lips and broad hands and feet. Mehy was not only the treasurer of Thebes, with a matchless understanding of money and of how to manipulate figures, but also the commander of the Theban army and a very popular one – he'd made sure of that by seeing to it that his troops did extremely well out of their service.

Mehy had wealth and high position and they had given him great self-confidence. In addition, he was sure women found him irresistible. Yet he was not content.

He was obsessed by an apparently impossible goal: to get his hands on the immense treasures of the Place of Truth. He had spent a long time spying around the village. He knew that, in the shrine known as the House of Gold, the craftsmen produced work worth incredible sums; and he had even seen the magic Stone of Light, which lit their way when they entered the dark depths of a tomb in the Valley of the Kings. It had been risky, though: he was nearly caught, and had had to kill one of the guards in order to escape.

Mehy turned on his heel and paced back across the room. The whole affair was most unsatisfactory. The anonymous letter to Sobek had not produced the hoped-for result: Nefer the Silent had been acquitted, largely thanks to the meddling of the mysterious Wise Woman of the Place of Truth.

Still, at least Mehy had got away unscathed, and it was obvious that no one had the faintest suspicion who the real murderer was. Indeed, he'd risen in rank and status, becoming treasurer after his father-in-law's death, which he had prudently arranged. That thought gave rise to thoughts of his wife, and Mehy smiled. Serketa was delicious, as charming as a scorpion, and as ambitious, ruthless and greedy as himself.

Greed was not Mehy's only motive. Long ago, he had applied to join the Brotherhood of the Place of Truth, but had been rejected by the Brotherhood's Court of Admissions. The insult still rankled: Mehy had sworn to avenge it. That resolve was coupled with a determination to transform Egypt, bogged down in its ancient traditions and beliefs, into a modern, all-conquering country, its people shaken out of their slumber by new discoveries made by people like his inventor friend Daktair.

Bringing this grand design to fruition meant unearthing the secrets of the Brotherhood, which the pharaohs protected jealously so as to ensure that they alone had access to them. Ramses had been a formidable adversary and Mehy's one attempt to kill him, by sabotaging his chariot, had failed.

Now Ramses was dead, and the Place of Truth must be in upheaval, for it was by no means certain that Meneptah, a man of the North, would be as well disposed towards the Brotherhood as his father had been. Mehy had not been able to obtain precise news from the Northern capital, Pi-Ramses, where Meneptah had been crowned. All he had was rumour. People said that Meneptah was backward-looking, that he had no intention of trying to modernize Egypt, and that he had made up his mind to follow slavishly in Ramses' footsteps. But, Mehy wondered, would supreme power alter his personality?

During this interminable mummification period, anything might happen – the death of Meneptah, for example, and a struggle for the throne. Mehy hoped it wouldn't come to that, because he wasn't ready for it. What he wanted was a king he could manipulate, one who'd strut around the centre of the stage while Mehy lurked in the shadows, wielding the real power. He'd succeeded in his scheme to control the mayor of Thebes like that, and saw no reason why he shouldn't repeat his success at the very highest level. A sluggish, mediocre pharaoh, mired in outmoded beliefs and unable to see the country's unstoppable evolution: such a pharaoh might prove to be his best ally.

Plots and intrigues were likely to grow ever larger and more complex. Certain people would make the most of a transitional reign – which would probably be only brief – so as to prepare themselves better for a new world. In that world, Mehy would play a principal role if he was guardian of the secrets of the Place of Truth.

The Place of Truth . . . To test the craftsmen's morale and their will to resist attacks on their privileges, Mehy had persuaded his ally Abry to send a tax-collector to the village, escorted by a troop of soldiers. If they succeeded in forcing an entry, Mehy would rush through the breach and begin stripping the Brotherhood of every single one of its privileges.

This time, Sobek saw instantly, things were serious. For the first time since taking up his post at the Place of Truth, he found himself confronting soldiers – and experienced, battle-hardened soldiers, at that. They halted in front of the fort and deployed in two ranks.

Sobek thought fast. His men were strong, and he'd trained them well in the use of their cudgels and swords. Most of them were, like himself, Nubian. They regarded him as their tribal chief, and would unquestioningly obey whatever orders he gave.

He walked forward. 'Who's your commanding officer?'

'I am,' replied a middle-aged soldier, visibly impressed by the tall Nubian who spoke to him so informally, 'but the tax-collector is in overall charge.'

A plump scribe, who had been hidden by the soldiers, emerged from their ranks and addressed Sobek in a thin, shrill voice. 'I have been ordered by Governor Abry to count the village animals and calculate the taxes due on them. I can discover no tax declaration for previous years, so obviously retrospective payments will have to be made. As you represent public authority, you must cooperate and help me carry out my orders.'

Sobek gaped. An attack like this was the last thing he'd expected. Pulling himself together, he asked, 'Do you intend to go into the village?'

'Of course. It's essential that I do.'

'My orders are absolutely clear: access to the village is forbidden to anyone who is not a craftsman or a member of his family, and who is not registered as such at my office.'

'Be reasonable,' said the scribe. 'I represent the governor of the west bank of Thebes.'

'The only exceptions to my orders are Pharaoh himself and the tjaty. You are neither.'

'When it's a matter of collecting taxes, you should be more flexible. Go and fetch the Scribe of the Tomb: he'll explain the law to you.'

Sobek thought for a moment. Actually, that wasn't a bad solution – evidently the scribe was unacquainted with Kenhir the Ungracious. He nodded. 'Very well, but the soldiers stay right here. If they try to pass this fort, my men will force them back.'

'I don't care for that tone of voice, Commander Sobek. You have fewer men than I have, and anyway I am in the right.'

'If you take that attitude,' snapped Sobek, 'I shan't go and fetch anyone, let alone the Scribe of the Tomb. I'll deal with this matter myself, here and now.'

The guards grinned and hefted their cudgels. Younger and faster than the soldiers, they were not in the least worried at being outnumbered two or three to one.

'There's no need to lose your temper,' said the scribe hastily. 'After all, we're both here to see that the law is obeyed.'

'My orders are clear, and I must follow them to the letter.'

'Go and fetch the Scribe of the Tomb!'

'Make sure you don't move a muscle while I do.'

The scribe pursed his lips and did not reply. He had been warned that his mission would not be easy, but he had not expected anything like this tall, frightening black man – and if fighting broke out, he might get hurt. No, for the time being, it was better to avoid using force and to discuss the matter with the Scribe of the Tomb, presenting him with an unanswerable case.

Sobek did not hurry back to the village. His men would have no trouble handling these soldiers if need be; but after these others would come, more formidable and in greater numbers.

He found it interesting that the man behind the incursion should be Abry. Their paths had crossed twice before. Abry had first tried to bribe him and then, when the bribe was contemptuously refused, had tried to get him moved to a post well away from the Place of Truth. It had been almost, thought Sobek, as if the governor found him a threat whose sting must be drawn.

Now Abry was attacking for the third time, and this time the attack was aimed not only at Sobek but also, and more directly, at the Place of Truth. Why? Could it be that Sobek's suspicions were right, and Abry was trying to conceal his complicity in the murder of the guard? Did he want to get rid of a potential accuser?

Well, all that would have to wait. The most urgent thing today was this matter of the tax-collector. Avoiding a confrontation might be impossible, because merely warning Kenhir would not be enough. The Scribe of the Tomb must agree to take action.

3

The Scribe of the Tomb was nagging his young servant-girl, Niut the Strong. 'Above all,' he said, 'keep your accursed broom out of my office. I'll clean that room myself.'

The girl simply shrugged. It was the same sermon every morning.

Kenhir was sixty-two, and more ill-tempered than a solitary old book-seller. He had the lumbering gait and corpulent body of a scribe who held high office, but also keen, bright eyes which missed nothing.

Thanks to an infusion of mandragora, Kenhir had overcome the insomnia that had troubled him since Ramses' death. He knew that the village was in danger and that it could not survive under a pharaoh hostile to its way of life. But he continued to fulfil his office as though it must last for all eternity.

The Scribe of the Tomb was always appointed by the tjaty, with the pharaoh's approval, and he carried a heavy burden of work. It was his task to ensure the village's prosperity, to maintain good relations between overseers of the two crews, to pay the workers, to keep the Journal of the Tomb, in which he meticulously recorded absences and the reasons for them, to receive and distribute the raw materials the craftsmen needed, and to carry out the Great Work begun by his predecessors. It was a crushing load, but Kenhir still found time for his favourite pastime: writing.

As the adopted son of the famous Ramose, who before his death had been raised to the great and rare dignity of Scribe of Ma'at, Kenhir had inherited his mentor's beautiful house and office and, above all, his rich library. It contained all the most celebrated authors, whose works Kenhir had copied out in his unattractive and almost illegible handwriting. A lover of epic poetry, he had composed a new celebration of the Battle of Kadesh, which had seen the victory of Ramses over the Hittites and of light over darkness, and he had begun a romantic account of the great pharaohs from Ahmose I to the time of Horemheb. When he eventually retired, Kenhir intended to devote himself to a definitive *Key of Dreams*, the fruit of lengthy research.

His musings were interrupted by Niut, who said, 'A craftsman wants to see you.'

'Can't you see I'm busy? Am I never to be left in peace?'

'Do you want to see him or not?'

'Show him in,' grumbled Kenhir.

Ipuy the Examiner, a sculptor from the starboard crew, was slightly built and rather nervous, but remarkably skilful. He knew how to tame the most recalcitrant rock and never balked at a difficult problem.

'What's the matter?' asked Kenhir.

'I had a bad dream,' said Ipuy. 'I need to consult you.'

'What was the dream?'

'First, the ram-god Khnum appeared to me and said: "My arms protect you. I entrust the stones born in the belly of the mountains to you to build temples." It was frightening.'

'Don't be afraid: that's an excellent omen. Khnum embodies the energy of creation, which builds men and gives craftsmen the ability to harness its power. Then what happened?'

Ipuy shuffled his feet uncomfortably. 'Then . . . Well, it's rather delicate . . .'

'I haven't got time to waste. Either tell me, or go away.'

'I dreamt I was making love with a woman who . . . who wasn't my wife.'

'That's bad. There's only one solution: dive into the cool water of a canal, in the early morning, and you'll find peace again. But tell me, why are you here? Why haven't you gone to work in the Valley of the Kings with the rest of the crew?'

'I took offerings to my father's tomb, and, besides, my wife isn't well.'

Kenhir noted down the two reasons, which were considered valid, in the Journal of the Tomb. Ipuy did not deserve the dreaded epithet 'lazy', which would have carried severe penalties, but all the same his story must be checked. The Scribe of the Tomb had not taken anyone's word since a craftsman had claimed to be absent because of the death of his aunt – who had died for the second time.

The sculptor had hardly left the pillared hall that served as Kenhir's office when tall, slow-moving Didia the carpenter came in.

'The overseer has given me some tasks to do in the workshop,' he explained, 'and he asked me to remind you that the wages are to be paid tomorrow morning.'

Paying the wages: it was a chore that had to be done every twenty-eight days, without fail. The Scribe of the Tomb and the two crew-overseers each received five sacks of spelt and two sacks of barley, while each craftsman was entitled to four sacks of spelt and one of barley. To that were added meat, clothing and sandals. Every ten days, Kenhir supervised the distribution of oil, ointments and perfumes; and each day, every villager was given a generous daily ration of bread and cakes, fish, several sorts of vegetables and fruit, milk and beer. Surpluses enabled them to barter in the market.

'Do you think I don't know my duties?' demanded Kenhir.

'These are worrying times, and many people are wondering if we can rely on getting the usual deliveries.'

'If we couldn't, I'd be the first to let you know. Tomorrow

the wages will be paid as usual, and not one single handful of grain will be missing.'

Reassured, the carpenter withdrew.

Though Kenhir couldn't say so, Didia's fears were well founded. If the new pharaoh, who had never been to the village, gave in to pressure from the Place of Truth's enemies, the deliveries of food and water would stop. The Brotherhood's well and grain-stores would enable them to survive for a little while, but what then?

The Scribe of the Tomb was an unrepentant grumbler about everyone and everything, who complained about his working conditions, and often conjured up the glittering career he could have had in Thebes. But he loved the village more than his own life. He knew he would end his days there as his predecessor and adoptive father had done, because to Kenhir, as to Ramose, the Place of Truth was the very heart of Egypt, the place where each day simple men, with all their good qualities and their faults, did wonderful work in the service of the gods.

The trouble was that he had to get them all to live together without too many quarrels, and that all the problems came back to him, Kenhir.

Niut interrupted him again. 'The housework's finished,' she said. 'I'll get lunch ready.'

'No cucumbers – I can't digest them. And not too many spices on my fish.'

He should long ago have got rid of this little pest who had taken over his home, but she worked remarkably hard and, moreover, put up with his bad temper with steadfast stoicism.

'There's someone else to see you,' she went on.

'Is there no end to this? Tell him to come back later.'

'She says it's serious and urgent.'

'Oh, very well,' said Kenhir crossly.

The visitor was the wife of Pai the Good Bread, a painter in the starboard crew. She looked very distressed.

Kenhir groaned silently and thought, 'Yet another boring tale of domestic troubles. He's deceived her, she wants to bring a complaint against him, and the village court will have to be convened.'

'Th-the gate-keeper h-has delivered a message from C-Commander Sobek,' she stammered. 'It's terrible!'

'Calm down and give me the gist of it.'

'Soldiers, at the first fort. They want to invade the village!'

4

The great gate opened to allow the Scribe of the Tomb through, and Sobek came straight up to him.

'What's happening?' demanded Kenhir.

'We have a problem with a tax-collector. He's brought some soldiers to back him up, and they're waiting for you at the first fort.'

Walking was not Kenhir's strong point. He preferred the calm of his study to sandy pathways. Nevertheless he trudged on valiantly.

At the fort, a very irritated tax-collector pounced on him. 'Are you the Scribe of the Tomb?'

'Yes, I am. What do you want?'

'The village hasn't paid tax on its animals. I must go inside to identify the culprits and set the level of the fines.'

'What animals are you talking about?' asked Kenhir.

'Cows, sheep—'

Kenhir burst out laughing.

'There's nothing funny about the law,' protested the scribe.

'No, the law isn't funny, but you are! If you're as incompetent as you seem, you aren't worthy to hold your office, and I shall write a detailed letter to the tjaty, demanding your dismissal.'

The tax-collector was taken aback. 'I don't understand, I—'

'You should know what you're talking about before you start threatening people. Inside the village, there are only domestic animals: cats, dogs and small monkeys. For reasons of cleanliness, no others are permitted within the walls. You will find donkeys, cattle, sheep and pigs outside the walls, and on the lands belonging to the craftsmen. Naturally, all of them have been declared and the taxes on them paid. So you have disturbed me for no reason at all, and that,' said Kenhir fiercely, 'is something I resent.'

The scribe realized there was nothing to do but beat a hasty retreat and hope Kenhir would not carry out his threat. A complaint from someone as important as the Scribe of the Tomb might destroy his career.

'When shall we finally be rid of insects like that?' grumbled Kenhir, as he watched the defeated tax-collector scurry away. He turned to Sobek and saw, to his surprise, that the commander still looked grim. 'Is something else wrong?' he asked.

'Yes, there's been a rather disturbing incident,' said Sobek.

'What's happened?'

'The objects concerned are in my office.'

When they got there, Sobek handed Kenhir several pieces of limestone covered with astonishing drawings. They were of a cat bringing flowers to a mouse, a female rat dressed in a skirt, an ape in petticoats, a fox playing the double flute, a goat dancing, a crocodile standing up on its tail and playing a mandolin, a swallow climbing a ladder to reach the high branches of a tree where a hippopotamus was enthroned, a rat driving a chariot and firing arrows at an army of rodents armed with shields, and a monkey sitting on a heap of wheat.

The drawings were very funny, but Kenhir was not in the least amused, for he recognized in them the stylized features of several members of the Brotherhood. Still more serious, the rat archer could be none other than Pharaoh fighting his enemies. As for the monkey, he bore several notable points of resemblance to the Scribe of the Tomb!

'Where did these horrors come from?' he demanded.

'They were put here in my absence.'

'They must be destroyed at once.'

'And what if the culprit does it again?'

'That will not happen, believe me.' Kenhir was sure he knew exactly who the guilty party was. The style, the precision of the drawing, the originality, the irreverence: everything bore the hallmark of Paneb the Ardent.

The Scribe of the Tomb had voted to allow Paneb to join the Brotherhood because, even though discipline was not that young man's strong point, the Place of Truth could not exclude such a talent. This time, though, he had gone too far.

There was still a gleam of laughter in Sobek's eyes.

'There is nothing funny about a bad joke like this,' snapped Kenir. 'It's an insult to the seriousness and strictness that must be observed in the Place of Truth.'

'I agree, and I know you'll know how to deal suitably with the offender. But there's a more serious matter. That tax-collector was sent by none other than Abry, and Abry, as you know, tried to bribe me and make me switch my allegiance to him.'

'Do you still suspect him of plotting against us?'

'More than ever.'

Kenhir's face darkened. 'I'd dearly love you to be wrong, but . . .' The two men exchanged speaking glances, then Kenhir went on, 'I've made a few inquiries, and he seems the sort of man who'll do almost anything to further his career. In the current circumstances, that's all I can tell you. We have no way of knowing what the new pharaoh has in mind for him. It might be dismissal, promotion or merely leaving him in his current position.'

Sobek nodded. 'His attempt to use force failed, but he'll try again, I'm sure of it. If he threatens the village's safety again, I'll have to take firm action – whatever his rank is.'

'Don't be too hasty, Commander. Let's wait until Meneptah has made his decision; then we'll have a better idea of what to do. But don't lower your guard while we wait, will you?'

Kenhir took his leave of the big Nubian, and set off back to the village, his mind full of troubling thoughts. Although he would not admit it publicly, for fear of unsettling everyone, he was becoming increasingly anxious. If Meneptah was overthrown, and as a result plotters like Abry became more powerful, the Place of Truth had only a few weeks left.

As he neared the great gate of the village, the lay workers poured out of their workshops and houses and surrounded him, almost threateningly. They were all there – the blacksmith, the butcher, the laundry-men, the pot-maker, the brewer, the cobbler, the weavers, the fishermen, the wood-cutters and the gardeners – and they were all in a state of turmoil.

Their leader, Beken the potter, shoved his way to the front. 'We may be called "Those who Carry",' he said, 'but we have rights. And the most important one is to know what's going to happen to us.'

'Nothing has changed for the moment,' said Kenhir.

'But we've just had a visitation by the army!'

'That was a ridiculous administrative error. It's all settled.'

'Is the village going to be closed?'

'That fear is completely unfounded.'

'You're just saying that to reassure us,' said Beken.

'Wages will be paid tomorrow as usual, and no one has lost his job. What better guarantees do you want?'

Kenhir's confidence calmed the men.

'Let's get back to work,' urged the potter.

The blacksmith's vague protests were lost in the murmurs of the group, which broke up reluctantly as the Scribe of the Tomb entered the village. Almost immediately, he was stopped by Pai the Good Bread's wife, who was visibly upset.

'My little cat's disappeared. I'm sure my neighbour's got him hidden away in her house. She's always envied me him because of his shiny black coat, and now she's stolen him. You must search her house and have her punished.'

'I have other things to worry about and I—'

'If you don't, I shall complain to the village court.'

Kenhir could well imagine how terrifying the quarrel between the two housewives would be, but it was up to him to resolve this kind of problem to maintain harmony between the families. 'Very well,' he sighed. 'Lead the way.'

Fortunately, before they got there the runaway cat jumped down from a roof and landed at his mistress's feet. She picked him up, hugged him and covered him with kisses, at the same time gently scolding him.

Baffled by feminine pettiness, Kenhir hurried away without a word. How many more trials would he be burdened with during this awful day?

'Lunch is ready,' announced Niut the Strong as soon as he arrived home. 'For dessert, you're having a cake stuffed with dates.'

'I hope it will be light.'

'Wait and see.'

Kenhir gave his usual scowl. How dare this little pest show such insolence! One day, he was going to put her in her place. But he had other, much more serious, things to worry about now.

Would Nefer the Silent succeed in completing Ramses' house of eternity in the time allowed, according to the conditions laid down? Nefer was certainly exceptionally gifted, but he had never before undertaken anything on such a tremendous scale, and Kenhir was worried that he might not be able to bring it to a successful conclusion.

And if Nefer failed, that would be the Place of Truth's death sentence.

5

Paneb the Ardent was deliriously happy.

His childhood dream had been fulfilled ten years previously when, aged sixteen, he was accepted into the Brotherhood of the Place of Truth to become an artist. The path had been a taxing one, but Paneb had never been discouraged; he was fed by the fire that burned within him and which nothing and no one could extinguish.

And now, this very day, he had entered paradise: the Valley of the Kings, this jewel amid the desert, sun-crushed and forbidden to unbelievers. Here, protected by the pyramid-shaped Peak of the West, rested the mummies of many illustrious pharaohs, whose souls were reborn each morning in the secrecy of their houses of eternity.

For almost all Egyptians, entering the Great Place was an impossible dream. But he, Paneb, had this good fortune because he had persevered, overcome innumerable obstacles and succeeded in becoming one of the members of the Brotherhood's starboard crew.

No one would have thought, seeing this huge, athletic young man, that his enormous hands could execute extraordinarily fine, precise designs, that power and grace were united within him. But he was still only an apprentice and he had a lot to learn yet – a prospect which filled him with excitement.

His fellow painters and colourists had made him carry to the valley all their cakes of paint, brushes of different types and sizes, and all the rest of the materials they needed for the final work on decorating Ramses' tomb. Paneb didn't mind; the weight seemed as light as a feather to him. He hardly noticed it as he looked around, admiring the high, vertical rock walls of the forbidden valley, where only the sun-baked stone could survive. The ochre cliffs stood out sharply beneath a perfectly blue sky, and at noon the sun left not an inch of shade in this sacred cauldron where the supreme mystery of life and death was played out.

This was the time of day Paneb liked best, for he loved the merciless heat, especially when no breath of wind disturbed the still air. Here, in this silent, peaceful, rocky valley, he felt at home.

'Are you day-dreaming, Paneb?'

The man who asked was Nefer the Silent himself, overseer of the starboard crew and Master of the Brotherhood. He was of average height, slender, with chestnut-coloured hair, grey-green eyes, a high forehead, a serious face and a quiet, calm voice. It had taken him only ten years to become the craftsmen's leader, an office he had not sought.

Paneb and Nefer had met before they were admitted to the Place of Truth, and Paneb had saved the life of Nefer, who would never forget his bravery. By following the path of the sculptors, Nefer had reached a high level in the Brotherhood before being admitted to the House of Gold, where he had become guardian of the secret of the Great Work; now he must transmit and embody it in solid form.

Paneb smiled. 'When I was a boy,' he replied, 'I dreamt of a perfect world, but I soon came up against men. With them there can be no peace: they have to fight all the time, and at the least sign of weakness they trample their opponent underfoot. Today, though, I know that the perfect world of my dream really does exist: here, in this valley where our

Brotherhood creates and adorns houses of eternity for the pharaohs. Man has no place here; we're only passing through, and that is fitting. Only a fiery silence reigns here, and I'm grateful to you for letting me feel it.'

'Don't be. You may be my friend, but I'm the overseer of this crew and I won't do you any favours. I wouldn't have ordered you to come and work in the sacred valley if you weren't good enough.'

So far, all Paneb had done was carry brushes and paints, and guard Ramses' tomb, which he had not been given permission to enter. From Nefer's tone, though, he sensed that the situation was about to change.

'Today's going to be a long, hard day,' Nefer went on. 'We're running short of time, and it's vital that we finish the decoration according to the instructions Ramses left. Ched the Saviour is going to give you some new and extremely important work.'

Ched was the starboard crew's painter, its greatest colourist and the very embodiment of haughtiness. For several years he had altogether ignored Paneb, the better to make him understand that, in Ched's eyes, he did not even exist as an artist. But Paneb had choked back his pride and resentment, for he knew Ched was truly outstanding, a master of his craft, an unequalled talent.

Paneb looked closely at his friend, who had sounded strained. 'You seem to have a lot on your mind, Nefer.'

'For some people, the seventy days of mummification seem a very long time; for us it's very short.'

'I don't understand. Surely all but the very last work on the tomb was finished a long time ago?'

'Most of it was, yes. But it is customary to wait for the king's death before bringing the walls to life, drawing in the last signs and figures, and completing the house of eternity where his body of light will dwell for ever. No mistakes are allowed; we must neither hurry nor waste time.'

'For your first undertaking as Master, destiny has spoilt you! It could have given you a pharaoh much less great than Ramses. But we all have complete confidence in you.'

'Yes,' said Nefer, 'I know. But I also know that the very survival of the Place of Truth hangs in the balance. If Meneptah isn't satisfied with his father's house of eternity, he might decree that the Brotherhood be abolished.'

'What's he like? What do people say about him?'

'Let's get on with our work instead of listening to rumours. If we work as hard and as well as we can, we shouldn't have anything to fear.'

Nefer was thirty-six, a mature man of quiet but compelling authority. By his presence alone, and without ever having to raise his voice, he brought a vital cohesion to the heart of the Brotherhood and motivated the craftsmen to give of their best. No one would have dreamt of questioning his orders, which were always concerned with how to perfect the Brotherhood's work and the harmony of the community. Even Paneb, with his undisciplined nature, recognized Nefer's stature and rejoiced that the Place of Truth had him at its head. With him, neither injustice nor corruption could gain a foothold.

Paneb asked, 'What would you do if Meneptah did decide to abolish the Brotherhood?'

'I'd show him that he was making a tragic mistake and that he'd be putting Egypt's wellbeing in danger.'

'But what if he refused to listen?'

'Then he'd be a tyrant, not a pharaoh, and our whole civilization would rapidly come to an end.'

The crew's three artists, Gau the Precise, Unesh the Jackal and Pai the Good Bread, came over to them, and put down at Paneb's feet a large number of cakes of brightly coloured pigments and little terracotta and copper pots.

'What shall I do with them?' he asked.

'Ched will show you. The sun's baking hot. Shouldn't you

get into the shade?' asked Pai, who found the heat in the valley hard to bear.

'I don't want to catch cold,' said Paneb with a grin.

The three artists headed slowly towards the entrance to the tomb. Even Pai, usually so quick to laugh and joke, was serious today. Like his colleagues, he thought of nothing but the intricate work he must accomplish.

'What about you, Paneb?' asked Nefer. 'What would you do?'

'If words proved useless, I'd take up arms and fight.'

'Against Pharaoh, his security guards and his whole army?'

'Against anyone who tried to destroy the village. It's become my homeland and my soul, even though I didn't exactly get a rousing welcome and my ten years here have been quite tough.'

Nefer smiled. 'Well, it's said we undergo only the ordeals that we deserve and that we can endure. If you go on like this, you'll make me believe your capacity for endurance is truly out of the ordinary.'

'With respect, I sometimes get the impression you're making fun of me.'

'That would be unworthy of my office and—' He broke off as Ched the Saviour came up to them.

Ched had well-groomed hair and a little moustache, a straight nose, thin lips, and pale-grey eyes in which there was sometimes a glint of irony. The glint showed now as he glanced at Paneb and said to the Master, 'Are my artists already at work?'

'They've just gone into the tomb.'

'The deadline's very tight.'

'We can't extend it,' said Nefer. 'So I'm giving you Paneb to help you.'

The painter raised his eyes to the heavens. 'An apprentice who'll have to be taught every single thing!'

'Be a good teacher, then. Come back to me if you need to.' Nefer smiled at them both, then he, too, went off towards the tomb.

Ched picked up what looked like a small red brick and showed it to Paneb. 'Do you know what this is?'

'It's a cake of colour – it can't be used in that hard form.'

The painter seemed devastated. 'It's just as I feared – you can't even see what's right front of you.'

6

It took an immense effort, but Paneb managed not to lose his temper – if Ched had decided to humiliate him, much good would that do!

'Colour,' declared the painter, 'is much more than mere matter. The word "*iun*", "colour", is a synonym for "existence", "skin" and "hair". Thanks to *iun*, a secret life is revealed and the whole of nature is brought to life, from apparently inert matter right up to man, that creature who is so often in a state of turbulence. Have you really looked at the ochre-yellow of the sand, the brilliant green of the palm leaf, the soft green of the fields in spring, the pure blue of the sky, the charming blue of the Nile or the gold of the sun? They have secrets to teach us, but no one pays them any heed. And yet it is Pharaoh in person who brings the colours to the Place of Truth, for he alone knows why and how they give life to the figures the artists draw. Our patron god is Shu, the god of sunlight and air, he who allows creation to set forth its marvels. My calling may make me biased, but I believe nothing in the world is more important than colour.'

Paneb looked with new eyes at the materials laid out before him. Ched had never spoken to him like this before.

'Before painting,' Ched went on, 'you must learn how to make colours. And you'd better be good at it, my lad! Ordinarily, you'd have had several months or even years in which to learn, but not this time. Ramses demanded that his tomb be bursting with life, so we're going to need large quantities of absolutely perfect colours – and quickly, too. I'll show you what to do, and then you must keep on making the colours while I paint. If you get it wrong, you'll hold everyone up, and if we don't get the work done in time you'll be responsible for our failure. Now, pick up those things and follow me.'

'Where are we going?'

'To my workshop.'

In a deep cleft in the side of the valley, Ched had set up planks, trestles and a cauldron. There were at least a hundred pots, cooking-vessels and vases of various sizes, protected by a white sheet stretched between two walls roughly smoothed with copper chisels.

'Sit down on that three-legged stool over there,' Ched told Paneb, 'and listen carefully. Our colours are obtained from minerals, which must be crushed as finely as possible in order to obtain a powder. You mix the powder with water, to which has been added something which not only binds the mixture together but is strongly adhesive. That something – and it's one of the colour-maker's most important secrets – is egg-white. It isn't affected by either hot or cold water, and it gives colours which fill every pore of the stone. Fish glue is another good binding material, and also an excellent adhesive.'

As he spoke, Ched lifted the lids of the pots containing the materials he was describing. He looked like a cook preparing to taste some delicious dishes he had prepared.

'The glue's perfect,' he went on. 'I boiled up extracts of bone, cartilage, tendons and skin, and poured the mixture into a mould where, as it cooled, it turned into a compact mass. Then there's my beautiful resin, mixed with powdered limestone – and just look at this!' He lifted the lid of a little rectangular terracotta cooking-pot. 'Top-quality beeswax, which I use to bind adhesives and which I apply to the painted surface to protect it. Of course, a novice would stick red ochre directly on to plaster, but the use of an adhesive is the mark of good work. And now I'm going to show you the best adhesive of all, my favourite: acacia gum.'

Ched removed the stopper from an alabaster vase. 'Acacia gum guarantees that a painting will last. Time doesn't affect it; it renders material stable and mocks variations in temperature. The word "*seped*", "acacia thorn", also means "to be precise, intelligent", and acacia gum is one of the light-filled powers that enable the sun to give life. One day, perhaps, you will encounter the acacia.'

He fell silent for a few moments, as though he were immersed in very old memories.

'Where was I? Ah yes, the binding materials. Good, now you know the basics. Let's move on to the colours themselves.'

Paneb would never have dreamt that this cold, withdrawn man could show so much passion. His eyes shining, his hands forever gesticulating, Ched seemed happy to open the gates of his universe, and the young man passed through them with delight.

'To obtain black,' Ched went on, 'well, nothing could be easier. You simply collect the finest-grained soot from the sides of the cooking-stoves in the kitchens and the black deposit left on lamps by smoke. Powdered wood charcoal gives a beautiful black, but I also have a store of manganese from Sinai. Be careful with black: its name, "*kem*", "the complete, the totality", signifies that it's the sum total of all colours. When Osiris is black, he embodies all the forces of resurrection.'

'Isn't "*kemet*", "totality", the name of Egypt?'

'Yes, because of the black earth, the silt which contains all the potential elements of life and rebirth. White, which is joy, purity and shining light, you get by crushing local limestone. For grey you mix gypsum with wood charcoal or lampblack, and for brown you add a bit of red to black or else mix red ochre with gypsum. As for the best brown ochre, that comes from the oasis of Dakleh, and I have a small stock of it.'

'What about red?' asked Paneb.

'Ah, red! The colour that frightens as much as it attracts. The red of the desert, of violence, of blood which transmits life, of heavenly fire, of the sail of the ship that carries souls to the afterlife, this red which surrounds doors so that destructive demons may not pass, which lights the eye of Set when he fights against Apophis . . . Your favourite colour, isn't it? You get it by collecting the red ochre that's so abundant in our land; or you can burn yellow ochre, which turns it red. Yellow ochre's abundant, too. You'll find it in oases in the western desert and, in the form of stone, in the hills. I also use yellow arsenic, which, in this mineral form, isn't poisonous. It comes from the East and from small islands in the Red Sea, and it gives the walls a sheen like that of gold, the flesh of the gods.'

On a fragment of limestone, Ched the Saviour drew a delicate butterfly, after dipping his brush into a colour which surprised Paneb.

'Pink,' explained the painter. 'It's made by mixing gypsum with red ochre, and it has the power to convey the grace of a woman or the elegance of a horse. Are you satisfied?'

'No,' replied Paneb. 'You haven't said anything about blue or green.'

Ched looked at him sharply and said, 'Perhaps you aren't quite as stupid as I thought. Some people still think that, to obtain those two colours, which evoke celestial mysteries and the dynamism of life, all you have to do is crush mineral pigments. But that's not how to do it if you want to be a painter in the Place of Truth.'

He went over to the cauldron and lit the fire laid ready beneath it.

'Nature gives us these pigments, and the art of the painter

is to make them effective in the form of colours which remain stable. For blue and green, the process is complex. Watch everything I do and engrave each stage in your memory.'

In a mould, Ched mixed sand, powdered limestone, malachite, azurite, natron and vegetable ashes. 'I'm going to make this mould very, very hot. What you have to do is vary the intensity of the heat by regulating the fire, and through this variation you can obtain different shades of blue, between turquoise and lapis-lazuli. You must also take account of the crushing: the smaller the grains are, the brighter the colour will be. And if you powder and compact the pigments and then heat them a second time, the colour will intensify.'

'What about green?'

'You use the same ingredients as for blue, but in different proportions, increasing the calcium and reducing the copper. Blue makes us think of immaterial things, green of spiritual fecundity. Now, when you've got your coloured powder, you must compress it into cakes, some long, some disc-shaped, and I'll dissolve pieces as I need them. Those are the first steps of our magic, Paneb. If you learn and understand the art well, it will lead you to the heart of our Brotherhood.'

Ched's concentration on the heating process was so intense that it was almost as if he felt its slightest variations – as if he was himself the mould. And the painter showed his apprentice how to go from an intense blue to a diaphanous green.

'Do you feel ready to start creating colours, Paneb?'

'Have I any choice?'

'I need red for this afternoon and blue for tomorrow. I hope we've got enough raw materials, because it isn't certain that the new pharaoh will agree to obtain them for us. And no more coloured pigments means no more painting . . .'

'That's impossible!'

'It's not for you or me to decide, my lad. But I have a feeling that things aren't going in our favour.'

Carefully, Paneb began to stir the pots of glue and acacia gum. 'I'm puzzled,' he said. 'Up to now you've looked down on me, but today you've taught me several of the secrets of your craft. Why this sudden generosity?'

'The overseer told me to teach you, and I'm obeying. But you have no chance of succeeding.'

7

The desert fox was exhausted; its thick, russet tail drooped. Panting, it took refuge in a cleft in the rock, where its pursuers might lose its trail.

But Mehy, at the head of a group of avid hunters, was a much more formidable predator than the little carnivore whose trail he had followed across the desert.

His nerves frayed, angry that he had been unable to find out what the new pharaoh's plans were, Mehy needed to kill. Slaughtering quail and doves was no longer enough, so he had taken his bow and ridden out into the desert to the west of Thebes in the hope of finding more interesting prey.

The fox saw the man enter the narrow tunnel that led to its refuge. The walls were too smooth for it to climb. It looked in every direction, but saw no means of escape.

At a peak of excitement, Mehy drew his bow. Not for nothing had he sweated in the chase in this hostile environment; once again, he had proved stronger than his prey.

The fox could have hurled itself at its attacker, but instead it looked its death full in the face, staring at Mehy with the courage of a creature which knew how to face the inevitable. Faced with those eyes, and the animal's courage, many hunters would have decided not to fire. But Mehy loved killing, and his arrow flew through the burning desert air and pierced his victim's body.

*

'Bring me a drink,' ordered Mehy as soon as he arrived home, 'and take this away.'

He threw down the bloody remains of the fox, which one servant hurriedly picked up while another brought some cool beer.

'Where is my wife?'

'Beside the lake.'

Serketa was lying on cushions in the shade of a pergola. She had covered herself with a fine linen veil as protection from the sun, so as not to have tanned skin like country girls. She was plump, with dyed blonde hair, opulent breasts and faded blue eyes, and was cruel and greedy as her husband.

Mehy grabbed her by the breasts.

'You're hurting me, darling!'

Although her husband was a poor lover, Serketa liked his brutality. His principal qualities were unbounded ambition and greed, and, thanks to his talent for calculation and management, he was making them richer and richer. Serketa had thought about getting rid of Mehy, and was convinced he had considered killing her; but they had preferred to become inseparable accomplices, bound by their crimes and their insatiable thirst for power.

'Good hunting, my sweet?' she asked.

'I enjoyed myself. Any news from the capital?'

'Unfortunately not, but I do have something interesting to tell you.'

Mehy lay down next to his wife. She had all the charm of a scorpion and the magic of a horned viper.

'Our informant,' she went on, 'that marvellous man who is betraying the Brotherhood, has just sent me a letter through our devoted friend Tran-Bel.'

Tran-Bel was a second-rate but compliant crook, with whom the traitor from the Place of Truth was amassing illicit earnings by selling quality furniture under the counter. In order to be able to continue his little deals, Tran-Bel had become the faithful servant of Mehy and his go-between, Serketa, to whom he could refuse nothing.

'Don't keep me waiting, Serketa, or I'll rape you.'

She kissed her husband's knees. 'Why not, my sweet darling? But first listen to this: Master Nefer has serious worries, arising from his inexperience. Ramses' tomb isn't finished, and it's likely that the deadline won't be met.'

'That's wonderful!' said Mehy. 'It means the Brotherhood will be charged with incompetence and its leaders discredited – which is unprecedented. There'll be a huge scandal. Abry will issue an official reprimand, and the supply deliveries will be stopped. We may be about to see the death of the village, Serketa, and be able to get our hands on its secrets more easily than I thought. In choosing this man Nefer as their leader, the craftsmen made a serious mistake.'

Serketa removed her linen veil, but she took care to remain in the shade. Judging by the lust in his eyes, her husband was about show to her just what he was capable of.

Given the urgency of the situation, the starboard crew stopped returning to the village at night, and slept on mats in the open air, close to the tomb.

Nefer thought he had detected a weakness in the rock. He asked the stone-cutters, Fened the Nose, Casa the Rope, Karo the Impatient and Nakht the Powerful, to take soundings, which, fortunately, revealed nothing alarming. So the four men continued their work, trying to make up for lost time.

The leader of the sculptors, Userhat the Lion, and his two assistants, Ipuy the Examiner and Renupe the Jovial, were putting the finishing touches to the royal statues, which were made of of wood and stone, and to the 'answerers', figurines of workers in the afterlife, which would be set out in the king's final dwelling.

The carpenter, Didia the Generous, was finishing the

funerary beds, which Thuty the Learned was covering with gold leaf, while the three artists, Gau the Precise, Unesh the Jackal and Pai the Good Bread were finishing drawing the hieroglyphs containing the vital forms of knowledge that would enable the reborn soul to pass through the gates of the afterlife and travel the beautiful pathways of eternity at will.

And Ched the Saviour painted on, at his own pace, as if he had many months at his disposal. His genius was so dazzling that Nefer was almost ashamed to remind him that the date of the funeral ceremonies was approaching fast.

Fortunately, Paneb had not failed. Enthralled by Ched's revelations, of which he remembered every tiny detail, the young man had worked tirelessly, faithfully repeating what his teacher had done. However, he soon found that, though this method produced excellent results, the quantities were too small. He began to experiment. Still following Ched's basic instructions, he tried using several different pestles so as to vary the fineness of crushing, and he changed the proportion of adhesive to colour. As the painter had stressed, the best binder was indeed acacia gum. He had a few failures, but he learnt a lot from them and he never made the same mistake twice.

When he saw Paneb's first cakes of red, Ched had reacted with a grimace of disgust, but all the same he agreed to use them. Paneb kept his face expressionless, though he wanted to shout for joy. At last, after all the years of patient endurance, he was working with colours. He knew how to make them, and they were good enough to be used by the craftsman charged with bringing the divinities to life on the walls of Ramses' house of eternity! He had done far more than realize his childhood dream. He had entered a world of unlimited riches and he was beginning to learn a language which would, one day, enable allow him to paint in his turn.

Paneb had, though, to rein in his joy when he heated the mixture destined to become blue and green. Although he had strictly followed the ingredients and proportions set out by Ched, he produced only hybrid colours. He had to repeat the process again and again, working all night until he fully understood how to vary the heat of the fire. Here again, he tried new ways of doing things, and the way he found worked best was not quite the same as Ched's.

By the time dawn broke, he had made cakes of bright blue, mid-blue and blue as dark as lapis-lazuli, then cakes of soft and dark green. He would have liked to check their quality, but Ched appeared, looking elegant, shaven and perfumed as if he had just emerged from the bathroom at his home in the village.

'Is my blue ready?'

Paneb handed him the coloured cakes.

'Bring me a terracotta palette and a pot of water.'

Paneb did so.

With a grater, the painter shaved off a few fragments of blue which he dissolved on the palette, pouring out the water drop by drop. Then, using an extremely fine brush, which he barely dipped in the lapis-lazuli blue, on a fragment of limestone he drew one of Pharaoh's crowns, which conferred a celestial dimension to his thoughts.

Paneb was as nervous as he'd been the day when he took the admission test to enter the Brotherhood. If he failed, he knew Ched could not, in these circumstances, give him a second chance. And even Nefer would be obliged to support Ched's judgment.

Interminable seconds rolled by. The painter allowed light to play on the crown and examined it from many different angles.

'There is one serious defect,' he concluded. 'Your cakes of blue are half a handspan longer than the ones I use. The rest are acceptable.'

8

There were four of them, a man and three women, and they stopped in front of Paneb the Ardent.

The man was of average height and build, and looked insignificant, with his little black moustache and his habit of not looking people in the eye. His name was Imuni and he belonged to the port crew. He prided himself on his knowledge of literature, and was forever flattering Kenhir, whom he considered a great author. Paneb had little time for Imuni, and found his behaviour thoroughly irritating.

The women were priestesses of Hathor; they wore short wigs and red dresses with shoulder-straps, and each carried an acacia-wood box. They were all, for different reasons, dear to him.

Uabet the Pure was a small, discreet but determined blonde, and she was his lawful wife. She had made up her mind to be so, and Paneb had been vanquished by the stubbornness of a perfect housewife. She was expecting their first child; her belly was swelling, and her happiness, and the ease of her pregnancy, made her blossom more each day.

Turquoise was a tall, voluptuous redhead, and she was Paneb's mistress. With her he indulged in unbridled games of love, and this burning passion, which had already lasted several years, showed no sign of cooling. Turquoise had vowed never to marry, used herbs and other methods to ensure she never became pregnant, and led the life of a free woman, paying no attention to tittle-tattle. Uabet tolerated the situation, on condition that Paneb never spent the whole night with Turquoise.

The third woman was glowingly beautiful. She was Ubekhet, wife of Nefer the Silent; she had been admitted at the same time as he to the Place of Truth. Slender, lithe, ethereal, with blue eyes and a sweet, melodious voice, she was loved by all the villagers and had become assistant to the mysterious Wise Woman, who had passed on the main body of her secrets to her.

'Where is the Master?' asked Imuni, in the honeyed tones he always used.

'In Ramses' house of eternity,' said Paneb.

'Go and find him.'

'In the first place, I'm not permitted to enter the tomb; and in the second place, it's not for you to give me orders.'

Imuni's dull eyes shone with satisfaction. 'That's where you're wrong. Kenhir has just appointed me Assistant Scribe, and in that capacity, I pass on his orders to the craftsmen. So they must obey me – and that includes you. These three priestesses have brought things for the tomb, and I must give them to no one but Nefer. Go and find him.'

'Are you deaf? I've just told you I'm not allowed to enter the tomb. You'll have to wait until Nefer comes out. This site is run by him and nobody else.'

Annoyed, Imuni scratched his little moustache. 'What work are you doing?'

'Oddly enough, I thought it was none of your business.'

'An Assistant Scribe must be kept informed about everything.'

'Give the boxes to me, and I'll give them to the Master.'

'That's out of the question!' Imuni's eye fell on the cakes of colour Paneb had made, and he looked closely at them. 'What ingredients did you use, and in what quantities?'

'We've got a lot of work to do here. You'd better go back to your office and have a nap.'

A malicious smile twitched Imuni's thin lips. 'I have the impression that not all these colours have been correctly registered. That's fraud, and if you're using the secrets of precious colours for your own profit—'

Paneb seized Imuni round the waist and lifted him off the ground. 'Say that again, runt!' he growled.

'I . . . I'm required to keep detailed records of everything and I—'

'Go on squealing like that and I'll smash you against the rock!'

'Let him go,' ordered Nefer, who, alerted by the sounds of the squabble, had come out of the tomb. He was bare-chested, and wore a calf-length pleated kilt which fastened below his navel; bracelets were clasped round his wrists.

Because it was the Master who demanded it, Paneb obeyed; he sent Imuni rolling in the dust.

Furious, the scribe sprang to his feet. 'Paneb attacked me!'

Nefer looked inquiringly at the three priestesses. None of them supported the accusation, and they were all having difficulty suppressing their laughter.

'The incident is closed,' decided the Master. 'Have you brought me lamp-wicks, Imuni? Or perhaps the priestesses have brought them, while you come empty-handed?'

'Indeed I have not. I've brought my writing-materials and I shall count the wicks, according to regulations.'

'Why isn't Kenhir here?' asked Nefer.

'He's having an attack of gout and he's chosen me as his assistant.'

Ubekhet, Uabet and Turquoise set down their boxes on a flat-topped rock. It was they who had made the precious wicks of twisted linen; each box contained twenty. Imuni counted them, one by one, and noted down the total.

'You may leave now,' said Nefer.

'But I need to know how the wicks will be used.'

'As Assistant Scribe, you play a strictly administrative role. Go back to the village, Imuni; I don't want to have to ask Paneb to escort you.'

The young giant was more than ready to do so. Imuni threw a hate-filled look at the Master but judged it advisable to leave.

Each priestess had also brought a pot of grease made from three derivatives – 'the healthy one', 'the creamy one' and 'the eternal one' – of linseed and sesame oil. Ceremonially, they put them down on the rock, beside the boxes of wicks.

'What about me?' asked Paneb. 'Can I stay?'

'Yes, but we need a pan of water and a huge amount of salt,' replied Ubekhet.

Paneb hurried off to fetch them; luckily, his makeshift workshop had plenty of both.

Turquoise poured salt into the pan, then more and still more, until the water could no longer dissolve it. The three priestesses in turn dipped the linen wicks into the solution several times, and laid them in the sun to dry.

Ubekhet poured some salt water into a jar, Uabet added an equal quantity of sesame oil, and Turquoise shook the jar to mix the water and oil together. After it had settled for a while, the mixture was purified, and the three priestesses sat down facing the Master.

The most delicate part of the operation was beginning. To ensure the wicks would not give off smoke, which would damage the paintings in the tomb, it was necessary to oil and grease them with great skill and care.

Paneb hadn't realized his wife knew such an important secret, and he admired her greatly for it, all the more so since she proved just as skilful as her two companions, who were obviously much more experienced.

Nefer watched attentively, as if the fate of the site depended on these wicks.

'The priestesses know the secret of fire,' he told Paneb, 'and one of my duties is to check their work and reject anything that isn't absolutely perfect. One single bad wick, and the work of the sculptors, artists and painters would be harmed. Usually, the priestesses prepare these wicks in a village workshop and give them to us in the morning, under the watchful eye of the Scribe of the Tomb, when we are working in a dark place. But this time, in view of the urgency, I asked them to complete our supply as quickly as possible, so that we'll have bright light.'

Paneb did not miss a single movement the priestesses made. He was acutely conscious that new treasures were being offered to him at the heart of this valley of miracles, and that the veils that hid the Place of Truth's secrets were being peeled away, one after another.

'Each cup-shaped lamp need three wicks,' Nefer told him, 'and each wick lasts about four hours.'

'How many are used in a tomb?'

'That depends on its size and depth, and on the extent of the work to be carried out. Ordinarily, around thirty wicks a day are enough. But for Ramses' house of eternity I want many more: a hundred and fifty lamps containing four hundred and fifty wicks.'

'A hundred and fifty lamps!' marvelled Paneb. 'That must be magical.'

'Would you like to see that light?' the Master asked him.

9

Paneb was silent for a long moment. He felt as though he were having a wonderful dream, from which he didn't want to awake. Then reality dawned: he had misunderstood the Master's question.

'Would I like to see one of those lamps lit, you mean? Yes, very much.'

'I expressed myself badly,' said Nefer. 'I intended to ask if you feel ready to enter Ramses the Great's house of eternity.'

It wasn't a dream! He, Paneb the Ardent, a peasant's son, a mere apprentice in the starboard crew, had been given permission to enter one of the most secret places in the whole of Egypt!

'Why do you hesitate?' asked Nefer.

'Me, hesitate? I swear to you that my wish to know this marvel isn't tainted by curiosity and that I'm not afraid. But I feel a sort of strange respect, almost a veneration, as if entering the tomb will turn my life upside down again.'

'You're right to feel like that. No one comes back untouched from a universe like this one.'

'Why are you doing me this favour?'

'I've told you before, I'll never do you any favours. Your work has given satisfaction, and now it is opening to you the gates of this site. The whole starboard crew has worked here. It is right and proper that, like the others, you should see the finished work. Come with me.' Nefer set off towards the tomb.

Paneb followed on his heels. Because he had longed to be an artist, because he had refused to settle for anything less, because he had continued to forge his way along his chosen path, refusing to heed those who urged him to choose an ordinary, colourless life, the gates of the Place of Truth had opened to him, and now so too would those of the house of eternity where the great pharaoh Ramses would be resurrected.

At the monumental threshold of the tomb the Master halted and looked about him, as if he were checking the proportions of the great entrance gate hewn into the rock.

Then he turned to Paneb. 'You are about to leave the world of humans and enter the world of the secret Light that gives life to the universe,' he said. 'Don't try to analyse or understand: just watch, with your whole being. See with your heart and feel with your spirit.'

The moment he crossed the threshold, which the texts called the 'first passage of Divine Light', Paneb was dazzled. The lamps arranged at regular intervals gave out a light which was at once soft and clear, turning Ramses' tomb into a world pulsating with life. It had been decorated everywhere with hieroglyphs and carved panels, and the whole was painted with a genius which left Paneb dumb with admiration.

Thanks to his lessons with Kenhir, he could read the texts lining the corridors; they evoked the changes in the sun, corresponding to the phases of resurrection of the royal soul.

The last dwelling of Ramses was nearly two hundred and fifty cubits long. It ran in a straight line into the heart of the rock, until it reached the Hall of Ma'at, the place of the ritual of the Opening of the Mouth, during which the apparently inert mummy came back to life. Then the passage turned sharp right and opened out into the eight-columned sarcophagus chamber which now awaited only the dead king's body of light.

The starboard crew had gathered there. They were all sitting in the posture of scribes, with the exception of Ched the Saviour, who was adding a gold highlight to a portrait of the king making offerings to Osiris.

'You are welcome among us, Paneb,' said Pai the Good Bread with a broad smile. 'Now you really are part of the crew.'

One by one, the spiritual brothers greeted him.

At last consenting to lay down his brush, Ched did the same. 'I thought you'd fail,' he admitted, 'and I had good reason to think so. But, to my astonishment, you've succeeded. This Brotherhood never ceases to amaze me. Don't let it go to your head, though. Your path has only just begun, and I'm not at all sure that even the combined efforts of all the artists will be enough to overcome your ignorance.'

Ched turned to the Master. 'For my part, all is finished. Pharaoh's wishes have been carried out to the letter, and he will live eternally in company with the divinities painted on the walls.'

'The work of the sculptors and stone-cutters is also finished,' said Userhat the Lion, whose powerful torso recalled the proud chest of that wild beast.

Didia the carpenter and Thuty the goldsmith said that they, too, had finished.

'I thank you all for the dedication with which you have worked,' said Nefer. 'Thanks to you, there will be no criticism of the Place of Truth, and Ramses will rest in the shrine he himself designed.'

'Don't thank us,' objected one of the sculptors, Renupe the Jovial. 'You did your duty by organizing the building work and guiding us, and we did ours by following your orders.'

Three times, the crew gave their Master the Brotherhood's ritual salute, with the left hand held away from the body to form a right-angle and the right folded across the chest. Nefer tried not to show how moved he was. He coughed and said,

'Our Brotherhood is a ship, we are a crew, and each of us has a particular role to play, vital for the unity of the whole. Whatever trials may come, we have respected our oath and kept our promises.'

'Was this tomb our last task?' asked Karo the Impatient, folding his short, powerful arms. He was frowning with anxiety, which, with his bushy eyebrows and broken nose, made him look decidedly unattractive.

'I don't know,' said Nefer. 'Some people were probably convinced we wouldn't be able to finish in the allotted time, and their reaction may be violent.'

'Whatever the authorities do,' said Nakht the Powerful, 'even if they decide against us, we must remain united, train young men and pass our secrets on to them.'

'That would be tantamount to rebellion,' objected Gau the Precise. 'We'd be punished very severely.'

Casa the Rope nodded his agreement. 'Our leader is Pharaoh. Anyone who rejects his authority becomes a rebel.'

'Let's not waste time on pointless debates,' advised the Master. 'As soon as Kenhir, Hay and I know Meneptah's wishes, we shall call a meeting of the villagers. There are only three days to the end of the mummification period, and from now on this tomb is to receive the treasures that will surround Ramses' mummy. That's the only reality that counts. Until further orders, you're all on holiday.'

Paneb the Ardent let his gaze wander into the little rooms surrounding the vast burial chamber. During the funeral ceremonies, they would receive a thousand and one precious items to ease the passage of the pharaoh's soul into the afterlife.

Standing at the heart of the empty shrine, Paneb had the feeling that he was experiencing creation at its origin, even before divine thought had made the stars visible. And he could not take his eyes off the extraordinary limestone sarcophagus, which the sculptor had shaped like the mummy of Osiris, the supreme body of resurrection. Inside and out, carved and painted hieroglyphs traced passages from the *Book of Gates*, knowledge of which would allow the resuscitated soul to cross the landscapes of the otherworld in safety.

The sarcophagus had been placed upon a stone bed painted yellow to symbolize the indestructible flesh of the gods. Recognized as having a 'just voice', Ramses would experience his ultimate triumph by becoming associated with their immortality.

Despite the beauty of the masterpiece the craftsmen had created, Paneb felt a strange sensation.

'It's as though it's inert, like an unworked block,' he confided to Nefer.

'Let the Stone be brought, and put out the lamps,' ordered the Master.

Nakht the Powerful and Karo the Impatient laid a stone cube at the head of the sarcophagus, while the other members of the crew plunged the tomb into darkness.

'Light is hidden in matter,' said Nefer. 'It is for us to liberate it so that it can vanquish chaos. Our art is that of magicians who abolish time in order to re-create the first instant from which all forms sprang. The memory of the Light is preserved by the work, not by the individual who carries it out.'

The Master laid his hands on the Stone. For a few minutes, darkness and silence reigned. Then a bright light sprang from the cut surfaces of the Stone and lit up the Hall of Resurrection, whose walls turned gold. The rays were concentrated on the sarcophagus, entering the very heart of the limestone so that every grain of it radiated light.

'The secret name of this sarcophagus is "the Master of Life",' said the Master. 'It has become a new Stone of Light which will maintain this dwelling outside death for ever.'

Guided by the brightness from the Stone, the crew left the tomb. They stood for a long time in deep contemplation under the starry vault of the sky. Then, in silence, they left the Valley of the Kings.

10

Nefer and Paneb had scarcely walked through the village gates when a black dog bounded towards them, jumping up first at the Master, then at Paneb. The dog had a long, powerful head, short, silky fur, a long tail and bright hazel eyes.

Fed and cared for by Ubekhet, who permitted no misbehaviour, Ebony had imposed himself as the village's mascot and master of the canine clan. Even the cats and monkeys of the Place of Truth watched respectfully when he passed by, for they knew he guarded all their territories.

Paneb liked Ebony's energy, Ebony liked the young giant's strength. They often indulged in wild tussles, from which the dog always had to emerge the victor. Paneb was the only person who never got tired, no matter how long they played. Now, the dog gave Paneb's face a thorough licking, then fell into step at his heels.

Paneb had not yet fully emerged from his waking dream. 'Did I really see those things?' he asked Nefer.

'How would I know?'

'The light that entered the sarcophagus came out of the Stone. I've seen that light before, at our Brotherhood's meeting-place. It came from that same Stone, and it passed right through the wooden door of the shrine. No one would talk to me about it, but I know what I saw.'

'Did I say you didn't?'

'You really do deserve your nickname of Silent! Shall I see the Stone again?'

'If its presence is needed.'

'Did you shape it with your hands?'

'Don't credit me with powers I haven't got. The Stone is one of the Brotherhood's essential treasures, passed on from Master to Master in the secrecy of the House of Gold.'

'So your lips are sealed, and all I can do is follow the path that leads to the Stone.'

'Well, that shows you can still think clearly.'

Uabet came rushing up to her husband. She was normally calm and peaceable, yet now she seemed in a terrible state. 'Imuni came to our house to warn me that the Scribe of the Tomb wants to see you urgently.'

'Why?' asked Paneb.

'Imuni wouldn't tell me, but he says it's very serious.'

'It must be a misunderstanding. Don't worry, I'll sort it out straight away.'

Paneb strode off to Kenhir's house, where Niut the Strong was sweeping the front step.

'I believe I'm expected,' he said.

'My employer talks about you a lot,' she said.

'Nicely, I'm sure.'

Niut smiled and went into the house.

The Scribe of the Tomb was taking advantage of a few rare quiet moments to devote himself to his literary work. Seated in a low chair, a papyrus spread out on his knees, Kenhir was writing the history of the foreign campaigns of the great pharaoh Tuthmosis III. He was explaining that the Egyptian army had fought few battles and that its main object had been to find and import exotic plants. The doctors and herbalists at the temple workshops had studied them minutely, and had learnt how to extract from them substances which had medicinal uses. One of these substances was used in the treatment the Wise Woman prescribed for gout, and had greatly eased Kenhir's pain.

Since the Master had promised him that Ramses' tomb would be finished within the timespan laid down, Kenhir had been sleeping better, so he was a little less irritated by his thousand and one daily cares.

Niut showed Paneb into the office.

'You wanted to see me?' asked the young man.

'Ah, there you are at last. What fiend from the desert perverts your work?'

'What do you mean?'

Kenhir rolled up his papyrus. 'I take it you are the author of scandalous drawings representing the king in the form of a rat drawing a bow? Not to mention caricatures of the members of the Brotherhood – and even of me!'

Paneb said calmly, 'Yes, those are mine all right. Didn't you think they were funny?'

'This time, my lad, you've gone too far.'

'I don't see why. Aren't I allowed to amuse myself?'

'Not like that.'

'I didn't show them to anyone. Who told you about them?'

'Commander Sobek. He found them in his office.'

Paneb thought for a moment. 'Well, I don't know how they got there. I left them in the artists' workshop, on a pile of limestone fragments destined for the rubbish heap.'

'And that's exactly where such horrors belong. You may be assured that they'll be utterly destroyed. And you are never to do anything like that again.'

'I can't promise not to. It's my way of relaxing, and it doesn't do anybody any harm.'

'Outrageous drawings like that are intolerable. They're an insult to our Brotherhood and its work!'

'If we can't laugh at ourselves and our faults, how can we be worthy of the work that must be done? Even the great sages wrote stories poking fun at human failings.'

'Perhaps, perhaps,' said Kenhir impatiently. 'But I cannot overlook your offence, and I shall be obliged to call you before the village court.'

'Because of my drawings? That won't stand up in court!'

'One of us has seen your caricatures, considers them irreverent and has decided to bring a complaint against you.'

'Who?'

Kenhir seemed annoyed. 'Imuni, my Assistant Scribe.'

'Why did you give that little runt such an important job? He should have remained a second-rate artist in the port crew.'

'First, he knows his craft well. Second, he makes me an efficient assistant – whether or not he is pleasant is of no importance. Lastly, I do not have to justify my decisions to you. You're in serious trouble.'

Paneb looked downcast.

'At least you see the error of your ways. When you're before the court, try to repent and so earn its lenience.'

Paneb bowed his head low, and went out. Kenhir was pleased to see that at least the young man no longer behaved like a mad bull at the least provocation. With maturity, he was at last learning to control his tremendous energy.

Paneb went home, where he found Uabet waiting anxiously for him.

'What are you accused of?' she asked.

'Don't worry, it's nothing serious.'

'But Imuni said that—'

'Is it true that he lives in the little house in the western district, next door to the house of the port crew's senior artist?'

'Yes, but—'

'Prepare me a good lunch: I'm starving and I shan't be gone long.'

Uabet clutched her husband's arm. 'Don't do anything rash, I beg of you!'

'I'm only going to clear up a misunderstanding.'

Imuni was preparing the accusation against Paneb when Paneb forced open his door by ramming it with his shoulder.

'Get out of my house immediately!' yelped the Assistant Scribe.

Paneb took him by the shoulders and lifted him off the ground, so that his weaselly face was exactly on a level with his own.

'So you're planning to lodge a complaint against me because of my caricatures, are you?'

'It's . . . it's my duty to do so!'

'Who showed them to you?'

'I shan't tell you.'

'You went into the workshop that belongs to the artists of the starboard crew, you searched it and you found my drawings. That's the truth, isn't it?'

'I carry out my work as I think best.'

'I shall accuse you of theft, Imuni, and drag you before the village court. And we both know you'll be found guilty.'

The scribe paled. 'You wouldn't dare! You—'

'Forget all about my drawings, little man, or else your reputation will be destroyed and you'll be expelled from the Place of Truth. Well, what about it?'

The scribe didn't have to think for long. What Paneb said was all too true.

'All right, I agree. The affair is closed.'

Paneb set the scribe roughly back on his feet. 'If you ever do anything like that again,' he warned him, 'I'll squash you into pulp.'

11

With the exception of Paneb the Ardent, who never got tired or ill, the artisans always went to consult the Wise Woman and her assistant, Ubekhet, at the end of a period of hard work like that on Ramses' tomb. The craftsmen set great store by the Master's wife, and some of them considered her, too, a true sorceress.

Using substances extracted from the bark, twigs and leaves of the willow,* Ubekhet could cure pain and stiffness. First, though, as a precaution she always examined each man throroughly, taking his pulses to hear the different voices of the heart and find out if the energies were circulating correctly in the various channels that criss-crossed his body. If in any doubt, she took account of the quality of the blood, whose major role was to link together the vital forces.

She was concerned about Gau the Precise. When she had placed her hands on the nape of his neck, his belly and legs, Ubekhet had detected a serious weakness of the liver, that essential organ whose ailments could cause severe problems. So she prepared a remedy composed of lotus flowers, figs, powdered jujube wood, juniper berries, sweet beer, milk and terebinth resin; filtered after standing overnight and mixed with dew, the potion would improve Gau's condition. In

* These substances form the basis of our modern aspirin.

addition, he must drink a great deal of chicory infusion to improve the functioning of his bladder.

For Fened the Nose, who had an abscess forming in the small of his back, Ubekhet prescribed a decoction based on lupins; an abscess was easy to cure.

As she was putting away in a wooden chest the papyri she had consulted during the day, the Wise Woman handed her another, rolled and bearing a seal of dried mud.

'I have no more to teach you,' said the old woman, smoothing her cloud of fine white hair. 'All that remains is for you to consult this old text from the time of the pyramids, the better to combat serious illnesses. Remember that an illness is unleashed by a dark and destructive force, and medicines alone will not be enough to overcome it. You must remove this harmful force and reduce it to nothing, otherwise it will move around inside the body and gnaw at it, often without the patient realizing. You must not rely simply upon symptoms; your task is to track down the energy disturbances before they cause incurable damage. At every moment, opposing forces run through the human body, which is not an independent entity but is linked to the earth as it is to the heavens.'

The Wise Woman broke the seal and unrolled the papyrus. 'I have taken my predecessor's teachings and added my own observations after checking several times that they were well-founded. Be wary of theories and concentrate on only one thing, curing your patients – even if you don't always understand how you've done it.'

The writing on the papyrus was fine and easily readable.

'The human body is a place of mystery,' the Wise Woman went on. 'In it a daily battle takes place between harmonious powers and their opposites, which try ceaselessly to corrupt and destroy. These destructive powers are disease-causing breaths which enter the organism in a thousand and one ways to immobilize it, render it inert and kill it. The majority of harmful agents are found in food; when putrefaction occurs, in the intestines, they try to spread into the vessels to cause inflammations, which make the organs age rapidly. The first key to health is therefore drainage, the removal of internal obstructions and the good functioning of the digestive system. I have perfected a preparation with precise dosages which you will find in the papyrus. The second key consists of maintaining in good condition the conduits and channels through which blood, lymph and the other forms of vital energy pass. Some are visible under the skin; together, they form a network similar to the weave of a piece of cloth, thanks to which vitality is transmitted, as long as they remain supple. As soon as they harden, the fluids no longer circulate correctly. The third and last key is the good working of what we call "the heart", that is, the energy centre of the being from which all the channels radiate out. You must constantly refine your powers of perception to hear its messages.'

Tired, the Wise Woman lay down on a mat. 'We must rise before dawn. Good night, Ubekhet.'

The Wise Woman and Ubekhet neared the summit of the Peak of the West as night was ending, and the snakes were going back to their holes. The old woman had abandoned her walking-stick at the beginning of the climb and was walking on steadily. At the summit, hollowed into the rock, there was a little shrine.

The birth of the dawn was accompanied by a light wind and, little by little, the Temple of a Million Years emerged from the shadows. Soon, the blue of the Nile and the green of the fields shimmered in the rays of the reborn sun. At the moment when the peak burst into the light, the Wise Woman raised her hands towards it in prayer.

'Goddess of silence, you who have guided me all through my life, guide my disciple who is climbing towards you. May she rest in your hand by night and by day. Come to her when she invokes you; be generous and show her the greatness of your power.'

The Wise Woman gestured to the shrine. 'Make your offerings,' she ordered.

Ubekhet laid on the ground the lotus-flower she had used to decorate her hair, her necklace and her bracelets.

'Prepare yourself for the supreme battle. The goddess who knows the secrets dispenses life or death.'

Suddenly a female royal cobra with eyes of flame darted out of the shrine. Its size stunned the young woman. Anger swelled its throat and it would not hesitate long before biting.

'Dance, Ubekhet, dance as the goddess is dancing!'

Although almost paralysed with fear, Ubekhet somehow managed to follow the movements of the terrifying snake. She swayed from left to right, then right to left, and backwards and forwards, following the rhythm of the cobra, which seemed disorientated.

'When she attacks,' said the Wise Woman softly, 'bend towards me, but do not take your eyes off her.'

Ubekhet had gone beyond terror. Fascinated by the goddess's beauty, she began to understand her intentions. And when the goddess struck suddenly at her throat, Ubekhet did as the Wise Woman had said.

Ubekhet avoided being bitten, but her dress was spattered with the venom spat by the cobra, whose failure unleashed its fury.

'She will attack twice more,' warned the Wise Woman.

The reptile was still undulating, and Ubekhet imitated it. And twice more it tried in vain to sink its fangs into her flesh.

'Now,' said the Wise Woman, 'exert control. Kiss her on the head.'

As if it were running out of strength, the cobra was moving less vigorously. And, almost imperceptibly, it shrank back when Ubekhet advanced towards it. Although terrified, she stared deep into the reptile's eyes and set her lips to the top of its head. Surprised, it did not draw back.

'We fear your sternness,' said the Wise Woman, 'but we hope for your gentleness. She who worships you is worthy of your trust. Open her spirit and permit her to cure those whom she cares for in your name.'

The snake was scarcely moving now.

'Take in the power of the goddess, Ubekhet. Let it enter your heart.'

A second time, Nefer's wife kissed the snake, which seemed almost docile.

'Seal your communion with a third and final kiss.'

Ubekhet obeyed.

'Now step back quickly!' ordered the Wise Woman.

If Ubekhet had not been alert, she would have been bitten when the snake suddenly struck. But she ducked away, and received nothing but a final jet of venom.

'The secret fire has been passed on to you,' said the Wise Woman.

Slowly, the cobra withdrew into its shrine.

'Take off your dress and purify yourself with the dew from the stones at the summit.'

The Wise Woman handed Ubekhet a white robe; it would have served as her winding-sheet had she not emerged victorious from the test. Then she sat down on a rock and watched while Ubekhet cleansed herself.

'I am going away, and you shall succeed me. No, don't protest! My life has been long, very long – over a hundred years – and it is good that it is ending. Remember that plants were born from the tears and blood of the gods, and that that is how they acquired the power to heal. Everything lives, but there are wandering souls and destructive demons who will never allow peace to reign on this earth. Thanks to your knowledge, you will constantly battle against them. God creates that which is above and that which is below, and he will come to you in a breath of Light. You do not have to believe in it, but know it and experience it.'

'Why don't you want to live any longer?'

'I am near the end of my hundred and tenth year. Even if my spirit is intact, my body is worn out. Its channels are hardened, the energy no longer flows around them, and the best medicine will not give them back their youth. Your training is complete, and you will watch with love over the village. Before leaving, I must pass on to you my last secret. The body ages and degrades in an unalterable way, but thought can remain alive and strong if you know how to regenerate it. Pass your hand over the stone of the peak, and you will gather the dew that gave birth to the stars. It is with this that the sky goddess washes the face of the sun, just before its birth; it is this which Pharaoh drinks each morning, in the secrecy of the temple, when he makes offering to Ma'at. When tiredness seizes your soul, climb to the summit, worship the goddess of silence and drink the stone's dew. In that way, your thoughts will never grow old.'

'I still have so many questions to ask you.'

'For you, Ubekhet, the time has come to give answers. Each day, people will come to question you and demand that you cure their ailments. You will be the mother of the Brotherhood, and all the villagers will be your children.'

The young woman would have liked to protest and reject this great burden, which was going to weigh heavy on her shoulders, but the intense brightness of the morning dazzled her.

The Wise Woman got to her feet. 'Come, let us go down,' she said. 'Walk in front of me.'

Ubekhet started off down the narrow path, unsure how fast she should go. Should she walk at her own speed, or slowly so that the old lady would not have to hurry? Worried, she paused after the first winding stretch of the path, and turned round.

The Wise Woman had vanished.

Ubekhet hurried back towards the summit, looking for the woman who had given her everything, but she found no trace of her. The Wise Woman had melted away, no doubt disappearing into a cave where she would breathe her last, in the silence of the Peak of the West.

Ubekhet tried to collect her scattered thoughts. She had spent wondrous hours in the company of the Wise Woman, who had opened many paths to her, paths she must now extend, alone. Slowly, step by step, she descended to the village, savouring the last moments of quietness before becoming the Wise Woman of the Place of Truth.

12

The craftsman had taken the ferry across to the eastern bank and as usual he had spoken to no one, apart from exchanging the occasional casual greeting. At this hour of the morning, the peasants were dozing, sitting on the boxes of fresh vegetables they were taking to the great market on the riverbank. Lost in the laughing crowd, all of whom were delighted at the prospect of indulging in the pleasures of haggling and trading, the man from the starboard crew headed for Tran-Bel's warehouse.

True, he was betraying his Brotherhood and his oath, but he had plenty of good reasons for doing so. First, it was he who should have been named as crew leader and not Nefer the Silent; second, he too deserved to make his fortune; and lastly, caught in a trap, he had no choice but to collaborate. The more contact he had with those who paid for the precious information he gathered, the more his scruples evaporated. The Place of Truth had certainly taught him a great deal, transforming a second-rate workman into an elite craftsman, but he preferred to forget that and think only of his future, while taking the precautions necessary to avoid being caught. Skilful and sly enough to do so, he no longer doubted that he would succeed.

In his office at the back of the warehouse Tran-Bel was waiting. He was dressed in an over-long kilt and over-sized shirt, and wore his black hair plastered to his round head.

'I have excellent news,' he said. 'Our beautiful furniture is selling very well, and I am building up a nice little hoard for you. But you must think up some new ideas.'

'I'm working on it.'

Suddenly, the trader's face froze. 'Ah, here's the person you must meet. I'll get out of the way. When you've finished, come and see me in the workshop.'

Serketa was unrecognizable in a heavy black wig, which hid her forehead, and painstaking make-up. She gave the craftsman a triumphant smile. 'Anything new?'

'Ramses' tomb is ready for the funeral ceremonies. We underestimated Nefer. He organized the crew surprisingly well and has earned everyone's respect. If he goes on like this, he'll become a great Master.'

'Not as great as you would have been.'

'That's true, but he'll soon gain the experience he lacks. By succeeding in this affair, he's enabled the Place of Truth to fulfil its obligations and justify its usefulness to the new pharaoh.'

'You were supposed to slow the work down,' said Serketa angrily.

'I tried, but it was impossible. The whole crew was working in the tomb, everyone had a specific task to accomplish, and Nefer was always there, watching carefully.'

'Let's hope Meneptah looks unfavourably upon him. Is there anything else?'

The craftsman hesitated. He was determined not to give up all the Brotherhood's secrets without a substantial reward.

Like a viper ready to strike, Serketa sensed that the man was trying to hide vital information from her. 'Don't play games with me,' she hissed, 'and don't forget I hold your fate in my hands. What have you found out?'

'What are you offering in exchange?'

'If you do what I want, I'll make you rich, with a house,

fields and a herd of milk cows. Servants will see to your comfort, and you'll drink good wine every day.'

'Promises like that are easy to make,' sneered the craftsman.

Serketa showed him a small papyrus. 'This title deed is in your name – is that nothing but a promise?'

The man tried to seize it, but she snatched it away.

'Gently now! Before becoming owner of your little paradise, you still have work to do. Now, what have you found out?'

The traitor gave in. 'Nefer has the power to handle the Stone of Light.'

'What's that?' demanded Serketa.

'All I know is that it comes from the House of Gold. It gives out an intense light and gives life to everything it touches. But only the Master, who has to undergo a special initiation ritual, can use it.'

Serketa's eyes shone with excitement. So Mehy was right: the Place of Truth did indeed possess prodigious treasures.

'Where is this Stone hidden?'

'I don't know.'

'Then find out!'

'That'll be very difficult – in fact, impossible.'

'Then you can forget your little earthly paradise.'

'You must understand that we make up a community and that we respect a rule of life. If I transgress that rule, I'll be expelled from the village and then you won't have anyone to find things out for you.'

Despite her anger, Serketa had to admit he was right.

'I'd love to know this secret myself,' he went on. 'But only patience and extreme caution will enable me to ferret it out so that you can profit from it.'

As Ubekhet passed through the great gate in the village wall, a large ibis with dazzlingly white feathers began circling in the sky above her head.

A little girl immediately alerted the villagers; and Kenhir forgot the pain of his gout and hurried as best he could to greet the Master's wife.

'The Wise Woman has vanished into the mountain, hasn't she?' he asked.

'She believed her life had run its course.'

'She followed tradition. According to the archives, her predecessors also chose to let themselves be absorbed by the peak. And you, Ubekhet, are the new mother of the village. May you protect it and cure it of all the ills that may afflict it.'

The little girl who had seen the ibis was clutching a small black and white cat.

'He isn't well,' she told Ubekhet. 'Can you make him better?' And, indeed, it looked half dead.

Ubekhet laid her hand its head. After a few moments a gentle heat spread through it, and it began to purr, softly at first, then more loudly. Then, annoyed, it put out its claws. The little girl loosened her grip and it jumped out of her arms.

'Come here, you naughty cat!' she shouted, running after it.

'She who has left has passed on her powers to you, Ubekhet,' observed Kenhir. 'We are fortunate. Do you want to live in her house?'

'No,' she said. 'Let it be given to the youngest mother in the village. I shall set up my workshop and see my patients in my own house.'

'In that case, you can also have the house next door. That arrangement is provided for in the village's finances, and you'll need more space. The office of Wise Woman is sufficiently important for its holder to carry it out in the best of conditions. Speaking of which, my gout is still painful. May I come and see you first thing tomorrow morning?'

Ubekhet looked at him closely. 'Your colour's all right. Very well, come tomorrow morning.'

Watched with wonder and a little fear by the villagers, she

walked home. Everyone already knew that the new Wise Woman had taken up her post.

Nefer was waiting for her in the doorway. He took her tenderly in his arms, and she laid her head on his shoulder.

'She used up her last strength to pass on her knowledge to me, and then she left us.'

'No, Ubekhet, for as long as the Peak of the West looks down upon the Place of Truth, she will be there within it. And you will make her thoughts and her life live.'

'But what if I can't do it?'

'She chose you, but you no longer have a choice.'

Arm in arm, they recalled their arrival in the village, ten years earlier, when they had been so afraid of being rejected. How brief had been the almost carefree time of apprenticeship; how restful it had been to know that others were taking care of the lofty responsibilities and that all you had to do to make progress was follow their instructions.

But now Nefer was Master and crew-leader, and Ubekhet was the Wise Woman. Their tastes and preferences no longer mattered. The only things that did were the wellbeing of the Brotherhood and the harmony of the work. And they knew that, in order to preserve her healing power, Ubekhet would bear no children: instead, the villagers, no matter what their age, would become her cherished sons and daughters. This sacrifice was immense, and only their love allowed them to make it.

At the main gate of the village there was a sudden disturbance. People had gathered, jostling each other, shouting. Fearing another attempt at force, Nefer ran to the gate. When they saw him the villagers parted to allow him through. Lying on the ground was Uputy, the village's messenger, who had been almost suffocated in the crush.

Nefer picked him up.

The unfortunate man fought for breath. 'I . . . I bring important news . . . A letter bearing Pharaoh's seal.'

The entire village gathered around the Master as he broke the seal and read the brief letter, which had been sent from Pharaoh's palace at Pi-Ramses.

'The royal ship and its escort left the capital several days ago,' he announced. 'King Meneptah is coming to Thebes to direct his father's funeral rites, and he will honour the Place of Truth with his presence.'

13

Never before had the village buzzed with such activity. Everyone set to with brooms, brushes and dusters to clean it from top to bottom and make the Place of Truth as spick and span as possible. The lay workers were also hard at work, and the Scribe of the Tomb had even called upon housewives, who although they already had a lot of work to do, took on all kinds of extra tasks, including the preparation of food. The priestesses of Hathor, meanwhile, made themselves look as beautiful as possible to welcome the pharaoh.

The gatekeeper didn't know whether he was coming or going. He was lost in the middle of a veritable free-for-all – though in fact things were not nearly as disorderly as they seemed. Turquoise had been put in charge of co-ordinating this vast operation, and she allowed no one to stand around chatting.

Two craftsmen from the port crew complained of neck pains which meant they couldn't, alas, use a broom. But Ubekhet applied a balm which soon eased the pain, allowing them to work after all. Even Ched the Saviour, who was not at all enthusiastic, had bowed to the discipline.

When Turquoise arrived at Paneb's house, she saw that the front step was immaculate. Because of her pregnancy, Uabet the Pure had been excused from the most strenuous work, but she had given every room in the house a thorough cleaning, leaving not one particle of dust.

'Where's Paneb?' asked Turquoise.

'He's finished the work he was allotted – as you should know – so he's gone for a swim in the Nile.'

'At a time like this? He's crazy!'

Uabet was overcome. 'I tried to reason with him – but when he wants to work off some energy . . .'

'Pharaoh will be here this afternoon. We should be thinking about getting ourselves ready and putting on our festival clothes. What a scandal there'd be, if Paneb wasn't back in time.'

'I warned him, but he didn't even listen to me.'

'Do you want me to tell the Master?'

'I think you must.'

The annual Nile flood was beginning.

A flood which the specialists, after studying the information provided by the river-gauges, announced was going to be excellent, perhaps even exceptional. There could be no better omen for the new pharaoh, the husband of Egypt and the guarantor of the fecundity of the cultivated lands.

The river water was turning red, and for several days would be undrinkable. Strong currents churned it up, whirlpools forming near the little islands.

This was the time when Paneb most loved to dive into the turbulent waters, swim to the eastern bank and then back again. Nothing was more fun than dodging the traps set by the raging tide. He wasn't afraid of the river's whims, for he sensed them, moved with the current and knew how to avoid its snares. But the exercise was not for novices, who would have stood no chance of survival.

When he reached the western shore again, scarcely out of breath, Paneb was hailed by three young men aged around twenty. The look in their eyes was far from friendly.

'You think you're really strong, don't you?' said a sturdy, red-haired youth.

'Come on, lads, I'm not asking anything of you. Just ignore me.'

'I can swim better than you. How about a wager?'

'I haven't got time.'

'That's funny. I told my friends here you're just a coward.'

Paneb sighed. 'Well, what's the wager?'

'A race across the river and back. If you lose, you owe us three sacks of barley; if you win, we'll let you leave without teaching you a lesson.'

'That seems fair,' said Paneb. 'Come on, then. I'm in a hurry.' And he dived in.

Taken by surprise, the red-haired youth also threw himself into the water, determined to make up for lost time. He had swum the river dozens of times, and he felt confident. His adversary must already be tired, so wouldn't last the distance.

The lad was swiftly proved wrong. Paneb used the overarm stroke,* his rhythm astonishingly fast and not weakening for a single second. His pursuer had to take risks, because if he slowed down he would lose the race. With an effort that took his lungs to bursting-point, he managed to keep in contact. When Paneb touched the eastern bank, the youth hoped that he would rest for a few moments, but Paneb made a somersault-turn in the water and immediately set off for the other bank.

To give up would mean losing face . . . Despite his fatigue and stiffening muscles, the youth set off again, hoping desperately that the big man would be caught by one of the river's traps. His movements jerky and his breathing laboured, the young lad was falling further and further behind.

He only caught sight of it out of the corner of his eye, but he panicked instantly: a crocodile was bearing down on him.

* The hieroglyphic signs used in the *Pyramid Texts* show that the ancient Egyptians used the crawl.

He tried to turn back, but got caught in a whirlpool which swallowed him up in a few seconds. The reptile plunged into the depths, delighted with such easy prey.

Paneb reached the western bank. He climbed out and turned round.

'Where's your friend gone?' he asked the two boys.

They looked at him with hatred in their eyes. 'He's drowned,' replied the elder.

'Poor lad. Hc didn't know his limits.'

'It's because of you that he's dead.'

'Don't talk rubbish. Go and tell his family.'

'It's all your fault!'

With an effort, Paneb kept his temper. 'It's said that the Nile carries drowned men directly to the kingdom of Osiris. So rejoice for your friend and leave me in peace.'

The two boys each picked up a large stone and brandished it. 'We're going to break your bones and throw you in the river – then we'll see how fast you can swim.'

'If you attack me I shall defend myself, and you might not win.'

'You think you're so strong, don't you!'

'Get out of my way.'

The younger boy threw his stone so suddenly that Paneb was taken by surprise. He jerked his head aside, but the stone grazed his temple and blood welled up.

'This is your last warning,' he growled. 'Get out of my way this minute.'

The other boy tried to throw his stone, but he was far too slow. Paneb punched him hard in the face and he collapsed, unconscious.

His friend threw himself at Paneb, who elbowed him in the chest, then delivered a decisive uppercut. The youth fell to his knees, blood pouring from his nose, and passed out.

'The world is populated by fools,' observed Paneb with distaste.

On the earthen track at the top of the dyke, two men appeared, running towards him.

'If those are friends of these two,' thought Paneb, 'the peace won't last long.'

As they got nearer, he saw that they were Nakht the Powerful and Karo the Impatient, and they looked angry. Paneb had already fought the first and had words with the second.

'The Master sent us,' said Nakht. 'We have orders to bring you back to the village.'

'I was coming back anyway. Why the fuss?'

'The pharaoh is visiting us this afternoon, and the crews must be up to full strength.'

Karo spotted the two lads lying on the ground like broken dolls. 'What's been going on?'

'These two idiots attacked me because their friend had drowned. I had to defend myself.'

'You're could get into serious trouble about it.'

'But I couldn't just let myself be beaten up!'

'When they wake up, they'll probably lodge a complaint against you,' said Karo.

'But you can testify for me, can't you?'

'We weren't here when it happened,' Nakht objected.

'We must go back to the village,' Karo said. 'As for the rest, we'll see later.'

Paneb was revolted by the idea of being the victim of an injustice. Fortunately, he still had one chance of escaping from it. He hauled one of the lads up on to his right shoulder and the other on to his left. The double burden weighed as much as he did, but the young giant carried it easily.

'Come on,' he said. 'Unless I'm very much mistaken, there's no time to lose.'

14

Paneb slung the two youths down at the feet of the guards posted at the first fort. One moaned, the other was still unconscious.

'Don't worry,' he said, 'they're not applicants for admission. Watch them. I'll be back.'

The Place of Truth was spotlessly clean and adorned with beautiful flowers. The white houses shone brilliantly, and the villagers had once again put on their brightly coloured festival clothes.

Ignoring the children who wanted to play with him, Paneb ran to the Master's house, where he was greeted by Ebony. The black dog had been brushed until his coat gleamed.

'Ubekhet, I need help.'

Nefer appeared. 'We're in the middle of getting dressed – Pharaoh will be here soon.'

'I know, but it's an emergency. If the Wise Woman doesn't act now, I may have serious problems.'

'Can't your emergency wait until tomorrow?'

'Not really. And it would be a good idea if Ubekhet brought remedies – I'll carry them, of course. The two fellows who need treating have been rather bashed about.'

The first one had a deep cut over his eyebrow. Ubekhet probed it and established that no bones were broken. Holding the edges of the wound together, she sewed it up, then applied two strips of gummed linen and a bandage soaked in honey and fat. To prevent infection, she prescribed a mixture of cow's milk and barley flour, to be applied several times a day until the wound was completely healed.

The second youth had a broken nose and had lost a lot of blood. The Wise Woman cleaned it with soft cloths, then inserted a honey-soaked wad of linen in each nostril and applied two linen-covered splints to re-set the nose. She prescribed a dietary regime to speed up healing.

Happy to have been well cared for, and certain they'd make a full recovery, the two lads went off without demanding compensation. They had no wish ever again to meet the young giant with fists of stone.

'Thank you, Ubekhet. Without you . . .'

She shook her head at him. 'A mother sometimes has difficult children, Paneb, and you know how to make sure you're not forgotten.'

'I warned them, but they behaved like idiots. I'm not responsible for other people's stupidity!'

'Let's go and get ready. You wouldn't want to miss Pharaoh's arrival, would you?'

Thebes, with its hundred gates, was buzzing with activity. The royal flotilla would soon arrive at the main landing-stage, and all the city worthies would be present at the event. The people had gathered on the riverbanks to cheer the royal couple, in whose honour a great festival would be organized. Strong beer would be drunk, and food provided by the palace would be eaten. Everyone had grieved deeply at losing a ruler of the stature of Ramses the Great; now came the joy of being governed by Meneptah, whose presence at Thebes was a guarantee of the continuity of power and the maintenance of traditions.

After being greeted by the High Priest of Amon, the royal couple would receive the homage of the mayor of the

Southern capital. Then they would cross the Nile to the western bank, and be welcomed by the local officials, before going to the Place of Truth and the Valley of the Kings, there to preside over Ramses's funeral ceremonies.

This fine programme did not delight Mehy, who had a tendency to bite his fingernails.

'Meneptah is indeed a traditionalist, as we feared,' he told Serketa, who was trying to decide between several necklaces.

'Is that really a surprise, my sweet?'

'No, but I'd hoped for better things. The king could easily have been represented by the High Priest of Amon, but no, he's coming in person, with the queen and all the court. And he isn't content just to meet a few old dignitaries. What's more, he is going to visit that damned village and give the craftsmen still more privileges!'

'Don't give up hope – and put on a fresh pleated shirt. The one you're wearing isn't splendid enough.'

Mehy eyed her narrowly. 'You seem to be taking the situation rather lightly.'

'What good does complaining do? Everyone knows we'll never have a pharaoh like Ramses again. So we're faced with a much less powerful enemy, whom we may be able to manipulate.'

'Have you got something in mind?'

Serketa smiled. 'I might have.'

'Tell me.'

'First change your shirt. I want you to look like an elegant, rich dignitary whom men admire and women fall in love with. But if one of them comes near you, I'll scratch her eyes out!'

Mehy seized his wife's wrists, so tightly that he hurt her. 'Tell me – and quickly!'

'We know from our spy that Nefer has become Master of the Brotherhood. Why don't we destroy his reputation? If the king were to receive documents proving the Master isn't worthy of his office, the Place of Truth would be discredited, because it would be seen as incapable of choosing a good leader. Meneptah might want to dismantle it or hand over its running to an outsider.'

'Someone like our friend Abry . . .'

Serketa was radiant. 'Don't you think it's time we made full use of his services?'

'But we haven't got time to prepare convincing evidence.'

'It's already done, my precious. I copied several people's writing and drew up official-looking documents accusing Nefer of incompetence, of refusing to obey the civil authorities, of wanting too much independence and, above all, of being a tyrant. There'll certainly be one or two craftsmen who'll jump on that bandwagon and help bring about the Master's downfall. There'll be chaos, and we can use it for our own ends.'

'I like the sound of that.'

'Are you pleased with me, my sweet love?'

Mehy smiled at his wife, and thought, 'She's more dangerous than a scorpion; I was right to make an ally of her.'

Abry had flabby cheeks, sweat-soaked hair and eyes that never seemed to focus on anything. All he wanted was to be a model, quiet, senior official. When he'd met Mehy, he thought fate was offering him a chance to escape from an impossible situation he couldn't get out of alone; and by the time he realized he had surrendered to a fearsome predator, capable of absolutely anything, it was too late. Abry was deeply afraid of Mehy. Face to face with him, his strength drained away and he could see no way out but absolute obedience.

He listened with anxious attention as Mehy told him about the false documents. 'This plan is as dangerous as it is daring, my dear Mehy. I don't think—'

'There's no danger and no risk. You are to give this information to the king as soon as he sets foot on the west bank. Coming from you, the documents cannot be anything but genuine. Meneptah will have time to read them before he reaches the Place of Truth, and he'll be convinced Nefer isn't worthy of being Master. He'll designate you leader of the Brotherhood, and charge you with the task of bringing it back into good order. You can capitalize on it by reminding him that you warned Ramses about the intolerable privileges enjoyed by these craftsmen.'

'You're putting me in the front line,' said Abry fretfully.

'It's to your own benefit. The king will give you credit for your clear-headedness.'

'I'd have preferred to remain in the background and not get involved so directly.'

'If this information reaches Meneptah anonymously, and if he maintains the sages' outdated morality and ignores hearsay, our efforts will come to nothing. So we need official action, and only you can take it.'

'All the same, this is very delicate.'

'Look, you have nothing to lose and everything to gain. Have a little courage, Abry, and the Place of Truth will lie at our feet.'

'But I don't know Meneptah. He may refuse to listen to me.'

'Refuse to listen to the governor of the west bank of Thebes, the most senior official in the region? You're mad! Quite the contrary: he'll congratulate you on acting to put right such a serious problem.'

'It would be wiser to see how Meneptah conducts himself, and act only after full consideration of —'

'You will give these documents to Meneptah, Abry, because I have decided that you will. Now go and get ready for the official welcome – and don't make any mistakes. Until we meet again, faithful ally.' And Mehy swept out.

But his shadow still fell on Abry, so Abry hurried off to consult the documents. Falsehood had been distilled in them with consummate skill. Vicious and venomous, the accusations would surely bring Nefer down.

As governor of the west bank, and theoretical protector of the Place of Truth, had he the right to ruin a Master's career like this? But such scruples did not trouble him for long: it was his own career that he must save. Besides, if he didn't obey Mehy, retribution would be swift and violent.

So he would hand over the information to King Meneptah.

15

The royal procession made its way through the Five Walls, watched attentively by the guards. True, the pharaoh was protected by his personal guard, but Sobek had nevertheless ordered his men to exercise the utmost vigilance.

Outside the village, all the lay workers and their families had gathered; not one single person was missing. The blacksmith and the potter were at the front of the crowd, and so got an excellent view of the pharaoh who had the onerous task of succeeding Ramses the Great.

Meneptah had an oval face, with a broad forehead, large ears, a long, thin, straight nose and a wide mouth. He wore a round wig and on his brow was the *khat*, the golden cobra whose task was to destroy the king's enemies. His pleated kilt was fastened with a belt whose buckle was shaped like a panther's head. Gold bracelets encircled his wrists.

Beside the king was his sixty-five-year-old queen. Like the king's mother, Ramses' second wife, she was named Iset the Fair. She had borne the king two sons, one of whom they had called Seti, 'Man of Set', after the formidable god; only one pharaoh, the great Seti I, Ramses' father, had dared adopt that name.

The queen was supremely elegant in her robe of exceptionally fine linen, and was brisk and lively for her years. In her right hand she held an ankh, the symbol of life.

The royal couple were accompanied by the tjaty and numerous civil and religious dignitaries.

Shaven and perfumed, the gatekeeper nervously stood before the main gate of the village, unsure how to hold his spear and cudgel.

The tjaty handed Pharaoh a strange golden apron which bore the secret of measurements and proportions, enabling the plan of a temple to be drawn. And the most senior priestess from Luxor hung a figurine of the goddess Ma'at from the queen's long golden necklace.

'Gatekeeper,' intoned Meneptah, 'you see before you the Master of the Place of Truth and the earthly representative of the law of harmony. May the gate of this village be opened to them.'

Mightily relieved to be given a clear order, the gatekeeper obeyed it with alacrity, then quickly closed the gate again, leaving the rest of the procession outside.

Nefer the Silent stepped forward from the mass of villagers, who had gathered to greet the royal couple. The locks of the Master's wig were arranged like rays emerging from the top of his head; the wig itself was held in place by a broad band of cloth. He wore a ceremonial kilt, with a red scarf slung across his body, and carried a heavy staff whose upper end was shaped like a ram's head crowned with a sun-disc. This symbol marked the presence of Amon, the Hidden God, among the little community. It was to him that their prayers rose, and to him that entreaties must be addressed.

As the villagers watched their Master, their hearts were chilled by anxiety, and Meneptah's austere, almost hostile, expression only added to it. Paneb, who was so tall that he could easily see over the heads of the throng, thought the new king looked like someone who wouldn't be swayed easily.

Hay, leader of the port crew, and the Scribe of the Tomb had left the worry of preparing a speech to Nefer.

He said in a clear, carrying voice, 'Majesty, Ramses' house

of eternity is ready to receive his body of light, and I surrender the Place of Truth into your hands.'

And that was all.

Paneb couldn't help smiling: not for nothing was Nefer known as 'the Silent'. But then he began to worry. Perhaps the Master was wrong to make his speech so short. The king might well have expected something more flattering. Would he be offended?

'God created the sky,' declaimed Meneptah, 'the earth, the breath of life, fire, the gods and goddesses, animals and all men, who are mere elements of creation and not its crowning glory. He is the sculptor who has sculpted Himself, the mould-maker who has never been moulded, the unique one who traverses eternity. The purest gold cannot compare to His radiance. All lands are surveyed according to His law, and the royal cubit measures the stones of His temples. It is God who makes the cord lie straight upon the ground and raises buildings with strong foundations. No wall raised on this earth must be deprived of His presence, for He alone expresses true power. In creating worlds, the Divine Architect made himself perceptible and He passed on the secret of His work. Here, in the Place of Truth, it is taught that only what God builds comes into being. Is it indeed thus, Master, that this Brotherhood lives and believes?'

'In the name of Pharaoh, I swear that it is so.'

Kenhir shivered. Meneptah's words revealed a profound knowledge of the Brotherhood and of the significance of the solemn oath its Master had just sworn. If the king found fault with anything the Master had done, he might consider that the Master had committed perjury and condemn him to death.

'Whether a country or a brotherhood, men cannot be ruled justly except by gifts and offerings,' continued Meneptah. 'The richer one is, the more generous one must be. Pharaoh, to whom the gods have entrusted the prosperity of the Two Lands, cares for the wellbeing of each of his subjects. To you, craftsmen of the Place of Truth, I shall continue to supply the tools, foodstuffs, clothes and all other things needful for you to do the work of Ma'at and live happily in your village. To celebrate my coronation, nine thousand fish, nine thousand loaves, countless haunches of meat, twenty large jars of oil and a hundred of wine will be given to you.'

Paneb could have shouted for joy, but anxiety kept the villagers silent. Despite this excellent news, which ensured the Place of Truth's survival, its people still felt a heavy threat hanging over them.

Meneptah went on, 'The role of this Brotherhood – its very reason for existing – is to embody the gods' map in matter. To succeed, it requires leaders who can direct and guide it. It is for them to open the sealed papyrus, and to wield the rod of discipline if necessary. A true leader must know how to serve the work and its Brotherhood, pilot the ship and handle the rudder without weakening. He must show that he is as great in his office as a well which overflows with pure, life-giving water. If he commands an ignorant man or an imbecile to carry out work which that man cannot do, he is unfit to rule. The overseer who behaves like a tyrant, or amasses wealth and privileges for himself: he too is unfit to rule.'

The tension increased suddenly. Everyone knew that the grievances Pharaoh had spoken of amounted to accusations against Nefer.

Ubekhet gazed at her husband, trying to convey to him all the intensity of her love; she knew he was in danger of being destroyed by the royal fire.

Meneptah looked Nefer full in the face. 'The governor of the west bank of Thebes has handed me a very grave report concerning you. I have read it carefully, and can reach only one conclusion: for what you have done, you must be dismissed.'

'If that is Your Majesty's will, it shall be obeyed. But may I know of what I am accused?'

'In the first place, of accruing personal wealth to the detriment of the Brotherhood.'

Kenhir stepped forward. 'Majesty, as Scribe of the Tomb and the official responsible for the day-to-day running of the Place of Truth, I can bring proof that this accusation is without foundation. In accordance with our rule, Nefer occupies a house allocated to him with the agreement of the tjaty, to which have been added a consulting room and a workshop which are needed by the Wise Woman, his wife. Like our venerated Scribe of Ma'at, Ramose, the Master could have acquired fields and flocks perfectly legally, but he has devoted himself exclusively to his work.'

'I take note of your words, Scribe of the Tomb. Next, the report states that Nefer was not chosen unanimously by the craftsmen, and that he behaves tyrannically, using force and threats against those who challenge him.'

'That's a bare-faced lie, Majesty!' Paneb burst out. 'All here present recognized Nefer as Master without question – the only person unhappy with the decision was Nefer himself.'

'One man's word is not sufficient,' said the king. 'Let each man speak freely about the Master's conduct.'

Paneb silently swore to punish anyone who lied, and he glared fiercely at Ched the Saviour, who was the first to speak. But he need not have been concerned: not only Ched but all the other craftsmen and then the priestesses of Hathor confirmed his fiery words and praised the way Nefer had acted as Master. Even the traitor sang Nefer's praises, for fear of standing out and attracting attention to himself. And Kenhir concluded by stating that the Brotherhood had indeed had the skill to choose the honest, competent man it needed.

The final decision, however, rested with Pharaoh; and it was unheard-of for a pharaoh to speak out publicly against one of his senior officials. The villagers held their breath.

'My father warned me that there would be devious attacks

on the Place of Truth,' said the king. 'He sensed that its Master would be slandered, so as to cast discredit upon the whole Brotherhood and bring about its destruction, so I was not surprised by these accusations. Nevertheless, it was important that I should hear all of you, to reassure myself of the strength of the bonds that unite you: and I am duly reassured. Approach, Nefer.'

Pharaoh tied the golden apron about the Master's waist. 'To you I delegate my sovereignty over the Place of Truth, and to you I entrust two all-important tasks: to create my house of eternity in the Valley of the Kings, and to build my Temple of a Million Years on the western bank.'

At his words, the villagers erupted in shouts of joy.

16

Standing among his fellow dignitaries outside the Place of Truth, Abry heard loud cheers inside the village. The first were in honour of the king, then Nefer's name was shouted.

He needed to hear no more. Obviously, the plot was a complete failure and the Master had succeeded in refuting all the accusations. By confirming Nefer in his post, Meneptah was dissociating himself from Abry and supporting the Place of Truth.

Abry trod on several people's feet on his way back to his chariot.

'Don't you feel well?' asked one of his scribes.

'It's probably the heat. I need to rest.'

'Comc and lie down in the shade for a few minutes.'

'No, I'd rather go home.'

'If he notices you're not here, the king might not be happy about it.'

Abry did not reply. He climbed into his chariot and gestured to his driver to set off.

Several senior officials had seen the little incident. They were astonished. Something serious must be up for the governor to behave so strangely.

When Abry got home, the house was empty. His wife had been invited to the royal palace at Thebes, where the queen was receiving the great ladies of the province, the children were taking part in the festivities on the banks of the Nile and the servants had two days' holiday.

This time, the abyss yawned at his feet.

Some well-meaning individual would undoubtedly point out to Meneptah that this wan't the first time Abry had tried to cause the Place of Truth's demise. Only because of Ramses' clemency had the governor kept his job. The new pharaoh would probably not be so lenient, particularly as he might have committed a grave injustice if he had acted on the false documents.

Disgrace, public failure, at best exile, at worst a death sentence . . . at the thought of those tortures, Abry trembled from head to foot. He was painfully hot; he felt as though he was burning up. In search of coolness, he went out into the garden and sat in the shade of a vine-covered pergola, next to the pool with its blue and white lotus-flowers.

Sitting there, he took a momentous decision: he would not suffer alone. Mehy, that vile schemer and blackmailer, was responsible for this appalling mess. Abry had no chance of coming out of it unscathed but at least, if he confessed everything, the most guilty party would also be punished. Small consolation, it was true, but it was his last chance to do the right thing.

'Abry, are you alone?' asked a woman's voice.

As though stung by an insect, the governor leapt to his feet and swung round to the clump of oleanders from which the voice had come.

'It's Serketa – we mustn't be seen together.'

'Of . . . of course,' he managed. 'Don't worry, the house is empty.'

If he hadn't known who it was, he wouldn't have recognized Serketa: her wig, make-up and dress made her look completely different.

'Mehy sent me to help you,' she said.

'Ah.'

'It's a difficult situation, but he's found a way to sort everything out.'

'He can't have!'

'Don't be so pessimistic. I have here a document which will calm the pharaoh's anger.'

Abry stared in astonishment at the papyrus Serketa held out to him. He was even more astonished when he read it. He, Abry, was explaining that he had tried to discredit the Place of Truth and to slander its Master because he had always hated the village, because he could not bring it under his control. Eaten away by remorse, he had no solution but suicide.

Dumbfounded, he handed it back to Serketa, who rolled it up.

As she did so, another thought struck him. 'Anyone would swear that that's my handwriting.'

She smiled. 'I had no difficulty at all in imitating it, and I shall seal the scroll with your seal to show that this sad little document is authentic.'

'I have no intention of killing myself. In fact, I'm going to denounce you – you and your husband!'

'I was afraid of that,' said Serketa with cold anger. 'So you see, my dear Abry, I'll just have to see that you don't.'

She gave him a violent push, sending him tumbling into the lotus pool. He tried to shout but his mouth filled with water. A poor swimmer, dragged down by his festival clothes, choking on the water he'd swallowed, Abry offered only feeble resistance. Serketa held his head under the surface until he stopped moving.

Then, smiling serenely, she went into the house and put the scroll on Abry's desk. It would be clear that he had chosen to atone this way for his treason.

To transport Ramses' funerary goods, it took no fewer than a hundred soldiers, eighty carriers of offerings from the neighbouring temples, forty sailors and two hundred officials, not counting the two crews from the Place of Truth and the priestesses of Hathor.

Acting as priests, the craftsmen had donned brand-new linen robes and papyrus sandals. In accordance with the rule, they had abstained from sexual relations on the night before the funeral ceremonies and had eaten special food.

The proudest of them all was Ipuy the Examiner, who had just finished painting his own tomb, mostly with scenes of daily activities such as fishing or washing laundry. He had been chosen as fan-bearer at the pharaoh's right hand. He wore the star-spangled robe of the Priest of Resurrection, whose task it was to open the mouth, eyes and ears of the mummy to transform it into the agent of daily regeneration in the secrecy of the house of eternity.

Paneb marvelled at the fabulous treasures that would accompany the dead pharaoh on his voyage to the hereafter: gold statues of the gods; caskets containing precious metals, perfumes, unguents, fabrics or preserved foods; sceptres, crowns, all sorts of sizes of model temples and shrines; boats, mirrors, offering-tables, bows, jet staffs, papyrus, a chariot ready to be assembled; and all sorts of other masterpieces; Paneb himself had been given a great bed of gilded wood to carry. This was the world of Ramses which would thus be associated with the transmutation of the royal soul.

The objects were set down at the entrance to the tomb, which was lit by a hundred lamps. It fell to the Servants of the Place of Truth, who alone were authorized to enter, to put them in their proper places in the halls and shrines of Ramses' last dwelling.

Absolute silence reigned as Meneptah began the resurrection rites on the mummy, which the Master, overseer Hay of the port crew and the stone-cutters placed in the sarcophagus. Nefer directed the delicate manoeuvre of positioning the stone lid that sealed the posthumous destiny of the Son of the Light.

Meneptah ordered all the craftsmen except Nefer to leave the tomb. Then he went to the far end of the shrine, beyond the sarcophagus chamber, and checked that the work, whose smallest detail had been done with great care, ended in bare rock.

'Beyond that which humans can imagine,' said Pharaoh, 'there is the unknowable, that from which we came and to which, if we have led a righteous life, we return. Have you brought life to the sarcophagus with the Stone of Light, Master of the Brotherhood?'

'The "Master of Life" has itself become a Stone of Light which will guard Ramses' being and keep it safe for century upon century.'

Meneptah thought of faithful Ahmeni, the aged secretary and friend of the dead pharaoh. He had retired to Karnak to write a chronicle of Ramses' life, which, sent out into every land where people could read, would contribute to his glory.

The king placed a lamp at the head of the sarcophagus and lit it. When the flame sprang up, a halo of soft light surrounded the head of the sarcophagus. The light would allow the soul-bird to feed from it before crossing the trial of darkness and flying off towards the sun. Nefer began to put out the other lamps. As he did so, the stone of the 'Master of Life' absorbed their energy and itself became a light-emitting source of ever-greater power.

When the two men left the tomb, the sarcophagus was radiating its light throughout the shrine, where the shadows were no longer hostile but fecund.

The Master closed the door of the house of eternity. There, far from the eyes of men, the hieroglyphic texts and ritual scenes would live in their own right, enabling Ramses to continue to reign, in the invisible world, over his country and his people, to whom he would henceforth show the path to the stars.

Finally, Nefer applied the necropolis seal, made up of nine jackals above bound and decapitated enemies. Thanks to the presence of Anubis, no malign force could penetrate the closed door.

'I never doubted you, your integrity or your abilities,' Meneptah told him. 'I set you a harsh test so that you might be judged worthy, by all members of the Brotherhood, to wear the golden apron.'

17

Sobek grabbed Kenhir's arm. He was in such a rage that he could hardly speak.

'Y-you heard what the k-king said. That miserable worm Abry tried to ruin Nefer – and he's been trying for years to smash the Brotherhood. What more proof do we need?'

The Scribe of the Tomb was still reeling with shock. 'How could an important official like Abry do such a terrible thing? It's his duty to protect the Place of Truth, but all he thinks of is destroying it.'

'You must make an official complaint!'

'Don't you think the king's anger will be enough? Abry will be accused of lying, of falsifying documents and probably, because he tried to deceive Pharaoh, of high treason. He'll lose his job, and be punished harshly besides.'

'Yes, but I want to take advantage of the situation to find out who murdered my guard. Did Abry do it himself, or did he have an accomplice? If we're involved in the case, I can interrogate him and make him confess.'

'I knew you'd say that,' said Kenhir resignedly. 'The complaint is ready.'

'And you must authorize me to investigate in the name of the Place of Truth and outside its boundaries.'

'A request for authorization has already been sent to the tjaty.'

Sobek realized why Kenhir, despite his difficult personality, had been appointed Scribe of the Tomb: for him, as for the overseers, the village was what mattered.

Because of the king's presence in the village, Sobek could not leave his post to question Abry, though he was longing to do so. Vulnerable and friendless, the criminal would talk.

'I only hope,' said Kenhir, 'Abry isn't the head of a network of our enemies.'

'I'm afraid he may well be, which means the danger is by no means over.'

They were interrupted by the arrival of the messenger, Uputy, who was visibly agitated.

'Terrible news,' he said. 'Abry has killed himself, at his home, when his family and servants were out.'

'How do you know it was suicide?' demanded Sobek.

'He left a letter confessing that he'd lied to the king and imploring forgiveness. He was afraid his punishment would be pitiless – perhaps even the death sentence – and couldn't bear the thought, so he killed himself.'

The royal couple were staying in the little palace Ramses had built in the Place of Truth, and were celebrating the morning rites in the adjoining temple. At that same moment, in all the temples of Egypt, from the smallest to the most enormous, the image of Pharaoh came magically to life to speak the same words and carry out the same gestures. The celebrants could only officiate in the name of Pharaoh, fashioned by the gods to maintain the presence of Ma'at on earth.

Then Meneptah and Nefer went to the House of Life, the sacred library built next to the village's principal temple. Kenhir was waiting for them with the keys to the library, which contained the 'Powers of Light', the Brotherhood's archive of the rituals and works written by Thoth, god of knowledge, and by Sia, god of wisdom. Thanks to them, it was written, Osiris could come back to life and the secret of resurrection could be passed on to men.

The most precious books of all were one encased in hammered gold and another in silver, which preserved the decrees creating the Brotherhood and its temple. To these were added vital texts, like the *Book of Festivals and Ritual Hours*, the *Book of Protecting the Sacred Ship*, the *Book of Offerings and the Inventory of Ritual Objects*, the *Book of the Stars*, the *Book for Warding Off the Evil Eye*, the *Book of Going Forth into the Light*, the *Book of Shining Magic* and manuals for the symbolic decoration of temples and tombs.

But the one the king wanted to consult was very different. 'Show me the plan of the houses of eternity in the Great Place,' he ordered Kenhir.

Up to now, no one but the Scribes of the Tomb had ever been allowed to see this priceless papyrus. For safety, it was kept, under a false name, among old records which no one ever consulted, and the secret of its hiding-place and false name was handed down by each Scribe to his successor.

Kenhir went and fetched it, and unrolled it on a low table. There before them were revealed the plans and construction details of each tomb in the Valleys of the Kings and Queens, and its precise location. Knowledge of what was in the scroll enabled successive Masters to create new tombs in untouched ground, and there was no risk of disturbing existing ones.

Meneptah studied the papyrus for some time, then said, 'You are to build my Temple of a Million Years on the fringes of the cultivated lands, north-west of the tomb of Amenhotep III and south of Ramses' temple. As to my house of eternity, Master, where do you suggest?'

'Majesty, we must take account of the quality of the rock and the orientations desired by previous pharaohs, so that the whole is of harmonious composition. Therefore I suggest this location here on the mountainside, west of your father's tomb and just above it.'

'An excellent choice, Master. But be always aware that

you are attempting to express the Great Work and that failure is unthinkable.'

Playing or listening to music was one of the villagers' favourite entertainments: most people had at least some skill at playing the flute, the small harp, the lute, the tambourine or the cythara. No one could imagine working without music, and it was even more essential at festivals and banquets.

Since Meneptah's coronation and Nefer's official endorsement as Master must obviously be celebrated properly, the players gave vent to the joy in their hearts, and the whole village was filled with music. The men were less skilful than the women, for the priestesses of Hathor were the guardians of the sacred music, whose performance was part of their initiation. Best of all was a group consisting of a female harpist, a flautist and tambourine player, whose melodies and rhythms enchanted everyone. Even crotchety old Kenhir felt the urge to dance – though of course his dignity did not permit him to do so.

Paneb abruptly stopped listening to them: a seductive little tune played on a lyre had caught his ear. He looked round.

The lyre-player was as beguiling as her music. She wore a wig of long black hair, which fell forward over her shoulders and hid most of her face; he could just see her eyes, exotically made up in black and green. At her waist was a belt of pearls separated by golden leopard-heads, and round her ankles were bracelets shaped like the claws of birds of prey. She wore a short, gauzy dress and her voice was as sweet as the evening breeze.

Skilfully, she plucked her instrument's eight strings. They were fastened by copper hooks to the sounding-box, which was hollow and flat, and were held in place by two bent arms of unequal length. She switched effortlessly from plucking the strings to strumming them, then held the lyre to her breast, muffling the vibrations, and sang very quietly to convey deliciously sensual nuances.

Paneb went towards her. She retreated step by step, still singing and playing, and led him into a shady corner. At last she halted, and he came close enough to touch her.

Suddenly he recognized her. 'Turquoise!'

'Aren't you ever going to be faithful to Uabet?' she asked.

'I never promised her I would be, and she's never demanded it.'

'Do you at least understand why I'm playing this music?

He kissed her passionately. 'To attract me – and you've succeeded!'

'No, I'm playing to ward off danger and evil: Pharaoh's intervention won't be enough to drive them away from the village. And you, Paneb, you are mad enough not to fear them and to confront them without taking precautions. So I am playing the music with which the priestesses dispel evil forces and I'm surrounding you with my protective magic.'

'You really are amazing!'

'Did you think you knew everything about me?'

'Of course not – though I do know how to play your body like a lyre.' With unexpected gentleness, he took the instrument from her and put it down on the ground. 'And there's one other thing I know about you,' he said seriously.

'What's that?'

'The dress you're wearing is completely unnecessary.'

Turquoise did not resist when he removed it. Then he took her in his arms and carried her to her house, where they made their desires sing in unison.

18

'My mistress is not receiving anyone,' said the doorkeeper at Abry's house.

'I am Commander Sobek, in charge of guarding the Place of Truth, and I am here on official business.' With Kenhir's agreement, and after checking that the king's safety was assured, Sobek had thought it vital to interview the widow as quickly as possible.

'In that case . . . I'll go and tell her. Please wait in the garden, Commander.'

Sobek went outside and stood in the shade of a palm tree.

A tall, brown-haired woman came out of the house. She looked listless and deeply unhappy. 'The police have already questioned me,' she said, her voice cracking with emotion. 'I was away when it happened, so I can't tell you anything. All I know is that some of my husband's colleagues saw him leave the official procession suddenly, when cheering started inside the village. Why . . . why did he kill himself?'

'He tried to destroy the Master of the Brotherhood, and he failed.'

'Why didn't he give up attacking the Place of Truth? He has left me alone, all alone, with a daughter to bring up . . . and the shame . . . the shame is so hard to bear . . . I didn't deserve this!'

'I have to ask you something very difficult,' Sobek said gently. 'You knew Abry better than anyone. Did you think him capable of suicide?'

'With all this turmoil, I hadn't even thought about it. But you're absolutely right to raise the question.' She was silent for a moment, then said firmly, 'No, he'd never have killed himself. He was too self-satisfied – and anyway he'd never have had the courage.' Almost at once the harsh reality came back to her. 'But he really is dead, and he even left a letter saying why he'd done it.'

Sobek changed the subject. 'Had your husband recently had any meetings one might call . . . suspicious?'

'Of course not! He received all the foremost citizens of Thebes, as his office required, people like the mayor, senior officials, principal scribes. The one I hate most is that upstart Mehy, but Abry saw him very rarely. Actually, I hate them all – especially Abry! Because of his weakness and laziness, he'd never have risen any higher in his career. He should have obtained a promotion at Pi-Ramses and introduced us to court. But all he ever thought of was Thebes.'

'Did he talk to you about the evidence he was planning to give to Pharaoh?'

'He never spoke to me about his work at all. The shame of it . . . To end like this . . .' She burst into tears, and Sobek judged it was time to leave.

The conversation troubled him. If Abry's death was in fact not suicide but murder, the murderer must have set a fiendishly cunning trap. The dead man sounded a weak character, easily influenced and incapable of doing anything either subtle or extreme. Had he really drawn up those skilfully forged documents, which he must have known would point straight at him if the plot failed?

Sobek had no hard evidence, but his instinct told him Abry had been only the instrument of the plot, not the instigator. Unless he was much mistaken, dark days lay ahead and even

Meneptah's support might not be enough to save the Place of Truth.

But how could he pick up the slender thread so brutally severed by Abry's death?

The bull had a black face and a dark hide. Horns lowered, it had charged. The other bull had not been quick enough. Gored in the belly, it slumped forward with its head hanging and its back legs raised, in an attitude of powerlessness and despair.

Tragedy was followed by comedy, in the shape of a flock of geese with white or grey heads and pointed beaks. They were all running in the same direction, except for one indisciplined bird who turned round suddenly and attracted everyone's attention.

As for grace, that was expressed by an elegant sketch of a gazelle with bluish horns, black eyes, a greyish-pink body and legs of an almost unreal slenderness.

This was how Paneb's first three paintings were presented, on three large slabs of highest-quality limestone. Ched the Saviour had been examining them one after the other for over a quarter of an hour, and the young man still didn't know what he thought of them.

Suddenly, Ched opened the door of the workshop.

A black and white cat was sitting outside. It gazed back at him with proud eyes.

'Observe that cat well, Paneb,' said Ched, 'Observe it more carefully than you have ever done before. When you paint it on the wall of a tomb, it will be no longer a simple cat but the incarnation of the Light which wields its rays, in the form of knives, to slash the dragon Apophis, the bad spirit who is determined to dry up the vital flux.'

'Does that mean you think I might make a painter?'

'Let's go out and look at the sky.'

Hordes of swallows were dancing in the azure blue.

'The souls of kings can be embodied in that bird,' said Ched. 'When you show a swallow perched on the roof of a chapel, you will symbolize the triumph of Light. But you will never achieve anything good without looking carefully.'

He led Paneb to a tomb in the western necropolis, where Gau the Precise and Pai the Good Bread were working. A ladder leant against the wall of the tomb.

'What do you think of the quality of the wall, Paneb?' asked Ched.

Paneb checked that it had been correctly levelled with mortar made of silt and chopped straw, then covered with a layer of gypsum to plug the holes. Next, two very thin coatings of filler had been applied with care, the second of high enough quality to give a suitable surface for painting.

'It looks good.'

'You're wrong,' said Ched. 'Show him, Pai and Gau.'

Pai climbed the ladder. He held one end of a fine cord soaked in red ink, and Gau the other. The cord was tightly stretched down the length of the wall, and Gau let go of it suddenly so that it whipped against the wall, leaving a straight line. They repeated the procedure several times, both along the wall and up and down, so as to make a grid.

'This grid must precede drawing and painting, so that each figure conforms to a system of harmonic proportions,' explained Ched. 'For a standing figure, three squares deep from the hair to the base of the neck, ten from the neck to the knees, six from the knees to the soles of the feet: nineteen in all. Fifteen squares for a seated figure.

Gau told Paneb several other rules of proportion relating to particular subjects There was one firm general principle: a tightly drawn grid for small motifs, a larger-scale one for themes with more substantial elements.

'Learn from this wall,' Ched advised, 'but don't get mired in calculations. Your hand must learn proportions, and without rigidity, for it alone possesses the freedom of creation. One day, if you become a true painter, you won't need this grid. While you wait, try to draw a woman's body – without spoiling the wall.'

Superimposing layers of variable thickness demanded great dexterity, but Paneb took the time he needed to obtain a subtle texture of red and white which reconstructed delicate flesh, on top of which he added an almost transparent white to form the fabric of a light dress. Then he covered his work with a varnish based on acacia resin, in order to preserve the brilliance of the colours.

Pai and Gau watched in open-mouthed admiration, but Ched was unimpressed.

'In the upper left-hand corner,' he ordered, 'show a falcon taking flight.'

That was a particularly difficult thing to draw, but in Paneb's huge hands the brushes became delicate instruments of utmost precision. Using one brush per colour, he created a bird of prey so full of vitality and life that it seemed hemmed in by the little room with a sky that was too low.

'What you must paint,' said Ched, 'isn't nature but that which is beyond reality, the hidden and supernatural life. The tomb is a house of eternity where the peasants carry out perfect, tireless tasks, where nothing withers, where frail papyrus boats sail without danger on tranquil waterways, where the happy couple are young for ever. It's a universe of light, which you must re-create without your personal preoccupations obscuring it. Each of your paintings must illuminate an aspect of the mystery of life. If they don't, they'll be useless.'

With black ink, Ched corrected one of the falcon's feet, which he felt wasn't precise enough. And Paneb, whose heart was starting to take fire, realized that he was still only a beginner. The master's eye had noticed the one tiny detail that prevented the bird of prey from really taking flight.

'There's still a lot of work to be done in this tomb,' said Ched, 'but I'm not sure you're up to it.'

Paneb gritted his teeth. 'I'll learn whatever skills I need.'
'That isn't the problem.'
'Then what must I do?'
'Answer this question: will you become my assistant?'

19

During Meneptah's coronation celebrations at Thebes, the tjaty was authorized by the king to reward men and women who had served their country well during Ramses' reign, and the tjaty took advantage of this event to make promotions and appointments.

Although he was not yet friendly with any of the influential members of Meneptah's court, Mehy was not too anxious about the future. He had learnt that the tjaty's men were asking the senior army officers about him. Mehy had taken steps to ensure that he was very popular with his officers and men, so he knew all the answers would be favourable; they should result in his promotion in the army. And he had no worries about his performance as treasurer of Thebes: it was faultless. Thanks to him, the city and the province had grown wealthier.

Since the old commander-in-chief of the Theban armed forces had just retired, Mehy had hopes of obtaining that post, which had to be given to a scribe with a good knowledge of the army. The pharaohs had always been suspicious of the army, and preferred it to be headed by civilians, who would be less likely to start insane wars.

The little world of the dignitaries who wished to please the new regime had only two preoccupations: would the mayor of Thebes be replaced, and who would be appointed governor of the west bank in Abry's place?

When the tjaty entered the council chamber, wagers were running high. It was obvious that the new pharaoh would put his stamp on the Theban region by appointing faithful followers from the North, and that local ambitions would be disappointed. The city of the god Amon would undergo profound upheavals, which would cause much gnashing of teeth and the formation of a more or less feverish opposition, fed by the resentments of those who had been rejected.

The tjaty began by handing out the awards, which ran from the Golden Collar down to simple rings. Then he called Commander Mehy, who bowed before him.

'Mehy, you are appointed general, and are to be commander-in-chief of the Theban troops. You will take charge of the troops' wellbeing and see that all weapons are maintained in good condition, and you will go regularly to Pi-Ramses to present a detailed report to the king.'

Spending time in the capital, getting close to power . . . Mehy was delighted. He swore the oath to carry out his duties, then rejoined the ranks of the senior officials, who smiled condescendingly at him. As the pharaoh was the supreme head of the armed forces and the tjaty was his right arm, the fine-sounding title of 'general' concealed its lack of true importance. Mehy was leaving the sphere of real influence to become a well-paid, lazy functionary.

Lastly, the matter of the mayor of Thebes's office was addressed, and the decision left the courtiers open-mouthed: the mayor was to retain his post, as were all his counsellors, to whom would be added a new treasurer, a Theban scribe of the traditional school of thought.

Mehy applauded Meneptah's political skill. By avoiding the feared upheaval, he would gain the approval of the rich Theban region and would have no trouble there. He was probably busy with problems in the North, and did not want to create any in the South.

There remained only the position of governor of the west

bank to fill. This appointment was considered particularly delicate after the tragic death of its holder.

'I call upon General Mehy,' said the tjaty calmly.

Astonished murmurings ran through the assembly. Mehy himself hesitated for a moment, thinking he had mis-heard. But all eyes were upon him, and this impelled him forward to present himself before the first minister of Egypt. The tjaty indeed conferred the office of the deceased Abry upon him, and the new general had no alternative but to accept.

The tjaty had accorded Mehy the privilege of a private audience in the palace garden, in the shade of the perseas and sycamores.

'You were expecting to be promoted to general, but you were surprised to be given the post of governor of the west bank, weren't you?'

'Those are both demanding jobs, with heavy responsibilities. I thought they'd be kept separate.'

'The king and I think the opposite, because of what has just happened. Abry was a fierce opponent of the Place of Truth, and he tried to trick the king by bringing false accusations against the Master. What we don't know is whether this was individual madness, or part of a plot whose ramifications are not yet clear. Until we find out, we must envisage the worst and take all necessary precautions. During the last years of Ramses' reign, you reorganized the Theban troops; both officers and men are grateful to you for that. They'll accept your authority without question, so you'll be able to ensure the region's security, according to instructions from the capital.'

'Forgive my curiosity, but do you think there might be disturbances in Thebes?'

'Not in Thebes, but the Libyans and others are still potentially dangerous. And the Nubian tribes of the Great South sometimes become belligerent again. So it's important that Thebes remains a region of stability and peace, qualities which might be threatened by troublemakers like Abry. The wealth of the west bank is immense: so many treasures in the royal tombs and the temples of a million years! If evildoers ever dreamt of seizing them, with the aid of corrupt senior officials, and if their appalling venture succeeded, what would become of Egypt? It will be your task to watch over the wealth of the western bank of Thebes, Mehy, and you will have both administrative power and armed soldiers with which to do so. In our eyes, it is a vital mission. Be aware that we shall be watching you with great care.'

'I shall try to prove worthy of your trust.'

'Trying won't be good enough,' said the tjaty. 'We require that the west bank be safeguarded from all attack, from whatever source. Do I make myself clear?'

'You can count on me.'

'If you have the slightest suspicion that something's amiss, or if there is even the smallest unrest, inform Pi-Ramses immediately. Nothing like the Abry affair must ever happen again.'

As the tjaty walked away, Mehy felt briefly amazed by the whims of destiny and he almost laughed aloud. He, the very person who was the main enemy of the Place of Truth, had been charged with protecting it!

Many leading citizens had been waiting for the tjaty's conversation with Mehy to end, so that they could congratulate the general and assure him of their complete loyalty. He took the time to enjoy their compliments; whether or not they lied, their words were agreeable and he savoured them.

When the last of them had gone, Mehy strolled slowly down the path to the gate, musing. On one hand, by acquiring great power he was reaping the fruit of long, arduous work; on the other, he was bound hand and foot, unable to attack the bastion he so much wanted to take. Would he have to abandon his grand scheme and settle for being a Theban dignitary with limited ambitions? Serketa would never forgive him if he did, and he himself knew he was capable of much higher things than mere regional powers, however great those might be. To achieve his aim, he must adopt a different strategy, though the modification would demand great skill. Still, thought Mehy, fate had smiled on him, almost miraculously clearing the way for him to see if new obstacles hindered his progress.

He had reached one of the guard-posts.

'Do you want something, General?' asked a soldier.

Mehy emerged from his thoughts. 'No, nothing.'

'Allow me to tell you how proud the Theban soldiers are to serve under you.'

'Thank you, soldier. If all the men feel as you do, we shall continue to do good work.'

The soldier saluted, and Mehy went out of the gate.

Mehy profoundly despised soldiers but, since the start of his career, he had known how to use them to best advantage by flattering them and giving them sought-after privileges.

When he got home, Mehy received the homage of his servants, who were proud to serve such a powerful master, and Serketa give him a come-hither glance, inviting him to follow her into their private rooms.

'Aren't you tired of all these formalities, my sweet?' she cooed.

'No, they amuse me enormously. After all, it's enjoyable to have one's true worth recognized.'

Serketa lay down on a pile of cushions and slowly bared her breasts.

Stroking them, Mehy asked, 'Did you have any difficulty in getting rid of that imbecile Abry?'

'None at all. And I was right: he was going to denounce us. In future, in your new position, we must be particularly careful in our choice of allies. I do hope these honours haven't made you give up our plans?'

'Of course not. But, as you've just said, we must be very

careful. Indeed, one false move would be fatal.'

'Our adventure is getting madly exciting.' Serketa stretched out like a cat, offering herself. 'And we have so many weapons . . .'

Unable to resist any longer, Mehy embraced her roughly, but he had only one thought in his head: as long as he never recoiled, even in the face of crime, success lay at the end of the road.

20

Ubekhet marvelled at the gifts the Brotherhood were presenting to the Master, to celebrate his recognition by the king. They had been prepared in the greatest secrecy, and Casa the Rope, Nakht the Powerful, Karo the Impatient, Pai the Good Bread and Didia the Generous had brought them to Nefer's house. Renupe the Jovial, with his mischievous genie's face and his big fat stomach, had been chosen to present the gifts.

He began with a finely crafted chair, high-backed with feet shaped into lions' paws resting on cylinders, its rush seat so solid that it would last for centuries. It was decorated with spirals, diamonds, lotus-flowers and pomegranates surrounding a sun to symbolize the perpetual rebirth of the architect's thoughts. This was paired with a useful folding chair, whose legs and uprights ended in ducks' heads; this little masterpiece was further embellished with marquetry in ivory and ebony.

Another chair with a curved, sloping back was made up of twenty-eight pieces of wood held together by tenons and mortises; its legs ended in lions' feet resting on bulls' hooves, embodying shining light and power, and it was decorated with a vine and fine bunches of grapes which evoked the rites of the wine-press, during which the wine was likened to the blood of the reborn Osiris.

Several leather-seated stools, low rectangular tables,

pedestal tables consisting of a circular top resting on a central leg which flared out at its base, several storage chests for linen, clothes and tools, baskets for bread, cakes and fruit, oval, oblong and cylindrical baskets made from the ribs of palm or rush stems, tied together so well that they were stout enough to withstand any test . . . Ubekhet was witnessing a veritable procession!

'This is too much, much too much, I . . .'

Pai laid on the table a delicate cylindrical jewel-box with a conical lid. It was made of plastered and painted cartonnage, and was decorated with a lotus in full bloom.

'This is crazy! I can't—'

'And here's our last gift,' said Renupe.

Paneb entered, smiling broadly. On his back he carried a new bed, of such fine quality that it was worth at least five sacks of grain. From the base with its interwoven crosspieces to the boards at the head and foot, which featured the laughing face of Bes, the protector of sleep, the craftsmen had surpassed themselves.

'Ubekhet,' said Paneb, 'I ask permission to enter your bedroom.'

'What on earth is going on?' demanded Nefer. He was standing, rooted to the spot, in the doorway.

'The Brotherhood has decided to turn our house into a palace,' said Ubekhet. 'Look, we're being inundated with presents.'

Like his wife, the Master was stunned.

'That's how it is and there's no more to be said,' declared Renupe. 'The important thing is to respect custom. When you have a good leader, you have to look after him because he only ever thinks about other people.'

'You'll at least stay and have a glass of wine, won't you?'

Renupe smiled broadly. 'There you are: more proof that we made the right choice.'

Paneb served the wine.

'Meneptah has decided to build his tomb in the Valley of the Kings where we spent the morning,' Nefer told Ubekhet. 'This evening, the royal couple wish to see you.'

'Me? Why?'

'To crown the Wise Woman.'

Ubekhet would have liked some time and peace to prepare herself for the ceremony, but she was given neither. Her cleaning-woman, bewildered by all this new furniture, kept asking what to do. Then several people came to consult her: a little girl with the beginnings of bronchitis, a stone-cutter with toothache, and a woman whose hair was falling out. The Wise Woman dealt patiently with them all – she knew and could cure their ailments. But the time flew by, and soon it was almost nightfall.

Ubekhet thought of her predecesssor, who had taught her so much before vanishing into the mountain to be united with the goddess of silence. She felt her beside her, encouraging and protective.

Nefer came rushing back from the House of Life, where he had been studying the maps of the royal tombs in order to draw up a plan and put it to Meneptah. Absorbed in his work, he had not stopped until the rays of the setting sun lit up the papyrus scrolls.

'I'm sorry I'm so late,' he said.

'I'm even later,' said Ubekhet ruefully.

All the same, they flew into each other's arms and kissed lovingly before dressing in their ceremonial clothes.

The royal couple greeted the Wise Woman in the pillared hall of the temple of Ramses the Great's *ka*. Out of respect for his father, Meneptah would not build a similar temple in the Place of Truth before he had passed the test of holding power for a long time. Because his age, sixty-five, made that rather unlikely, he would be content with this shrine, which was at once modest and splendid, the better to associate himself with the great pharaoh's posthumous destiny.

On a throne to the left of the king sat the Great Royal Wife, Iset the Fair; to his right stood the Master, Nefer the Silent. Seated on the stone benches that ran along the walls were the priestesses of Hathor, dressed in long white robes.

'Go and seek out the Wise Woman,' ordered Meneptah.

Turquoise bowed before the royal couple, left the pillared hall and joined Ubekhet, who had just been purified by two priestesses. She dressed her in an ankle-length robe of pleated white and pink linen, a broad gold necklace and narrow bracelets of the same metal, and placed upon her head a black wig, held in place by a band surmounted by a lotus.

Then Turquoise led Ubekhet into the sacred place, where she stood facing the pharaoh and the queen, her hands crossed in front of her breasts.

'We call "Woman" the father and mother of the gods, the stellar womb from which all forms of life issue forth,' declared Iset the Fair. 'Without it, neither Egypt nor this Brotherhood would exist. The Divine does not take flesh unless the primordial woman can attract and hold it. That is my role at the head of the state and it is yours, Ubekhet, in the Place of Truth. If the village disappeared, the country would be in peril. It is up to you to perpetuate the life that flows in the veins of this community, to maintain the fire that enables it to create.'

Iset rose, stepped forward and placed a circlet of gold on Ubekhet's head. 'Thanks to your presence, Wise Woman, the sun rises and death moves further away. Know how to link words and sounds so that the rituals may be celebrated and the offerings consecrated. Know how to bind people together so that they may form one body, whose unity is unshakeable.'

The Master handed the queen a golden dovetail, which she pinned to Ubekhet's robe, over her heart.

'Be the mother of the Brotherhood, feed it and care for it. Uphold peace and harmony between humans and the gods, who are quick to anger at our weaknesses and afflict us with sicknesses and accidents; know how to decipher the messages of the Invisible One at the right moment, identify the origin of ills, prepare remedies, master venoms, be "she who understands and knows".'

As the queen returned to her throne, Ubekhet trembled. The recitation of her duties suddenly gave them a hugeness she had not yet comprehended. She was afraid, afraid to the point of giving in and confessing to the royal couple that she was a simple woman, incapable of fulfilling such terrifying responsibilities.

But her eyes met Nefer's. At that moment he was looking at her not only as a husband but as the Master of the Place of Truth. And in his eyes she found so much trust, love and admiration that she could not bear to show herself unworthy of him.

'On the recommendation of the Great Royal Wife and with the unanimous agreement of the initiates present in this temple,' declared Pharaoh, 'we name you High Priestess of the community of priestesses of Hathor at the Place of Truth.'

21

Meneptah and Iset the Fair were happy at the little palace in the Place of Truth. Far from the court, from flatterers and supplicants, the royal couple celebrated the rites, visited the workshops, and enjoyed the music played by the priestesses of Hathor. They visited the site where Meneptah's Temple of a Million Years would be built; and Nefer took Iset to the Valley of the Queens, to show her the location of her house of eternity, which would be magically linked to that of the pharaoh.

More than once the king and queen invited to dinner the Master, the Wise Woman, the Scribe of the Tomb and Hay, overseer of the port crew, to hear them talk of the Brotherhood's work and way of life. Kenhir had an inexhaustible fund of stories about the community. He made the king smile several times as he described the craftsmen's foibles and the proliferation, at certain times of the year, of reasons for absence from work, which, said Kenhir, he checked very, very carefully.

Even here, though, Meneptah could not escape the cares of state. During a banquet to celebrate the memory of the pharaohs who had protected the Brotherhood, the tjaty appeared, looking very grave.

He bowed before the king and said, 'May I speak with you privately, Majesty?'

'Can you not wait until the end of the meal?'

'I should like to know your wishes as soon as possible, so that I may immediately send instructions to the capital.'

The king rose at once and followed the tjaty out of the dining-hall. The conversation lasted a long time, and when Meneptah reappeared, there was concern on his face.

'I shall leave for Pi-Ramses first thing tomorrow,' he announced.

'Shall I have time to show you the first plan I've prepared for your tomb, Majesty?' asked Nefer.

'Let us go and look at it now,' said Meneptah.

The document had been laid out in the House of Life, and the pharaoh, Nefer and Kenhir pored over it. The Master had adhered to the rules in force under the pharaohs Seti and Ramses.

'I approve this plan,' said Meneptah, 'and I require no changes. As regards the choice of texts and illustrations, and their arrangement on the walls, you are to send me other, very detailed plans. And don't forget, Master: no mistakes. Each element must be in its proper place.'

Nefer knew that a royal tomb was like no other monument and that it must be conceived like a magic furnace whose fire produced eternity. By taking his inspiration from his predecessors' example and assimilating all the dimensions of sacred lore, he must produce a composition whose every component harmonized with every other and with the whole.

When he thought about the difficulty of achieving that, Nefer felt dizzy. To rid himself of the feeling, he set to work by consulting the papyri in which the words of the gods had been preserved.

Mehy had never in his life worked so hard. He had to divide his time between his two offices: army headquarters on the eastern bank, and the main administrative office on the west bank. He had ordered both to be repainted and luxuriously furnished and, when he thought the work was going too slowly, had demanded and got more workmen.

This hectic existence, constantly crossing from one bank to the other, attending meetings, studying files and taking decisions, suited Mehy perfectly, for his energy seemed inexhaustible. His responsibilities might be only regional, but the region in question was as wealthy as it was prestigious and would enable him to become one of the most important people in the country, especially if he succeeded in gaining admission to Meneptah's court at Pi-Ramses.

Standing at the window of his office at army headquarters, Mehy contemplated the future. He was determined to carry out his official duties excellently and thus acquire the stature of a statesman. Everyone would think him one of those high dignitaries who were satisfied with themselves and their good fortune. Who would suspect his true aims?

A senior officer came in and saluted. 'General, your presence is requested urgently at the quay.'

'Why? What's happened?'

'The king will be leaving Thebes shortly. All the security forces are to be deployed.'

'I'll come at once.'

Indeed, the royal flotilla was about to weigh anchor. Mehy made the necessary arrangements to keep onlookers away, and bowed low before the king as he embarked. He noted that Meneptah looked worried. The tjaty was waiting for the king on the bridge, and the two men immediately went into the central cabin.

Mehy talked to several leading Theban citizens, to try to find out why the king was leaving so suddenly, but no one knew anything, and everyone was worried.

The only person whose opinion seemed worth heeding was an old man leaning on a stick. 'Either Pharaoh's opponents are trying to seize power in Pi-Ramses,' he said, 'or there's a threat of invasion. Whatever the truth may be, the skies over Egypt are darkening.'

*

Though he refused to be the slave of a rigid geometry which would have sucked the life from his work, Paneb had absorbed Gau's teaching and made no further mistakes with the grids. That didn't stop Gau correcting several details and scolding him for making imprecise calculations, and the two men had quite a few arguments. Sometimes Paneb gave in, but he often proved, once the motif was coloured in, that he was right.

Pai was happy to see Paneb becoming assistant to Ched the Saviour. Unesh the Jackal, however, was not. Unesh had long recognized Ched's genius, and superiority over the artists who prepared his work for him, but was not ready to obey young Paneb, whatever his gifts might be.

Ched followed every step of his pupil's progress, and permitted nothing that was not perfect. Before taking him into the Valley of the Kings to work on decorating Meneptah's tomb, Ched wanted to put Paneb to a decisive test of skill: if the young man failed, he would never be a real painter. So Ched had asked the three artists to prepare the corner of a wall in the big tomb that Kenhir would occupy. Paneb was charged with painting a craftsman, dressed in the white robe of a priest, offering incense to Ptah.

When he arrived in the tomb, armed with his brushes and paints, he found that not even the preparation of the wall had been done. Leaning against it and munching an onion was Unesh, whose expression made him look more than ever like a jackal.

'Where are the others?' asked Paneb.

'Gau has stomach-ache and Pai has a bad cold. And I stupidly cut my finger while I was cooking. It seems to be one of those days when everything goes wrong. Unfortunately for you, Ched will soon be arriving to examine your painting, and you haven't even started.'

'It's really kind of you to have waited here to tell me, but hadn't you better go home now?'

'You're right. My cut might get infected, so I'll go and get it seen to.'

Paneb should have given in and admitted defeat but he preferred to fight, even if the result was a foregone conclusion. He checked that the plasterwork was of good enough quality, then drew in the grid. After preparing his colours, he did no preliminary drawing but painted the figure directly on to the wall. This was a serious infraction of the rules, but there was no time to do anything else. When Ched arrived to check on his pupil's work, Paneb might have failed, but at least Ched would see that he'd done everything in his power to finish the work.

The morning went by, then the early afternoon . . . still no Ched. Paneb had time to put the finishing touches to his work, refine details here and there and check that the scene was balanced.

He stepped back to take a final look, and suddenly a thousand faults leapt out at him.

'Pleased with yourself?' demanded Ched, who was standing behind him, arms crossed.

'No, it's only a sketch.'

'When you paint, you must view your work face-on, in profile and in three-quarter profile. You must eliminate deceptive perspectives which take away the life force, and you must exclude over-dramatic effects of light and shade, link multiple points of view by stressing the essential details: the face must be seen in profile, the eye face-on, the torso face-on in all its width, the pelvis three-quarters on with the navel visible, the arms and legs in profile. Create a space which does not exist and make us see the hidden reality. When you draw a falcon, bring together several moments of its flight in a single image; when it is a human figure, unveil all its characteristics at once. And never forget that our work is not written in time; these are eternal moments, which we are charged with making flesh. We never evoke a particular time of day, for what matters is the day as the fruit of the light. You must always live in unmoving movement; let it be the central point of your hand. And respect the order of beings: Pharaoh is of greater stature than men, for he is the great temple that shelters his people; the master of an estate is larger than his servants because he exercises more responsibilities than they do and must ensure their wellbeing. And a priest, like the one on this wall, should have his eyes raised slightly to the heavens.'

Paneb drank in Ched's words.

'For a painting produced rather quickly,' Ched went on, 'I've seen worse. But you must prove that you can correct its failings. Otherwise, just imagine what Kenhir will say!'

Everything that had seethed within Paneb's heart since his boyhood was at last going to be able to express itself, for Ched had opened his eyes to another reality, one that was more intense, more beautiful and more vital than the visible world.

Pai the Good Bread rushed into the tomb. 'Paneb, come quickly. Uabet's having her baby!'

22

The Wise Woman had called upon six priestesses of Hathor to help Uabet give birth. Their faces were grave, for they all knew that a child's journey into the world was a perilous one. They must separate it from its mother's body without any evil touching it, in the hope that the creative powers would enliven it and not leave its spirit at the moment of its birth.

Ubekhet had thrown bird-fat and incense into the fire, then positioned two stones covered with magical texts according to which Thoth fixed the newborn baby's lifespan and destiny. Her assistants had reduced Uabet's pain by smearing her vagina with a paste made of milk, fennel, terebinth resin, onion and salt.

Though Uabet's belly had swollen spectacularly during the last days of her pregnancy, she looked frail, and she could not hide her anxiety. 'Is everything normal?'

'Don't worry,' said Ubekhet, 'the birth is imminent, and you won't even need to take drugs to reduce the pain. The child is lying in the best possible presentation.'

'But it feels enormous. Won't it tear me?'

'No, don't worry about that. Your pelvis may be small but it was made for childbearing.'

The contractions came closer together. The priestesses undressed Uabet and helped her to squat, while supporting her back.

As Ubekhet had predicted, the child was born without complications. The cry it let out was so loud that it let half the village know it had arrived.

'Why can't I go in?' said Paneb furiously.

'Because the ritual of birth is women's business,' replied Pai. 'Your being there would be both pointless and dangerous.'

'But it's my child that's being born!'

'Just calm down and let the Wise Woman and her assistants do their job.'

Paneb paced up and down in silence for a few minutes. Then he asked, 'Pai, how do you bring up a child?'

'A child is a twisted stick with two defects: deafness and ingratitude. As soon as possible, you must open the ear on its back,* tell it what its duties are, make it understand all that it owes to its parents and teach it respect for others. Then the twist will be straightened, and the child begin to be righteous so that it can grow up.'

'If my child's anything like me, I'll have no chance of straightening it.'

The bedroom door opened and Ubekhet emerged, beaming. 'It's a boy, a beautiful boy. And a very big, strong one.'

Paneb rushed into the jasmine-scented room where his wife lay on a comfortable bed, holding an enormous baby in her arms. He had a fine mass of black hair and two teeth, which his father ran an astonished finger over.

'I've never seen that before,' confessed the eldest midwife. 'The umbilical cord was so thick that we had difficulty cutting it.'

Paneb was amazed but delighted. If appearances were

* An expression used by the sages, who believed an uneducated child was deaf because 'the ear on its back' had not been opened by 'the staff' (*medu*), that is, the word of the teacher, which equipped a child with the staff needed to undertake the journey of life.

anything to go by, this giant of a son would be as strong and healthy as his father.

'Are you pleased with me?' asked Uabet in a tired little voice.

He kissed her on the forehead, and asked, 'Can I hold him?'

'Be careful!'

'He's going to be a real fighter, I'm sure of it.'

The mother gave the child its flesh, the father its bones; and it was in a boy's bones that his sperm was formed. In view of the baby's weight, Paneb felt sure his son would have no difficulty fathering children.

Ubekhet gave the young mother some honey and a birth-cake known as 'the Sweet Eye of Horus'. A priestess ground up the ends of some papyrus-stems to make a powder which she mixed with some of the new mother's milk. She would make the baby drink the mixture before it was suckled by a wet-nurse with generous breasts.

'Have all the proper precautions been taken?' asked Paneb.

Round the baby's neck Ubekhet had fastened a thin linen necklace with seven knots, to which was attached a little piece of folded papyrus containing a clove of garlic and a tiny onion; on the papyrus were written magic words to protect him against the forces of darkness,

'Only the light will save this child from death which comes like a thief,' she said. 'No demon will come forth from the shadows to carry him away, for we shall keep a lamp lit through the night and watch over him.'

Reassured, Paneb broached another vital subject. 'What shall we name him, Uabet?'

It was up to the mother to choose. She could give him one name, to be used during infancy, and another secret one, to be revealed only when the child's character became clear.

'One name will be enough,' Uabet decided. 'Our son shall be called Aapehti, "He Who Has Great Strength".'

*

The din began in the middle of the night. At first there was just one deep, drunken voice singing, then a second, more halting but louder, and finally a third which tried, very loudly indeed and appallingly out of tune, to join in the song.

The three revellers roared their love of wine, women and freedom so loudly that they woke the whole village. Children whined, dogs barked. Eventually, at the end of her tether, Pai the Good Bread's wife got up, dressed and stormed out to find the troublemakers and order them to be quiet.

To her astonishment, she found Pai clinging to one of Paneb's arms; clinging to the other was Renupe the Jovial, who couldn't have stood upright without this support. Paneb was swigging from a jug of wine.

Panicked by the sight of his wife, Pai let go of Pancb and fell over. He peered owlishly up at her. 'I can exshplain. We've been shebrel . . . shelebrating Aapehti's birth and I—'

'Your're coming home with me – at once.'

'We're free men,' declared Renupe proudly, 'and we haven't finished our song!'

Pai's wife slapped him, and grabbed her husband by the scruff of his neck and hauled him to his feet so roughly that he yelped with pain. She dragged him away down the street, and Renupe followed, still protesting about their song.

Paneb burst out laughing, and emptied his wine-jug. Still singing, he went on down the street and halted in front of Turquoise's house. He'd had an amusing idea which would both dazzle the village and prove how talented he was.

When Turquoise opened her door next morning, she found a crowd outside. They were admiring the half-finished portrait of his mistress that Paneb had drawn on the wall of her house. It showed her playing the lute, dressed only in a delicate pearl-studded belt whose fine detail emphasized her seductive curves. Paneb himself lay fast asleep in the middle of the narrow street, a paintbrush still clutched in his hand.

Comments rang out on every side, and they were not flattering. Already, Nakht the Powerful had started to rub out this scandalous creation, and Paneb was being accused of having a burning mouth and a lustful heart.

'Do you know what he dared do?' shouted a priestess. 'He stole wine from the offertory tables, wine destined for the dead!'

'Don't talk rubbish,' snapped Turquoise. 'Everything he drank came from my wine-jars. There's only one person who might be offended by his painting, and that's me – and I'm not in the least offended. It's no sin to celebrate.'

'It is when it's done like that!' objected Pai's wife. 'The village has always lived quietly, and we don't want that hot-head Paneb changing things.'

'Weren't you ever young?' demanded Turquoise.

'Yes, but I'm glad to say I never got so drunk that I didn't know what I was doing. Paneb much be punished severely.'

Ched the Saviour, perfumed and impeccably shaved as always, spoke up. 'Don't forget that he's now my assistant and there's a lot of work waiting for him. Personally, I think this incident should be ignored.'

An animated discussion ensued. After a while it was interrupted by the arrival of Nefer, who had worked late into the night on the plan of Meneptah's tomb. The upshot was inevitable: 'Let's ask the Master,' shouted Casa the Rope. 'He'll know what's the right thing to do.'

Everyone began talking at once and, faced with so many contradictory statements, Nefer had some difficulty in finding out exactly what had happened. Fortunately, Turquoise's account, brief and to the point, enlightened him.

'Go home, all of you,' he said, 'and leave me alone with Paneb.'

At the sight of his angry face, Pai's wife was sure that the reveller – who had slept soundly through all the uproar – was going to have an unpleasant time.

The Master took a terracotta cupful of water from a large jar and threw it over Paneb.

He awoke immediately and sat up, ready to defend himself. 'Who did tha—'

'Your Master, Paneb, the man to whom you owe respect and obedience.'

23

Ignoring his terrible hangover, Paneb stood up and leant against the wall of Turquoise's house.

'Why has her portrait been rubbed off?' he demanded indignantly.

'Because the walls of our houses must be pure white. You yourself restored them, remember? You cannot allow them to be soiled by lewd drawings.'

Paneb threw his brush in the air. 'I want to conquer the sky, the stars and the whole earth, capture them in my painting, make the most secret reality appear, make it vibrant and hot like the body of a loving woman! And I will paint it where I want – even on the wall of a house.'

'No you won't.'

The young man's still-bleary eyes met Nefer's challengingly. 'What do you mean, no? You're not going to dictate how I behave.'

'I'm your overseer and I have the power to expel you from the Brotherhood if you commit a serious enough offence – such as refusing to obey the Master.'

The threat sobered Paneb at once. 'You're not serious?'

'I'm very serious. Whatever happens to us, whether good things or bad, we have no right to behave like unbelievers, and we must always show that we are worthy of the Brotherhood. Your attitude is unacceptable.'

'In other words, you aren't my friend any more.'

'The hive is more important than the bee. It is also more important than friendships and personal likes or dislikes. You're the one who's making me have to act as Master, and I warn you that I shall do my duty, no matter what it costs me.'

Paneb clenched his fists. 'The drawing has been erased and the wall is white again. What else are you going to scold me about?'

'Drunkenness, disturbing the peace and a lack of self-discipline. When will you finally understand that you are part of the Great Work?'

'That's your affair. I'm just Ched's assistant.'

'You're wrong again,' said Nefer. 'All the inhabitants of this village, in varying degrees, are taking part in the same adventure. Whatever your gifts may be, I will not authorize you to use them alone.'

Paneb could tell the Master wasn't joking. He tried to explain. 'Do you at least understand what it is that's seething inside me? I could paint dozens of houses of eternity without ever tiring.'

'I hope that one day you will. In the meantime, either you accept your punishment or you leave the Place of Truth.'

Paneb turned his back on his judge. 'Will the punishment be dishonourable?'

'You don't know me very well, do you? You're an assistant painter, and even a punishment must benefit the Brotherhood.'

Mehy worked quickly and well. He had used his knowledge of the army and government in establishing efficient networks of informants. Through them he gathered a great deal of confidential information on every possible subject, which enabled him to understand how the situation was developing and to avoid making any mistakes.

The general demanded the strictest discipline and

surrounded himself with subordinates to whom his word was law, men to whom he promised substantial rewards if they pleased him. Promising, not keeping the promise, explaining why the promise had not been kept, and promising again: Mehy was a past master of that subtle art, and to it he added the use of slander, refined day after day. Using such methods, he set his collaborators against each other and created a climate of distrust which would be extremely useful when it came to blaming someone else for a failure or a bad move.

The general lied with an assurance and conviction which carried the day with all he talked to; and since, unlike most high officials, he worked extremely hard, he knew exactly what was in his files and had no need to fear criticism.

Some senior officers still had flashes of integrity, or even clear-headedness, which might prove threatening. Mehy watched them closely and even invited them to dine with him so as to get his loving wife's opinion. She had taken such pleasure in killing that she would not hesitate for a moment to do so again, if necessary. Having an ally with that talent meant that many problems would be resolved before they even fully emerged.

When the Theban soldiers who had escorted the royal party back to Pi-Ramses returned to Thebes, Mehy sent for their commander.

'Did the king's journey go smoothly?' he asked.

'Yes, General, and there are no incidents to report. The country is calm, Pharaoh's fleet was cheered throughout the journey, and Meneptah arrived at the capital in excellent health.'

'What did you think of Pi-Ramses?'

'To be frank, General, I found it less impressive than Thebes. True, the temples and palaces are magnificent, but they haven't the history that gives our city its glory. And nothing can equal Karnak.'

'What did you find out about the political situation?'

'It's rather uneasy. No one challenges Meneptah's ability to govern, but ambitious men are already clashing in anticipation of the accession of another pharaoh, which, given Meneptah's age, probably won't be long in coming.'

'He's Ramses' son, don't forget, and he might live as long as his father did.'

'You're right, sir,' said the soldier, 'but people do seem to be forgetting it. There's beginning to be serious friction between the two main candidates, Meneptah's son Seti and Seti's son Amenmessu, whom even his own father seems unable to control.'

'Get me detailed information about both of them,' ordered Mehy.

'Yes, sir. We have a few good friends at Pi-Ramses, officers of Theban origin.'

'Why did the king return to the capital so suddenly?'

'Someone had begun a rumour that Meneptah had died at Thebes, and Amenmessu at once had the word spread that his father was so grief-stricken that he wouldn't have the heart to mount the throne. Several denials of the rumour arrived by official courier, but not everyone believed them, so the king had to return as soon as possible to prove he really was still alive. Everything seems to have quietened down again, but Meneptah will have great difficulty re-asserting his authority and crushing the plots.'

Mehy thought, 'So that's why he is so determined to keep the Theban region loyal and submissive. If it rebelled, he might not have the means to re-establish order.'

'There's one other thing you ought to know, General. All garrisons on the western and north-western frontiers have been put on alert.'

'That's vital information,' said Mehy furiously. 'Why didn't you tell me straight away?'

'Because it turned out that the alert was only an exercise. Meneptah wanted to be sure that his orders would be correctly passed on and obeyed. It seems there were no weak points in the system.'

'All the same . . . Are you sure the exercise wasn't being used to mask a threat of invasion?'

'Quite sure, sir. Everything's quiet on the frontiers. However, some officers think their weapons are too old, that there aren't enough good soldiers, and that long years of peace have weakened the army's fighting-instinct.'

'That's exactly why I reorganized the Theban troops so thoroughly.'

'The elite regiments that would defend the borders in case of attack are based at Pi-Ramses, but their training may not be not intensive enough. Still, there's no serious threat to Egypt, and the peace Ramses established should last.'

Mehy disagreed. Ramses was dead, and his magic along with him. He had been adept at compelling the Libyans, Syrians and others to accept peace, but their aggression would soon revive and an ageing Meneptah would not be able to counter the vengeful plotting of these war-hungry peoples. It was up to Mehy to work out how best to use these last years of peace to make the Theban army even more powerful. One day it would be Egypt's last defence, and he would be Egypt's saviour.

'What about the queen?' he asked. 'What do people say about her?'

'She's utterly loyal to her husband and has no reason to complain of the way he treats her. The bond between them is very strong, and Meneptah has never shown the least interest in the young beauties who flaunt themselves at court. In the past, his austere character meant he spent most of his time working, and he seldom honoured a banquet with his presence. Now that he's king and the weight of his responsibilities has grown, he probably won't even go sailing in the marshes any more.'

'A pity about the queen,' Mehy said to himself. 'A second-rate, treacherous one could have been manipulated with some profit.' Aloud, he said, 'And the queen's household?'

'Iset rules her staff very strictly. Actually, of course, she's controlled the household for years, with Ramses' agreement, and it's ages since there was any scandal at court. She's said to be an excellent manager, and no one would dare try to trick her.'

In Mehy's eyes, this report contained many positive points which he must be ready to exploit. Readiness alone would not be enough; he must find new weak points, and enlarge existing ones. And he still had to find an answer to a very delicate question: how should he behave towards the Place of Truth?

24

Commander Sobek was good at his job and, like any good officer, he had an acute sense of danger. Now, as he sat in his office waiting for his patrol-leaders to come and make their reports, he felt it was very close, almost certainly inside the Place of Truth. The years of fruitless investigation had not blunted his resolve to find out who had murdered one of his men and tried to pin the crime on Nefer the Silent.

With Ramses' death and Nefer's appointment as Master, had the criminal decided to keep quiet for ever? Sobek didn't think so. The murderer was patient and determined, and was in ruthless pursuit of his aims. Nefer was more at risk than ever.

Abry was dead, but Sobek was convinced that the criminal within the Brotherhood must have other accomplices on the outside. That Abry had been designated protector of the Place of Truth was a bitter irony – and one that underlined the deadliness of the threat. His death had severed an important thread of the plot, but Sobek might manage to tie the severed ends together by identifying the craftsman who had betrayed his oath.

So the big Nubian came to a decision which he decided he would not mention to anyone else: using all the means at his disposal, he was going to keep watch on every single member of the starboard crew. The murderer, if he had indeed gone to ground at the crew's very heart, would make a mistake sooner or later, and then Sobek would pounce. This was his last chance of success, and he was not going to let it slip away.

The patrol-leaders arrived and saluted.

'Sir,' said one of them, 'the donkey has arrived.'

'The donkey? What donkey?'

'The one you ordered, sir . . . didn't you?'

'Oh yes, so I did. Tell the seller I'll pay him within the week.'

The officers reported that they had nothing to report: nothing out of the ordinary had happened, the Valley of the Kings was well guarded, and no suspicious persons had tried to approach. Everything was quiet; so quiet that they ventured to complain about all the extra hours they were, for no apparent reason, having to work and about how badly the extra work was paid.

'Where do you think you are, you fat-witted imbeciles?' roared Sobek furiously. 'You aren't guarding a grain depot, you're ensuring the safety of the Place of Truth! Serving here is an honour, and any bonehead who doesn't want that honour can hand me his resignation here and now!'

There was dead silence.

Sobek dismissed them and, after they had gone sheepishly back to their posts, went outside to examine his donkey, which one of his men was feeding and watering.

'How much is the seller asking?'

The guard said woodenly, 'A piece of fabric, a pair of sandals, one sack of rye and another of flour, sir.'

'Does the damned man take me for a fool? This pathetic creature's old and ill. It'd never be able to climb the mountain paths. Take it to a palm grove, where it can end its days peacefully.'

The donkey-seller bowed before Mehy and said, 'I have obeyed your instructions, my lord'.

'You delivered an old animal to Commander Sobek?'

'So old that it can barely walk.'

'Did you ask a good price?'

'The price of a donkey in good health.'

'Was the delivery note registered?'

'Certainly, my lord, but the description on it was that of a fine healthy animal – the one that several witnesses saw leaving my field.'

'Good. Sobek will have to pay you. You are not to harass him. Just let time pass. Now I have good news for you, my man. The government is ordering a hundred donkeys from you. Make sure they're good, strong animals and that the price is reasonable – I have to keep a sharp eye on expenditure.'

Paneb worked day and night in order to finish, as quickly as possible, the work Nefer had given him by way of punishment. When it was done, he would have the opportunity to learn a new technique, that of sculpting stelae, and perfecting a type of drawing which he had not often practised before now.

Turquoise's wine was so good that his hangover had not lasted long; and, since Aapehti and Uabet were both thriving, Paneb did not regret the little celebration for a moment. The villagers were still angry about it but, shut away in his workshop, the guilty party had the good fortune not to hear their complaints.

When Nefer appeared, Paneb was putting the final touch of green on an ear intended for a statue of Osiris.

He had made more than a hundred ears: black ones, like those of the illustrious Queen Ahmose Nefertari, founder of the sisterhood of the Place of Truth; yellow ones, like those of her son, Amenhotep I, revered by builders; dark blue ones to evoke the sky where the air created by the gods circulated; limestone ears; and others sculpted in relief or cut into stelae which would be placed in chapels.

'I asked for only ten pairs of ears as an offering to the temple,' said the Master.

'I developed a taste for them. With all these, the gods should easily be able to hear the prayers of the whole village.'

'The magic must operate in two directions. May they hear us indeed, but above all may we, and particularly you, hear them. Have you forgotten that a Servant of the Place of Truth is "He Who Hears the Call"? By listening only to yourself, you risk becoming deaf to the spirit of the village.'

'I know, I know,' grumbled Paneb, '"Listening is the best thing of all." But that's all I've been doing for the last ten years, listening!'

'First, you're exaggerating; second, do you believe that a craftsman ever finishes listening?'

'Don't moralize at me! Do I have to hand out these ears myself?'

'Of course.'

Nakht the Powerful came running up. 'A tragedy,' he said, getting the words out only with difficulty, 'a terrible tragedy. It's the child. He . . . he's dead.'

Paneb shot out of the workshop and ran like an arrow to his house. Why had destiny dealt him such a cruel blow? Getting drunk wasn't such a serious sin against the gods! Yes, he was vain of his talent and his head had swollen these last few weeks, but the child wasn't to blame for that.

He found Uabet resting in the living-room.

'Paneb,' she said in surprise, 'why aren't you at work? What's the matter? You look frantic.'

'How did it happen?'

'What are you talking about?'

He seized her by the shoulders. 'Tell me, Uabet! I must know!'

'Know about what?'

'My son! How did he die?'

'What on earth do you mean? He isn't dead – the wet-nurse is suckling him.'

Paneb rushed into the bedroom. Sure enough, Aapehti was suckling greedily, not pausing for breath.

'He's already put on weight,' said the nurse. 'He really is a fine boy.'

When he went back into the living-room, Uabet looked up anxiously. 'Why did you think he was dead?'

'Nakht said that "the child" was dead, and I though he meant Aapehti.'

What had happened was that a little boy had been walking along the edge of a balcony to impress a little girl. He had lost his balance and fallen, landing head-down on a flight of steps. Ubekhet was fetched at once, but all she could do was confirm that the child was dead. His mother had fainted, and Ubekhet went to tend to her.

The horrified villagers had assembled at the scene of the tragedy, but no one had dared touch the dead child. It was Paneb who gently lifted the broken little body and cradled it against his chest, as though the child were sleeping.

His face lined with grief, Thuty the goldsmith stepped forward out of the crowd. 'That's my son,' he said, 'my second son. He was only five.'

'Do you want to take him?'

'No, Paneb, I haven't the courage. Thank you for your help, thank you with all my heart.'

The Master arrived, dressed in the starry robe of the Priest of Resurrection and asked several craftsmen to purify themselves in order to assist him in the funerary rites.

Still in a state of shock, the villagers processed to the eastern cemetery, where, in a low-lying area, children who had died young were buried. Urns held foetuses and stillborn children; round or oval baskets held infants whom Death the Abductor had stolen away, defeating their magic protection.

For Thuty's son, Didia the Generous had donated a little flat-lidded, rectangular sycamore chest, which he had been keeping in reserve in his workshop.

While Nefer the Silent led a ritual announcing the return of the child into the immense body of his celestial mother, Paneb wrapped the little corpse in a linen cloth and laid it in the sarcophagus, where Turquoise had placed two vases containing bread, grapes and dates which would feed him on his journey to the afterlife. Then the coffin was lowered into its grave and the god of the earth absorbed it, to transform it into a boat which would sail across the waters of the heavens.

In accordance with their rule, the craftsmen of the Place of Truth were their own priests and they had no need of any outside help. The entire village would wear mourning, and no one would forget the tears of Paneb, who, right up to the moment when he had to lay the child in the coffin, had hoped against hope that his own warmth and energy would bring him back to life.

25

'It's no good, Mehy. My patience is exhausted, and I'm not prepared to wait any longer.'

The fat, bearded little man who dared to address the general thus was Daktair, the son of a Greek mathematician and a Persian alchemist. He was an unattractive creature, with aggressive black eyes, red hair and unusually short legs.

Appointed to run the central workshop at Thebes, situated on the west bank not far from the Place of Truth, Daktair had dreamt up a grand plan: to force old Egypt to enter the era of new learning and progress, to strip away its outdated beliefs and at last realize its formidable potential. Daktair had, by stealing other people's ideas, become a well-known and respected man of learning. He wanted to enforce his views and press nature into the service of man.

But he still lacked two important things: support from a politician of the highest rank, and knowledge of the Place of Truth's secrets. Mehy, he thought, was the only Egyptian who could supply both. Mehy's spectacular rise to power was matched by his desire to seize the Brotherhood's treasures: he had seen them, and could confirm they were no mere legend. But Mehy had left Daktair kicking his heels in a boring job, where, despite his position, he had not been able to put his talents to work.

Mehy smiled at him. 'You feel forgotten, don't you?'

'Exactly.'

'Well, you haven't been. I simply had other priorities.'

'But my discoveries—'

'Aren't independent of power and never will be. You see, Ramses' death and its consequences seem to me much more important than what you want.'

'I'll accept that, but you're a general and governor of the west bank. Why can't you move now?'

'You're a brilliant man, Daktair, and we'll bring your grand ideas to fruition, but you don't know Egypt very well. I am indeed master of Thebes, but I'm also the designated protector of the Place of Truth. And Pharaoh – in person – will demand an accounting from me.'

'Does that mean we're hamstrung?'

'Not at all, my dear fellow! But we must be as cautious and cunning as wild animals.'

Daktair's shoulders slumped in disappointment. 'So the secrets of that damned Brotherhood are still out of reach.'

'For a man who has shown such patience up to now, you give up hope very quickly.'

'I see things clearly. Your appointments make you powerless.'

'No they don't. I never give up and I know better than anyone else how to manipulate a situation. My power is an advantage, not a disadvantage.'

'Well, what do you propose to do?'

'First, I shall get rid of that inconvenient Commander Sobek. He refused a bribe, but a legal case will see him discredited and will at last breach the village's formidable security. Next, I shall force the Scribe of the Tomb and the Master to fulfil their obligations. Didn't you tell me about a very special expedition which must be organized at regular intervals?'

'Yes, though I don't know why the Brotherhood are involved with it.'

'The end of Ramses' reign and the start of Meneptah's have meant the overthrow of many customs, but I shall see that they're re-established. I imagine you're short of galenite and bitumen in your workshop?'

Daktair's ugly face blossomed into a smile. 'You'll have a detailed report on it first thing tomorrow, and an urgent request for supplies.'

'Do you enjoy travel, my friend?'

'I don't mind it.'

'You'll be the leader of this expedition, Daktair. That way, you'll be able to control everything.'

The craftsmen of the Place of Truth were divided into two categories: those who practised a skill which they had perfected without being 'introduced into the presence of God', and those who, like Nefer the Silent, had experienced the mysteries of the House of Gold and could therefore officiate in the manner of the high priests of Karnak.

Both craftsman and ritualist, the Master went each day to the temple, there to carry out the primordial task: the unveiling of the divine Light which gave life to wood, stone and other materials.

As he purified himself before entering the shrine, Nefer thought of the qualities demanded of a wise man: the ability to do what is righteous and just, to be coherent, silent and calm, to have a firm character capable of bearing both happiness and sadness, a vigilant heart and a tongue which knew when to be silent. He knew he was far from possessing all of them, and yet they were all necessary if he was to carry out his duties without faltering.

The only solution was to go forward, day after day, thinking of the Brotherhood and not of himself. The celebration of the morning rites gave him back energy, while he wondered how to shoulder his many burdens.

Dressed in the golden apron given him by Pharaoh, Nefer

entered the principal temple of the Palace of Truth, dedicated to Ma'at, the eternal regulator of the universe, and to Hathor, creative love. Two paths which made one, two faces of the same divine power.

The first islet to emerge from the ocean of possibilities, the shrine was the eye of God, who watched the world. A living being in perpetual metamorphosis, he fed upon his own substance, the Light hidden in the stones.

Here, all was resonance, heavenly music, harmonious numbers and proportions; here chance and destiny were abolished to make way for a sublimated life which no imperfection could stain. Like the sky in all its parts, the temple was the dwelling of the Mother of builders, she who was named Ma'at, Hathor or goddess of silence; it was there that she caused her children to be reborn in spirit.

After making the offering of Ma'at to herself, at the very moment when Pharaoh was celebrating the same rite in the great temple at Pi-Ramses, Nefer went to the boat-room which, on this site, had a special importance. For the Place of Truth was compared to a great ship in which the two crews took their places.

On this day of mourning for the son of Thuty the goldsmith, his companion in the adventure, the Master wished to link the child to the Brotherhood's great voyage. So he drew a sun on a new cup, which he placed at the bow of the sacred ship, whose oarsmen were the imperishable stars. They would carry the little boy's soul away with them.

When the Master left the temple, the early-morning sun was already shining brightly. The priestesses of Hathor were decorating the altars of the ancestors with flowers, housewives were going to fetch water, and the shouts of children were heard, dispelling the atmosphere of tragedy and pointing to the future.

On either side of the gate in the encircling wall there was

an eared stele, put up by Paneb. Their presence made Nefer smile as he headed for the sculptors' workshop. To his great surprise, he found its door locked.

Renupe the Jovial ran up. 'Don't worry. Everything's all right.'

'Why isn't the workshop open?'

'There's a small problem.'

'Is Userhat the Lion ill?'

'No, I don't think so.'

'Shouldn't he have given you the key?'

'Yes, he should, but . . . but he's lost it. He's looking for it now, and that's why he's late. As soon as he's found it, he'll unlock the door and we'll set to work.'

Nefer frowned. 'You lie very badly, Renupe. Why not tell me the truth?'

The sculptor tried to maintain his usual jollity. 'It's nothing serious, I assure you. A simple misunderstanding which will be sorted out very quickly, I'm sure.'

'Could you be more specific?'

'You know Userhat. He's a difficult man, and now and then he loses his temper.'

'Why has he lost it this time?'

'Let's say . . . a small difference of opinion with Ipuy the Examiner. But it's nothing dramatic, I promise.'

'Why should this quarrel stop Userhat unlocking the workshop?'

Renupe dared not look the Master in the face. 'Well, he . . . he's refusing to come back to work.'

26

In the living-room of his comfortable home, Userhat the Lion had paid homage to the ancestors by laying flowers on the offertory table. When Nefer arrived, he was passing the time by turning a piece of sycamore wood into a duck with articulated wings, a toy for his two daughters.

'I was expecting you, Master,' he said.

'And I'm expecting an explanation.'

Userhat put down the chisel and the half-finished duck, then turned to face Nefer. His powerful craftsman's body shook with indignation.

'I'm the senior sculptor of the starboard crew, and even my colleagues in the port crew consider me their superior. That's true, isn't it?'

'Certainly.'

'In that case, I cannot tolerate Ipuy the Examiner's insulting behaviour towards me. Ever since he held a fan to shade the pharaoh, that pretentious idiot thinks he can do anything – it's intolerable! My mind is made up: until he's expelled from the Brotherhood, I shan't return to work and the sculptors' workshop will stay locked.'

The Master could have got angry, too, and pointed out to Userhat that his attitude was not in accordance with the Brotherhood's rule and that he was behaving as badly as Paneb. But that would only have fanned the flames and risked making the situation worse, just when Nefer needed a united crew to undertake two huge projects.

So instead he sat down on a stool, to try to lance the abcess. 'What exactly has Ipuy done?'

Userhat also took a seat. 'Do you know the price of a good pig?'

'About two ordinary baskets,' hazarded the Master.

'I wanted to buy three, and was offering an excellent price: one luxury basket. The deal seemed done, then the seller told me he had a better customer, who was offering him a bed – a plain bed, it's true, but all the same . . . That's outrageous, way above the real value of three pigs! And who was the dishonest person having fun at my expense? Ipuy the Examiner, my fellow sculptor. He knew perfectly well those pigs were supposed to be for me, and he paid that ridiculous price just to spite me.'

'I see. But why did he do it?'

'Because we disagree over the selling-price of a limestone statue which we have to deliver to the overseer of the granaries at Karnak. Ipuy's asking far too much, and he refuses to listen to my point of view. If I really am his superior, he should obey me. If not . . . no more sculpture.'

'You're right,' said Nefer.

Userhat's face lit up. 'I've always supported you, and I don't regret it. When will you convene the court to pronounce Ipuy's expulsion?'

'There is something more urgent that I must do first.'.

'Oh? What?'

'Warn the pig-seller that he'll sell no more animals at absurd prices. If he tries, no one will buy his pigs, and if that leaves him with Ipuy as his only customer he'll be ruined.'

'Good, good. But what about the price of the statue?'

'I told you, you're right: no more sculpture. The overseer's order is cancelled, and you won't deliver the statue. Ipuy will have lost everything, and your honour will be safe.'

'Well, yes, but it's a high price to pay for winning.' Userhat rubbed his chin. 'Perhaps we might be able to reach a compromise.'

'You? Reach a compromise with Ipuy?'

'No, of course not, but all the same . . . With your authority, you could speak to him and make him admit his mistake. We could finish the statue and sell it at whatever you think is a fair price.'

'If I do that, will you accept a reconciliation with Ipuy?'

Userhat said gruffly, 'Deep down, he's not a bad fellow – but I'm still the head sculptor!'

'Shall we go and open the workshop?'

'It's my duty, and I am proud to carry it out. Tell me, Nefer . . . you think I'm a bit pretentious, too, don't you? And maybe even more stupid than Ipuy?'

'The important thing is the work we have to do. I don't wish to judge either of you.'

Watched by Nefer, Renupe sawed wood while Ipuy smoothed a supporting pillar with an adze. In a corner of the workshop were a funerary mask and a sarcophagus.

Userhat had finished the rough version of the granary-overseer's statue, which was of a kneeling dignitary, his hands held flat against his thighs and his eyes raised to the heavens. The sculptor had drawn the contours of the statue in red on the limestone. Now he was finishing the first polishing with abrasive paste based on powdered quartz, which he applied gently.

Watching him work was fascinating: he caressed the statue, whispering to it of how he was going to bring it to life, and working to a regular rhythm which demanded total control of his breathing and his hand.

When he'd done, Userhat picked up a saw and held it out to Ipuy. 'Your turn.'

Their eyes met. Userhat's held sternness but no hostility;

Ipuy's held respect and friendship.

Ipuy sawed along the red lines with remarkable sureness of touch, cutting away the unwanted stone to obtain the silhouette Userhat wanted. The figure of the praying man was beginning to be born.

Renupe the Jovial did the second polishing with much enthusiasm, happy to see his colleagues reconciled.

'When you've finished,' said Userhat, 'I'll hollow out the ears, the eyes and the hands with a flint drill; Ipuy will separate the legs with a hollow copper tube which he will turn in his hands; and I myself will do the final polishing, which is the most delicate, since it will fix for ever the form of the face and body. This will be a beautiful statue, colleagues, I promise you.'

'Hurry up and finish it,' said Nefer. 'There's a lot of work to be done in the coming months. We shall need new wooden statues for the festival of Amenhotep I, our founder, and several cult statues of King Meneptah.'

The three sculptors had been expecting this decision, but hearing it from the mouth of the Master himself gave it another dimension. Suddenly, the extent and difficulty of the work loomed large.

'We shall need a lot of first-rate stone,' warned Userhat.

'I'm sending messages to the main quarries this very day,' promised Nefer. 'You'll also have brand-new tools and all the materials you need.'

'Will we have to work on our rest days?'

'To be frank, that's possible. The Place of Truth must show itself worthy of its reputation, and I have a feeling that we can't afford to lose any time at all.'

'Well, at least we shan't get bored,' remarked Renupe, scratching his head. 'When will we be getting an official portrait of the king?'

'Right now – here it is,' said Nefer. He went over to a small statue veiled in cloth, and removed the cloth to reveal a plaster model of Meneptah. The king looked austere, and his noble features were worthy of Ramses the Great.

'You haven't lost your touch,' said Userhat. 'You're the real master sculptor.'

'You taught me everything,' said Nefer, smiling. 'And I'm counting on you to create colossi, statues standing in the posture of Osiris, seated statues and others making offerings.'

Ched the Saviour came into the workshop and looked interestedly at the work in progress. 'It's good to have competent colleagues,' he said with slight disdain. 'May I steal the Master from you for a few minutes?'

It was clear from his tone that it was a matter of some urgency, but Ched maintained his usual elegant gait as he led Nefer into Kenhir's tomb.

'Master, you must see Paneb the Ardent's latest exploit as soon as possible.'

Yet another thing to worry about . . . Nefer wondered how many more surprises this stressful day had in store for him.

Ched halted before the wall on which Paneb had painted the priest making offering to Ptah. It was illuminated by soft lamplight which threw into relief the fine lines and the beauty of the colours.

'It . . . it's splendid!' exclaimed Nefer.

'It is indeed. A great painter is born.'

27

Niut the Strong's broom was as busy as ever, and she had tried several times to mount an attack on Kenhir's office; he was having more and more difficulty in preserving his domain. The girl was gaining in confidence, arguing about his orders and sometimes doing only what she wanted. But her cooking was still excellent, and the Scribe of the Tomb couldn't imagine what he'd do without her.

'The messenger has just brought this letter,' she told him, handing him a papyrus marked with Mehy's seal.

Kenhir read it immediately. Politely phrased, it requested nothing less than a vital meeting the next day.

'I have to go out,' he said.

'But lunch is almost ready.'

'I shan't be long.'

He found Nefer at the sculptors' workshop, where he was studying Userhat's designs for statues.

'Master, Mehy has summoned me to a meeting,' said Kenhir.

'Is that unusual?'

'No, he's simply acting in accordance with the duties of his office. He's well within his rights in wanting to talk to me, but I'm not obliged to comply with his request.'

'If you get on the wrong side of him, mightn't that cause unnecessary friction?'

'Yes, it might. From what I hear, he does his job very well and conscientiously, and, besides, he should be our main defender in any future administrative wrangles. It would be as well to keep in his good books.'

Nefer looked at him closely. 'But you don't seem very enthusiastic about meeting him.'

'No, I'm not,' agreed Kenhir, 'because I suspect that in the future he may make all sorts of demands. Like most officials, he doesn't understand what the Brotherhood does, and he'll probably try to put an end to what he sees as unwarranted privileges. If he does, our conversation will come to an abrupt end. Mehy must acknowledge that he has no hold over us and that we'll make no concessions.'

The gatekeeper at Mehy's villa bowed before the Scribe of the Tomb and called the steward, who ran up.

'My master is expecting you,' he said, also bowing. 'If you would care to follow me . . .' He escorted Kenhir along a paved pathway bordered with carob trees, through a large garden with a small lake in the centre, and up to the entrance of an imposing house.

As soon as he crossed the threshold, Kenhir was invited by two servants to sit down on a low chair. They washed his hands and feet, wiped them with scented cloths and gave him a pair of beautifully worked sandals. Then the steward led him through an antechamber whose ceiling, decorated with intertwined foliage, was supported by two porphyry columns, and ushered him into a vast hall with four columns, decorated with scenes of hunting and fishing in the marshes.

'My lord, your guest is here,' said the steward.

Dressed in the latest style of pleated shirt and a long kilt clasped by a leather belt, Mehy put down his writing-case and came forward to greet the Scribe of the Tomb.

'My dear Kenhir, what a pleasure to meet you. I thought it better that we should talk in private, at my house, rather than in the rather formal surroundings of my offices. And I have a little surprise for you.'

On a low table stood a red wine-jar bearing the legend 'White wine from the Khargeh oasis. Ramses, Year Five'.

The cupbearer filled two cups and withdrew.

'An exceptional vintage,' said Mehy, 'from the year when Ramses defeated the Hittites at Kadesh. Between ourselves, I have only three jars left. Do taste it, won't you?'

Kenhir settled himself on a lion-footed chair; it was excellently made, as was all the furniture. The new general loved having wealth and displaying it; and he knew how to feign warmth and good humour to put his guests at ease. But his charm did not work on Kenhir the Ungracious, who did, however, fully appreciate the excellent wine.

'Would you like some fruit or cakes?' asked Mehy.

'I'm quite content with the wine. It's truly admirable.'

'To give a friend pleasure is one of the joys of life. We are fortunate to live in a country which can produce such good wine. But tell me, are you in good health?'

'I'm not a young man any more, but the beast is sturdy and free of serious ailments.'

'Let's drink to long life.'

They drained their cups, and Mehy refilled them. The second cup was as delicious as the first.

Kenhir looked at his host out of the corner of one eye, and thought, 'If he wants to get me drunk, he's in for a disappointment – unless he proposes to empty his wine-cellar. And the threat of that vile gout won't stop me, either.'

'You may know that Pharaoh has entrusted me with two offices, that of general of the Theban armed forces and that of governor of the west bank. In spirit, the two are linked, for it's my duty to ensure the security of this region with its immeasurable riches; and indeed I intend to fulfil my duty to the letter. Actually, this concerns you directly, since the Place of Truth lies within the the region I administer.'

'It may be located on the west bank,' Kenhir corrected him haughtily, 'but it answers to no one but Pharaoh or the tjaty.'

'Of course, my dear fellow, of course, as has been the rule since its foundation. My role consists simply of safeguarding it against attack, by adding my protection to Commander Sobek's. King Meneptah, like his predecessors, holds your Brotherhood in high esteem and wants to see it carry out its work in the most perfect serenity.'

'As long as Egypt is herself,' said Kenhir, 'that will be so.'

Mehy wondered how to thaw this frosty old scribe, whose head for wine was remarkable. Kenhir was going to be a more formidable adversary than he'd expected.

He said, 'I have to ask you an indiscreet question, my dear fellow.'

'In everything that concerns the Place of Truth, I am bound to absolute secrecy.'

'Obviously it's not about that; it's about my predecessor, Abry. His horrible end troubles me a lot, I confess. He was charged with watching over the safety of the Brotherhood, but all he thought of was attacking it, and he even went so far as to try to submit a false report to the king. After a crime like that, his only way out was indeed to kill himself. But I have learnt something from the incident: there may be a group of influential people seeking to harm the village.'

The theory did not seem to move Kenhir. 'That's nothing new,' he said, 'and it's inevitable. The Place of Truth's secrets have always been well guarded, so people imagine things and their greed is fed by their imaginings.'

'But it might be very dangerous.'

'It's good that you don't underestimate the danger. Thanks to you, we shall sleep soundly.'

'You may indeed count on me; and I should like to be able to count on your cooperation.'

'I repeat, I answer to no one except Pharaoh or the tjaty.'

'Yes, of course. I understand that. What I meam is that we

ought to cooperate in the fight against all threats to the Brotherhood. So please, if you can, answer me three questions. Did you meet Abry often? Did you suspect him? And do you think he acted alone or as a member of a plot?'

'I met him very seldom, and the last time we met he tried to bribe me.'

'The scoundrel!' exclaimed Mehy. 'And what do you think he was after?'

'Abry was a weak, opportunistic man. He believed in constantly increasing taxes and enforcing the government's power. The very idea of freedom was foreign to him, and he couldn't bear the fact that the Place of Truth was outside his control. As for the rest, I can't tell you. Commander Sobek believes there was – and may still be – a plot, and he won't lower his guard until he finds one. Nor will I, for that matter.'

'I was hoping for more reassuring words. I thought the king was anxious, and now I know why. Fortunately, Abry's death and my appointment change things radically. Anyone who tries to harm the Brotherhood will have do deal with me besides yourself and Commander Sobek. Between us, we should make an effective defence.'

'May the gods hear you,' said Kenhir.

'We must not disappoint either the king or Egypt. At the least suspicion, the smallest cause for concern, don't hesitate to tell me and I'll act at once.'

Kenhir preferred this kind of talk to Abry's. On the evidence, the general was taking his duties seriously, and the Place of Truth had benefited by the change.

'I have to ask you a favour,' Mehy said.

The Scribe of the Tomb stiffened.

'Oh, don't worry, it's nothing personal, just an administrative problem I'd like to resolve as smoothly as possible.'

'Go on.'

'Could you arrange for me to meet the Master of the Brotherhood?'

28

Kenhir's expression became openly hostile. 'That is utterly impossible. Even the identity of the Master must remain unknown.'

Mehy called his cup-bearer and ordered another jar of the Khargeh wine. When the man had gone, he went on, 'In theory, that's true, of course. But during the king's visit to the Place of Truth, everyone in the official delegation, even though we were outside the walls, heard the villagers shouting two names: Meneptah and . . . Nefer the Silent. Everyone knows Nefer was consecrated as Master by the royal couple and that he is the true leader of the Brotherhood, though you undertake all the administration. But let me immediately reassure you: those are the only two small secrets that have passed outside the village walls, and they don't compromise its safety in any way.'

'Why do you want to meet the Master?'

'He can help me sort out an administrative problem.'

'Can't I do it?'

'I am afraid not,' said Mehy. 'There's one aspect of the matter on which only the Master of the Place of Truth can decide. I'm afraid I can't tell you any more, because it's highly confidential. Of course, if Nefer wishes to tell you about it, he's free to do so.'

'You know he can refuse your . . . invitation.'

'Yes, I do know that, but I beg you to plead my cause eloquently. If I can't obtain his advice, I'd find myself in a rather awkward situation because I don't know what the best solution would be, whereas I'm sure he does. Will you ask him?'

'Very well, but I can't promise you anything. The decision rests with him.'

'I'm in your debt, Kenhir.'

Kenhir took another sip of his wine. 'You know, this jar is even better than the first.'

'Then let's finish it, to thc glory of thc Brotherhood!'

As soon as Kenhir had left, Serketa came in. She sat down at her husband's feet and said, 'I heard every word of that fascinating conversation.'

'What do you think of Kenhir, my sweet?'

'He's a crafty old devil, stubborn, suspicious and almost impossible to bribe. That fool Abry certainly wasn't up to the job.'

'Do you think I convinced him?'

'Yes – and worried him, too. And of course you weren't stupid enough to offer him a jar of that wine he likes so much. He just wanted to see if you'd try to bribe him, as Abry did. I don't think hc knows any great secrets, but he'll defend the Brotherhood tooth and nail.'

'Why did you say I worried him?' asked Mehy.

'He could tell you aren't going to be as passive as Abry when it comes to dealing with the Place of Truth. But I think the firmness of your promise reassured him: who wouldn't be glad of a protector of your calibre?'

'Tell me frankly, my sweet, do you think we ought to get rid of him?'

'Absolutely not! We're going to get to know him well, and I advise you to ensure that he remains in place as long as possible. If I killed him, which in any case wouldn't be easy, he'd be replaced at once, and we might come up against someone even more intransigent. I'm sure he has weak spots – and they'll be useful.'

Mehy pulled his wife's hair. 'You've convinced me. He won't know it, but the Scribe of the Tomb is going to become our ally.'

Casa the Rope had gone off to see his sick ox. Fened the Nose was making a stool for his parents-in-law, Karo the Impatient a linen-chest for his grandmother, Didia the Generous a bedhead for his niece, while the other members of the starboard crew were working on things destined for the outside world.

They were interrupted by a summons from the Master to the Brotherhood's meeting-place, at the foot of the northern hill, on the edge of the necropolis. They all purified themselves, then took their places on the stone benches.

Nefer sat down on the easternmost chair, which previous overseers of the starboard crew had occupied before him. His gaze rested on the seat reserved for the *ka*, the creative power which gave life to the craftsmen's hearts and hands; it would for ever remain empty of any human presence.

'I have a proposal to put to you all,' he announced, 'and it's one you may not like. First, I stress the enormous size of the two projects we are about to begin, the creation of Pharaoh Meneptah's house of eternity in the Valley of the Kings, and the construction of his Temple of a Million Years. All our energies must be gathered together to carry out these two all-important tasks, so I'm asking you to stop all work for outside customers.'

A heavy silence followed this declaration.

Eventually Karo the Impatient dared to break it. 'It is an ancient custom which has never been questioned before. Outside work enables us to earn more and ensures that our families live comfortably.'

'I know that, but you must understand that it's essential we focus our efforts.'

'Why can't we do both?' asked Casa the Rope. 'Let's get on with these two projects at a good, steady pace, and do our outside work as well, as we've done in the past.'

'That is impossible for two reasons,' explained Nefer. 'First, I'm absolutely certain that we haven't much time.'

'Because of the king's age?' inquired Nakht the Powerful.

'Yes, that's a real concern. It's no use deceiving ourselves. Meneptah's succession may well be difficult, there may be serious upheavals, and we must move forward as though the allotted time is short.'

'Have you had any reliable information about what's happening at Pi-Ramses?' asked Gau the Precise.

'Unfortunately not, but I ask you to trust me. Ordinarily, I don't like rushing and I'd have preferred to take plenty of time to design and build the tomb and the temple; but I'm convinced that time is a luxury we can't afford.

'Then there's my second reason, which has to do with to the very nature of our work. We put the last touches to Ramses' tomb, but it had been almost finished for a long time. Meneptah's tomb will be our Great Work, the first royal tomb we will create together so that it produces eternity, like its predecessors. As for the temple, it will preserve the king's *ka* and will therefore require work of exceptional quality. All this is going to be exciting, but it won't be easy, so I'm asking you to make a very special effort. We must excel ourselves in order to justify, once again, the existence of the Place of Truth.'

'I heard a rumour that our holidays and rest days are going to be cut,' ventured Pai the Good Bread. 'If they are, our wives won't like it at all.'

'Necessity knows no law,' replied the Master.

'But,' protested Unesh the Jackal, 'if we have to turn down outside work and our rest days are cut, life will be unbearable.'

'The Scribe of the Tomb has given me his word to pay you extra, to compensate for your extra time.'

'Less free time,' insisted Unesh, 'means less leisure, fewer pleasant moments with the family, fewer visits outside.'

Pai and Gau agreed, as did Renupe the Jovial and Karo the Impatient.

'This is pathetic!' exploded Paneb. 'The Master summons you to take part in a wonderful enterprise, the most essential work undertaken on Egyptian soil, and you moan about your privileges and think about nothing but your pay and your comfort. What a wonderful crew! Do we really want to set sail, or would we rather stay in port for ever, dozing in a warm breeze? If our ship is so decrepit, worn-out and soulless, it would be better if it sank!'

Most members of the crew went pale, except for Pai and Renupe, whose faces turned bright red.

'You have no right to speak to us like that,' said Userhat the Lion.

'And what right have you to behave like state workmen,' demanded Paneb, 'more interested in counting your hours than in working, and with your only ambition a longer mid-day break? If that's how things are, the Place of Truth will soon be dead.'

Ched the Saviour asked permission to speak. 'My assistant has no tact whatever, and his manner of self-expression is not exactly subtle, but basically he's right. Because Ramses' reign was so long and happy, we've acquired a taste for the easy life, for which our old skills and knowledge are perfectly adequate. The building of Meneptah's tomb and Temple of a Million Years is a vast and perilous enterprise, and it frightens us because we're bogged down in routine. And yet we have the inestimable good fortune to be able to join together in the Great Work. Faced with such a prospect, do we really dare impose conditions unworthy of the spirit of the Brotherhood and the ancestors who watch us work? Let the Master decide what we must do, and we shall obey.'

The crew agreed unanimously.

29

Ubekhet and Nefer had made love as passionately as they had the very first time, with the same fire, now tinged with a tenderness and intimacy which grew more beautiful day after day. Time could not corrode their love, which seemed eternal, never to become prey to the vagaries of human feelings.

Even when naked and sweaty from lovemaking, thought Nefer, Ubekhet retained the innate nobility that had won the villagers' hearts. The Master admired the Wise Woman, the husband his wife.

She looked up at him. 'You're worried, aren't you?'

'The crew said they accepted my proposals, but did they mean it?'

'You won't find perfection among men, but you may find it in their work. If you give them an ideal and enable them to achieve it, they'll overcome their weaknesses.'

'Yes, but will I overcome mine?' said Nefer. 'I'm not cut out for this office. Sculpting would be enough for me. And how good it used to be to follow the overseer's instructions!'

'Aren't you forgetting who chose you? It'll do no good to chafe against your duties, like a horse against its harness, and still less to doubt yourself. I'd be the first to admit that neither of us is up to the responsibilities we must fulfil. All we can do is fulfil them as best we can and, each day, begin to climb the mountain again.'

'So much fuss,' said Nefer wearily, 'so many trivial problems, so many ridiculous demands from people. That's what I find exhausting – much more than the vast scope of the work itself.'

'Do you think I fare any better? There is stone and wood, eternally ready to receive the Light, but there are also human beings, always ready to lie, to be lazy and to compete in vanity and selfishness. That's how people are, and they'll never change; but the Place of Truth turns them into a crew capable of sailing to realms which none of them could have discovered if he had travelled alone.'

Nefer kissed his wife passionately.

'I am all yours,' she said, 'but don't forget that we have a guest.'

Kenhir savoured every mouthful of the succulent kidneys in white wine, accompanied by lentils with garlic and pounded aubergine.

'It's a very simple meal,' apologized Ubekhet. 'The girl who helps me in the house is on holiday, and I hadn't time to cook anything elaborate.'

'You are gifted in every way,' said Kenhir. 'Thanks to you, my gout has almost disappeared.'

'Perhaps it might be wise to drink a little less wine and a little more water,' she suggested.

'At my age, it is bad to change one's habits.'

Ubekhet smiled. 'Are you satisfied with Niut the Strong?'

'She's a thorough nuisance, impertinent and stubborn, but she's efficient. She hunts down every speck of dust, she doesn't disturb my furniture too much and she cooks decently. I may even have to pay her more. But what worries me is that she keeps trying to clean my office – she's probably doing it at this very minute, now that I'm not there to watch her. Ah well, so long as she puts every writing-brush back in its place and doesn't touch any of the papyri . . .'

'How did your meeting with Mehy go?' asked Nefer.

'Rather well. He is an energetic man, and seems determined to fulfil his office. Above all, he's very ambitious, which should make him an excellent protector of the Place of Truth. That's the task Pharaoh has entrusted to him, and he has no intention of failing. What's more, he didn't try to bribe me – there wasn't even a hint of anything like that. But he did make a curious request.'

'What was it?'

'He wants to meet you, Nefer.'

'Why?'

'He says he has an urgent administrative problem which only the Master can help him resolve.'

Nefer was puzzled. 'But surely that's a matter for you, Kenhir, not for me.'

'Apparently not, in this case, because there's one aspect of the problem on which only the Master can advise. I of course invoked the rule of secrecy, but your official recognition by the royal couple means that your name has spread abroad. It's not important that Mehy knows you're Master, and you aren't obliged to grant his request.'

'Well,' said Nefer thoughtfully, 'if he's favourably disposed towards us, it might be impolitic to turn him down.'

'I agree.'

'Very well, I'll meet him at the first fort. And if I can help him, I will.'

The traitor in the starboard crew knew he would have to take great care in order to reach Tran-Bel's warehouse unseen. As luck would have it, several other craftsmen had taken advantage of the additional week's holiday the Master had granted before the Great Work, and had left the village. Some were tending their fields and their flocks, others were visiting relatives, and others were shopping.

If Sobek's watchful gaze was anything to go by, the

commander was becoming more and more suspicious. The traitor took comfort from the thought that, if there had been any firm evidence against him, he'd have been arrested and interrogated by now. All the same, Sobek's attitude had definitely changed recently, as if he suspected someone inside the Brotherhood – he might even be having the craftsmen followed. If he was, and the traitor led his follower to the warehouse, all would be lost. The traitor should probably have stayed in the village and not taken any risks, but he needed to speak urgently with the woman who was making him rich.

Instead of taking the ferry, on which there might be an informant in Sobek's pay, the craftsman hired a fisherman, who took him across the Nile in exchange for a round loaf of bread; he would hire someone else for the return journey. No boat followed them.

After disembarking at an isolated spot far from the main landing-stage, the craftsman stayed crouching in the reeds for a good hour. No one came near his hiding-place.

Reassured, he climbed up the bank and headed for the town, casting frequent glances over his shoulder.

Twice he turned into a blind alley and then retraced his steps, to surprise anyone who was following him, but there was no one there. If there had been a tail, it was broken.

The craftsman hurried into the warehouse and went to the office, where Tran-Bel was doing his accounts.

'Ah, it's you,' said Tran-Bel. 'I'm glad to see you. Our business is doing marvellously.'

'Tell you-know-who I'm here.'

'In a moment, in a moment. Have you designed any new chairs?'

'Yes, but you'll have to wait for them.'

'That's annoying, very annoying. I've got customers clamouring for them.'

'My safety comes first. Tell her, and quickly.'

'All right, all right.'

Tran-Bel was already thinking about making copies, but they would have flaws. So, for a while anyway, he would have to resort to clients with money but no taste.

When Serketa arrived, as usual her disguise made her unrecognizable.

'Well?' she demanded. 'What's this important information you've got for me?'

'The Master has decided that the craftsmen of both crews must devote all their time and energy to the construction of Meneptah's tomb and Temple of a Million Years.'

'That isn't important. Have you found the Stone of Light's hiding-place?'

'Not yet. It just isn't possible.'

'What do you mean, "It just isn't possible"?' she sneered. 'Are you going to let me down?'

'I have almost nothing to go on, and if I sniff around all over the place someone's bound to get suspicious.'

'Can you go wherever you like inside the village?'

'No. Some places are kept locked, and only the Scribe of the Tomb and the Master can open them. I'd never be able to break in.'

'Well, it's up to you to get the information I want.'

'My crew is going to be working incredibly hard, and for a long time I shall be out of contact with the outside world.'

The look in Serketa's eyes became ferocious. 'If you think you can escape me by hiding in that damned village, you're wrong.'

'You don't understand!' protested the craftsman. 'The projects we're about to begin will affect the whole future of the Brotherhood, and the Master is adamant that we shall have to work extra hours and, if problems arise, have less time off. But that's not all: Sobek is getting more and more suspicious.'

'About what?'

'I'm sure he suspects that one of us is involved in a plot against the Place of Truth. He may even think it was one of us who murdered that guard. Sobek is a formidable man. He's quite capable of having people followed and setting a permanent watch on a suspect. I had to take endless precautions on my way here.'

'That was sensible. But aren't you seeing dangers where none exist?'

'I don't think so.'

Serketa walked slowly in a circle round him. 'All you ever bring me is bad news. What a pity. And I've got such good news for you: while you're vegetating in your village, your inheritance is growing. Another milk cow, a piece of land beside the Nile, a field . . . When you retire, you'll be a rich man. But before then, you must get me the information I want.'

The traitor had a vision of himself reclining on soft cushions in the cool hall of a beautiful house where he would spend his time counting his possessions and then counting them again. But it was still a long way from the dream to the reality, and he was determined not to give up all his secrets until he was certain that he'd enjoy his reward in perfect safety.

'I haven't changed my mind,' he said, 'but I'll be unable to contact you until work on the tomb and temple is fairly well advanced.'

'Don't forget that our alliance cannot be broken,' Serketa warned him. 'When we see each other again, I'm sure you'll have a lot to tell me.'

30

Ubekhet had been summoned urgently to the bedside of Userhat the Lion's wife, who was complaining of severe chest pains. After a detailed examination, the Wise Woman decided it wasn't a heart attack and gave her a treatment to calm her nerves. She also gave a spinal manipulation, for the poor state of her patient's back was at the root of many of her troubles.

When she got home in the middle of the morning, Ubekhet found Paneb standing on her doorstep, looking anxious.

'I wanted to speak to Nefer about a problem with the supplies for the painters' workshop,' he said, 'but no one knows where he is. He was seen leaving the temple after the morning ritual, but where did he go then?'

'To see the sculptors, I expect.'

'I've been there. They haven't seen him, either.'

'He might be talking to Ched the Saviour.'

'No, I've just come from him.'

Ubekhet and Paneb questioned the neighbours, but in vain. Children claimed to have seen him all over the village, most of them believing that this was a new game and that they had to show as much imagination as possible. More and more villagers joined in the discussion, but no one knew where the Master was. Eventually they had to face up to the fact that he had disappeared. People began to panic.

Ubekhet closed her eyes and composed herself, shutting out all the sounds around her. She filled her mind with Nefer's face, so as to bring him as close as if their faces were touching.

'Don't be afraid,' she said calmly. 'I know where he's gone.'

Many kinds of date palms liked to live with their heads in the sunshine and their feet in the water. Forming walls of vegetation against the wind, they lived for a hundred years and, in the autumn, they gave lavishly of their honey-tasting fruits. Some clustered around olive groves and vines, others formed thickets away from the pathways, but all were models of generosity, for each part of the tree was useful. It provided wood for building and furniture, fibre to make sandals and baskets, and leaves to cover the streets and keep them cool.

But Nefer had chosen to meditate in the shade of a very old, solitary palm tree, at the edge of the desert. According to legend, Thoth, the god of knowledge, had written words of wisdom here, and Amenhotep I, the founder of the Brotherhood, had come here to receive them. The tree drew its sap from the ocean of energy that had bathed the universe when, during the 'first time', the earth had appeared as an island.

The Master had come to beg the god's help in calming the fire that consumed him. Paneb might able to struggle against his flames, but Nefer was sure he himself would fail to do so. And this fiery torture had taken the form of a question which was as devastating as it was painful: was he capable of leading the Brotherhood to success? Carrying out the Great Work seemed to him an objective far beyond his reach, and he had no right to lie to those who had chosen him as their guide.

The real Silent One, said the sages, resembled a tree with abundant foliage and sweet fruit, which lived out its tranquil lifespan in a well-tended garden. Nefer's heart was now no more than an arid landscape where anguish and uncertainty had made weeds grow. So he had come to pray to Thoth to keep him safe from futile words and to offer him water from his well, which was sealed against the loose-tongued. If there was no response to his appeal, he would die of thirst, and the Brotherhood would appoint a new Master.

'Have you discovered the spring?' asked a wonderfully sweet woman's voice.

'Ubekhet! How did you know about this place?'

'I saw it and I saw you lying prostrate under this palm tree.'

'The god hasn't spoken, and I'm not strong enough to continue my task.'

'Listen harder, Nefer, and create what you lack.'

The Wise Woman knelt down and dug into the sand with her hands, uncovering the edge of a small circular well. Nefer helped her, and soon they reached damp earth.

'At the foot of a palm tree of Thoth,' she said, 'there's always a hidden spring. Unblock this well and drink its water, which comes from the stars. It will put out the fire burning you, and free the energy you don't realize you possess. Nothing will prevent you from doing your work, Master, for your path has been traced by the gods.'

Intertwined, they indulged in the unheard-of luxury of an afternoon of meditation and silence in the shade of the palm-leaves. And the Master understood that, without the Wise Woman, the Brotherhood would have been nothing but a sterile group of men, incapable of fashioning the Great Work.

A strong wind swept the guard-post, raising clouds of sand which stung the guards' eyes. Through the sandstorm, they saw a chariot approaching fast, and they immediately levelled their spears while their senior officer drew his bow.

The chariot stopped suddenly, and the two horses reared up, neighing. A sturdy, broad-chested man jumped down. He walked towards the guards as confidently as if their weapons didn't exist.

'I am General Mehy, governor of the west bank. Tell the Master of the Place of Truth that I'm here.'

A guard ran to the fifth fort to alert Sobek, and he ordered the village gatekeeper to inform Nefer. Nefer was working on the plan of Meneptah's tomb, but he at once put down his writing-brush and, not bothering to change his clothes, went to meet his visitor, accompanied by Ebony, who was delighted by this unexpected walk. Bareheaded and barefoot, and wearing only a simple kilt, compared to Mehy, whose ostentatious elegance oozed wealth, Nefer looked like a humble workman.

Mehy greeted him courteously and said, 'Thank you for agreeing to this meeting.'

'What do you want?'

'May we talk where indiscreet ears can't hear us?'

'Follow me.'

The Master turned away from the guard-post and walked about a hundred paces into a dried-up riverbed. Mehy followed, careful not to spoil his beautiful leather sandals. As for the black dog, which was ordinarily so demonstrative, it kept its distance from the general, watching him suspiciously.

'We'll be completely alone here,' said Nefer, 'but the only seat I can offer you is a block of stone.'

'That will be fine. Meeting you is such a privilege that material comforts are unimportant.'

'Your time is as precious as mine, Mehy. Perhaps you could come to the point?'

'It concerns a delicate, confidential matter which I can't resolve without your help. Daktair, the head of the central workshop, has just drawn up a list of things he needs. There's no problem with most of them, but he's asking urgently for bitumen and galenite, because stocks of them are exhausted. He says the shortage has arisen because there should have been an expedition to collect more, but it never took place because of Ramses' death.'

'Even if I had stocks of those minerals, they'd be reserved for the Place of Truth.'

'Oh yes, of course. There's no question about that.'

'In that case, there's no more to be said.'

'No, please don't go yet, Master. I haven't finished. You must know that a craftsman from the Place of Truth always goes on these expeditions, to advise the miners and to collect the share reserved for the Brotherhood.'

'You're well-informed.'

'I simply consulted the official reports,' said Mehy. 'But now we come to the heart of the problem. Daktair wants permission to lead a troop of soldiers and miners to the sites where these things are mined, and I can see no reason to refuse. But the expedition has to include a member of the Brotherhood, and only you can nominate him.'

While the Master considered the matter, Mehy watched him closely, to get the measure of him. Without any doubt, this was a great man. A serious face, penetrating gaze, powerful personality, resolute character, stern words . . . The leader of the Brotherhood was a true leader, a dangerous adversary.

At that moment, in that hostile desert, facing the Master, whom he was seeing for the first time, Mehy fully realized the magnitude of the battle to come. At the thought of conquering such a formidable enemy, and at last subjugating the arrogant Brotherhood that had dared to reject him, the general felt his strength grow tenfold.

'Couldn't the expedition be postponed?' asked Nefer.

'According to Daktair, no, but I'll bow to your decision.'

The Master knew he should not deprive Thebes of these minerals and, besides, he himself needed them for a very special purpose.

'I shall appoint a craftsman,' he said. 'Make sure the

expedition is ready to leave in five days' time, and provide plenty of strong donkeys.'

'Thank you. Daktair was being a real thorn in my flesh, and you've pulled it out.'

'I should like as little working-time as possible to be spent at the mines. The craftsman musn't be away too long.'

'I'll give strict orders to that effect. Once again, thank you. Will you do me the honour of accepting an invitation to dinner?'

'I'm sorry, but I've renounced all worldly pleasures.'

As agile as a mountain goat, Ebony jumped from stone to stone to get back to the village. Nefer followed him.

Mehy watched them go. If he'd been armed with a bow, and certain he could act with impunity, he'd gladly have brought down the Master with an arrow in the back. For he'd prefer not to fight such a warrior face to face.

31

At four in the afternoon, one gatekeeper relieved the other and took his place in the hut beside the main gate. He didn't find the work unpleasant, and his wages were supplemented by deliveries of firewood, for which the two gatekeepers were responsible. They also received a small fee when they served as witnesses in transactions between craftsmen or when contracts were drawn up.

A small man approached. 'I'm a donkey-seller.'

'Good for you, friend.'

'The lay workers told me that you can see that overdue fees are paid.'

'Does a craftsman owe you money?'

'No, not a craftsman.'

'Then go and bother someone else,' said the gatekeeper.

'But you must be able to help me. I want to lodge a complaint against Commander Sobek.'

'Sobek! Why?'

'Because he hasn't paid me what he owes me.'

'Are you quite sure of what you're saying?'

'I have all the necessary proof, and I want you to take my complaint to the village court.'

'But Sobek's the commander of the village's security guards!'

'Yes, and do you know how to recognize a security guard?

By the fact that he never pays a debt, whether it's for a pot of grease or a donkey.'

The Place of Truth's court had the symbolic name of the Assembly of the Square and the Right Angle, the *genbet,* and it could be convened at any time, even on a festival day if the case was urgent. It was generally made up of eight members, a crew-leader, the Scribe of the Tomb, the commander of the guards, a gatekeeper, and two experienced craftsmen and their wives.

It dealt with both private and public affairs, among the latter the registration of declarations of succession and acquisitions such as land. Totally independent, the court had the power to order exhaustive inquiries, and it pronounced sentences, whatever crime had been committed. If it felt the matter was too complex, it passed it on directly to the highest legal institution in the land, the tjaty's court. But it also dealt with minor matters such as the donkey-seller's complaint, which could not be ignored.

Kenhir greeted him outside the village, in the small office which he had set up in the lay workers' area. 'Bringing a complaint against the commander is very serious,' he said. 'He has a reputation for scrupulous honesty.'

'Reputation is one thing, the facts are another. I have proof that he's a thief and I want him punished.'

'Do you understand the risk you're taking? If this proof is invalid, you're the one who'll be punished.'

'When you're in the right, you have nothing to fear from justice.'

'So you're determined to go ahead with your complaint?'

The donkey-seller nodded vigorously.

The court was headed by the Scribe of the Tomb, and was made up of the Master, the gatekeeper who had received the complaint, the Wise Woman, Uabet the Pure, a Nubian guard,

Thuty the Learned and Userhat the Lion. When both accuser and accused were members of the Brotherhood, the court sat in the courtyard of the main temple in the Place of Truth. In this case, both were outsiders – though Sobek came under the Scribe of the Tomb's authority – and could not enter the village, so the court was convened just outside the great gate.

The jurors had put on heavy robes and they wore large wigs which changed their appearance and their faces. If the donkey-seller hoped to identify a particular craftsman, he would have great difficulty.

Under the court's system, the accused and the accuser had to appear in person before the court and each put their case, taking as much time as necessary. Seated on stools, the donkey-seller and Sobek avoided looking at each other. Both seemed confident.

'Unfairness is an abomination to God,' declared Kenhir. 'This court will act towards those who are close to it in exactly the same way as it will act towards those it does not know. It will not show injustice to the weak in order to give advantage to the powerful, and it will protect the weak from the strong by distinguishing truth from lies. Let us pray to the Hidden God who comes to the aid of the unfortunate in distress, and beg him to enlighten this court and enable it unanimously to pronounce the correct sentence.'

The Scribe of the Tomb directed his gaze first at the accuser, then at the accused. 'You are required to speak clearly, so that your words can be understood by all, without specious arguments or involved explanations. Make your accusation, donkey-seller.'

'Commander Sobek ordered a donkey from me. We agreed on the price, and the animal was delivered to him, yet he refuses to pay me the agreed sum, which is a piece of fabric, a pair of sandals, a sack of rye and a sack of flour. The delivery note was duly registered and the price cannot be contested.'

'How do you answer the charge, Sobek?' asked Kenhir.

'This man is a thief and a liar. A donkey was indeed delivered to me, but it was old and sick. So I owe him nothing – in fact, I'm the one who should have brought a complaint.'

'That's not true,' retorted the man. 'The donkey I delivered was a strong young male, in perfect health. And here, to prove it, is a document signed by witnesses when I drew up the delivery note.'

He handed Kenhir a wooden tablet, on which an inscription in cursive writing described the donkey and gave its price. The names of three witnesses certified the validity of these details.

'I have a witness, too,' said Sobek, 'the guard who saw this old animal and whom I ordered to take it into a palm grove to end its days peacefully.'

'Did you get his evidence in writing?'

'Of course not. Why would I have done that?'

'Let Userhat the Lion go and find this guard so that he may give his testimony,' ordered Kenhir.

Sobek's man appeared before the court. He was very nervous, and had trouble getting his words out.

Kenhir asked him, 'Do you remember a donkey which was delivered to Commander Sobek and about which he gave you an order?'

'Er . . . yes, yes . . . it was definitely a donkey.'

'Young or old?'

'Very old and weak – it could hardly walk.'

'What did Commander Sobek order you to do?'

'He didn't want it, because he'd ordered a young, healthy animal, so he told me to take it to a palm grove. After notifying my superior officer that I'd be absent, I obeyed the commander's order.'

Kenhir turned towards the Wise Woman, whom he expected to speak, but she remained silent. He told the guard, 'The truth will be easy to establish. Go and fetch this donkey at once, and bring it here.'

*

Thanks to cool drinks and shady awnings, waiting was not too gruelling. The donkey-seller looked cheerful, as though he had nothing to fear from this decisive measure. Such assurance was a bit worrying, though Sobek was still certain that he'd be acquitted and that the liar would be suitably punished. The man must be completely mad to mock the court in this way!

It was a breathless guard who reappeared before Kenhir.

'Where is the donkey?'

'I . . . I looked for it everywhere, but I couldn't find it.'

'Are you sure you looked in the right grove?'

'Definitely: I chose the nearest one. Besides, its owner has several donkeys . . . But the old one wasn't where I left it.'

The donkey-seller was exultant. 'Obviously, Commander Sobek and his man invented this story so as to get out of paying me for the healthy donkey, which they have hidden somewhere. Sobek thought a humble tradesman like myself wouldn't dare lodge a complaint against him and that he could steal with impunity. But the truth has been established, and I demand reparation, compensation, penalties and the dismissal of this dishonest officer.'

'What have you to say in your defence?' Kenhir asked the Nubian.

'This man is a liar!'

'To my accusations,' shot back the donkey-seller, 'I add slander, which all the members of this court have witnessed.'

'Has either of you anything to add?' asked Kenhir.

'Let justice be done!' cried the tradesman.

'I am innocent, and this is all a plot!' protested the furious Sobek. 'Let me interrogate this rogue, and he'll soon tell you the truth, I promise you!'

'That's enough, Commander! Guards will escort you to the first fort, where you will await our verdict.'

32

A prisoner in his own domain: Sobek's mood was bleak. He'd fallen into a trap that was as simple as it was cunning, and he could see no way out of it. He'd be found guilty of theft and lying, he'd be sentenced to several months in prison, and he'd lose his job. In view of the responsibilities he had exercised, the court would make an example of him. The honesty of the head of security, of all people, must be above suspicion.

Sobek could feel the shackles tightening round his neck; they'd end up strangling him. Despite his anger, he saw things clearly: the enemies of the Place of Truth had bought the donkey-seller and organized the plot, which was designed to get rid of Sobek and his Nubians once and for all. Another commander would be appointed, at the head of another detachment of guards, and – there could be no doubt about it – the village's protection would be destroyed.

The plotters hadn't killed Sobek, because his death would have led to an inquiry and the craftsmen would have suspected the truth. Kenhir would have demanded reinforcements and sealed off the sacred area even more securely. Instead, they'd found an ideal way to discredit him.

One of his men came in and saluted. 'Sir, the court is about to pronounce sentence,' he said with great embarrassment.

The late evening was gentle and quiet. Sobek walked slowly, the better to savour his last moments in the austere place he had grown to love so much. The Place of Truth had become his home, a harmonious space which he had kept safe by always being on the alert. And now he had failed, and all because of an old donkey . . .

The donkey-seller was already sitting on his stool, a smile on his lips. Sobek noticed that the Wise Woman had not returned to her place.

'I would prefer to remain standing to hear the sentence,' said Sobek.

'Very well,' said Kenhir. 'I shall pronounce sentence now.'

The big Nubian closed his eyes.

There was a long silence, which was eventually broken by the sound of hooves coming slowly towards the court.

Sobek opened his eyes, turned and saw the Wise Woman leading a frail old donkey with a shabby coat, stroking its head as she walked.

'That's – that's the one!' exclaimed Sobek. 'Ask my witness. He'll recognize it, just as I have.'

'He has already done so,' said Ubekhet.

A broad smile spread over Sobek's face. 'How did you find it?'

'I went to the palm grove and questioned the peasants. I had little hope of finding it, for I feared it would have been killed, but luckily for you greed won the day. This man's accomplice had kept it, in the hope of trapping another buyer.'

The Scribe of the Tomb glared sternly at the accuser. 'What have you to say to this?'

'You can't prove that this old donkey really was delivered to Commander Sobek. You could have got it from anywhere.'

'Not at all,' said Ubekhet calmly. 'I could have explained everything after you had both given your evidence, but it was better to keep this information secret until now.'

The tradesman's voice became less confident. 'What do you mean?'

'On what date was the donkey you sold to Commander Sobek delivered?'

'Precisely eighteen days ago.'

'The donkey is vital to Egypt,' the Wise Woman said sternly. 'Without it, Egypt would not have become a rich country. But it sometimes contains the dangerous energy of Set, so every donkey which enters the domain of the Place of Truth must be magically calmed. As is customary, Sobek asked that a priestess of Hathor paint a hieroglyph on the inside of the left foreleg, and the animal was not taken to the palm grove until after this had been done. The hieroglyph varies according to the seasons and the festivals. Eighteen days ago, as the whole Brotherhood can bear witness, the chosen sign was a ringlet of hair. The court can check this.'

Userhat the Lion gently lifted the old donkey's leg and showed the court the sign, painted in red ink.

'I warned you,' Kenhir reminded the tradesman. 'You brought a false accusation against Commander Sobek, and you piled lie upon lie in order to have him convicted. Do you accept those facts?'

'No, no – I'm not to blame!'

'You still dare to deny it?' said Kenhir icily.

The donkey-seller bowed his head. 'No, I beg your forgiveness . . . I just wanted to make an easy profit.'

'First of all, the court sentences you to give five donkeys to Commander Sobek.'

'Five! That is a huge number, I—'

'In addition, you shall give him two days' work each week for five years; if you fail in your duty a single time, your punishment will immediately be doubled. Do you wish to appeal to the tjaty's court?'

'No, no.'

'Then swear to accept this judgment.'

The convicted man took the oath in an almost inaudible voice.

'Now go,' said Kenhir, 'and bring the five donkeys first thing tomorrow morning.'

The donkey-seller left, a broken man.

'He should have been arrested,' said Sobek.

'If you have other charges to put, we shall convene another court.'

'Don't you understand? The Brotherhood's enemies were trying to get rid of me.'

'Do you realize the gravity of what you're saying, and what it implies?'

'How can you be so blind? If I'd been ruined, who would have been appointed to protect you?'

'Calm down,' said Kenhir firmly. 'You're forgetting that it is the tjaty who appoints the commander of the guards.'

'Who's to say he might not also be manipulated?'

'This trial has exhausted and confused you. Go and rest. We'll discuss this later.'

As soon as the big Nubian had set off back to his quarters, Kenhir asked the Wise Woman the question that was burning his lips. 'I've never heard of this magical custom . . .?'

'Ask Uabet the Pure,' replied Ubekhet, smiling. 'It was her idea. But the important thing was to find the donkey and obtain the tradesman's confession.'

'Well done! But what are we to make of Sobek's astonishing claims?'

The Wise Woman took the Master's hand. 'The sky will be covered with dark clouds, and lightning may well strike us. But the priestesses of the Place of Truth will drive away evil destiny.'

The donkey-seller was beside himself. He had expected an easy victory, and instead this had been the most painful day of his whole life.

In the evening, he went to his stables to await the arrival of General Mehy's messenger, who would pay him his fee –

though it would be small compensation for what he had gone through. The court's sentence would not only impoverish him but also ruin his reputation.

Mehy must not only compensate him but prevent Sobek from bringing any other charges against him. The commander would be angry and resentful. He'd pursue his accuser mercilessly and, if he succeeded in having him arrested, would interrogate him brutally until he confessed everything. The only solution was to go to see the general at once, and ask for his protection.

As he was leaving the stable, he bumped into a peasant woman.

'What do you think you're doing here?' he demanded.

'I am Serketa, Mehy's wife.'

'But . . . you're dressed like a pauper!'

'I didn't want to be recognized.'

'*You're* his messenger?'

'You've worked for us and you must be suitably rewarded.'

'But the court didn't convict Sobek. The old donkey was found, and the court saw through the whole plot. Now I need you to protect me.'

'Did you mention Mehy?'

'No, they think I was working alone. But if Sobek arrests me, I won't be able to hold out under his questioning – I'll have to confess everything to save my skin.'

'We haven't reached that stage yet,' Serketa reassured him. 'It's a pity we failed, but all hard work should be rewarded, and you shall have what you were promised.'

'And will you protect me?'

'Where you're going, you'll have nothing to fear from Commander Sobek.'

Reassured, the donkey-seller gazed in admiration at the two silver ingots that she placed on a linen-chest. A small fortune indeed! Despite the setbacks, he had been right to accept the general's proposal.

While the merchant was feasting his eyes on the silver, Serketa slipped behind him. Taking from the pocket of her rough dress a long, slender needle, she thrust it suddenly into the back of his neck, between two vertebrae. After all her practice on animals and a model of a human head, Serketa's first real-life experiment succeeded wonderfully.

The donkey-seller's mouth opened wide. He gave a death-rattle, stretched out his arms to clutch at empty air and collapsed, stone dead.

Serketa removed the needle, which had drawn a few drops of blood. She wiped them away carefully, so as to leave no trace of her crime. As her victim would not receive a first-class mummification, no one would notice the tiny hole.

Then she untied the donkeys and, with one of the ropes, hanged the man from the end of a roof beam in the stable. The man weighed no more with her now he was dead than he had when he was alive.

Before vanishing into the night, Serketa retrieved the two ingots.

33

The starboard crew had gathered in the Brotherhood's meeting-place, where the Scribe of the Tomb was addressing them. He reminded them that they needed rare products like galenite and bitumen, and that the Master required at least one craftsman to take part in the expedition. Following precise instructions, he would bring back to the village the necessary quantities for the Great Work.

Ordinarily, it was Thuty the Learned who performed this duty; but because of his recent bereavement the Master could not ask him to do it. So he called for a volunteer, who must be ready to leave the very next morning.

On his return to his office where, as he feared, Niut the Strong had wielded her broom, Kenhir did not even have time to fly into a rage, for a message from Sobek summoned him urgently to the fifth fort. Although he detested unexpected disturbances, the Scribe of the Tomb nevertheless abandoned his beloved papyri.

Sobek couldn't conceal the fact that he was on edge. 'Have you heard the news, Kenhir?

'I am here to learn it.'

'The donkey-seller . . .'

'He hasn't dared defy the court by not failing to bring the five donkeys he owes you?'

'No, it's much worse than that. He's just been found dead,

at his stables. He hanged himself.'

'The miserable wretch couldn't face being ruined.'

'Another suicide, so soon after Abry's?' exclaimed the Nubian.

'How can you compare the governor of the west bank with a donkey-seller? The man was afraid of you and what you might do.'

'I am certain that he was murdered to stop him talking. Exactly like Abry.'

'Have you any proof? In either case?' asked Kenhir irritably.

'Unfortunately, no.'

'It isn't altogether a bad thing that you see conspiracies everywhere, Sobek, because it keeps you alert. But don't let it become an obsession. Can you at least get the donkeys back?'

'Someone untied them, and they wandered off.'

'Why couldn't the merchant have freed them, before killing himself?

'That would be very simple.'

'And that's what it is: simple! Aren't you due for a few days' holiday?'

'I don't want a holiday!'

'Well, you should have one anyway. A rest would do you a great deal of good.'

'The village's safety is all I care about. And the people who tried to destroy me made a very big mistake in failing.'

The page of the Journal of the Tomb that Kenhir would have to write would be as long as it was exceptional. No one could leave the village to go on the expedition: Casa because he had eye problems; Fened because he was taking offerings to his parents' tomb; Karo because he was repairing the door of his house; Nakht because he was brewing beer for the next festival; Userhat because he had been stung by a scorpion; and all the others for equally good reasons.

All except Paneb.

'You are the father of a small baby,' Kenhir reminded him.

'He gets bigger every time I see him, and Uabet is taking very good care of him. But surely I'm not the only volunteer?'

'I'm afraid so. Let's go and see the Master.'

Nefer could not hide his embarrassment. 'Thank you for your bravery, Paneb, but I wasn't thinking of you – you do not know the sites or what products to bring back.'

'Who does know?'

'The best person would be Thuty, but his bereavement—'

'Does he belong to the Brotherhood, yes or no? When we're entrusted with an important task, we have to put aside our joys and our sorrows. I shared his distress; but today we need him, because I don't suppose this is exactly a simple walk in the desert. The things to be brought back are vital, aren't they?'

'Even if the Theban workshop and the governor of the east bank hadn't requested this expedition, we'd have had to organize it. The House of Gold uses bitumen and galenite for special reasons which I can't tell you.'

'I shall go and see Thuty and persuade him to go. If there are two of us, the journey will be easier.'

Daktair could not keep still. Constantly tugging at his beard, he counted and re-counted the two hundred donkeys and the two hundred miners who were about to set off. They would be led by thirty prospectors who had long experience of searching for minerals and precious stones, and who were used to danger and hardened to discomfort. They had drawn up their own maps and were discussing the precautions to be taken against attacks from 'sand-travellers', cruel and thieving nomads. Daktair had ordered maximum protection for the caravan, so there was also a guard detail of twenty veteran soldiers.

The route was lined with wells, but the caravan carried ample supplies of water and food. The donkeys had been carefully checked, to make sure they were strong and healthy, and their panniers and girths were brand-new.

The only thing they needed now was the craftsman from the Place of Truth.

'How much more time is he going to make us waste?' demanded Daktair indignantly. 'We can't wait all day for him.'

'Do you want me to go to the village?' asked one of the prospectors.

'Look,' said another. 'Perhaps that's him.' He pointed to the landing-stage.

All eyes fixed on a small boat which was – rather ineptly – trying to come alongside and tie up. Clumsily handled, it failed twice before it was safely moored.

Two very different passengers jumped out on to the landing-stage, a young giant and an older, sickly-looking man, who seemed fragile enough to break. Immediately the soldiers surrounded them, brandishing their cudgels.

'Who are you?' Daktair asked aggressively.

'Can't you tell?' replied the young giant in surprise. 'A novice who's learning to sail. I didn't do too badly for my first crossing.'

'Go back where you came from, my lad. This is a military area.'

'Isn't an expedition about to set out from here?'

Daktair was worried. 'You're well-informed. Who told you?

'The Master of the Place of Truth.'

'I was expecting one craftsman, not two.'

'My name is Paneb, and this is my companion, Thuty.'

'I need to know details of your ranks and your skills.'

'Well, you'll have to be content with our names.'

'Do you know who you're talking to? I am Daktair, head

of the central workshop at Thebes, and leader of this expedition. You owe me total obedience, so you must tell me what I want to know.'

Paneb stared at the soldiers, one by one: one by one, they looked away. Thuty realized that his companion was preparing to charge into the fray and would not easily be subdued.

'Paneb, no,' he whispered. 'Remember, we have a mission.'

'You're right – I can't do as I'd like. Fine. Let's go home, then.' Paneb turned on his heel and headed back to the boat.

Daktair rushed after him and seized him by the wrist. 'Where are you going?'

'Let go of me immediately, or I shan't answer for the consequences.' He looked so menacing that Daktair hastily obeyed. 'Thuty and I are going back to the village.'

'But aren't you supposed to be coming with me?'

'With you, yes, but not under your command. We're free men and we know what we have to do.'

Daktair went red in the face. 'I remind you that I am the leader of this expedition and that, if it's to succeed, there must be strict discipline.'

'Use it on your underlings; we answer only to the Place of Truth. If you can't grasp that, you'll be responsible if the expedition's a failure.'

'Will you at least tell me where we're going?'

'You'll know soon enough. Right, that's agreed, then. Thuty will take the lead and show everyone the way.'

'You're defying my authority, Paneb!'

'Whatever are you talking about? I'm just not bothering with it, that's all.'

'I'm not accustomed to being spoken to in that tone of voice. Whether you like it or not, I'm in charge of this expedition, and I won't tolerate your attitude.'

'Then leave without me.'

Daktair turned to Thuty. 'I hope you're more reasonable than your friend.'

'In accordance with our Master's wishes,' said the goldsmith calmly, 'I shall lead this expedition to the mines. But on one condition: the instructions I've been given will be followed to the letter. Either you accept that – regardless of all your titles and prerogatives – or you stay in Thebes.'

Daktair stared at him in silent astonishment. No wonder this Brotherhood was such a formidable enemy.

'Let's stop all this useless arguing,' said Paneb, 'and get moving.'

34

The expedition sailed down the Nile from Thebes to Gebtu, where the animals and men disembarked and set out across the desert to the Red Sea and the Sinai peninsula. The region was rich in turquoise and copper, which had been mined since the days of the pharaoh Djoser. Led by Thuty, who knew the area well, they travelled for some time along a track which led eventually to a granite quarry, then turned off and headed for Gebel Zeit.

Although rain hardly ever fell in the region, there was some moisture because of the Red Sea, and little islands of greenery blossomed here and there, notably at the foot of an impressive chain of mountains with towering peaks.

Most Egyptians feared the desert, which was inhabited by strange, dangerous creatures; but everyone knew that it preserved bodies for eternity and that it contained immense treasures, gold, silver, and all the 'pure stones born in the belly of the mountains'. You could cross the desert, but you could not live there, for it was the afterworld present on earth. And you needed experienced guides if you were not to fall victim to one of its many hazards.

Despite his frailty, Thuty set a good pace. Paneb strode along beside him.

'I have the feeling,' said Thuty, 'that you're enjoying this journey.'

'Oh, more than enjoying it!' exclaimed Paneb. 'What a magnificent place. The sand looks like fire, but it's soft under my feet. It's good that our village is in the desert; it needs the desert's power to help men and stop them getting flabby.'

'What do you think of that man Daktair?'

'As far as I'm concerned he doesn't exist. He's just a fat, petty little scribe, whose privileges have gone to his head.'

'All the same, be wary of him. When I worked at Karnak I met men like him, though they weren't so dangerous. It's not surprising that he doesn't like us, but I have a feeling there's something more serious behind it.'

Paneb looked at Thuty in astonishment. 'What? You used to live in the domain of Amon?'

'Yes. That's where I learnt to work precious wood, gold and electrum, to carve decorated panels, to cover doors, statues and boats with gold. I'd have reached high rank if Kenhir hadn't called on me when the Place of Truth needed an experienced goldsmith. I was the third on the list, but the court of admissions had rejected the first two.'

'Why didn't you stay at Karnak?'

'I'd never dared knock at the Brotherhood's door, but I knew the village held professional secrets which weren't known anywhere else. I'd never have been able to learn those secrets anywhere else, so when the opportunity arose I took my chance.'

'Did you hear the call?'

'The first time I held gold in my hands. But I didn't know what it was, or that it made me different from other goldsmiths. The Brotherhood did know, of course, and accepted me into the starboard crew. What a wonderful day that was. Now, I must put up with the suffering . . .'

'You could have another child,' said Paneb awkwardly.

'No, I prefer to keep my son's memory intact – his laughter, his games, the happiness I've lost . . .' Thuty cleared his throat, and went on, 'I'm grateful to you for making me come out of my trance and join you on this expedition. I couldn't have done it alone, but with you here as well we have a good chance of success.'

'What makes you think Daktair's dangerous?'

'Because the minerals we're going to collect are dangerous – there are strict rules governing their use. As head of the central workshop, Daktair might be intending to break those rules.'

'Isn't one of our duties to make sure they're obeyed?'

'Yes, so if Daktair really is up to something we may become a stumbling-block. The expedition isn't dangerous in itself; but since I met Daktair. . .'

Paneb smiled eagerly. 'Let's hope he tries to take us on.'

'But there are only two of us!' protested Thuty.

'From what I understand, you've got friends among the miners and prospectors.'

'Well, yes. Crossing the desert several times creates bonds between men, it's true. Very few of them would turn against us.'

'Don't worry,' said Paneb. 'Daktair doesn't stand a chance.'

Daktair was the only man to ride on a donkey. Despite this privilege, which was due to his rank, he drank much more water than the men on foot. He'd known the journey would not be a pleasure-trip, but he hadn't foreseen that these vast stretches of desert would be so horrifying.

He was in a thoroughly bad mood. As he rode along, he tried in vain to think of a way of dealing with Paneb, who, he sensed, was as wary and as fierce as a wild animal. How could he get rid of Paneb without making Thuty suspicious? If Thuty refused to go on, Daktair would lose the chance of getting his hands on one of the Brotherhood's greatest secrets. No, he couldn't do anything now. He'd have to wait until the minerals had been collected; then he'd think again.

Up ahead, the miners slowed down and stopped.

'I didn't give the order to halt,' said Daktair.

'Well, we're halting anyway,' said one of the men.

Angrily, Daktair rode up to the head of the caravan. He found Thuty sitting on a block of stone, his back to the sun. Around him, men and animals were having a drink of water.

'What's going on?' demanded Daktair.

'An unexpected pause,' replied the goldsmith. 'It shouldn't be long, and a short rest won't do anybody any harm.'

'Where's your companion?'

'He and two prospectors have gone off to that little mountain over there.'

'Why? That isn't our destination.'

'Go and have a nap.'

'Call those men back immediately!' snapped Daktair.

'Just wait quietly till they get back. The more worked up you get, the thirstier you'll be.'

Thuty offered Daktair a fig but he refused it and rode back to his place at the rear of the caravan. Not one miner showed him any sympathy, while many of them came up to reminisce with Thuty about previous expeditions.

When Paneb returned, he was carrying a small bundle.

'Thuty, it's incredible!' he exclaimed. 'Just look what we found!'

He unwrapped the bundle and laid out several twelve-sided pieces of rock containing cornelians, red jasper and garnets. Some of the bigger garnets were already out of their coating and were in the form of chains of spheres.

'They weren't making fun of you,' said the goldsmith.

'Our friends say there's no need to show these stones to Daktair and have them registered. After all, they're only big pebbles.'

'From an unbeliever's point of view, that's true. And there's already so much paperwork to be done . . .'

'Will you cut some of them for me?'

'Yes, of course. But now we'd better get moving again. Daktair must be getting impatient.'

A soldier ran up to them. 'We spotted two sand-travellers up there,' he said, pointing to one of the surrounding hills. 'They watched us for a few moments, then disappeared. Scouts, probably.'

'Should we prepare for an attack?' asked Paneb.

'Not necessarily – those cowardly thieves don't usually attack well-defended caravans. All the same, though, we're going to take precautions. Archers will travel at the head of the column with you, and at night we'll set a guard.'

They started off again, more slowly now, casting anxious glances around in case an armed band suddenly came charging out of nowhere. But as the hours passed, their alarm subsided. All was quiet, and, besides, none of the wells along the route had been blocked up or polluted. The guards were alert, the caravan was well protected, and morale was high. From time to time, the prospectors checked their maps and filled their leather pouches with samples of minerals, which they labelled with care.

A young miner collapsed, sunstruck. Paneb picked him up and carried him on his back, attracting covert looks of approval and admiration. No one complained about the pace Thuty was setting.

Thuty called a halt. 'This will be our last stop before we reach the site late tomorrow morning,' he said. 'This evening we'll have a bit of a feast: dried beef and red wine.'

And a feast it seemed, after the long, arduous crossing of the desert. After they'd eaten, the miners began roaring out songs to the glory of the pharaoh and to Hathor, queen of precious metals.

Daktair came over to Thuty and Paneb. 'We haven't exchanged a single word during the journey. Perhaps it's time we called a truce,' he said.

'Why not?' replied Thuty. 'Sit down and have a drink.'

'Thank you, but I never drink alcohol.'

'It might put you in a better mood,' suggested Paneb.

Daktair ignored him and said to Thuty, 'We'll be starting work tomorrow, I suppose?'

'That's right.'

'Isn't it time you showed me how you plan to go about it? I'm here to help you and give you the benefit of my knowledge.'

'We don't doubt that,' said Thuty, 'but for the moment it'll be better if you concentrate on seeing that the caravan's safe.'

'The soldiers are doing that. What I'm interested in is what sort of minerals, and how much, we'll be taking back to Thebes.'

'It's time we were asleep,' decided Thuty.

35

Gebel Zeit was a mountain range which towered over the entrance to the gulf at the head of the Red Sea. Being so isolated – it was far from all the usual caravan routes the site was mined rarely: only when galenite was needed

Daktair watched impatiently while Thuty prepared for the ritual prayer to Hathor. The fat man had heard several miners say that galenite was as precious as gold, which made his mouth water. He now understood why Thuty had come here several times, but he did not yet know how the Brotherhood used the mineral.

'Let us now pay homage to Hathor and ask for her protection,' said Thuty.

Daktair muttered to himself that they were wasting time, but he knew that eradicating the old superstitions wouldn't be easy.

All the members of the expedition stood in contemplation before plain stone stelae raised before little shrines of dry stone, erected among the rough shelters the miners slept in. Each made an offering to the goddess – an amulet, a porcelain scarab, the terracotta statue of a woman, a piece of fine linen – and they also prayed to the gods Min, protector of desert mines and miners, and Ptah, patron of craftsmen.

When the ritual was over, Thuty assigned the men their work. He sent five prospectors to hunt gazelles, five others to fish and gather shellfish, and he appointed two stewards to take charge of the site's day-to-day running and cleanliness. They began to unload the donkeys, and the soldiers who were on guard took up their positions.

Paneb was put in charge of handing out the stone tools, picks and hammers, most made of basalt, and choosing twenty or so miners who had enough energy left after the journey to go to the mine, about half an hour away.

The well-organized bustle took Daktair by surprise. He hardly knew where to turn, in case he missed something the two craftsmen did. At any moment they might reveal the goal of their mission and, therefore, the secret he was so desperate to get his hands on.

'Let's go,' said Thuty. 'Steward, make sure the meal's ready when we get back.'

Daktair joined the party heading for the mine; neither Thuty nor Paneb paid him any attention.

The closer they got, the greater the abundance of strange minerals, some bluish-grey, others very dark; Daktair had never seen anything like them. He got another surprise when he saw the mine, part of which was open to the sky while the rest was underground. The seams of galenite had been detected on the surface, running from north to south; it had been quarried there, and then galleries sixty cubits deep had been excavated. One particularly rich seam was a full two hundred cubits deep in the earth; it was reached by means of a shaft so narrow that only one slender miner at a time could use it.

Daktair was excited, as though he were on the threshold of a great discovery. 'These rocks, are they galenite?'

'Galenite is greyish-blue,' said Thuty. 'The rocks that vary from dark brown to black are bitumen. Do you want to go into one of the galleries?'

'Of course!'

'You're sure to get dirty – and you're too fat to get into some of them.'

Fascinated, Daktair would have followed him to the ends of the earth, but the climb down was not easy, and Paneb had once to catch him by the waist when he started sliding dangerously.

The previous expedition had worked well, creating chambers tall enough for a man to stand upright. Ventilation shafts about half a cubit across provided fresh air.

With a pick, a miner broke off a piece of rock, which he hammered into pieces to extract the nuggets of galenite.

'This is what we shall be taking back to Thebes,' said Thuty.

Daktair peered at it. 'What's it used for?' he asked.

'The bitumen is used to waterproof grain silos, to caulk certain types of boat, to seal the lids of jars and to fit handles on to tools. As a poultice, it's effective against coughs. As for the galenite, it provides that most precious of products, the cosmetic that beautiful women use to make up their eyes. It would be worth the journey to obtain just this – our wives love it.'

All that secrecy over something so trivial! Daktair was cruelly disappointed, and couldn't help wondering if the craftsmen were making fun of him and telling a pack of lies. Being careful not to show his suspicion, he watched the miners as they worked. He moved about as he liked in the accessible galleries and even ventured into a shaft which had just been excavated, though he saw nothing interesting.

After a few days, bored with nuggets of galenite, he decided to spy on Thuty and Paneb. Unfortunately, they worked long and hard, and not until nightfall did they return to their hut, where they slept on two sturdy travelling-mats. Daktair faced a dilemma: how could he find out what Paneb was doing while he was watching Thuty, and vice-versa? And why did Thuty always look so haggard and eat so little? He managed to bribe two miners, but they provided him only with uninteresting information.

Under Thuty's direction, galenite was extracted; under Paneb's, the nuggets were listed and arranged in panniers to be transported, and the tools were cleaned and repaired. The two men made full use of their experience of construction. They organized the work efficiently, adapting to the particular conditions of each day and never wasting the workmen's energy on unimportant tasks, something which brought them growing popularity.

Daktair was still brooding over what Thuty had said about galenite. If it was used just for make-up and as a sealant, why go to such lengths to mine it? No, there must be more to it than that. The Place of Truth was too important to devote itself to such superficial things. If Thury and Paneb were acting according to precise instructions from their Master, if they had left their village knowing that their faces and names would henceforth be known, they must have done so for a serious reason.

So Daktair changed his strategy. During the day, he rested for much of the time; at night, he stayed awake to watch the two men's hut, in the hope that they would give themselves away.

After three interminable nights of vigil, his patience was rewarded. While the camp was fast asleep, Paneb and Thuty left it soundlessly and headed for the mine. Daktair followed them; the moon was up and he could see quite clearly.

They walked round one of the guard-posts and turned off towards a ravine outside the mined area.

Daktair hesitated. If he stumbled, they'd hear the noise and might spot him. And if it came to a fight, he'd stand no chance against Paneb; he'd be easy prey. But this was his only chance to find out what the craftsmen were up to.

Fortunately, they were going slowly, as though unsure which path to take; then he realized they were avoiding the sentries. The two men passed far behind the last one, who did not see them, and began climbing the side of the ravine.

Daktair did likewise.

Suddenly they halted, as though they had come up against an invisible adversary. Paneb moved away from Thuty and picked up a stone. When he raised his arm, Daktair thought that he was going to strike Thuty down. Had he decided to get rid of him so that he could seize all the treasure for himself?

Paneb hurled the stone down, and the two men continued.

When Daktair passed the place, he saw a dead black cobra, its head shattered. Fear seized him by the throat. Ordinarily, no one walked in the desert at night, for it was the realm of reptiles and scorpions.

In spite of his fear, Daktair's feet carried him on. He had no choice: he didn't know the way back to the camp. He dared not look around him, and stared at the craftsmen's backs, afraid of hearing a sinister hiss.

The climb was painfully difficult. Twice Daktair almost slipped on the rocks.

When they reached the top, the two craftsmen suddenly disappeared.

'It must be the entrance to a mine,' thought Daktair. 'They must have gone into the gallery where the treasure is hidden.'

Forgetting the snakes, the slippery stones and the hostile desert, he climbed rapidly to the top of the ravine wall, lay flat on his belly behind a rock, and peered round it.

Thuty and Paneb were standing not at the entrance to a mine but in a sort of crater. But what were they looking at? Daktair strained his eyes to see. Had the two men simply lost their way?

What froze his blood was not a snake's hiss but the hiss of an arrow. It grazed his brow, producing a bloody furrow. He looked round frantically. Running towards him were three men armed with daggers.

'Help!' he screamed. '*Help!*'

36

Paneb lunged forward to the edge of the crater.

In the moonlight he saw Daktair, pinned to the ground by three sand-travellers and yelling his head off.

'Why don't you take me on, you cowards,' roared Paneb.

The looters abandoned their prey and leapt at him. Sure they'd easily be able to stab this madman to death, instead of surrounding him they all rushed at him together. At the last moment, Paneb bent down and butted the middle one in the belly, then grabbed the other two by the testicles and flung them aside. Before they could get up and regain their breath, he let fly. He smashed the first man's skull with a stone, broke the second one's neck and slit the third one's throat with his own dagger.

Daktair got shakily to his feet. 'Don't hurt me!' he begged.

'What are you doing here?' demanded Paneb.

'I'm nothing to do with them. I . . . I lost my way.'

'You were following us, weren't you?'

Daktair clapped his hand to his head. 'Blood! I'm wounded, seriously wounded.'

'You'll be taken care of if you tell the truth.'

'You can't treat me like that. If my wound isn't tended at once, I'll die!

Thuty drew Paneb aside, and said quietly, 'Let's take him

back to the camp. If he brought a complaint against you, he might cause serious problems.'

Against his better judgment, Paneb lifted Daktair with one hand and slung him over his shoulder like a sack of grain.

Daktair was resting in his tent. Although spectacular, his wound was only superficial and his life was in no danger.

The three men Paneb had killed were notorious bandits; a soldier recognized two of them. They were known to have attacked encampments in the middle of the night, and to have killed, raped and pillaged. Their corpses were left for the jackals.

The incident made the atmosphere sombre, and the miners were eager to get home to Egypt. When Thuty announced that there were only two more days of work, everyone felt reassured.

'Your trick worked very well,' Paneb told Thuty. 'Daktair obviously believed we were going to lead him to a treasure-trove. Now that we needn't worry about him any longer, tell me honestly: does that treasure exist?'

'Galenite and bitumen are indeed vital to us – and not only for the uses I told Daktair about. I am required to take a certain quantity back to the Master.'

'Is this connected to the Stone of Light?'

'It may be – and that's all I know.'

Paneb narrowed his eyes. Either Thuty was lying, or he'd been ordered not to reveal the the secret.

'The crater Daktair followed us to was only a decoy,' the goldsmith went on. 'He could go back there a hundred times and he'd never find anything. But there's another place I must show you.'

The two men walked out beyond the mine site, checking that they were not being followed. Paneb noticed that the rocks were becoming darker and darker.

'Tread carefully,' Thuty warned him. 'The ground gets very slippery.'

'You'd swear the stone was oily,' said Paneb, puzzled.

'It is. We are on the mountain of stone-oil, which oozes out of the cracks. Look closely at this spring.'

On the surface, Paneb noted a nugget of grease, which floated on the water but did not mix with it.

'Peculiar stuff,' he said. 'What is it and what's it used for?'

'It is a kind of oil, but it's animated by a dangerous energy which the ancients forbade us to use. It burns easily, but it soils and pollutes – in tombs, it blackens the walls and ceilings. Because of the destructive power within it, it can only be transformed into a ritual unguent, during certain mummifications, and in the preparation of the mysterious Stone of the Place of Truth where it undergoes such a transformation that all harmfulness is driven away. If ambitious, greedy men like Daktair succeeded in exploiting it and spreading its use, terrible misfortune would strike down our country. Men would become mad; the sand-travellers might even invade Egypt and the surrounding lands to take power, accumulate wealth and subjugate humanity. In his wisdom, Pharaoh has ordered that none but the Brotherhood shall be authorized to use this oil, which is a terrifying poison. Now, Paneb, you belong to those who know.'

Complaining of his aching head, Daktair was carried on a litter by four soldiers. The expedition moved as quickly as possible along the homeward path, keen to reach the banks of the Nile and their verdant landscapes. The desert was even more dangerous now, because at any moment a band of sand-travellers might materialize, determined to avenge their dead.

In that hostile, desolate country, Paneb felt his strength growing. The spirits that lived in the sand and the sun-scorched rocks wiped every trace of tiredness from him and increased his vitality tenfold. He thought of the first builders who had dared to venture into the desert, there to master the stones' fire. Egypt was truly a miracle, accomplished day after day, because she knew how to celebrate the wedding of the black, fertile, generous earth to the power of the desert.

'Daktair wants to talk to us,' said Thuty.

The two craftsmen went over to the litter.

'You saved my life and I want to thank you. If it hadn't been for Paneb, those bandits would have killed me.'

'Why were you following us?' asked Thuty.

'I was convinced that treasure was hidden on that site and that your mission was to bring it back to the village. I didn't want to steal it, I just wanted to satisfy my curiosity.'

'Well then, when we get back have all the panniers reserved for the Place of Truth searched: all you'll find is nuggets of galenite. That is the treasure: a rare substance, difficult to mine. I repeat, your workmen will use it to seal the stores where grain is kept to provide for bad years, and it ensures that handles are more securely fixed. And we shall, of course, take enough to make the cosmetic that Pharaoh generously gives to our wives and daughters.'

'But . . . if the expedition was merely routine, why did you have to come?'

'A royal decree makes it obligatory.'

'But you wanted to come, didn't you? Why?'

Thuty smiled. 'Oh, that's simple. We don't altogether trust the government you represent, so we prefer it to be one of us who checks that we get all the galenite we're entitled to. Also, as you may have noticed, we know how to organize and manage a work-site.'

Daktair couldn't think what to say. Thuty's explanation made perfect sense and left nothing unexplained. And yet, deep down, he was sure it wasn't the whole truth.

He pulled himself together. 'Will you forgive me?'

'Of course,' replied the goldsmith. 'There are so many absurd stories about our village . . . If you believed the street pedlars, you'd end up convinced we hold all the secrets of creation! The reality is much simpler: we belong to a

Brotherhood devoted to the service of Pharaoh, and that is where our pride and our reason for existing lie.'

Convinced, Daktair drank a mouthful of water and let the matter drop.

The fires of the encampment, the last in the risky area, were being put out, and the caravan was preparing to take the broad track towards Gebtu. Thuty had partly regained his appetite and, despite his weariness from the journey, he looked less gaunt.

'This journey has been good for me,' he confided to Paneb. 'The suffering will never go away, but I am can bear it better. I owe that to you – it's as if you've given me a little of your strength – and I thank you from the bottom of my heart.'

'My brother, you have nothing to thank me for. When a member of the crew is in difficulty, shouldn't the others help him so that the boat doesn't get into danger? The Master is always saying so, and I'm beginning to wonder if that secret isn't as important as the secret of the House of Gold.'

A sentry blew a warning blast on his trumpet.

'Sand-travellers!' shouted a frightened miner.

'Don't panic!' ordered Paneb's powerful voice. 'The soldiers and prospectors will form a circle. Stay inside the circle and you'll be safe. We have weapons and we know how to use them.'

His confidence calmed the men, and the circle was formed quickly and without panic. Paneb craned his neck to see the enemy. There were about a hundred of them, led by a man riding a black mule. They were all bearded, long-haired and clad in gaudy robes. They brandished bows and daggers, and were clearly spoiling for a fight. A lot of men were going to be killed on both sides, and the prospects did not look good for the Egyptians.

A stone in either hand, Paneb walked forward out of the circle.A sand-traveller let fly an arrow. Paneb waited for it to fly towards him then threw his first stone and broke the arrow in half in mid-air; then he threw the second at the sand-travellers' leader.

At that distance, the man jeered, he was in no danger of being hit. The sand-travellers all laughed loudly at the Egyptian's boastfulness.

Then Paneb launched a third stone high into the sky. Gathering speed as it fell, it crashed down on the bandit leader's skull and he collapsed and fell off his mule. When he did not get up again, one of his men grabbed his weapons and the mule and fled, followed instantly by his comrades.

Loud cheers greeted Paneb's exploit.

37

Daktair was being massaged by a young Syrian girl with very gentle hands when Mehy burst into his bedchamber,

The general gestured to the girl to leave, and demanded, 'When did you get back?'

'Yesterday evening. I was in a bad way.'

Daktair turned on to his side with difficulty and sat up, moaning and clutching his bandaged head. 'I was almost killed by a sand-traveller during that horrible journey. The heat, the desert, bandits roaming the place . . . Don't ever ask me to go on another of those expeditions. Next time, I shall send one of my assistants.'

'Yes, but you're alive, and you'll soon recover. Let's get to the important thing: what did you find out?'

'Nothing.'

'What do you mean, "Nothing"? I don't like people mocking me, my friend.'

'But I'm not!' protested Daktair. 'I don't think there was anything to find out. Gebel Zeit is just a place where they mine galenite and bitumen, and I now know what they're used for. I brought back the same quantities as my predecessors and I shall get a good price when I sell them to the cosmetics merchants. There's no treasure and no secret down there, believe me.'

'Then why was the Place of Truth involved in the expedition?'

'For a reason which neither you nor I would ever have thought of: to acquire a mineral which fixes handles to tools. Those people are more simple than we thought. Having spent time with them, I can confidently say that they see no further than the efficient running of a site and the wellbeing of the workers.'

Mehy slapped him hard.

Dazed, he took a while to unscramble his wits. His left cheek was burning red, and his head was buzzing. 'Whatever has got into you, General?'

'You reason like an idiot and you've lost your memory! They made you go to sleep and I'm waking you up. Are you forgetting that I, Mehy, have seen the Stone of Light? The secrets we must uncover are indeed to be found in the Place of Truth – and only there. Our enemies are neither stupid nor simple. They're cunning creatures who know how to defend themselves. The ones who deceived you were obeying orders from their Master. And that man leaves nothing to chance.'

The donkeys halted before the great gate of the Place of Truth. Helped by a few lay workers, Paneb unloaded the baskets laden with galenite, and Thuty counted the nuggets so he could give an exact number in his report to the Scribe of the Tomb. Then the precious cargo was taken into the village by Nakht the Powerful and Karo the Impatient, after long, warm congratulations to the two travellers.

'With you watching over Thuty, we weren't too worried,' said Karo, 'but all the same it's a relief to have you back.'

'Is all well in the village?'

'Yes, but busy – we've no time to be bored, I assure you! Nefer made us repair the tools so that the sites could be opened soon, and the sculptors are already at work.'

At that moment, Nefer appeared. He greeted the arrivals and asked, 'Did everything go well?'

'More or less,' replied Thuty. 'The sand-travellers

attacked us twice, but Paneb saw them off. And then Daktair tried to find out why we were on this expedition, and what we were after, but we made sure he didn't find out.'

'Are you absolutely certain of that?'

'Well, pretty certain. But the fellow doesn't like us, and he seems extremely crafty. We'd better keep a watchful eye on him.'

'Have you brought back what we need?' asked Nefer.

'Yes, and plenty of it,' said Thuty. 'You should even have some to spare.'

'Does Paneb know about it?'

'I showed him the oil and he knows its dangers. Before I go, and while he's present, I must stress that he behaved impeccably at all times.' And Thuty went off to see his wife.

'Well, Paneb,' said Nefer, 'it seems the desert is still your ally.'

'The desert and I are alike, and we understand each other. Besides, without it, our village wouldn't exist. But tell me what's been happening here. When are we starting work on the big sites?'

'The day after tomorrow.'

'So much the better! Will I be in the first crew?'

'You weren't going to be, but, in view of what Thuty said, I've changed my mind.'

Paneb jumped for joy, then said, 'I'm off to kiss my wife and my son.'

He sped off but he did not go far. Delicious in a short red dress and a fine pearl necklace, Turquoise was standing in the doorway of her house, combing her long hair.

'The wife who runs her house well is a treasure beyond price,' she murmured. 'All you need do is admire her and congratulate her on all the work she does. Why are you stopping in front of my house?'

'May I come in?'

'You know very well that it's risky.'

'Can you imagine what it's like being stuck in the middle of the desert with not a woman in sight?'

Turquoise stepped aside. Paneb lifted her gently by the waist, carried her inside and laid her down on the love-bed in the living-room. He could never resist her charm and her beauty; nor did he want to.

When she was naked, he took from his belt a leather bag, untied the lace that held it shut, and poured on to her belly the garnets that Thuty had cut for him.

'Aren't they superb?' he said.

'Are you getting civilized, Paneb?'

'Certainly not!'

Giving Turquoise no more time to admire the jewels, he kissed her with all the fervour of a passionate young man who had been deprived of love for much too long. She responded just as passionately, and gave her lover pleasures more splendid than all the gems of the desert.

Sitting on a high chair equipped with a cushion, Uabet the Pure was taking a short rest while a serving-girl rubbed her feet. In the kitchen, a little monkey which had taken up residence in the village was eating a fig. He scampered from house to house, stayed for a few days in one or the other, and no one drove him out, for he played with the children, who loved him better than any toy.

Opposite Uabet, a well-endowed wet-nurse was feeding Aapehti, who was suckling greedily. He had grown even bigger.

'I've never seen anything like it,' said the wet-nurse. 'You'll soon have two giants under your roof.'

The wet-nurse drank fig-juice and ate lots of fresh fish to ensure that she had plenty of milk, sweetly scented like carob flour, but milk alone was not enough to satisfy Aapehti's appetite; he was already eating solid food.

From time to time, Uabet wondered if she would have

sufficient energy to carry out her duties as a priestess, look after the house and bring up this child; but she reassured herself by thinking that he'd spend most of the day outside and that Paneb would be sure to train him in wrestling and similar activities.

'My neighbour says she saw Paneb at the great gate,' said Uabet. 'Do you know if he's really back, Nurse?'

The nurse looked embarrassed and avoided Uabet's eyes. 'I didn't go that way this morning.'

'So he is back, and he's gone to see Turquoise,' concluded Uabet. 'That's probably just as well, because when he comes home tonight he won't be so demanding.'

The little monkey sprang out of the kitchen and leapt on to Paneb's shoulder as he stepped over the threshold. Sitting there, the animal seemed minuscule.

'I hope everyone is well,' said Paneb. 'Come and greet me, my son.'

The wet-nurse held Aapehti out to his father, who cradled him gently while the little monkey hesitantly fingered his black hair.

'What a fine boy he is!' exclaimed Paneb. 'He does you proud, Uabet. But are you well? You look a bit pale.'

'It's nothing. I'm just a bit tired.'

Paneb handed the baby back to the wet-nurse and laid a leather bag on his wife's knees.

'What is it?' she asked.

'Open it.'

Uabet untied the cord and looked inside. 'Cornelians . . . and red jasper!'

'I'm counting on you to have them made into necklaces which will turn all the other women green with envy.'

Uabet smiled. 'I've got something much less difficult to ask of you. We need more fresh fish for the wet-nurse. Aapehti's appetite is so big that she needs to eat more than the usual ration.'

'Don't worry, I'll see to it.' Paneb kissed her on the forehead.

Suddenly there was a knock at the open door, and Imuni put his head in. 'I apologize for interrupting your family reunion,' he said, 'but the Scribe of the Tomb wishes to see Paneb on a matter of some urgency.'

38

Paneb could cheerfully have punched the stuffy, pompous little pipsqueak, but a summons from Kenhir must not be ignored; besides, he was intrigued to know what it was about. So he dutifully followed Imuni out into the street.

'I warn you,' said Imuni, 'the Scribe of the Tomb is in a very bad mood.'

'No change there, then.'

'If it's because of you, I wouldn't like to be in your shoes.'

Paneb grinned. 'There's no risk of that, Imuni.' He quickened his pace, and the Assistant Scribe had to break into a trot to keep up.

When they reached Kenhir's house, Niut was sweeping the doorstep.

'He's waiting for you in his office,' she told Paneb.

Imuni tried to follow him, but Niut blocked the doorway with her broom. 'Not you. He said, "Paneb, and no one else."'

Annoyed, Imuni had to kick his heels outside while Paneb went into the office. There he found not only the Scribe of the Tomb but also the Master and the Wise Woman.

'Am I being hauled up before the court?' asked Paneb.

'Instead of talking rubbish,' replied Kenhir, 'sit down and pay attention.' He seemed deeply worried, Paneb thought.

Kenhir went on, 'I have to inform you all of a catastrophe,

and ask you to promise not to reveal a word of what I'm going to tell you.'

They all gave their solemn word.

'The most valuable tools are kept in a special locked room with strengthened walls; only the Master and I have keys. To prevent thefts, we still use the locks perfected by a master-carpenter in the reign of Amenhotep III.'

'Thefts?' gasped Paneb. 'Here in the village?'

'Men are only men, and I have just received another proof of that: someone has tried to break into the room.'

'That is unbelievable!'

'Alas, it is true. The thief broke the clay seal on which I had placed the seal of the necropolis, then he tried to saw through the first wooden bar. When he did, he must have realized he'd activated a second locking-system and must have feared there'd be a third, so he gave up and ran away before he could get caught. But the evidence that he'd been there was plain to see.'

'If anyone but the Scribe of the Tomb had said that,' declared Nefer, 'I wouldn't have believed a word of it. But we must accept the evidence. There's a dishonest craftsman among us; or, at least, someone who's greedy enough to think of stealing the Brotherhood's possessions.'

'That's a very serious crime,' said Kenhir. 'Shouldn't we warn Commander Sobek?'

'Oh no!' protested Paneb. 'This doesn't concern anyone but us. Let's sort it out ourselves, without involving outsiders.'

'It'll be difficult,' said Kenhir. 'You three are the only people in the village whom I can trust. The Master and the Wise Woman are the father and mother of this Brotherhood, and you, Paneb, were away in the desert when the attempted theft took place.'

'So was Thuty,' Paneb reminded him.

'True, but he could be the thief's accomplice.'

'And I couldn't?'

'You'd never help a wrongdoer.'

'Perhaps we're over-dramatizing the incident,' suggested Nefer. 'There's no doubt that someone did try to break into the locked room, but surely whoever it was wouldn't dare try again.'

'I wish I could be that optimistic,' said Kenhir.

'Tomorrow,' said Nefer, 'after consulting Hay about assigning the work on our two great sites, I shall be meeting all the members of the starboard crew. I'd like to believe that the greatness of the work to which we are called will purify everyone's thoughts.'

Kenhir smiled sardonically to himself, and thought, 'We need men like Nefer to touch the sky, but we also need men like me to keep everyone's feet on the ground.' Aloud, he asked, 'What does the Wise Woman think?'

'We must trust in the work and be vigilant towards men.'

Paneb went to the fishpond. All sorts of fish, including perch, mullet, tilapia and elephant-fish, were raised there, so that the Brotherhood could always be sure of a supply, whatever the fishing conditions on the Nile. The pond came under the authority of the government of the west bank, who had planted willows and sycamores all round it to keep it cool throughout the year.

Beside the pond was a salt warehouse used by the fishermen who slit open the fish open, gutted them and laid them out to dry in the sun before salting them. Fry and small fish were heaped up in baskets, while the big ones were hung on poles carried by two porters.

Paneb headed for a fisherman who, with a long, sharp knife, was gutting an enormous perch while one of his colleagues prepared a delicious meal of salted mullet-roes.

'Greetings, friend. I am Paneb, the husband of Uabet the Pure. I need a basket of fresh fish and a jar of dried fish for my son's wet-nurse.'

'Whoever you are, you won't get anything. We have

precise orders: to deliver the fish from the pool to the village and have the exact quantities noted down by the Scribe of the Tomb's assistant. It's forbidden to sell anything direct to a craftsman.'

'Not even when it's needed for a wet-nurse?'

'Not even then.'

Paneb felt like hitting the fisherman, but he thought he'd better not cause trouble among these peaceful people, who, moreover, seemed to be working hard for the village.

'Go to the river,' advised the fisherman. They'll be more understanding there.'

Sitting on the riverbank in the shade of a sycamore, an old fisherman was repairing his net. Other men were fishing, using a large landing-net made from two crossed rods reinforced by a crosspiece; the net was easy to handle when it was empty, but when it was full of fish plenty of brawn was needed to heave it out of the water.

'Greetings, grandfather,' said Paneb. 'Are there fish for sale here?'

'Not here, no. My lads work for the priests at Ramses' temple.'

'Where can I find the men who catch fish for the Place of Truth?'

'On the canal, a hundred or so paces to the north.'

When he got there, Paneb saw six men busy at their work. They were divided into two teams, one on the bank and the other in a boat, and had stretched a long net across the canal. The net ended in a point on either side and was extended at its two ends by a stout rope.

'Pull harder, you idle good-for-nothings,' ordered their leader, an ugly, bearded man with a fat belly.

'Do you think we're doing this for fun?' retorted an even uglier man.

'Get on with it,' said a third. 'It's a good catch.'

Mullet, eels, white carp and tilapia: the catch wasn't just good, it was excellent.

'Empty that net,' said the leader, 'kill the fish that are still moving and put them in the baskets under the willow over there. And get a move on.'

Paneb went closer. 'My name is Paneb, and I'd like to buy some fresh fish.'

The head fisherman cast him a sidelong glance. 'My name is Nia, and how much will you pay?'

'The usual: one amulet for a basket of mullet caught today.'

Nia rubbed his stomach. 'That's right. Have you got the amulet on you?'

'Here it is.'

Cut by Thuty from a cornelian Paneb had found in the desert, the amulet featured a flowering papyrus stem, the symbol of prosperity.

Nia weighed it and closed his fingers over it. 'Superb, really superb. It's well worth a basket of mullet.'

'Then give it to me.'

'I really would have liked to, but I can't. Why not? Well, my lad, I don't sell my fish to anyone. But finders keepers – and all my fishermen are witnesses that you never gave me any amulet. Go away, now. It's the best thing to do.'

His five men had gathered behind their leader.

Paneb glared at him. 'And this is how you treat a craftsman from the Place of Truth?'

Nia burst out laughing. 'Go away, I tell you. Otherwise we'll make you lose your fondness for fish.'

Paneb punched Nia in the belly so hard that he was hurled backwards, knocking his men over. The first two who got to their feet were knocked out by the young giant, the others fled.

Paneb stuck an empty basket on Nia's head and booted him in the backside. 'I am taking my fish and leaving you the amulet. Let's hope this teaches you not to be so dishonest.'

39

While Paneb and Thuty had been away, the starboard crew had completely refurbished the Brotherhood's meeting-place. When Paneb entered it, after the purification rite, he noticed two brand-new painted jars, and beautiful new rendering on the ceiling and the walls; and he breathed in the sweet smell of incense.

The Master invoked the ancestors, took his place on his chair and invited his brothers to sit down.

'Paneb and Thuty have brought back from Gebel Zeit the vital materials for the elaboration of the Stone of Light,' he said. 'The secret work of the House of Gold can therefore be completed, and its light will continue to illuminate our path. The moment has come to create King Meneptah's tomb and to build his Temple of a Million Years. In agreement with Hay, I have decided to entrust the first task to you while the port crew finish the work already in progress.'

For a few moments, each craftsman held his breath. At last, the great test!

'Has the site of the tomb been chosen?' asked Unesh the Jackal.

'The king has agreed to our proposal.'

'Exceptional work demands exceptional tools,' said Gau the Precise in his rasping voice. 'Have we really got everything we need?'

'The Scribe of the Tomb has guaranteed it,' confirmed the Master.

'Will we have to stay at the pass, far from our families?' asked Pai the Good Bread.

'Sometimes, yes. We'll have to, so that we don't waste time travelling to and from the site, and can make the best use of our strength.'

'It isn't as nice a place as the village.'

'I'm sorry, Pai, but the work must come before everything else.'

'I suppose my presence won't be required at the beginning of the work,' suggested Ched the Saviour haughtily.

'The whole crew must be on the site right from the beginning, so that the sum total of our talents may become a magical power. We shall need that power in order to succeed.'

'How long will the work in the Valley of the Kings take?' inquired Renupe the Jovial.

'I don't know. It will be a very large tomb, almost as big as that of Ramses.'

'Years and years of work ahead,' muttered Karo the Impatient. 'And I suppose everything has to be absolutely perfect.'

Nefer smiled. 'You can be sure of that.'

'Is there any news from Pi-Ramses?' asked Didia the Generous.

'Nothing new,' replied the Master, 'but King Meneptah has issued a decree confirming the role and duties of the Place of Truth.'

'So the Brotherhood has all eternity before it,' said Userhat.

'We shall act as if we had, but also as if each instant was to be the last. Giving the best of ourselves will not be enough. In creating this monument, we must reveal the mystery without betraying it.'

*

Paneb was leaving Turquoise's house when he bumped into Ched the Saviour.

'Are you still as besotted as ever?' asked Ched.

'Well . . . Turquoise is the most beautiful woman in the village.'

'Let's hope her beauty will inspire you. But do you really think this is the best way of preparing yourself for your stay in the Valley of the Kings?'

'To be honest, Ched, I haven't thought about it.'

'That's why you're still a novice, ignorant of the risks you run.'

'Well, since you're my teacher, what do you suggest?'

'Come to the workshop.'

The two men walked slowly along the main street of the village. Ched was more serious and less ironic than usual, as if preparing himself for something important.

'You may know I own a cabin near the Nile, a little field, a warehouse for jars of oil, a granary, a stable and a few head of livestock. It isn't an enormous fortune, but it gives me a regular income big enough to afford a measure of comfort and, more importantly, to buy my own colours. If you agree, I shall leave everything to you in my will.'

'Out of the question.'

Ched was taken aback. 'Why?'

'All I want you to leave me is your teaching. I'll earn the rest myself.'

'My suggestion would save you time.'

'I'm not afraid of time. Instead of wearing me out, it strengthens me. Besides, I distrust presents.'

'Surely you don't think I am trying to bribe or corrupt you?'

'My answer is no, and that's that. Leave your wealth to your family, and let's not speak of it again.'

Ched nodded, and they walked on in silence.

When they reached the workshop, Ched pushed the door open. The light inside was strange; it seemed to come from the brushes, which were so well cleaned that they looked brand-new. Sketches were arranged neatly against the walls.

'Perfect your skills, Paneb, but don't ever think that that's worth as much as knowledge. Nothing is more important than acquiring knowledge. It opens the doors to the magic of forms and colours, reveals the sacred nature of the craft, will be your only true source of joy and will dictate the right and honourable way to behave. Practising Ma'at means passing from ignorance into knowledge, and above all knowing in your heart and by heart.'

Ched made up some red ink, dipped in a very fine brush and, with one smooth movement, drew the eye of a falcon.

'What do you see, Paneb?'

'The eye of a bird of prey.'

'You're supposed to be an assistant painter, but you can't really see anything at all, can you? Don't you understand that our art needs seers, not sterile imitators? The eye is present everywhere, on the walls of temples, on sarcophagi, on stelae, on boats. The eye of the world beyond never stops watching us, not for one single second, and you, the painter, must share this gaze. But do you really want to?'

'Give me a test.'

'Don't let your heart succumb to pride because of what you know. Take advice from a servant-girl as readily as from a great man, for no one ever reaches the limits of art. Don't forget that even the little dewdrop makes the field prosper. Are you really ready to see, Paneb? Do you understand that you will discover an infinity of new worlds, from which you can never return?'

'No one will ever accuse me of cowardice.'

'Then wear this and never take it off.' Ched took off the amulet he wore round his neck and gave it to Paneb. It consisted of an eye in steatite in which, in symbolic form, were embodied all the measurements of the world.

'Iris, pupil, tear duct, cornea – each part of this eye is equivalent to a fraction of the whole. If you add up all the parts, you will get only sixty-three sixty-fourths. The missing sixty-fourth is your painter's hand, which will allow you to discover it if you become a true seer. For seeing is creating.'

Fascinated, Paneb contemplated the little masterpiece that would henceforth protect him. 'I'd like—'

'Be quiet and and prepare yourself.'

Abruptly, Ched left the workshop. He could not bring himself to tell his pupil that he was going blind.

Wearing his golden apron and ceremonial wig, and followed by the craftsmen of the starboard crew, the Master appeared before the Scribe of the Tomb, who was carrying a heavy wooden key.

'Do you agree to open the door of the locked room and entrust Pharaoh's tools to us?'

'Tell me the password.'

'The love of the Work.'

Kenhir used the key to deactivate the first lock and turned it to disarm the second. Then he opened the door of the room, which contained five hundred ordinary copper chisels, fifty large ones, thirty hoes and twenty-five adzes in the same metal, which came from Sinai. Nefer checked their quality before asking the Scribe of the Tomb the ritual question. 'Does this treasure harbour the celestial metal?

'Let the Master identify the tools that will render the works of eternity visible.'

Nefer found a set square and a level made from metal which had fallen from the sky, and raised them up before the craftsmen.

Watched by Kenhir, the distribution of the tools began. Each man received them with emotion and respect.

Suddenly, Unesh threw his chisel to the ground. 'This tool's no good. Look at it – it's split all along its length!'

'So's mine,' said Didia in horror.

'We've been struck down by the evil eye!' exclaimed Pai. 'There's no point in beginning work on the tomb. It would be a terrible failure.'

Neither the Master nor the Scribe of the Tomb could refute the argument. Only the evil eye, indeed, could have damaged chisels like that.

'Let us call upon the Wise Woman,' decided Kenhir. 'She alone is capable of overcoming this evil spell.'

40

The priesteses of Hathor had assembled in front of the main temple; they wore red dresses with shoulder-straps. Some were singing a hymn to the goddess, others were playing drums decorated to look like the sun, while seven of them formed a circle inside which stood Ubekhet, the Wise Woman; she wore a close-fitting white ceremonial dress and had a lotus-flower fixed to her wig.

Then there was a long, profound silence, during which the priestesses went away and the most senior member of the Sisterhood appeared on the threshold of the temple.

'When the Light creates life,' she declaimed, 'it takes the form of the sun, whose eyes opened inside the lotus. When the water of the eye fell on to the earth, it was transformed into a sublimely beautiful woman, to whom was given the name Gold of the Gods. She, the female sun, lights the world; you, the Wise Woman, you are her daughter. But will you have the courage to risk your life to accomplish the work of a man, to become the Mistress of the craftsmen, venerated by the Brotherhood, capable of vanquishing the evil eye?'

'The Place of Truth gives me life,' replied Ubekhet. 'I will give my life for it.'

'You who are the living one of the city of the tomb, enter this shrine and confront your destiny.'

Ubekhet stepped forward without hesitation, and crossed the threshold.

On a granite plinth stood the statue of a baboon, the incarnation of Thoth; in its left hand, it held a case containing a papyrus scroll. Its red eyes stared at the young woman, who gazed back to take in the words of knowledge the god wished to pass on to her. The stone hand seemed to come to life to hand the case to Ubekhet, who took it and prostrated herself before the statue.

'Come to me,' said a calm female voice, 'and pass through my door.'

Beyond the baboon of Thoth was a second stone plinth. When Ubekhet's eyes had grown accustomed to the half-light, she could make out a small gold statue of a falcon crowned with a gold sun-disc; at the foot of the statue reared up a cobra, its hood raised like that of the symbolic cobra worn on the forehead of the pharaohs.

From its posture, Ubekhet knew it was about to attack, but she did not step back. Strengthened by her experience at the summit of the Peak of the West, she gazed steadily at the snake, ready to imitate its slightest undulation.

But the creature did not move.

Intrigued, she went closer. The cobra was a stone one, made with such genius that it seemed alive. Ubekhet touched it gently and with caution.

'Take the gold sun-disc,' said the voice, 'and place it on your breast. It will permit you to see into the darkness.'

Ubekhet armed herself with the precious symbol, from which a gentle heat was emanating. The dark chamber grew bright, and she saw seven knife-wielding figures wearing terrifying masks, to which the papyrus gave names: Facing the Wrong Way, He Who Burns, Slanderer, He Who Barks, Sharp-Face, Howler and Worm-Eater.

Together, they moved towards the Wise Woman, encircling her. She opposed them with the only weapons she possessed: the sun-disc and the papyrus. The seven demons retreated and disappeared, giving way to a ritualist wearing the mask of Anubis the jackal.

'Walk with me upon the divine water,' he invited her.

Ubekhet followed him and stepped forward on to a silver floor which evoked the stretch of water where the first forms of life had appeared.

'Anubis washed the Wise Woman's feet, then dressed her in the white robe of resurrection, so tight that she could scarcely move,' chanted the ritualist.

He led her to the threshold of a darkened shrine.

'In this place takes place the transfiguration of the spirit that goes out by day among the living. Dare you submit to the energy which would enable you to ward off the evil eye?'

'I accept the trial.'

'Beware: this energy could destroy you. The ancients knew how to capture it and preserve it inside temples, but few mortal bodies are able to receive it. And no one knows if you will bear it.'

'Permit me to confront it, since I shall draw from it the strength necessary to help the Brotherhood.'

'Enter this shrine, Wise Woman, and may the goddess decide.'

Walking with difficulty, Ubekhet approached a statue of Neith, whose seven words had created the world. The statue was the same height as herself, and its stone eyes seemed alive. Shining like stars, they stared at the intruder. She halted less than a pace from the statue, whose hands were stretched out to her, palms open to the sky.

Suddenly, Ubekhet saw two rays of light spring forth from the stone hands and flow directly towards her heart. Two wavy lines which made the young woman falter. This energy flowed into the channels which made up her being but it was so intense and so burning hot that she could not bear it for long.

It was for the goddess to end the trial, and the Wise Woman must not hide. For it was vital to be energized by this power if she was to overcome the evil eye.

Kenhir told Nefer everything. Sooner or later, the Wise Woman must anyway have confronted Neith to find out if her vital energy was of the same nature as the goddess's. Ordinarily, though, she would have prepared herself for this trial with long periods of meditation, and would not have encountered the statue at a time of crisis.

'Someone tried to enter the locked room,' said Kenhir, 'but he failed. It is indeed the evil eye that is responsible for the deterioration of the tools. If its action is not countered, you will not succeed in building the king's tomb.'

'Why did you not call upon a court magician?'

'No one has a better chance of succeeding than the Wise Woman. As mother of the Brotherhood, she will fight to her last ounce of strength to help it.'

'No one doubts that,' said Nefer anxiously, 'but she's my wife, the being who is most dear to me, and without warning me you have put her in great danger.'

'Yes, I have, but it was my duty to do so. When circumstances demand it, the Scribe of the Tomb forgets individuals and thinks of nothing but the Brotherhood. Our only goal is to create the pharaoh's house of eternity, and so long as the evil eye hinders the craftsmen's hands, the Place of Truth will be sterile, unable to create anything.'

In Nefer's eyes, the Scribe of the Tomb took on his true stature. He was not a simple manager of the village but also, like the two overseers, the guarantee of its essential promises.

'Although your decision has caused me anguish,' he said, 'I have done nothing to oppose it.'

'And you are right, Master. If you had interfered Ubekhet would have been furious, and you know it.'

Nefer looked at the temple where his wife was undergoing

an ordeal which few could withstand. Would he see her alive again, with her sweet smile, her tranquil glance and her boundless love?

'I'm as anxious as you are,' whispered Kenhir, 'and I think the law to which we have submitted ourselves is sometimes very harsh.'

Turquoise and Uabet the Pure came out of the shrine supporting Ubekhet, who had changed her white dress for a loose robe tied at the waist with a red belt. Her eyes half closed, she seemed unable to stand upright without help.

Nefer wanted to rush to her, but Kenhir held him back. 'Wait a little. She must absorb the light.'

The Wise Woman opened her eyes, as though reborn to a new reality. She looked up at the sun for a few moments and regained her poise. The two priestesses left her and she saw Nefer. He ran to her and took her in his arms.

'I thought I was going to die,' she told him, 'because the goddess's energy was so intense, but she saved me from the darkness.'

'Come and rest.'

'Later. First we must go to the room where the tools are kept.'

'But you're exhausted,' he protested.

'I must give back without delay that which has been given to me.'

Filled with hope, the craftsmen watched the Wise Woman pass, reassured by her serenity.

The tools had been laid out on the ground, in front of the door to the room. No one else had dared touch them, for fear of damaging them further by attracting the negative energy of the evil eye.

Ubekhet closed the door and burned incense in the room in order to purify it and expel any destructive forces, then she gave life back to the tools one by one, lingering on those which had faults, even small ones. The cracks closed up again, and the copper shone with a new brilliance.

'The evil eye is destroyed,' she declared, 'and it will no longer hinder the works of the Brotherhood.'

Acclaimed by the craftsmen, Ubekhet embraced her husband, who was overwhelmed with admiration and love, so mingled that he was not sure which feeling was the stronger.

41

'This is the culprit,' Kenhir told Nefer. He showed the Master a small copper rectangle, covered with verdigris which hid part of the inscription incised into the metal.

'I know these texts,' he continued, scratching them with a fingernail. 'They come from a book of evil magic and cause the disintegration of objects which a greedy man cannot obtain and chooses instead to destroy.'

'Where was this found?'

'It had been inserted into the back wall of the locked room; I found it when I examined the room in minute detail. Thanks to the Wise Woman's magic energy, this piece of metal became visible and therefore harmless.'

'It's hard to believe one of us is wicked enough to do such a thing. But what if he tries again?'

'He probably will,' agreed Kenhir, 'but he won't find it easy. The Wise Woman and the priestesses of Hathor are going to create a protective shield over all the buildings in the Place of Truth, and our man won't have the skill to break through it.'

'No, he won't. So the attack will have to come from outside.'

'Let's hope so, Nefer, but the reality may well be more cruel. You do realize, don't you, that building the royal tomb is going to be dangerous?'

'Do you think I'm not as brave as my wife?'

'The Scribe of the Tomb is concerned with the Master's safety, and he requires that measures be taken to ensure that safety.'

'Paneb will be there. Does that reassure you?'

'That's the least we need. I'd prefer more safeguards.'

'I must think about building, not about protecting myself.'

If the slightest suspicion had fallen upon him, Kenhir and Sobek would already have taken action. So the traitor was unworried; he'd continue to work at the heart of his crew, scrupulously obeying the Master's instructions and strengthening the bonds of friendship with his colleagues.

However, he had taken many risks in hiding the evil-eye charm in the locked room. He'd hoped to make the tools unserviceable, cause trouble among the craftsmen, and delay work on the royal sites. But in his haste he hadn't hidden the charm as well as he'd have liked, so his plan had failed. The Scribe of the Tomb and the Wise Woman had joined forces to ward off his attack, and he couldn't try something similar again for fear of being unmasked.

The creation of a house of eternity in the Valley of the Kings would not only weigh him down with work, but also delay the time when he would get his hands on the fortune awaiting him outside the village. Besides, if the tomb's construction was a success, Nefer the Silent's prestige would soar even higher.

At the start, the traitor had thought only of himself and his future wealth, hoping he'd not have to fight the Brotherhood. But the more embroiled he became, the more he realized that confrontation was inevitable; and to save his own skin he'd have to help the enemies of the Place of Truth.

The craftsmen of the starboard crew had kissed their wives and children, knotted wide bands of fabric round their waists and donned leather kilts. It was time to leave for the Valley of the Kings, via a mountain pass where the crew would sleep for nine nights before returning to the village.

They assembled before the tomb of a former Master, Sennedjem,* to gather their thoughts, then, guided by Nefer, they crossed the necropolis and took a narrow, rocky path which led to the summit of the Peak of the West. They had to walk along the edge of a sheer cliff, taking care to watch their step. For Kenhir, it was a painful ordeal, but he had a sturdy walking-stick and, although he never stopped complaining about the mountain, he kept up with the others.

On their left, to the west, the pyramid-shaped peak loomed over them in all its grandeur; on their right, to the east, stretched out a magnificent landscape, containing the tombs of the nobility, the temples of a million years and fields stretching as far as the Nile.

Nefer paused to drink in this beauty, which he hoped to make even more beautiful by adding Meneptah's temple. Paneb, too, was dazzled; he could never thank the gods enough for granting him such an exciting life, punctuated by marvels like this.

As Nefer moved off again along the path, Nakht the Powerful caught his arm, and said, 'Be careful, Master, or you'll fall. This section is particularly dangerous, and there have already been accidents. Let me go first.'

'Don't worry, I'll be careful.'

Nakht seemed disappointed but he returned to his place, and the procession continued on its way to the pass. A little settlement had been established there, consisting of seventy-eight huts, built from large blocks of limestone joined together with mortar, and fifty or so small shrines backing on to the cliff.

The Scribe of the Tomb led the crew to the shrine

* Tomb no. 1 at Deir el-Medina.

dedicated to Amon of the Good Encounter, and they prayed silently for success.

Paneb was astonished by this strange place scattered with stelae on which Servants of the Place of Truth were shown worshipping the gods. It seemed that the pass was meant not only for rest, but, and more importantly, for meditation and establishing contact with the invisible powers that reigned here.

'The wind is strong and the voice of Amon is growing louder,' Kenhir told him. 'If he did not allow us to encounter him, we could not find our way again. Let us settle in.'

Each hut, roofed with flat stones and branches, consisted of two little rooms. In the first there was a stone bench into which a U-shaped seat had been cut, sometimes inscribed with the name of its owner. In the second, which had no window, there was another stone bench on which the occupant laid his sleeping-mat.

The Scribe of the Tomb was entitled to the largest hut, which was also the most comfortable as it had an extra room which served as his office. It was in the east of the settlement, where it was well sheltered from the wind and sun.

'Would someone be kind enough to sweep my hut?' asked Kenhir.

'At your service,' replied Paneb.

Pai the Good Bread, Renupe the Jovial, Casa the Rope, Nakht the Powerful and Unesh the Jackal went into the huts, laying out the provisions they had brought for the first two days. The next morning, under escort, lay workers would bring them what they needed, and the same would happen each day until the work was done.

Karo the Impatient and Gau the Precise handed out jars of water, while Didia the Generous and Thuty the Learned laid out bread, onions, dried fish and figs on a large flat stone which served as a communal table. It was forbidden to cook food or light a fire in the settlement. Living conditions were much harsher here than in the village, and everyone missed the comfort of a house and the warmth of a hearth.

Fened the Nose, Userhat the Lion and Ipuy the Examiner entered the modest workshops to make statuettes of craftsmen at prayer, which would be placed in the shrines, and amulets in the form of tools, such as the level, the hoe or the square. These would be worn around the craftsmen's necks, to protect them from the evil spirits that roamed the mountain.

Only Ched the Saviour did not make himself useful. Sitting in the entrance to his hut, he was drawing an offertory table laden with food.

The Master approached.

'I know what you're thinking,' said Ched, 'but you're wrong. It is good that one of us is not busy with menial tasks so that his spirit may remain free.'

'Even if I agreed with you, it would be up to me to decide who that man should be.'

'Ah, but I am the most observant man in the crew, aren't I? As I draw, I keep watch.'

'Do you think we're in danger?' asked Nefer.

'This mountain isn't exactly hospitable to people. It's as well to be on one's guard.'

Paneb had finished cleaning the Scribe of the Tomb's hut and was now cleaning his own.

'We shall sleep really well here,' he said to the Master, 'but I shall spend my first night watching the sky. What a wonderful place! You can feel the presence of those who came before us. They meditated here before creating their masterpieces, they fed on the silence and the grandeur of the Peak of the West. I'd like to stay here for ever.'

'It's a world between worlds, Paneb. No one could live here permanently.'

'Dinner's ready!' shouted Pai.

The craftsmen ate their meal but, apart from Paneb, they

had little appetite. Each man well knew the gravity of the tasks awaiting him, for working in the Valley of the Kings was unlike working anywhere else. Humans did not belong there, and the craftsmen needed all the magic of their initiation in the Place of Truth to venture there and to excavate the rock without angering the powers of the world beyond. Moreover, each man knew that failure would ruin his career and endanger the very existence of the village.

'Why do you all look as if you're at a funeral?' asked Paneb indignantly. 'Anyone would think you were about to die a shameful death.'

'Yes, well, you don't know the ordeals we're facing,' retorted Gau.

'What ordeals? We're together, our hearts beat as one, and we're taking part in an adventure which will enable us to touch eternity. What more could we ask?'

'My pupil is a spirited fellow,' commented Ched, 'and he's right to try to dispel our fears.'

'And you, of course, are afraid of nothing,' sneered Casa.

'I might be more scared than anyone else, but what good would it do to show it?'

'I still don't understand you,' Paneb went on. 'You're anxious, frightened, nervous – how can you feel like that? The unknown is every bit as powerful as love, and we must involve ourselves in it with all our strength.'

'That's enough of this pointless talk,' said Kenhir. 'Go and rest, all of you. In four hours, we set off for the Valley of the Kings.'

42

The descent into the Valley of the Kings was as easy as the climb towards the pass had been difficult. The Master led, followed by Paneb, who was deliriously happy to be entering 'the great meadow which those who have done evil may not enter'. And that was one of the reasons why Nefer was worried: if it was a member of his crew who had tried to use the evil-eye charm, he was about to bring an evildoer into this sacred place. But he could not be certain, and he had no way of identifying the guilty man, so he must go forward, bearing this extra weight on his shoulders.

'The fierceness of the light makes fire spring forth from the stones. Am I the only one who can see it?' Paneb asked the Master.

'We all see it, to differing degrees, and we know it will destroy us if we're unworthy of the work we must do. May the Peak of the West protect us.'

'Don't tell me you're getting scared and gloomy too!'

'Don't worry, Paneb, I've got too much to do.'

'What is it you're so worried about? It isn't the work, is it?'

'No, it isn't – in fact, the thought of the work is exciting. But it's possible that a traitor is hiding among us, intending to ensure that we fail.'

'Do you really believe that?'

'I can't rule it out.'

Paneb thought for a moment. 'If it's true, and there really is a traitor here, he'll probably try something simple but very effective: attacking you. Without a captain, the crew would be lost. But this snake has forgotten that I'm here. So long as I am alive, nothing will happen to you.'

'I can't tell you how much I—'

'Don't try. Just live up to your nickname of "Silent".'

The entrance to the Valley of the Kings was a narrow passage hewn out of the rock and guarded by men appointed by Sobek, who had come to welcome the crew. The Nubian greeted the Scribe of the Tomb and the Master, then each of the craftsmen.

'Anything to report? asked Kenhir.

'Nothing,' said Sobek. 'All my men are on full alert, and anyone trying to get into the area would be spotted at once.'

'I need your two best men to guard the workshop and the site.'

'Penbu and Tusa. Their service records are excellent, and no one will take them by surprise.'

The two Nubians reported to the Scribe of the Tomb; they had honest eyes and radiated good health.

'Right, let's begin,' said the Master.

One by one, the craftsmen walked through the passage that separated the Great Meadow from the rest of the world. Here, the reign of the Light was absolute, and the ephemeral gave way to the eternal. The vertical cliffs produced an other-worldly silence nourished by the blue of the sky.

'Penbu,' said the Scribe of the Tomb, 'you're to guard the equipment store. Only the Master and myself have keys to it, and we shall distribute the tools. If even one goes missing, you'll be held responsible.'

Kenhir opened the door of the store and checked the picks, chisels, cakes of colour and lamp-wicks. Their numbers tallied exactly with the inventory he had drawn up during his last stay in the Valley. Suspiciously he re-counted them and checked that the picks and chisels were in good repair. With those the starboard crew had brought along, there were enough to begin the work.

The tools were given out in silence, and Kenhir noted on a wooden tablet what was given to each craftsman, who must hand everything back in the evening. No theft would be possible, and the damaged tools would be taken back to the village to be repaired.

'Tusa,' Kenhir said, 'you're to guard the site from the moment we leave until we get back. If, by some extraordinary means, someone manages to get through all Commander Sobek's barriers and safety measures, you're to kill the intruder on the spot, whoever he is. I stress that point: *whoever* he is.'

Next to the door of the equipment store, Userhat placed a stele on which had been engraved seven ears. They would enable the guards to hear even the smallest suspicious sound.

Guided by Nefer, the crew headed for the site of Meneptah's house of eternity, to the west of Ramses' tomb.

Fened the Nose and Ipuy the Examiner scrutinized the rock for a long time.

'It won't be easy,' said Ipuy at last. 'Can't we dig a little further along?'

'The decision is Pharaoh's and mine, and it's final,' said Nefer.

'Then of course we'll obey. But accuracy's going to be as important as strength. The rock's tricky here, and there'll be all sorts of pitfalls.'

Fened put a hand on an outcrop of stone. 'The first blow of the pick must fall here. Its resonance will alter the rock's resistance and make it easier to follow the fracture lines.'

The Scribe of the Tomb handed the Master the gold and silver pick that, since the creation of the Valley of the Kings, had been used to deliver the first, ritual blow. Nefer wielded it and drove in the point at the place indicated by Fened.

Then, with a silver chisel, he enlarged the hole.

The rock gave out a strange sound, like a song that was at once plaintive and full of hope.

Fened smiled; once again, his nose had led him to the right place.

Wielding a heavy pickaxe made of hard stone, Nakht the Powerful led the first real assault. His colleagues followed suit, but only Paneb made any real progress. Nettled, Nakht hit harder, but Paneb matched him stroke for stroke. The competition lasted for a long time, and it was Nakht who tired first.

'You two, rest now,' ordered Nefer. He told the others to use lightweight picks; they comprised a bronze core enclosed in copper, which cushioned the blows and stopped the metal fracturing.

Exciting days of work followed; the stone-cutters used heavy, wooden-handled scrapers and copper chisels to detach the rock in small shards. Little by little the white strata of limestone appeared, one on top of the other, run through with layers of darker flint, and the sight filled Nefer with joy: the rock was of good quality and would form an excellent foundation for sculpture and painting.

To the left of the tomb entrance, Kenhir had had carved out a recess bearing a trenchant inscription: 'Seat of the scribe Kenhir'. Sitting there in the shade, he could keep a close eye on the work's progress.

'Apart from Ched,' he told Nefer, 'everyone is working enthusiastically. The great entrance is taking shape, and you'll soon be able to begin excavating the downward-sloping passageway.'

'The work can't be hurried in any way,' said Nefer, 'or the rock might be damaged. It may take longer, but we'll avoid making serious mistakes. And Ched isn't idle: he's preparing the plans for the tomb's decoration and making a lot of sketches.'

'He's always been like that. What matters is that when he's face to face with the stone wall he works with absolute sureness of touch. But what a strange man he is.'

'He never fails to do his share of the work, does he?'

'Oh no, never. But he is a peculiar character, and I don't like the way he behaves.'

'Have you anything specific against him?'

Kenhir hesitated. 'No . . . not yet.'

'But you think he might be capable of harming the Brotherhood.'

'It's only a very vague feeling. Perhaps I shouldn't have mentioned it.'

'Yes, you should. You mustn't keep anything from me, even if it breaks my heart. Knowledge is always better than ignorance.'

'Very well,' said Kenhir. 'But you must prepare to be cruelly disillusioned. Men, even those of the Place of Truth, cannot measure up to the standard you expect.'

'So long as our work is completed, that doesn't matter.'

'Yes, but what if it isn't completed?'

'So you think I'm going to fail.'

'In all honesty, I don't know. But I've been having alarming dreams, and I'm afraid this project may end in tragedy, no matter how skilful you are. And the attack by the evil eye confirms my fears.'

'But the Wise Woman destroyed it, didn't she?' Nefer reminded him.

'I really do wish I could believe that.'

'Stay sceptical, suspicious and pessimistic, Kenhir. Then you'll be the best ally I could hope for.'

The Scribe of the Tomb murmured a few inaudible words and settled down on his stone seat. Thanks to his watchfulness, not one tool had disappeared and sharpening had been carried out without the slightest delay.

Despite his warnings, he had not given up hope, and the

reason for that was Nefer the Silent. No one could help admiring his dedication and patience, which were reinforced by the firm grip of a true leader.

The excavations advanced at the pace he had set, and he examined each inch of the rock as if his life depended upon it. The craftsman were sensitive to his calm manner and, knowing that he would not tolerate any sloppiness, they gave of their best. With one word or one gesture, Nefer resolved difficulties and prevented mistakes. The stone-cutters could see that their Master had such a feeling for this difficult rock that he could sense its breathing and knew how to make it submit to his plan without humiliating it.

Once ten cubits or so had been excavated, Paneb and Unesh began collecting the spoil. They put it in leather bags which they heaved on to their shoulders, or on to sleds mounted on wooden runners and hauled by cables, while Karo and Nakht wielded the pickaxes.

At one point, Nakht got so carried away that he almost lost his balance, and the point of his pickaxe brushed Karo's head.

Karo was furious and brandished his own pickaxe at Nakht. 'You could have killed me, you fool!'

Paneb dived at him and bore him to the ground before things could get out of hand, while Nefer flattened Nakht against the stone wall, shouting, 'Don't you dare raise your hand against your Master!'

Nakht calmed down, and Paneb let Karo get to his feet.

'Resolve your differences at once,' ordered Nefer. 'The incident is closed and nothing like this is to happen again.'

43

Serketa's transformation from blonde to redhead had been a complete success. Skimpily clad in a filmy linen veil, her opulent breasts more alluring than ever, she greeted her husband seductively when he returned home.

'How do you like me this evening?'

Mehy threw his accounting papyri across the room. 'You are a real woman,' he said, kneading her breasts.

'Did you have a good day, my sweet?'

'Excellent.'

'Power suits you so well,' she cooed.

He ripped off her veil and leapt on her like a rutting goat. That was how she liked him, brutal and insatiable. Life was nothing but violence, and you must always prove that you were the strongest. Thanks to their complicity, Mehy and Serketa were not afraid of anyone.

'We're no longer getting any useful information about the Place of Truth,' she lamented as they lay together afterwards.

'Well, we know the Brotherhood has started work on Meneptah's tomb.'

'Yes, but that doesn't take us any further, does it? We still haven't got our hands on any of their secrets.'

'Patience, my lioness. You know perfectly well my position means I mustn't make any false moves. I haven't given up hope of getting more information, but I've got to make the Scribe of the Tomb and the Master trust me completely.'

'You've had an idea, haven't you?'

'A very clever idea, as you'll soon see.'

With his son in his arms, and the little monkey perched on his shoulder, Paneb watched the priestesses of Hathor dancing.

The monkey had chosen its perch so that it could examine the baby closely and gently touch his head with a mischievous finger. Aapehti reacted with smiles and little cries of pleasure, and his new playmate continued, though without going too far and alarming the child's father.

Paneb was wearing the amulet Ched had given him. He felt it enabled him to see reality in greater depth and clarity, as if from several different angles at the same time. This new perception gave him a greater appreciation of the dance.

There were seven dancers, all wearing short kilts cut low at the front and wigs with long tresses, to which were attached porcelain globes evoking the sun. The dancers revealed 'the secret of the women of the interior' only to the members of the Brotherhood, and the dance was intended to create magic protection for the village and the craftsmen's work. The priestesses took their lead from Turquoise, whose easy grace was dazzling. She held a staff whose top took the form of a hand holding a mirror.

Turquoise spun round and faced the other dancers. One of them put her left foot forward and looked at herself in the mirror, then another came forward and covered it with both hands. Turquoise then angled the mirror up to the sky, so that it received the sun's rays and reflected them all around.

'Let us not look at ourselves,' she chanted. 'Instead, let us turn our mirror towards the sun. Thus shall we be protected from evil.'

After giving little Aapehti a long examination, Ubekhet handed him back to his father.

'He's in excellent health, Paneb.'

'You are absolutely sure?'

'He shows not the slightest sign of illness, and he's every bit as energetic as you are. There isn't another child like him in the village.'

'So much the better. As soon as he can stand up properly, I shall teach him the rudiments of fighting.'

Ubekhet had no time to express her opinion of this educational programme, for Unesh the Jackal entered her consulting-room, looking glum.

'I've got a pain in my upper back,' he explained. 'I must have pulled a muscle when I was using my pickaxe.'

The Wise Woman put her right hand on the painful spot. 'One of the bones in your spine is out of harmony with the rest,' she diagnosed. 'I shall put it right.'

She told Unesh to link his hands behind his neck. Then she slid her arms under his and levered upwards, at the same time pulling him towards her. There was a loud *crack*.

'I can feel heat all the way up my neck,' said Unesh.

'Good. That means all is now well."

'That was interesting,' said Paneb. 'Will you teach me how to do it?'

'To be frank, I was thinking of taking on an assistant, because your colleagues are too sturdy for me. The Wise Woman before me taught me the right methods, but I'm not strong enough to apply them all. So, yes, I'll teach you how to cure back-pain like that. But we'll need someone to practise on.'

Unesh sidled towards the door, but Paneb grabbed him by the shoulder. 'I'm sure you've got other pains and that you'd be delighted to volunteer.'

'No, I haven't. I feel absolutely fine.'

'We must all make sacrifices for the good of the community. Don't you trust me?'

'Er . . . how can I put it . . . ?'

'Thank you for helping,' said Ubekhet with a beautiful smile and such gratitude that he could not refuse.

The Wise Woman taught Paneb the right method of correcting bad posture and poor alignment of the bones in all three sections of the spine. She taught him how to manipulate the bones to cure lumbago or a stiff neck, and told him that each bone in the spine corresponded to an internal organ and could cause many problems, from an uneven heartbeat to indigestion.

Paneb proved to be an exceptionally gifted pupil. He quickly absorbed Ubekhet's teaching, and even succeeded in correcting the misalignment of Unesh's pelvis, which had been causing pain in his hips for a long time.

'By the gods,' exclaimed his first patient, 'you've made me feel twenty years younger! Your new skills will be tremendously useful on the construction site. Thank you, my friend. Now I'm going home to show my wife how you've helped me.'

After Unesh had left, as good as new, Ubekhet taught Paneb more secrets of the craft.

'It will take several sessions to perfect your skills,' she said. 'On your rest days, I'll supervise you while you treat patients, and eventually you'll be authorized to work alone.'

'I'm glad I can help you.'

'Your strength is a gift from heaven, Paneb, but don't impose yourself by force. If you do so, others will do the same to you.'

Ubekhet was about to close her office when Ched the Saviour emerged from the shadows.

'Can you grant me a few moments?' he asked.

'Of course.'

He slunk inside as though he didn't want to be seen.

'What's the trouble?' asked Ubekhet.

'Nothing serious. I've been having a little trouble with my eyes, and my eyelids are sore.'

After examining him, she gave him two small pots. 'This one contains an ointment made from crushed acacia leaves, sawdust, galenite and goose-grease. At night, apply a little to your eyelids and cover them with a bandage. In the other pot is a solution of aloe and a special substance made from copper. Using a hollow vulture feather, put three drops in each eye three times a day, and it will relieve the irritation. It won't work miracles, though. It can't, because you haven't told me everything, have you?'

Ched looked at Ubekhet as if he had never seen her before. 'Does the Wise Woman think I'm lying?'

'You know the answer better than I do.'

'I should like the lamps put out.'

Ubekhet did so, and darkness reigned.

'So it is with all life,' said Ched in a weary voice. 'Life is born of the Invisible, is nourished by the light and returns to the darkness where forms dissolve, whether they be the hardest granite or the softest emotion. My pupil Paneb does not know this yet. He thinks his strength will be inexhaustible and will allow him to win all his battles. He's wrong, but what good would it do him to see clearly? It is better that he destroys obstacles one after the other until the day when his will and his fists are useless. Then, and only then, he will understand that he is manipulated constantly, and that death is the most welcoming of mistresses. But he must first open up new paths, paint as no one has ever painted before, and believe that man can be a true creator. He must be helped, Ubekhet, and his demons must not be allowed to conquer him, for the Place of Truth is going to have great need of Paneb.'

'You're going blind, aren't you?'

'You have become our mother, and you must love each of your sons, even when one of them despairs. Unless you can give me hope . . .?'

Ubekhet said gently, 'I cannot lie to you: you have a

sickness which I know but which I cannot cure. It will develop slowly, and I may even be able to slow it down, but that's all I can do.'

'What god is cruel enough to inflict blindness on a painter? I probably haven't worshipped the Peak of the West enough, but it's too late to have regrets. The most important thing is that no one must know. My name is Ched the Saviour and I don't want anyone else doing the saving.'

'You should consult the eye-doctors at Thebes and Memphis.'

'What's the use? They wouldn't have your magic. I'll accept my fate, as long as it doesn't turn me into an invalid. But I won't let you treat me unless you do so in absolute secrecy. I say again, no one must know.'

'There is one person from whom I can hide nothing.'

'Your husband, our Master. He is the Silent one, and I trust him.'

'At this moment, I can't cure you, Ched,' said Ubekhet. 'But I'm not going to admit defeat just yet.'

44

Niut the Strong's roast chicken was mouth-wateringly delicious, and altogether her cooking was so good that it revitalized Kenhir. Since she had taken charge of his house, he had enough energy to keep the Journal of the Tomb, oversee the construction work in the Valley of the Kings and pursue his literary work. He had completed his version of *The Battle of Kadesh*, in which he emphasized Ramses' supernatural role, and now he was compiling a list of the kings who had had temples built on the west bank, and putting the finishing touches to a history of the rulers from Ahmose I to Horemheb. Through a mixture of poetry, learning and symbolism, he was trying to bring to life the many facets of the extraordinary civilization to which he was lucky enough to belong.

'You have a visitor,' announced Niut.

'Oh no, not now! Can't you see I'm writing?'

'Shall I send the Master away?'

'No, of course not,' said Kenhir testily. 'Show him in.'

Nefer, ordinarily so calm, looked angry. 'The donkey-train bringing us copper to make chisels has just arrived,' he said.

'Oh good! We weren't expecting it until tomorrow.'

'The donkeys are here, but the copper isn't.'

'That's impossible!'

'Come and see for yourself.'

Kenhir abandoned his work and went with Nefer to the main gate. They found the head donkey-driver sitting on a travelling-mat and arguing with Obed the blacksmith.

'What have you done with the copper?' demanded Kenhir.

'The donkey-train was searched by the guards at Gebtu, and they said the load didn't comply with regulations. My orders were to come here, so I have. I don't want any trouble – just sign the delivery order, and I'll go back to Thebes.'

'What do you mean, "didn't comply with regulations"?'

'That's all they said, and that's all I know. Look, are you going to sign or not?'

Kenhir did so, and the caravan of donkeys left for the ferry.

'And what am I supposed to do?' asked the blacksmith, hands on hips. 'Without raw materials, all I can do is kick my heels.'

'There are picks and old chisels to sharpen,' replied Nefer. 'The stone-cutters will give them to you. Come, Kenhir.' As he and Kenhir walked away, he went on, 'If the copper we ordered doesn't arrive within the next two months, I shan't have enough tools. I'll have to suspend work on the site.'

'Things like this have happened before,' said Kenhir, 'but it couldn't have happened at a worse time. I can only see one solution: we must tell Mehy.'

The offices of the government of the west bank were a veritable anthill. Scribes ran in carrying urgent messages, others ran out to pass on orders, and still others were dealing with discontented taxpayers, peasants challenging rulings by the land registry, and people delivering provisions which had to be inspected.

A guard armed with a baton stopped Kenhir. 'Who are you?'

'The Scribe of the Tomb. I wish to see the governor immediately.'

There was no shortage of enterprising people demanding

to see Mehy, and as a rule the guard directed them to a scribe, who kept them waiting for a suitable time before seeing them. But the Scribe of the Tomb merited special treatment.

'Please follow me,' said the guard.

He led Kenhir to the main building, where the governor received important guests, and told the governor's secretary that the Scribe of the Tomb had arrived. The secretary at once told Mehy, who came out to meet his visitor.

'My dear Kenhir, what a pleasure to see you. Is there something I can do for you?'

'There may well be.'

'Do please come in.'

Furniture made from precious woods, oil-lamps wherever they'd be most convenient, cupboards and shelves for papyri and wooden tablets, jars of water and beer: Mehy's office was luxurious and comfortable.

'Do sit down.'

'I'm in a hurry and I must come straight to the point,' said Kenhir.

'Is it something serious?'

'The delivery of copper for the Place of Truth was blocked at Gebtu.'

'Why?' inquired Mehy in astonishment.

'The donkey-driver was told it didn't comply with the regulations.'

'Can you give me more details?'

'Unfortunately not. But the Brotherhood needs that copper urgently, to make tools and continue their work.'

'I understand, I understand. I should have been told about this.'

'You didn't know about it?'

'If I had, I can assure you I'd have dealt with it at once. I fear one of my subordinates may have blundered. Would you mind waiting for a few minutes while I go and find out exactly what happened?'

From Mehy's furious expression, the Scribe of the Tomb deduced that he did not like being caught out like this.

Shadows were creeping across the courtyard when Mehy stormed back into his office, a papyrus in his hand.

'A letter was indeed sent to inform me of a dispute over your copper, but the scribe responsible for dealing with Gebtu had classified it as non-urgent. Needless to say, the fool no longer works in my department. He will go and re-learn his trade in a little provincial office, and I shall ensure that he is barred from promotion for several years. I offer you my most sincere apologies, Kenhir. I consider myself responsible for mistakes made by any of my staff.'

'Do you know what the problem was with the consignment?'

'A stupid administrative error. The director of the mine didn't fill out the transport document properly, and the Gebtu guards suspect fraud. They've opened an inquiry, but it could take several months.'

'Several months! It would be a disaster if we had to wait that long. Is there anything you can do?'

'I shall draw up a strongly worded complaint and order Gebtu to send the copper to Thebes immediately.'

'Do you think that will work?'

Mehy looked none too pleased. 'Perhaps, but I can't be sure; and I'm afraid it won't stop the inquiry.'

'Can you get us a new consignment?'

'I'm afraid not. You were allocated that consignment and no other. The quotas are fixed rather rigidly, and I have no power to alter them.'

'Yes, but we're dealing with the Place of Truth here,' Kenhir reminded him. 'Surely an exception could be made?'

'If it was solely down to me, it would already have been done. But the decision depends on an adminstrative system whose complexity you know very well.'

'So I shall have to take bad news back to the Master,' said Kenhir reprovingly.

'There is one possible solution,' ventured Mehy.

'What is it?'

'I'll go to Gebtu myself, see the authorities there and put our case. There's no guarantee that I'll succeed, but you can count on me to be as persuasive as possible.'

He rolled up the papyrus on which the reason for the dispute was set out and marched towards the door of his office.

'I'll leave at once,' he said, 'and I hope not to return empty-handed.'

'Whatever happens, Mehy, the Brotherhood will be grateful to you.'

'Not at all – it's my duty to protect and support it. Forgive me for cutting short our conversation, but there's not a moment to lose.'

Mehy hurried down to the courtyard, hailed his chariot-driver and set off. He was delighted with the success of his plan, every detail of which he had honed. He'd have no difficulty in resolving a problem he himself had created, and the craftsmen would hail him as their saviour.

He was sure Kenhir suspected nothing. Mehy had played his part so cleverly that the Scribe of the Tomb had swallowed the bait. He'd tell the Master that Mehy would go to any lengths to defend the Place of Truth, even leaving his office and dropping everything to fly to its aid.

And when Mehy came back to Thebes at the head of the convoy bringing the vital copper, he'd be regarded as a hero.

45

The Master had decided to continue the excavation of Meneptah's tomb with what tools he had. He had explained the situation to the crew. Gau, Fened and a few others came close to despair and would have given up had it not been for Paneb, who convinced them Nefer would sort out the mess. So the pace of work had not slowed down.

Seven weeks later, the atmosphere had grown much gloomier. As they descended from the pass to the village for two rest days, the crew were wondering if they would be back in the Valley of the Kings that soon.

'We can't help doing inferior work with worn-out tools,' complained Karo.

'Don't worry, the Master won't let us,' said Nakht. 'If need be, he'll suspend the work.'

'I don't like the idea of that,' said Fened. 'When we start again we'll have lost our rhythm. An incident like this is a bad sign: there's bad magic in the air.'

'Perhaps,' suggested Gau, 'there's a serious reason why the copper hasn't arrived. No more metal, no more tools, no more work . . . What if it's because the authorities have decided to close the village?'

'Have a little faith,' advised Paneb. 'Everything will work out.'

'How can you be so sure?' asked Pai.

'Because it can't be otherwise. Pharaoh came to the village, and he supports us.'

'You're being naive,' objected Casa. 'If there's trouble at court, Meneptah will be fully occupied with keeping his throne and he'll forget all about us.'

'Ah, but you're forgetting that Pharaoh can't live without a house of eternity.'

The discussion continued all the way back.

As they neared the village, Paneb saw something.

'Look!' he exclaimed. 'Donkeys!'

'Don't get your hopes up,' said Didia. 'It's only a food delivery.'

'In the late afternoon? It'd be the first time ever!'

Paneb slithered down the slope at top speed and almost crashed into Obed the blacksmith, who was carrying a heavy wooden box.

'Is that copper?' asked Paneb breathlessly.

'It certainly is – enough to make hundreds of chisels. I'm getting straight to work.'

Mehy waited modestly behind the last donkey, which was being unloaded by Obed's assistants. The Scribe of the Tomb and the Master came towards him.

'Thank you for your invaluable help, Governor,' said Kenhir. 'The copper has arrived in the nick of time.'

'I have a pleasant surprise for you: there's much more of it than I thought. I told them you had vast projects planned and that the Place of Truth must never lack for tools. The authorities at Gebtu tried to turn a deaf ear, but I threatened to go right to the top, to Pi-Ramses, and deliver a detailed report on the case. They realized I wasn't joking, and all of a sudden they become thoroughly cooperative. I took advantage of that to demand compensation for the delay, and this is the result. It's good of you to thank me, but there is no need: I've only done my duty.'

'Nevertheless,' said Kenhir, 'I shall write to the tjaty to tell him of all the trouble you've taken on our behalf, and he'll tell Pharaoh. You have made a very significant contribution to the creation of the royal tomb.'

'That will be one of my finest claims to fame,' said Mehy, 'and no doubt I'll be weak enough to boast of it. Would you like to check the delivery note?'

Kenhir the Ungracious actually smiled. 'That would probably be advisable,' he said.

While Kenhir was doing so, the Master walked away; he had said not one single word.

Narrow-eyed, Mehy watched him go. His silence was a bad sign: the Master seemed even more suspicious than the Scribe of the Tomb, and it was impossible to tell what he was thinking. Convincing him that Mehy was a loyal ally was going to take all Mehy's efforts.

'Uputy has brought a message marked with the king's seal,' said Niut.

What?' demanded Kenhir. 'Why didn't you tell me before?'

'Because you've only just arrived,' she said coolly.

Grumbling, he broke the seal. What he read stunned him.

'I'm going to see Nefer,' he announced.

'But dinner's ready,' complained Niut.

'Keep it warm until I get back.'

She muttered something under her breath, but Kenhir ignored her. Despite his tiredness, he hurried along, swinging his stick.

When he entered Nefer's house, the Master was coming out of the bathroom. As for Ubekhet, she was worn out after a long series of consultations, and had stretched out on the bed in the front room.

'I'm sorry to disturb you, but it's an emergency: a message from the king.'

'Sit down,' said Nefer, 'while I pour you a drink.'

'Yes, thank you, my throat's dry. But this order is . . .

Meneptah demands that we begin the construction of his Temple of a Million Years immediately, no matter how far we have got with his tomb, but,' said Kenhir, tapping the table for emphasis, 'neither he nor the queen can leave the capital to bless the start of the work.'

'But how can we possibly begin work on the temple if they aren't present?' asked the Wise Woman.

'Since he is invested with a religious office, the Master can represent Pharaoh. And the Wise Woman, leader of the priestesses of Hathor, will act in the name of the queen.'

'Are you sure you've understood the letter right?' asked Nefer anxiously.

'Yes. The text is quite unambiguous.'

'Have we a text of the necessary rites?'

'Yes, it's our oldest document. From the king's haste, it seems that he needs the daily energy the temple will produce as soon as it is inaugurated. He must be engaged in a fierce fight to preserve Ramses' heritage.'

'We must tell Hay immediately,' declared Nefer, 'and make the necessary arrangements.'

Uabet had gone to the temple of Hathor, so Paneb cradled his son in his arms and soothed him until his ear-splitting howls quietened: Aapehti was teething. The wet-nurse had never seen such rapid growth or such a passionate nature, which only his father could control.

Uabet came hurrying into the house. 'Something strange is happening,' she said. 'The Wise Woman has summoned us all to the temple again this evening, and your colleagues are all standing around in groups, talking.'

'As soon as I've settled Aapehti, I'll go and find out what it's about.'

Even though she had to share her husband with Turquoise, Uabet was happy. Turquoise offered him intoxication of the senses, whose secret she alone knew, and Uabet had given up trying to fight her on that ground. But it was here, in his home, that he found peace, and she knew that, whatever his shortcomings, he would always come back.

Few women would have accepted such an arrangement, but Uabet loved him and the child he'd given her. She doubted that Paneb, even when he was older, would be any less impetuous and more level-headed; it fell to her, with her quiet, steady love, to prevent him from being consumed by the fire within him.

'You have a strange look in your eyes,' he remarked.

'I was looking at you, you and your son.'

'You gave birth to a fine boy, but he doesn't go to sleep easily!'

'Can it be that you've found someone stronger than yourself?'

'We shall find out when he's older. Ah, success at last.'

The baby had dozed off. Gently, Paneb laid him in his mother's arms, then left the house.

Before he'd gone far, Pai stopped him. 'I've just woken up from my midday nap. Is there trouble brewing?'

'I don't know anything about it.'

'After all that business about the copper, I was hoping we'd have some peace at last,' said Pai gloomily. 'Come on, let's go and see the Master.'

When they got to Nefer's house, they found most of the starboard crew gathered outside.

As so often, Nakht was complaining. 'It seems we've got to excavate several tombs for nobles. When will we have our rest days? The royal tomb was more than enough. Why can't we make more use of the port crew?'

'Who told you that?' asked Casa.

Nakht considered. 'Er . . . I'm not sure now. But that's what I heard.'

'Well, I heard something different,' said Unesh. 'Apparently, the king is going to summon some of us to the capital to build a new Temple of Amon.'

'That's out of the question,' declared Userhat. 'I was born in Thebes and I'll die here.'

'Same here,' said Didia. 'No one's going to make me leave the village.'

'Why don't we wait and see what the Master says?' suggested Paneb.

The craftsmen looked at him in surprise.

'No one knows where he is,' said Renupe. 'And that proves something's wrong.'

'He might be with Hay,' said Karo. 'They have to put their heads together before they tell us bad news.'

'Then let's go to Hay's house,' said Paneb.

The little band did not have to go far, for Nefer came to meet them.

'We want to know exactly what's happening,' said Casa. 'Is the work in the Valley of the Kings going to be stopped? Are we to be sent somewhere else?'

'The sages advise us not to listen to rumours,' said Nefer with a smile.

'Then tell us the truth.'

'Pharaoh has ordered us to begin the work immediately on his Temple of a Million Years. The two crews will be brought together on the site in order to inaugurate it. After that, we shall return to our work on the tomb.'

'Why all this haste?' asked Thuty worriedly. 'Does it mean there's trouble at court?'

'Like every pharaoh, Meneptah needs the energy the temple will give him, and it's up to us to bring the temple to life.'

'When will the king be coming to Thebes?' asked Thuty.

'The Wise Woman and I have been instructed to represent the royal couple.'

46

The traitor knew one thing for certain: when a site as important as that of a temple of a million years was inaugurated, the Stone of Light had to be used. The Master would have to remove it from its hiding-place, and this was an unhoped-for opportunity to discover where it was kept.

He had a plan, and a good one, though realizing it would be difficult. The Stone would necessarily be moved at night, probably shortly before the sun came up and the craftsmen awoke. He must leave his house without waking his wife and, above all, without being spotted by Nefer the Silent.

To resolve the first problem, the traitor first thought of pouring a sleeping-draught into the hot milk his wife drank at dinner, but he did not know the exact dosage and was afraid of getting it wrong. All things considered, he had decided to tell her a little of his plan.

'Do you trust me?' he asked.

'Why on earth do you ask?' she replied, astonished.

'Because I've decided to get rich.'

'Well, I've certainly no objection. But how?'

'Not like the others, who are content with very little. I can't tell you any more, and you must not ask. But I promise you that we aren't going to end our days in this village, where my worth goes unrecognized. I've tried being patient and it got me nowhere, so now I'm trying something different.'

'Isn't that risky?'

'You know how careful I am. One day, we shall live in a beautiful house, and we'll have servants, lands and flocks. You won't have to do the cooking or the cleaning any more.'

'I thought you weren't interested in riches, and that the only thing you really cared about was your craft.'

'It's vital that the whole village goes on thinking that.'

She thought for a long time. The traitor stared at her. If she showed the slightest opposition, she'd become an immediate and unacceptable danger.

'I'd never have imagined you behaving like this, but I understand,' she said. 'More than that, I approve. I want to be rich, too.'

The traitor hid a smile of relief. His wife was neither beautiful nor intelligent, but she had become his accomplice and, like him, was yielding to something he'd resisted for too long: the lure of gain. He'd speak to her only of future plans and of possessions he'd already acquired. He'd never mention his partners in crime – the less she knew about them, the better. Still, at least he could now be sure she'd keep her mouth shut, and he'd have room to manoeuvre.

As luck would have it, the night was very dark. Hidden behind an enormous water-jar, the traitor fixed his gaze on the door to the Master's house. If his reasoning was correct, Nefer would go himself to fetch the Stone of Light and carry it to the main entrance of the village before waking the craftsmen.

If he had been less watchful, the traitor would have missed the furtive exit of his crew-master, who had taken care not to make a sound. Keeping close to the fronts of the houses, the Master headed for the meeting-place. He turned round twice, and his follower was almost caught unawares. But Nefer continued on his way.

The Brotherhood's meeting-place . . . The traitor had

thought of it many times, for, when the craftsmen met, the Stone had to be placed in the innermost shrine; from time to time, the light could be seen radiating out of it. But he had discounted that hiding-place as too predictable. He'd been mistaken.

Using a wooden key, Nefer opened the door to the meeting-place and went inside. When he emerged, after several long minutes, he was carrying something heavy hidden under a cloth.

The traitor felt profound satisfaction. Now he knew. A mad idea flashed through his mind: what if he killed the Master, stole the Stone and fled with this priceless treasure? But unfortunately he had no weapon or tool. Besides, dawn was beginning to glimmer in the east and the darkness would soon be gone. If he didn't manage to knock Nefer out with a single punch and strangle him, the Master would defend himself and call for help. No, it was too risky.

The traitor followed the Master, to find out what he would do with the Stone. Perhaps he would hide it in another, more accessible, place before summoning the craftsmen. But the Master walked quickly towards the main gate.

There the Scribe of the Tomb and the Wise Woman were waiting. At their feet was a cube-shaped object, wrapped in an ochre-coloured cloth which allowed a strange light to filter through.

The Stone . . . Kenhir must have brought it!

The Master unveiled his burden. It was a wooden chest, from which he took several metal plates which he examined before putting them back.

The traitor had missed his chance this time, but there'd be other opportunities.

'Were you followed?' Kenhir asked Nefer.

'I don't think so, but I'm not sure.'

'I am still sure that whoever cast the evil eye on the tools will try to discover the hiding-place of the Stone of Light.'

'But even if he did, what good would it do him? He couldn't steal it and run away.'

'He'll try,' said Kenhir, 'and we must double our safeguards. If he did follow you, he'll have seen that he followed the wrong person. He may realize that we tricked him because we've become suspicious.'

'Surely,' said Nefer, 'that's one more reason for him not to do anything which would enable us to identify him. I agree that a "shadow-eater", a criminal, has gone to earth in the village, but I think all he can do now is lie low and hope he doesn't get caught.'

'You're much too optimistic,' said Kenhir.

'Don't forget the Wise Woman's power. She'll be able to protect us from all attacks, whether they come from within the village or from outside.'

A series of loud bangs destroyed the tranquillity of the dawn. Paneb was running through the village, hammering on every door to wake those who were still asleep.

'We're leaving at once,' he shouted. 'I'll drag any latecomers out of bed myself.'

After gulping down an enormous breakfast of hot pancakes, fresh milk, cheese and preserved duck, Paneb had kissed his wife and his son. He was in an excellent mood, and promised himself that he would give energy to those who lacked it.

As he was beginning his rounds, he glimpsed someone running away at top speed, as if to escape from him. An unfaithful husband in a hurry to get home, or the curse-layer who was roaming the village spreading his evil?

The previous evening the Wise Woman and the Master had at last managed to make Paneb face the sad reality that there was a traitor in the village, determined to do it harm. He'd been shocked and deeply distressed. Even at the heart of an elite brotherhood like that of the Place of Truth, men would never be anything but men, and some would even forget their sacred duties. But this realization had in no way reduced Paneb's enthusiasm, for no traitor, however skilful, would succeed in preventing the Great Work from being accomplished, so long as the Stone of Light still shone.

And the Stone was right here, in front of him.

'If anyone's still asleep, I promise never to drink another drop of wine!' he said.

'You should be more cautious,' advised the Wise Woman. 'What if I've given one of my patients a sleeping-draught?'

'In that case my promise would be void, because I didn't know the facts.'

'Your legal analysis leaves something to be desired,' commented Kenhir.

'I think I saw him,' said the young man, suddenly serious.

'Who? Do you mean the traitor?' demanded Nefer.

'Yes, I think it was him.'

The Master's throat tightened. 'Did you see who it was?'

'No, all I saw was a vague shape. And yet, the more I think, the more convinced I am that it was him.'

Ubekhet tried to read Paneb's thoughts to find anything he had forgotten, but there was no trace of anything unspoken.

'So he did indeed follow the Master,' said Kenhir.

'That's extremely dangerous!' protested Paneb. 'Why didn't you call on me to guard him?'

'Because I had decided to act as a decoy,' explained the scribe.

'That's insane! If you do things like that, Nefer, how on earth can I protect you?'

'I'm in no danger,' said Nefer. 'All that miserable creature wants to do is steal our treasures, and perhaps hamper our work.'

'Still the optimist,' said Kenhir disapprovingly.

The craftsmen assembled and the procession set off, the Master at its head.

The day promised to be hot. Paneb, who was laden with a dozen large water-skins, wished they'd walk a bit faster, but the gentle pace favoured Pai and Renupe, who were growing fatter by the day.

'I didn't get much sleep last night,' complained Renupe.

'Why not? Were you celebrating?' asked Paneb.

'My wife and I ate and drank a little . . . This morning, I have a terrible headache. It's because of all this work awaiting us. It's all right for you, with your strength.'

'A bit of exercise will put you right.'

'It seems we're going to use the Stone of Light,' ventured Renupe.

'Yes, it does.'

'Haven't you ever wondered where it's kept?'

'No,' said Paneb shortly.

'So you aren't curious.'

'Are you?'

'No, not really. It's nobody's business but the Master's.'

47

Daktair had been humiliated by Mehy, but he did not bear a grudge, for he knew Mehy had good reason to be angry with him. He, a man of learning, a man with an ever-vigilant, critical mind, had been deceived by two craftsmen from the Place of Truth!

Wounded in his pride, Daktair hated the village even more, and was determined to fight it with every means available, even the most vile, until he achieved its complete destruction.

In the meantime, he still needed to learn its secrets. So far, despite his persistence and his many official contacts, he had come up against an impenetrable wall of silence.

Perhaps galenite and bitumen gave him a place to start? He was convinced they were used for more far important things than cosmetics or caulking boats. He wasn't worried about their use in rituals, because those were just outdated customs which would eventually die out.

According to the regulations, Daktair should have given the temples the entire consignment from the desert mine, for he had been only its transporter and temporary guardian; but by falsifying his report and altering the quantities so slightly as not to attract attention, he had managed to keep back a few nuggets of galenite on which he had carried out numerous tests. The results were disappointing but he had kept trying new tests and, in the end, had made an extraordinary discovery which he knew he must tell Mehy about immediately. He had not taken notes. There must be no written record of his discovery, and only he and Mehy must know of it.

He hurried to Mehy's office, only to be told by Mehy's secretary that the general was out.

'When will he be back?'

'This evening, when he's finished inspecting the main army barracks at Thebes.'

'Can I wait for him here?'

'As you wish.'

Dusk was falling when the general's chariot halted in the courtyard.

Daktair ran to meet him. 'I must speak to you. It's urgent.'

'I have letters to dictate. Come back tomorrow.'

'It can't wait. When you know what it's about, you'll agree.'

Intrigued, the general took Daktair up to his office and closed the door himself. 'Now, what's this about?'

'This morning there was a fire in my workshop. The damage is serious, but no one was hurt.'

'What caused it?'

'I did.'

'What do you mean?'

'I've discovered the secret of bitumen. It's flammable and it gives off both heat and light.'

'Is it a clean light or does it leave soot behind?'

'It does leave some soot, but—'

'Can you imagine the craftsmen letting paintings in tombs and temples be damaged by this bitumen?'

'Of course not, but they've certainly found a use for it.'

Mehy thought of the Stone of Light, but galenite could be only one of its ingredients.

'The stone-oil will be very useful to us,' Daktair went on. 'It will enable us to burn down any building, including forts, and create terror among enemy troops.'

'Give up this idea.'

Daktair froze. 'I can assure you that—'

'Pharaoh has just ordered the closure of the mines at Gebel Zeit. The site will be permanently guarded, and no one will be allowed near it without authorization from the palace.'

'I'll wager the Place of Truth is behind his decision.'

'Very likely. The craftsmen must have realized that you would keep trying to find out its uses, so the Scribe of the Tomb alerted the tjaty and access to this dangerous oil is now impossible.'

'You must do something,' cried Daktair. 'You must ask the king to change his decree.'

'I shall do nothing so stupid. It is not yet time to confront Meneptah; we'd simply be accused of fomenting a rebellion.'

'But with the oil, General, we'll have the benefit of a terrifying new weapon.'

'Yes, but to get it,' said Mehy with exaggerated patience, 'we must conquer the king. Then we'll be able to use all the country's natural resources however we like.'

Daktair looked sullen. 'All the same, I've discovered one of the secrets of the Place of Truth.'

'You've done no more than scratch the surface. The Master may need a little bitumen to make the Stone of Light, but it's probably just one ingredient among many. Have you told anyone about your discovery?'

Daktair looked even more sullen. 'Only you, and I didn't even make any notes.'

'Good, very good. Your intelligence will take you far. Now to another matter. I shall officially order you to work on improving the weaponry of the Theban forces. I want better swords, better spears, better arrowheads. You'll have all the copper you need, and even some iron. Keep your work secret, and as soon as you have some interesting results let me know.'

*

Together with the Master and the Wise Woman, Thuty watched the sky night after night. They had plotted the positions of Mercury, which was under the protection of Set; Venus, linked to the rebirth of the phoenix; Mars, the red Horus; Jupiter, whose task was to illuminate the Two Lands and to open the gate of mysteries; and Saturn, the bull of the heavens. Thuty had consulted the books of astronomy and astrology in which the unchanging stars were studied, and also those which appeared and disappeared on the horizon, forming a zodiacal band divided into thirty-six decans. Every ten days a new decan rose; after passing through the heavenly workshop of resurrection, it became visible again.

'The time is favourable,' declared Thuty.

The sighting having been correctly carried out, the earthly location of Meneptah's temple would correspond perfectly to the harmony of the sky, which the finished building would reflect in all its parts.

The Master had placed the Stone of Light, still covered, on the spot where the innermost shrine would stand. Then he handed Hay the plan drawn up on a roll of leather which would be hidden in a crypt at the end of the building work.

Nefer checked that the angles were square. On the ground he drew a right-angle using a cord divided by knots into twelve equal parts and then formed a triangle whose sides were in the proportion 3–4–5, symbolizing the triad of Osiris the Father, Isis the Mother and Horus the Child.

With a hoe, the Master dug the foundation trench that put the temple in contact with the *Nun*, the ocean of primordial energy; then he moulded the mother brick from which the large stones would be born.

Paneb watched the rites from far away. He no longer felt at peace, for danger was prowling around the two crews who had gathered together on this site. Since he had been wearing Ched's amulet, he felt as though he could see in the darkness like a watchful cat.

And yet the ceremony passed off without incident and in a profound peace which entered the souls of the craftsmen, who were conscious of taking part in an event of eternal significance, defying the destructive power of time.

Carrying mallets, Nefer and Ubekhet stood before two stakes stuck at either end of the foundation trench. Between them a cord had been stretched, giving the measurements of the temple. Playing the parts of Pharaoh and the Great Royal Wife, they struck the heads of the stakes hard, to drive them further into the ground.

At that very moment, the flame of the divine eye, hidden in the Stone of Light, began to create the temple.

'How beautiful this dwelling is,' chanted Nefer. 'Its like does not exist; all its forms are accomplished in straightness; its plan was conceived in joy. Celebration reigned at its birth, and it will be completed in lightness of heart. May its life be as long as the life of the sky.'

'May the Great Work shine out brilliantly over the whole land,' prayed Ubekhet. 'May its light give it happiness and may this temple be in a state of perpetual growth, expressing the life of the universe.'

In the foundations, the Master laid the plates of precious metal and scale models of tools, including a set square, a level and the cubit on which the interplay of proportions in Meneptah's temple had been engraved. A flagstone covered up this treasure, which would be hidden from sight for ever.

Nefer purified the site with incense, opened the temple's mouth with a sceptre, touched its key points and, using the ancient form of words, 'gave back the dwelling to its master', the creative principle that had agreed to be embodied in this place.

Paneb stared around, convinced someone was watching them, but could see nothing suspicious. The ceremony ended and, very reverently, the two crews of the Place of Truth set off back along the path to the village.

Paneb turned and looked back. No one was following them.

Daktair was disappointed.

He'd used a device which he'd secretly imported from Phoenicia and which enabled him to see more clearly over long distances, but it had shown him nothing of interest. He'd chosen an ideal position to observe the different phases of the ritual, but it had been nothing but a series of ancient ancestral customs.

No one had touched the Stone of Light, which was kept covered all the time. At the end of the inauguration, the Master had picked it up again, replacing it with the first stone of the innermost shrine, the vital centre of the structure; it would be built first so that the morning rites could be celebrated there as soon as possible.

Daktair thought, 'Ritual, nothing but outdated ritual. The real secrets lie hidden inside the village.'

48

An event as important as the inauguration of the site of Pharaoh's Temple of a Million Years was naturally accompanied by a great celebration, which was added to the ritual rejoicing in honour of the gods decreed by the calendar. At the Master's request, the Scribe of the Tomb had therefore granted the two crews a week's holiday, during which the villagers would enjoy gifts of meat, vegetables, pastries and wine sent by the tjaty, who was pleased with their work.

The traitor could not take advantage of the holiday to disappear, for this was a family celebration which no villager would wish to miss. The houses were bedecked with flowers, food was cooked, tables were set up in the open air, jars were filled with fresh wine, and offerings were laid on the altars of the ancestors, linking them to the festivities. The laughter of men, women and children was the best possible proof that the work was progressing well.

Even Ebony had concluded a truce with the cats: stuffed full of beef and fresh vegetables, he had no desire to chase them. As for the monkey, he continued to delight the children. They also enjoyed their lessons with Paneb, who was teaching them the rudiments of combat, both unarmed and with small sticks.

'Why don't you fight someone your own size?' jeered Nakht.

'Like you, for instance?' said Paneb.

'A festival without a fighting-competition isn't a proper festival. Everyone knows we're the strongest, you and I, so shall we go straight to the final, this evening, by the forge?'

'I'm not interested.'

'Well, I'll be there. But you're probably right to say no. Have you at last realized you aren't up to it? Fear is a good counsellor and cowardice sometimes the only answer.'

Paneb seethed: if he hadn't been surrounded by children, Nakht wouldn't have insulted him much longer.

'Just watch out,' advised Nakht. 'One of these children might hurt you. I wouldn't want to beat someone who was already wounded.'

Turquoise stroked Paneb's hair; he had made love to her as passionately as though it was their first time.

'What ardour! Will you ever lose your appetite?'

'Will you ever stop being so beautiful?'

'Of course. The years will take their toll.'

Paneb gazed at her as she lay naked on the scented bed, more desirable than ever.

'You're wrong,' he said. 'In you there is a beauty which time can never erode.'

'You're the one who's wrong. The only person time can't touch is the Wise Woman.'

'My instincts never lie, and they tell me that our desires will always be just as intense as they are now.'

Amused, Turquoise pretended to believe him. He was intemperate and demanding, but generous – he gave as much pleasure as he took – and so in love with life that it felt good to burn in his fire. She stroked his hair.

'I'm going to fight Nakht,' he said, 'and teach him a good lesson. After that, he'll finally leave me in peace.'

Turquoise stopped caressing him. 'You mustn't fight.'

'Why not?'

'It frightens me.'

'You're like me, Turquoise, you aren't afraid of anything.'

'Do as I ask – please.'

'If I don't face up to Nakht, the crew will think I'm a coward and I'll have no place here. Don't worry, Nakht has no chance of beating me.'

The festival reached its height in the warm night air. From his seat made of plaited reeds bound together with straps, Aapehti watched everything that happened. Uabet had given up trying to put him to bed, because he only screamed until she got him up again.

Paneb and Thuty were sharing a jar of Khargeh red wine.

'I didn't know you were an astronomer,' said Paneb.

'To be honest, it was the Wise Woman who taught me how to observe what lives in the sky and to know the stars, "among which there is neither fault nor error". I was appointed to deal with matters of time, to make sure the rites begin at the right moment, to observe the rise of a new decan every ten days and to indicate its influence to the Master. The Place of Truth must be constantly linked to the movements of the heavens, so as not to lose its integrity. Do you know that the undying stars revolve around an invisible hub, and that this whole also moves, because of the precession of the world's axis? Knowing the movements of the stars and the planets, understanding how they move within the immense body of the goddess Nut – it makes one understand how the architect of the universe fashioned it.'

Paneb felt someone's eyes on his back. Turning round, he saw Ubekhet, who was not taking part in the general revelry but was heading towards the Temple of Hathor. He got to his feet.

'Stay here,' said Thuty. 'The festival isn't over yet.'

Paneb shook his head and began to follow the Wise Woman. He felt an irresistible call, as if he had had the good fortune to open a door which until then had been sealed. He did not notice Ched leaning against a wall, a little smile on his lips.

Ubekhet stepped over the threshold of the temple, and crossed the open-air courtyard. Entering the first covered chamber, which was lit by lamps whose wicks gave off no smoke, she set off up a staircase whose steps were small and made climbing easy.

Paneb joined her on the roof of the shrine, where she was watching the full moon.

'The universe is intelligent,' she stated, 'and it is that which creates and designs us. Life comes from this limitless space, and we are the children of the stars. Look closely at the night sun, the eye of Horus which Set tries in vain to break into a thousand pieces. We think the moon is going to die, but it is reborn to light up the darkness. When it's full, it embodies Egypt in the sky's image, with all its provinces; it is the complete eye which enables Osiris to return alive from the realm of the dead. You, the painter, pacify that eye and reconstitute it through your works so that they too become eyes, which illuminate our path. Three times each year,* Thoth rediscovers the lost eye, puts it back together and restores it to its place, and this is the third of those times. Henceforth, the amulet Ched gave you will link you to the drawings engraved in the heavens and will give your hand the power to see.'

Paneb remained alone on the roof of the temple, bathed by the light of the full moon, deaf to the festive sounds rising from the village. Ubekhet had told him to expose his amulet to the night sun, and he had obeyed.

In those moments when Thoth's full moon opened his painter's eyes, Paneb no longer dreamt of a miraculous

* The twenty-first day of the second month of the first season, the fifth and twenty-ninth days of the first month of the second season.

world; he would be capable of bringing that world to reality. To the skills he had learnt was added the most vital element: an interior vision which his hands would be able to translate.

The people who had made this possible were Ched and the Wise Woman. Ched, the cynic, had shown unequalled generosity in offering his pupil the sign of power that he had lacked, this modest amulet whose significance the Wise Woman had revealed. She, the Brotherhood's spiritual mother, had just granted him a new birth.

As he walked home, he thought of the hundreds of images that would soon spring from his brushes and he longed to talk to Ched about them. He might even have a chance to display them on the walls of a royal tomb!

'You forgot our meeting, Paneb.' Nakht's voice was full of drunken aggression.

'Go to bed. You're drunk.'

'I can hold my drink better than you can, my lad! And I've bet a sycamore-wood stool that I'll throw you and pin your shoulders to the ground.'

A stool? That was just what Uabet wanted, to rest her feet on while she was cradling Aapehti. But then Paneb remembered Turquoise's warning.

'Let's not spoil the celebrations, Nakht,' he said. 'I don't want to hurt you.'

'You are just a coward. All that drawing has made your muscles go soft. I'm a stone-cutter, not a woman!'

'You're a muttonheaded fool who's going to apologize to me.'

The only response was a burst of coarse laughter.

'All right, Nakht, let's settle this quickly.'

The other stone-cutters, Casa, Fened and Karo, were sitting nearby, wine-cups in their hands.

'There you are at last!' exclaimed Casa. 'We three will judge the fight. Let's have a good clean bout, and no low punches.'

The three craftsmen's eyelids were drooping, but Nakht's first attack, without warning, woke them up. Springing aside, Paneb dodged his opponent's joined fists.

'You're running away, you woman,' jeered Nakht. 'You're afraid of me! Come on, come a bit closer – if you dare!'

Nakht was impressively muscular, but he wasn't agile. So Paneb decided to topple him by diving at his legs and lifting them up. But his hands slipped on Nakht's skin, and he found himself on the ground. At once, he rolled aside, but he wasn't quick enough to avoid a brutal kick in the ribs, followed by coarse laughter.

Nakht said triumphantly, 'I oiled my body and you won't be able to catch me. I'm invulnerable, and you're going to suffer!'

If Nakht had seen the rage in Paneb's eyes, he would have stopped fighting and run. He was hit in the chest by what felt like a battering-ram and fell flat on his back, his arms outstretched. Paneb knelt over him and flattened his shoulders to the ground.

'Deliver the stool to my house tomorrow morning,' Paneb told the judges. 'If you don't I shall tear Nakht's house down, brick by brick.'

49

Didia knocked on Paneb's door. It was opened by Uabet, who was carrying her son in her arms.

'I've brought the stool,' said the carpenter.

'But . . . I didn't order one.'

'The stone-cutters told me it was very urgent, so I chose this one, which I had in stock. It's a good strong one, I assure you.'

'My husband's still asleep. I'll go and wake him.'

Paneb emerged from a sublime dream in which he had covered entire walls with pictures of Turquoise adoring the sun and the moon. On returning to reality, he felt a pain in his left side; that brute Nakht had broken one of his ribs. He looked up and saw Uabet standing by the bed.

'Didia's asking for you,' she said gently.

'Why's he disturbing us so early, on a rest day?'

'It's something about a stool.'

His mind cleared and he remembered. He laughed out loud and he hugged his wife and son. 'It's a present for you, Uabet.'

'I did want one, but it wasn't urgent.'

'We mustn't let good opportunities pass us by. I'm hungry! Shall we invite Didia to breakfast, to celebrate your present?'

From the street came the sounds of an altercation. Paneb hurried to the door and found Imuni and Didia quarrelling loudly. The cantankerous little Assistant Scribe didn't seem in the least afraid: he'd put his writing-materials down on the doorstep and was hitting Didia with a leather papyrus-bag.

'You're making my head ache, Imuni,' said Paneb. 'Go back to your office and leave my colleague in peace.'

Furious, the scribe rounded on him. 'There is a law in this village, and neither you nor he has the right to break it!'

'What have you invented this time?'

Imuni put a possessive foot on the stool. 'Did I invent this piece of furniture?'

'It belongs to me. It has nothing to do with you.'

'Oh, but it has! I must know whether it belongs to a set of funerary furniture destined for a tomb and if you and the carpenter are engaging in illegal trading.'

Paneb folded his arms and eyed Imuni with curiosity. 'That you churn out one stupidity after another doesn't surprise me. But it does surprise me that you should turn up at the exact moment when the stool was being delivered. It couldn't be, could it, that someone's been whispering in your ear?'

'That's irrelevant. Didia must prove that this stool isn't stolen, or I shall bring a complaint against both of you.'

'Before I've washed,' said Paneb, 'I'm always in a bad mood. And I haven't had time to wash this morning. Who told you?'

At the change in Paneb's tone, Imuni realized that he'd be wise not to play with this particular fire.

'It . . . it was Nakht. He said you'd forced Didia to give you a stool and that I must charge you with theft and blackmail.'

'Knowing you, I suppose the deed of accusation is already drawn up?'

Imuni lowered his eyes to the papyrus-bag. 'The facts seem clear to me.'

'To me too,' said Paneb with worrying calm.

'You mean you confess?'

'You shouldn't be allowed to write your lies, Imuni. If you

go on like this, you might become positively harmful. I must help you to return to the path of righteousness.'

Paneb snatched the leather bag and tore it open, ripping the papyrus inside. Then he stamped on the scribe's writing-materials and smashed them, brushes, cakes of ink, water-pot and all.

Afraid he'd be meted out similar treatment, Imuni fled.

Paneb picked up the stool. 'Uabet will be delighted,' he told Didia. 'Come and have breakfast with us.'

'My throat's burning,' complained Ipuy. 'My wife thinks I have an inflammation and am losing weight. I think I'm getting a fever and may not able to go back to work after the holiday.'

Ubekhet took his pulse in several places. Ipuy wasn't one of those sickly creatures who, at the slightest twinge, tried to persuade her to authorize extra rest days.

'The heart's voice is disturbed,' she said when she had finished. 'You should have come to see me sooner.'

'Is it serious?'

'Open your mouth and tilt your head back.'

The healer saw what she expected. 'It is a sickness which I know and can cure, but you've suffered in silence too long. There's no value in that sort of courage, Ipuy. Your infection could have deteriorated and caused an incurable condition.'

She prepared a mixture of garlic, peas, cumin, sea salt, yeast, fine flour, feverfew seeds, honey, oil and date wine, keeping to the proportions that her predecessor had specified in her book on infectious illnesses.

'You must take this medicine in the form of pellets,' she said, 'twenty a day for a week. The pus will soon disappear, and the pain with it. Then I shall reduce the dose until you're completely cured, and then—'

She broke off as she heard cries for help. Imuni was shouting himself hoarse, and the village was in uproar.

*

Nefer eventually succeeded in restoring calm, and obtained a clear accusation from a trembling Imuni, watched with astonishment by the craftsmen.

'He broke my writing-things. He's a madman, a destroyer!'

'Who is?'

'Paneb. You must have him arrested, or he'll lay waste to the village.'

Excep for Nakht, who was confined to bed, the stone-cutters were bursting with suppressed laughter. Imuni had fallen into their trap, and Paneb's reactions had exceeded their best hopes.

'Go and find Paneb,' the Master told Thuty.

Thuty returned with both Paneb and Didia; the latter was eating a hotcake filled with hot beans.

'Protect me!' yelled Imuni, hiding behind the stone-cutters.

'Did you break the Assistant Scribe's writing-materials?' Nefer asked.

'I simply wiped out his lies and I think I've done the Brotherhood a service. If I hadn't taught Imuni a lesson, he'd have ended up thinking he was all-powerful. Let him keep to his place, carrying out the Scribe of the Tomb's orders, and there'll be no problems.'

Red with rage, Imuni hit back. 'Paneb is a thief and a blackmailer, and he's destroyed the proof written down in my deed of accusation!'

'This time,' bellowed Paneb, 'you've gone too far!'

The Master hastily stepped between them. 'No violence, Paneb! How do you answer?'

'You mean I've got to answer this snivelling little hypocrite?'

'All that matters to me is the truth.'

'I'll tell you the truth,' cut in Didia. 'Three of the stone-cutters asked me to deliver a stool to Paneb urgently, and I took him one I'd made to sell outside the village. There was neither theft nor blackmail – and I'd very much like to know who is going to pay me.'

'Nakht the Powerful,' replied Paneb, revealing the nub of the matter.

'All the same, this is very complicated,' said Unesh. 'Shouldn't we convene the court?'

'The Staff of Amon will suffice,' replied the Master, 'for the case is clearer than you think.'

Paneb said resentfully, 'I have a witness, Imuni accused me falsely, and the stone-cutters just wanted to avenge Nakht's defeat. And you want to judge me anyway?'

'You committed an offence in breaking Imuni's materials,' Nefer reminded him. 'The Place of Truth teaches us to build, not to destroy. Whatever the circumstances, remember that.'

Hay, overseer of the port crew, stern as a gatekeeper from the other world, appeared. He carried a heavy staff topped with the finely sculpted head of a ram crowned by a sun-disc painted bright red.

The Wise Woman came and stood beside the emblem. 'Paneb, do you dare look into the eyes of the divine ram and state that you have not lied?'

'I place my trust in you.'

He stared at the gilded wooden head, whose eyes of black jasper seemed alive. It was to the ram of Amon that the villagers addressed their prayers or requests, and it was to his hidden power that the Master entrusted the care of judging his friend before the silent villagers.

Paneb felt immediately that the magician who had created this likeness, at the time of the village's birth, had given it a power which could break the will of a human being. He would have liked to look away from the invisible flame of this pitiless gaze, and beg the god to show mercy. But the force of truth enabled him to keep his head steady and not to yield to the sacred ram.

Suddenly, the sun-disc seemed less alive, and the heavy staff moved away.

'Paneb has committed no serious offence against the community,' decreed the Wise Woman, 'and he has not incurred the wrath of God.'

'Nevertheless,' said Nefer, 'I order him to provide Imuni with a new set of writing-materials.'

Paneb said nothing.

Hidden behind the stone-cutters, Imuni thought that the friendship between Nefer and Paneb might not be eternal.

50

The Scribe of the Tomb had summoned the Wise Woman and the two overseers to his house. The holiday was nearly over, and decisions must be taken.

'The port crew will undertake the construction of the Temple of a Million Years,' said Kenhir, 'according to the plan drawn up by the Master and approved by the king. Do you want to say anything, Hay?'

'No, nothing.'

'The site will be closed and guarded. In the event of the smallest incident, alert Commander Sobek at once.'

Hay nodded.

'The two other points to put to you are delicate,' Kenhir went on. 'Is it wise to begin work again in the Valley of the Kings and to trust Sobek with our dreadful secret?'

'Excavating the royal tomb is vital,' said Nefer. 'Whatever the risks, I shall continue.'

'In that case, let us warn Sobek that a traitor is hiding among us.'

'I don't think we should,' said Hay. 'It's our problem, and we shouldn't involve an outsider.'

'I understand why you say that,' said Ubekhet, 'but Sobek's our good friend. He loves the village, he wants it to survive, and we need his help.'

'But it'll bring shame on us all! It'll shatter the unity of the Brotherhood.'

'The person who wants to destroy the Brotherhood is the miserable creature who's betrayed his oath. And as for the shame, it's our own fault for not being more vigilant.'

'Very well,' said Hay reluctantly, 'I agree – but on one condition: that Sobek must swear not to say a single word about it to anyone.'

Kenhir was occupying the only comfortable chair in the fifth fort, so Sobek sat on a mat facing him.

The commander was worried. 'What you've said comes as no surprise. For more than ten years I've been trying in vain to find out who murdered one of my men, and I became convinced that he was hiding in the village – after all, what better hiding-place could he have found? And now this shadow-eater is seeking to harm you inside the Brotherhood itself. Look at the evidence, Kenhir. This plot has been a long time in the making. I can't make inquiries in the Place of Truth, so you'll have to do it. But be careful, very, very careful. The shadow-eater's already killed once, and he won't hesitate to kill again if he thinks his safety and his anonymity are threatened.'

'I'll be careful,' said Kenhir. 'But what about you? What are you going to do?'

'Our man must have some contact with his accomplices on the outside, and eventually he'll make a mistake.'

'He hasn't done so yet.'

Sobek sighed. 'I know, Kenhir, I know. You'd swear he cannot be caught, and I've lost many hours' sleep over it. But it's my only hope.'

'You must give me your word that you won't say a word about this to anyone.'

'I ought to write reports to my superiors and—'

'Your only superiors are Pharaoh, the tjaty and myself. I will answer for you, Sobek, and if necessary I'll explain everything to the king. But no other guards, no soldiers, no administrators must know what's happening in the village. You're the only one we trust.'

The big Nubian was touched. 'In the name of Pharaoh, I swear to keep silent.'

Someone was coming.

Tusa, the guard who'd been charged with watching over Meneptah's tomb, was sure of it: someone was coming. Bare feet on the sand made hardly any sound, but the Nubian's hearing was very sharp. He unsheathed his dagger and flattened himself against the rock, ready to strike the intruder down with a single blow.

Paneb, who was the first to arrive at the site, was astonished when there was no sign of the guard. Knowing how seriously Sobek's men took their work, he could arrive at only one conclusion: Tusa had been killed.

If the killer was still around, Paneb would catch him. But where was he? If he'd heard Paneb approaching, he'd be hiding, pressed against the rock face close to the tomb entrance. Paneb crouched down and crept silently along the rock.

The other man was there, he could feel it. He could detect both his fear and his desire to kill him.

Paneb charged at the tomb entrance, throwing himself to the ground and rolling over. Taken by surprise, his quarry struck at empty air. Paneb grabbed him round the legs, felled him to the ground and hit him so hard on the wrist that he dropped his weapon.

Then he stared in astonishment. 'But . . . but you're the guard!'

'And you're a member of the crew!'

Paneb grinned. 'You do your work well, my friend.'

Tusa grinned back. 'And if you ever want to change your job, Commander Sobek will gladly take you on.'

'Somehow I doubt that.'

The Master and the other craftsmen arrived, and Tusa and Paneb got to their feet.

'What happened?' asked Nefer.

'Nothing. I was just testing the security arrangements,' replied Paneb. 'Thanks to Tusa, the tomb's in no danger.'

Kenhir settled himself in his seat in the rock, sheltering from the sun, and watched the distribution of equipment. The starboard crew would continue to excavate under the Master's direction, except for Ched and Paneb, who were given fine copper chisels.

'For us,' said Ched, 'the precise work is beginning. In the part which has been dug out, we shall prepare a wall, making it as smooth as possible. Without an excellent base, we can't paint properly.'

Paneb touched the amulet at his throat.

'You've changed,' remarked his teacher. 'As much raw energy as ever, but more power.'

'You opened my eyes, Ched. How can I ever thank you?'

'By becoming a better painter than I am. The other artists will do as I tell them. From you, I expect more.'

'I have hundreds of ideas to show you.'

'I shall probably reject every one of them. That way, you may become more inventive, at the same time as conforming to the symbolic programme a royal tomb requires. If you're faithful to it, none of the remaining secrets of our art will be beyond your grasp.'

During the night he'd spent at the pass, Paneb had observed the stars and the moon. Charged with energy, the eye-amulet dissipated all tiredness, and it was with his usual energy that he used a short adze to cut away the last outcrops of stone before using pebbles to polish the surface. He, the gypsum specialist, would next have to apply a layer of fine plaster and transparent adhesive. Then the artists would draw a grid on the wall so that each figure would be in its proper place and would live in harmony with the unity of the scene.

The sculptors were finishing the lintel of the entrance. It was decorated with a scarab and a ram, evoking the resurrection of a sun with which the pharaoh's soul was identified, watched over by Isis and Nephthys.

While the rest of the crew got on with their work, Ched the Saviour began to disclose to his disciple the theme of the paintings that would bring the walls to life.

Serketa was wearing a green dress with purple fringing. With calculated slowness, she took it off and put on a bright yellow one, which left her breasts bare.

'Am I beautiful, sweetheart?'

'Magnificent,' said Mehy. He was throughly enjoying the display after a hard day's work during which, thanks to his talent for corruption, he had made more people indebted to him. On the west bank of Thebes, as on the east, he now had more and more fervent supporters who lauded his dynamism and his excellence as an administrator. And his charming wife's talent for flirting with important guests at banquets had induced several stuffy old fellows to lend him their support; men who liked this rich, influential couple.

Mehy continued to spin his web, so that not one influential person in the great Southern province would escape him. What better training-ground could he hope for before taking on the entire country?

While Serketa was undressing again, and striking lascivious poses, the steward came in to speak to Mehy.

Eyes lowered, he said, 'An army officer has arrived from the capital and wishes to see you, my lord.'

'Show him into the reception hall and give him something to drink.'

Serketa rubbed herself against her husband. 'Can I hide behind a wall-hanging and listen?'

'That's a good idea.'

'Shouldn't we get rid of this soldier?' she lisped.

'Probably, one day, but not yet.'

At the thought of committing another murder, Serketa was so excited that she used all her wiles to arouse Mehy as well. The officer would have to wait.

'What's the news?' asked Mehy.

'Meneptah is ruling with an iron fist,' replied the officer, 'but there are whispers that his health isn't good.'

'Who is best placed to succeed him?'

'His son Seti. But there's something more serious. In the barracks, the training exercises are being stepped up, and the king has ordered the armouries at Pi-Ramses and Memphis to make large numbers of swords, spears and shields.'

'Are manoeuvres planned?'

'That is the most likely reason. The tribal chiefs in Syria and Canaan seem to think Meneptah is weaker than Ramses, and they may start stirring up trouble. A demonstration of force would forestall any possible rebellions.'

'Are there any definite indications?'

'No, General. In my opinion, you should go to Pi-Ramses to obtain a clearer picture of the situation. Staying isolated in Thebes does you no good – and, besides, with the way your reputation is growing, several dignitaries close to the king would like to meet you.'

The officer was right, but Mehy would need a good excuse to undertake the journey. He smiled: the Place of Truth was going to provide it.

51

After a week of hard work, the craftsmen of the starboard crew were enjoying their two days' rest in the village before leaving again for the Valley of the Kings.

Paneb was amusing himself throwing Aapehti into the air and catching him at the last moment, making the baby laugh with pleasure. Uabet looked on, smiling.

Their tranquillity was abruptly shattered by the shouts of a couple hurling insults and crockery at each other.

'It sounds as if it's coming from Fened's house,' said Uabet.

'Probably an argument with his wife – it doesn't sound too serious.'

'It sounds more like a boxing-match. Shouldn't you do something?'

As Paneb was very fond of Fened, he handed his son to Uabet and set off up the street to the stone-cutter's little white-walled house. A fine alabaster dish flew through the open door, clipped the side of his head and smashed against the opposite wall.

'Hey! Calm down in there!' he called.

Fened shot out of the house and collided with him. 'We'd better run for it,' he advised. 'My wife's gone mad.'

Bearing in mind the alabaster dish, Paneb followed his colleague, who ran off without turning back.

Once they were out of range, Feneb panted, 'Thank you for your help, but even an army of giants would be powerless against a madwoman. This time she's gone too far – I am going to ask for a divorce.'

'Oh, come now, don't do anything rash. What's it all about?'

'We can't agree about anything. It's better that we separate.'

'That's a serious decision, Fened. Couldn't you make it up with her?'

'We just don't understand each other any more.'

Fened marched determinedly into Kenhir's audience chamber, where the scribe was busy writing the Journal of the Tomb.

'I want to get divorced,' he announced.

Kenhir did not look up. 'Are you aware that you'll have to move house and leave at least one-third of your possessions for your wife, who will no doubt demand more than that?'

'It's a question of life or death.'

'Well, if things have reached that stage . . . My assistant will prepare the necessary documents.'

Kenhir called Imuni, who was filing papyri. To Fened's surprise, the Assistant Scribe showed tact and understanding, and thanks to him the stone-cutter faced up to the ordeal with a degree of optimism. It would be for the village court to attempt a final reconciliation, to hear the couple's respective stories, and to share out their possessions. In the meantime, Imuni would take Fened into his house.

Paneb was pensive when he rejoined his wife and son.

'Was it serious?' asked Uabet.

'Fened's getting divorced.'

'That's . . . that's terrible!'

'To look at him, you wouldn't believe it. It's bizarre. I even got the impression he was acting.'

'Divorces are rarer here than in other villages, for the

craftsmen warn their future wives what to expect, and they know what their material and ritual duties will be. But why should Fened try to deceive people?'

'To make them believe that he and his wife can't get on.'

'Why should he want to do that?'

'I've no idea.'

'You intrigue me, Paneb. I shall speak to her and try to find out the truth.'

It was nightfall. Paneb had been to fetch water for cooking and he was lighting the lamps, when Userhat and Ipuy knocked at his door.

'The Master wants to see you,' said Userhat.

It was the last evening of rest before returning to the Valley of the Kings, and Uabet had planned a delicious dinner.

'Is that an order?'

'You're free to refuse,' replied Userhat.

His words intrigued Paneb, who turned to his wife

Uabet smiled at him. 'We'll eat later,' she said in a strange voice, as if she and the visitors were accomplices.

Paneb turned back to Userhat. 'What does Nefer want?'

Userhat shrugged. 'We don't know anything. What's your answer?'

'Let's go.'

'Good luck,' whispered Uabet.

The trio set off towards the great temple, where they found Nakht guarding the entrance. If this was about settling scores in front of the crew, Paneb felt ready.

'We are accompanying a craftsman who wishes to travel the two paths,' declared Userhat. 'Let us pass.'

Nakht stood aside, and the three men went into the open-air courtyard, where a large vessel had been filled with water.

'Take off your clothes,' commanded Ipuy, 'and step into the water to purify yourself.'

After immersing himself completely, Paneb climbed out of

the water and was invited to cross the threshold into the first chamber of the temple. Sitting in the half-light, on the stone benches which lined the walls, were the members of the starboard crew.

Suddenly, fire sprang forth.

'Do you dare cross this obstacle and enter the circle of fire?' asked Userhat.

Paneb darted forward, but Ipuy held him back and told him, 'Take this oar, on which an eye has been drawn. It will not burn in the flames, and the ancients used it to travel the pathways of water and fire.'

Holding the oar in front of him like a shield, Paneb passed through the curtain of flames.

The craftsmen got to their feet and formed a circle around him.

On the floor two winding paths had been drawn, one blue and the other black. Between them was a pool out of which more flames emerged.

'Two difficult pathways lead to the sacred vase of Osiris,' said the Master. 'The pathway of water is blue, the pathway of earth is black, and they are separated by a lake of fire where the sun and the spirit of the initiate are regenerated. These two pathways are in opposition to each other, and you may not travel them except by the Word and the intuition of facts. Do you wish to see the secret of knowledge?'

'I wish it with all my heart.'

'Let the rope of metamorphoses be uncoiled and may the just man follow the path of Ma'at.'

Userhat took back the oar, and Gau and Unesh arranged a rope on the two pathways.

'Follow me, Paneb,' ordered Nefer.

The two men walked into the darkness of a chamber which ended in three shrines with closed doors.

'I am going to draw the bolt,' announced Nefer. 'What you will see, you will never be able to forget, and your sight will be transformed. There is still time: you can retreat after hearing the voice of the fire.'

'Draw back the bolt.'

The Master opened the door of the centre shrine. On the Stone of Light, which was covered with a veil, stood a sealed golden vase, one cubit tall.

'The fire protects the Vase of Knowledge in the heart of the silence and darkness. In it was placed the lymph of Osiris, inaccessible for ever to unbelievers. Anyone who contemplates this mystery will not die the second death, for he will become the bearer of the words of knowledge, thanks to which he will not decay in the West.'

Nefer approached the vase, from which Paneb thought he saw aggressive flashes of light emerging, and presented it with a statuette of Ma'at. 'We are the sons of the Place of Truth and we offer you the goddess of righteousness who, alone, drives away the darkness. May Paneb's soul rise to the sky, traverse the firmament and become brother to the stars.'

The chapel filled with light.

On its front-wall pediment, Paneb made out a winged sun, whose light was as bright as that of noon.

'Light up the pathways for the Servant of the Place of Truth,' prayed the Master. 'May he go and come without being enmeshed by darkness.'

Nefer removed the vase's seal and the veil that covered the Stone. Its brightness made Paneb close his eyes, but he opened them again very quickly, protecting himself with his forearm.

'This Stone is the untameable one, which cannot be enslaved,' said the Master. 'In it are carved scarabs, charged with replacing the human heart for the voyage to the afterworld, but it loses no part of its substance, for the light remains eternally alike unto itself. Know that the sky is our quarry and our mine, from which we draw the materials for our work.'

Nefer tilted the vase towards the Stone. From its neck emerged a golden flame of incredible beauty.

When he turned back towards Paneb, the Master was holding a little scarab, carved from green stone.

'You already possess the eye; and here is your heart.'

52

Standing in the carefully excavated first corridor of Meneptah's tomb, Ched and his artists studied the representations of the pharaoh and of the gods which would feature on the walls, along with the hieroglyphic texts that they would draw sign by sign. They would begin with the *Invocation to Ra*, whose enigmatic words unveiled the many forms of divine Light.

'Master, we've uncovered a sacred bone!' shouted Karo in anguish.

Nefer, who was conversing with the sculptors outside the tomb, immediately went inside to join the stone-cutters.

'Look at that!' lamented Karo. 'An enormous block of flint. If we continue in a straight line, according to your plan, we'll have to cut all the way round it to remove it from the rock mass, and that will take ages.'

The Master considered the block. 'It's magnificent.'

'I agree,' said Fened, nodding. 'I'll wager there isn't one as beautiful in the whole of the valley.'

'We'll leave it in place and continue straight ahead,' decided Nefer. 'This rock shall belong to the tomb and protect it.'

When the starboard crew neared the village, on their way back for their two days' rest, they heard barking and shouts of indignation. Nefer saw women running along the main street and into the smaller alleyways. For a moment, he thought that the Place of Truth had been attacked and invaded, but he saw no armed men.

Turquoise ran up to meet them. 'Come quickly! There are so many monkeys that we just don't know what to do. They're stealing food from the kitchens and playing with the crockery.'

The hunt lasted a good half-hour and ended in the capture of around twenty female baboons. Terrified, emitting plaintive little cries, they were herded together in front of Nakht's house; threatened by the dogs, led by Ebony, and the sticks the artisans were brandishing, they clung together.

'Kill them,' recommended Casa, 'or they'll only do it again.'

Standing before them, with his well-muscled body, square-cut face, and large, angry chestnut eyes, the stone-cutter would have terrified a wild beast. The little green monkey jumped on to his shoulder, as if begging for mercy. Casa took it by the throat and squeezed; the animal's eyes filled with fear.

'Don't hurt him!' said Paneb. 'Don't you know he's our good spirit?'

'A good spirit who encourages his fellows to cause chaos in the village! Let's get rid of these monkeys before they hurt our children.'

The Wise Woman intervened. 'These animals are fig-gatherers. It's easy to calm them. Take this flute, Turquoise, and play.'

Turquoise began to play the melody that was played at the foot of a fig tree when the baboons climbed up to gather the fruit and place them in baskets. At the sound of the very first notes the baboons grew calm and looked at the humans with gentle eyes.

Casa went home sheepishly.

The little green monkey took refuge on Paneb's shoulder. Paneb looked at him curiously. 'Why this sudden madness?' he asked the little trickster. 'Why did you lure in the baboons and show them a new place to play?'

The monkey made himself as small as possible.

'Don't do it again,' Paneb warned him. 'Here, we don't like chaos.'

Ubekhet selected four women to take the female baboons back to their owners. Strips of fabric served as leashes, and the procession moved off gaily.

'Is all that fuss over at last?' Kenhir asked his assistant.

'Yes,' said Imuni. 'The baboons have gone.'

'I simply cannot deal with everything. If we carry on like this, it will soon be chaos.'

'I assure you everything's been sorted out,' said Imuni. 'May I inform you that we have just received a letter from General Mehy, who asks to see you and the Master?'

Kenhir groaned. 'Am I never to be left in peace?'

'And . . .'

'And what?'

'Niut is insisting on cleaning your office.'

Worn down, the Scribe of the Tomb decided to go and find Nefer, and take him to see the governor of the west bank.

Mehy closed the wooden shutters to keep the sun out of the audience chamber where he had received Kenhir and Nefer.

'The heat is unbearable today,' he said. 'I hope you aren't suffering too much.'

'Why did you request this meeting?' asked Kenhir.

'I must go to Pi-Ramses to present the king with a report on my activities. One of the most important of them is the protection of the Place of Truth, and I should like to know if you are satisfied with my government's behaviour towards you.'

Kenhir nodded. 'We are. I suppose you'd like that in writing?'

'If it's not too much to ask. And I should also like to be able to give Pharaoh news of the work in progress.'

'It's for us, and us alone, to supply him with that information.'

'I know that, but may I not serve as your messenger?'

Kenhir glanced at the Master, who voiced no objection. 'When are you planning to leave, Mehy?'

'As soon as you've given me your report.'

'You will have it the day after tomorrow.'

By the light of a large lamp, the Scribe of the Tomb was finishing off the report he would entrust to Mehy, while Nefer checked the plan of Meneptah's Temple of a Million Years.

'You still seem just as suspicious of our protector,' said Kenhir.

'I'm just being cautious.'

'He's consumed with ambition, it's true; but in that business with the delivery of copper, his help was invaluable.'

'I admit that.'

'I think I understand what he's really after. He wants to have the ear of Pharaoh and belong to the inner circle of courtiers, and perhaps to that of the king's counsellors. Even if he's been lying to us, he's shown no interest whatsoever in the Place of Truth and thinks only of the capital, where the country's policies are decided.'

'That may be, but is it wise to entrust him with a detailed report on the construction sites? Normally, we'd send it by special messenger.'

'You're worried that Mehy's curiosity might extend to opening the papyrus and reading it, aren't you?'

'Yes,' said Nefer, 'I am.'

'Then you underestimate old Kenhir. I know very well that the central government is full of traps and peopled by ambitious men who are past masters in the art of shady dealings and manipulating people to ensure they're promoted. I accepted Mehy's proposal in order to remain on good terms with him; but if he makes the mistake of reading what I've written, he'll get a nasty surprise. The detailed report will be sent in the usual way when we've passed the block of flint and finished the shrine of the Temple of a Million Years.'

Driven along by the Nile's strong current, Mehy's boat would carry him to the capital in ten days, if the captain and his thirty-strong crew of experienced sailors kept their promise.

Inside a comfortable cabin with a sliding roof, Serketa ate grapes and drank a cool white wine from Sais, light and fruity. She was delighted to be making the journey, and took care to appear on the bridge scantily dressed, to excite the desires of the sailors, who found themselves close to a desirable but inaccessible woman. Her little game amused her husband, who took her with his customary brutality and enjoyed the effect her cries of ecstasy had on the crew.

'Nefer really doesn't seem to like me, and he well deserves his nickname,' he confided in his wife, who was touching up her make-up.

'It is a strategy,' she said. 'While the Scribe of the Tomb talks to you, the Master watches you, the better to weigh you up. The important thing is that they agreed to entrust you with the report to the king.'

Mehy fingered the rolled and sealed papyrus.

'You should read it, my sweet,' said Serketa. 'Father taught me to imitate seals so perfectly that no one can tell the copies from the originals. So you'd be running no risk by reading this message and using the information in it.'

The general hesitated. 'They gave it to me a little too easily.'

'But you've given them proof after proof of your loyalty and friendship.'

'They distrust me, I can tell. And also these are craftsmen, skilled in the use of almost any material. Just supposing they've set a trap for me, and in breaking this seal I fall into it? They'd never trust me again.'

Serketa sat down on her husband's knee and looked at the scroll. 'Do you really think they're cunning enough to dream up something like that? It would be quite exciting. You're right, my love. Don't touch this papyrus. When the king reads it, we'll know if we've made the right choice. And now, while we wait, let's enjoy ourselves.' She pinned Mehy to the bed and climbed astride him.

53

Mehy and Serketa were not disappointed by Pi-Ramses, the City of Turquoise that Ramses had built in the Delta. It was close to the turbulent protectorates of Syria and Canaan, and it housed an enormous garrison ready to fly into action if need be. Ramses had realized that the north-eastern flank of the country offered an invasion corridor for the peoples to the east who, for centuries, had dreamt of seizing Egypt's riches.

The sun made the blue-glazed tiles shine on the fronts of the houses, and the royal palace looked superb, surrounded by gardens in which grew olive, pomegranate, fig and apple trees. 'What joy to live in Pi-Ramses,' proclaimed a popular song, 'for there the small is treated with as much consideration as the great, the acacia and the sycamore give forth their shade, the wind is gentle, the birds play around the lakes.'

Served by two branches of the Nile, 'the waters of Ra' and 'the waters of Avaris', the capital boasted four temples dedicated to Amon, Set, Wadjet 'the Verdant' and Astarte, the Syrian goddess; and four barracks where the soldiers were well-housed. Vast warehouses received the goods brought in by river, and the government occupied imposing buildings.

An officer showed Mehy up to the royal audience chamber, which was reached by a monumental staircase decorated with the figures of dead enemies, symbols of the darkness against which Pharoah must fight unceasingly. In the audience chamber itself, Mehy glanced admiringly at the pictures of flower-filled gardens and lakes filled with brightly coloured fish, over which birds soared, but his gaze was swiftly caught and held by the eyes of the master of Egypt.

Bare-headed, hollow-featured, Meneptah gave an impression of power and seriousness.

Mehy bowed low. 'Allow me, Majesty, to congratulate you on the first anniversary of your coronation, and to wish you many years upon the throne.'

'That is for the gods to decide, Mehy. You have read my thoughts in making this visit: I was about to order you to come to Pi-Ramses to report on the situation in Thebes.'

'It is excellent, Majesty. The region continues to prosper, and your subjects serve you faithfully.'

'What of the army?'

'You know the special attention I give it, Majesty. The troops are well trained and their weapons are in a good state of repair. The officers are skilful, and Thebes's security is assured.'

'Is the transport fleet in a state of readiness?'

'It is ready to cast off whenever you so order it.'

'And your subordinates? Are you confident in them?'

'They're good professionals, devoted – as I am – to the greatness and safety of our country.'

'As soon as you return to Thebes,' said Pharaoh, 'you are to step up training exercises. Footsoldiers and charioteers alike must be ready for action at all times.'

'Am I to understand, Majesty, that war is in the offing?'

'If there is trouble on our borders, we must be ready to deal with it.'

'May I give you a letter from the Scribe of the Tomb?'

Meneptah seemed astonished. 'This is very unusual.'

Mehy handed the papyrus to the king, who broke the seal, unrolled it and read it.

'Kenhir praises your behaviour towards the Place of Truth, and he is convinced of your loyalty, since you have handed me this document intact. He used a special ink, and if anyone had tried to open the scroll the hieroglyphs would have turned green when they came in contact with the air.' Meneptah looked up. 'Contact your colleagues at the main barracks and be present at my next council of war, the day after tomorrow.'

The general bowed before his sovereign and withdrew, his back soaked with sweat.

The reception was dazzling, the dishes succulent. Through his eloquence Mehy had won over two generals, one a charioteer, the other a commander of footsoldiers. Serketa was flirting with the director of the armoury, who let himself succumb to her child-woman whims.

The couple were savouring their first evening spent rubbing shoulders with the highest-ranking people in Pi-Ramses' society and meeting notable members of the civilian and military communities.

At the end of the banquet, the servants brought limestone bowls filled with scented water. The guests washed their hands and then went out to walk in the gardens, where the fragrance of flowers added to the sweetness of the night.

A young man of around twenty, elegant and proud of bearing, approached the couple.

'I am Amenmessu. You are General Mehy?'

'At your service, Prince. And this is my wife, Serketa.'

'You've no need to serve me, my dear fellow. I'm only the son of Seti, son and designated successor of our beloved pharaoh. I've been told that you're doing excellent work at Thebes – I was born there, and it remains dear to my heart.'

'I do my best,' said Mehy, bowing.

'Are your armed forces really the best-equipped in the South, as your friends claim?'

'I see that they lack for nothing.'

'I'd so love to return to Thebes. Here, the atmosphere is too serious: the security of our borders, the arsenal, the barracks – it's all so boring.'

'Do you think there'll be a war?' asked Serketa innocently.

'Officers are constantly coming and going between the capital and the garrisons on the north-east frontier. But whenever I ask my father about the reasons for all this fuss, he refuses to tell me anything because he thinks I'm just an idler, with no interest in affairs of state.'

'I'm sure he's mistaken,' purred Serketa.

'Of course he is. But you don't know him. He didn't take the name of Seti for nothing! He has a violent temper, and he flies into a rage if you challenge his authority. I'm suffocating in Pi-Ramses.'

'Do you like horses?' asked Mehy.

'Riding is my favourite pastime.'

'May I invite you to Thebes, where you'll be able to ride a superb stallion with a matchless turn of speed?'

'What a splendid idea, Mehy. At last, something to look forward to. Come, let me introduce you to a few friends.'

The general and his wife met the principal members of young Amenmessu's circle, most of whom were sons of dignitaries who had faithfully served Ramses. Serketa deployed her charms; Mehy explained his government, in such as way as to emphasize his abilities.

When the evening was over, Amenmessu seemed delighted with his new friends.

Mehy and Serketa were staying in a huge apartment reserved for leading provincial citizens visiting Pi-Ramses.

When they returned from the banquet, Serketa stretched out on a pile of cushions. 'I'm exhausted, but it's been wonderful. We've seen the king, and you've already been accepted into the capital's highest ranks of society.'

'We mustn't rejoice too quickly, and we must be wary of

hypocrisy among these people. What's more, today isn't over yet.'

Serketa was intrigued. 'What have you planned?'

'I'm expecting a visitor.'

The visitor, a senior officer posted to Pi-Ramses, knocked at the door.

Mehy let him in, and at once asked, 'Are you sure you weren't followed?'

'I was extremely careful and I'll leave by the garden.'

'Is there really a risk of war?

'It's impossible to say. Certainly, the troops in the capital have been put on alert and those on the north-western frontier have been reinforced, but it may be no more than a show of force, which isn't unusual at the beginning of a reign. Meneptah wants to show any would-be troublemakers that he'll reign just as firmly as Ramses did, and that he won't permit rebellion in Syria or Canaan. In my opinion, there's no cause for alarm, and if trouble did arise we wouldn't be taken unawares.'

'So Meneptah's consolidating his power,' said Mehy.

'That's right. Anyone who thought he was weak was badly mistaken.'

'Nevertheless, he's sixty-six years old,' Serketa reminded him. 'The court must be humming with rumours about his succession.'

The officer nodded. 'Meneptah has tried to dispel them by officially naming his son Seti as his successor. Seti's forty-six, so he's mature, experienced and accustomed to the art of governing. But he's a difficult man.'

'Is there any serious opposition?' asked Mehy.

'Not to Meneptah. When it comes to Seti, things are different – and rather unexpected. His main opponent is his son, Amenmessu, who hates his father.'

'Why?'

'After the death of Amenmessu's mother, Seti married

Tausert, a woman who's as beautiful as she is intelligent. His son hasn't forgiven what he sees as a betrayal. Moreover, Amenmessu resents being considered worthless and having to leading an idle life.'

'Would he go so far as to rise up against his father when Meneptah dies?'

The officer thought for a moment. 'I doubt it, but some people think conflict between the two is inevitable. Contrary to what Seti believes, Amenmessu isn't sitting idle. He's formed a group of determined young men who are urging him to declare himself and demand power.'

The officer went on to give Mehy precise details about the troops quartered in Pi-Ramses, then he left.

'Amenmessu seems wide open to influence,' observed Serketa.

'I agree, but we must be very cautious. This close to the highest in the state, a mistake would be fatal. Before returning to Thebes, we must pay a courtesy visit to Seti. Let's wager as much on him as on his son. That way we'll be winners regardless of who's the victor in their duel.'

54

The catfish was enormous and menacing. If Kenhir dived to escape it, he'd drown. There was only one way out: to fall upon the monster, sink his teeth into its flesh and devour it.

Just as he was swallowing the first mouthful, the Scribe of the Tomb awoke from his nightmare.

It was a bad start to the day. Eating catfish in a dream signified that one was going to be importuned by an official. Still, it could have been worse. According to an ancient *Key of Dreams* which Kenhir had copied out, dreaming that you were becoming an official meant you were close to death.

His neck hurt and his tongue was coated, and he walked with difficulty to the low table on which lay the papyrus he had drawn up the night before. Scrupulously, he re-read it once more to check that each word was correct. The text assured the king that the two crews of the Place of Truth had worked ceaselessly to create his temple and his tomb, and that the Master had overcome all difficulties.

Niut the Strong came in, bringing fresh milk and a hotcake. 'You're up late this morning,' she said.

'Is this all there is to eat?'

'At your age, you mustn't put on too much weight. Uputy has been waiting for you for half an hour.'

'Dreams never lie,' muttered Kenhir. 'Show him in.'

The messenger came in, carrying the Staff of Thoth.

'The letter to Pharaoh is ready,' said Kenhir. 'You, of course, are bringing me bad news, aren't you?'

'Indeed, it's not good. At Pi-Ramses the armed forces have been placed on full alert.'

'Is it war?'

'It's too early to say. The Syrians and Canaanites have always been rebellious, and Meneptah must show them he's as strong as Ramses.'

'You're not leaving for the North by yourself, I hope?'

'Since your letter is to the king, I'll have an escort. Don't worry; your message will arrive safely.'

Paneb had made spinning-tops, wooden soldiers with moving limbs, crocodiles and miniature hippos which amused Aapehti greatly. Paneb was thinking of making a rider, mounted on a horse with a harness and pulling a war-chariot, but his son must earn it. The little boy loved to open and close the crocodile's mouth, but he had already broken several toys by being too rough with them.

'Breaking things is always very wrong,' Paneb told the child, who watched him attentively, as if he understood every word. 'I'm going to give you a model boat, but you must show that you can take care of it. And if you're good, we'll play a game with a rag ball.'

Uabet came back from collecting provisions; she was carrying two baskets of fresh vegetables. She stood for a while, watching father and son play together. For her, no greater happiness could exist.

'I had a long talk with Fened's wife,' she said, 'She can't bear him any longer and she's determined to get a divorce.'

'Will she leave the village?'

'No, she's staying. But I'm afraid there's worse news than the divorce.'

As if he could see his mother's anxiety, the baby clutched his father's thumb with his little fingers.

'According to Uputy,' Uabet went on, 'the troops at the capital are on full alert.'

The memory of the battle of Kadesh, fought by Ramses against the Hittites, was in everyone's mind. The peace treaty with the Hittites had held, but there were other peoples, just as warlike, who coveted Egypt's lands and wealth.

Paneb went at once to the Master's house, to find out more. There he met Userhat, who was showing everyone a stele on which the Syrians' goddess Qedeshet was depicted standing naked, face-on, on a lion; she had a moon-disc on her head, flowers in her right hand, a snake in her left. The strange figure was unsettling.

'The Wise Woman asked me to place this stele by the main gate,' he explained. 'It will protect us against violence from outside.'

'Did she say anything about war in the north?' asked Paneb.

'No, but she thinks it best to take precautions. If you want my opinion, things don't look good.'

At that moment, Ubekhet came up. 'Paneb, I was looking for you,' she said.

'Has war broken out?'

'I don't know, but we must use magic to protect the village. Fortunately, we're entering the seventh month of the year and it's nearly time for the great festival of Amenhotep I.'

Portraits of Amenhotep I, founder of the Place of Truth and revered patron of the Brotherhood, featured on stelae, lintels, offertory tables and painted walls. During his festival the craftsmen carried in procession a statue showing him seated, dressed in the traditional kilt, his hands resting on his thighs.

'What are you expecting from me?' asked Paneb.

'His royal mother, Ahmose Nefertari, still stands by his side like Ma'at beside Ra, the father of the divine Light. Renupe has been working for several weeks on a cedarwood statue of her, and he will finish it today. It falls to you to give it its final colour: you must paint it black.'

Paneb was troubled. 'Why must she be black?'

'Because she's the spiritual mother of the Brotherhood, the bearer of all creative potential, like our black and fertile earth.* She guides us in the darkness and shows us the immensity of the night sky where the light of the origins of life shines.'

The black queen wore a heavy, luxuriant wig and a long linen robe, and held a flexible sceptre which ended in a lotus-flower. There was a faint smile on her lips, and she seemed almost alive.

Paneb had created a brilliant shade of blue-black which drew many admiring looks.

'Your reputation's growing,' remarked Ched. 'Your colleagues will end up thinking you talented.'

The procession set off. Stone-cutters and sculptors carried the statues of Amenhotep I and Ahmose Nefertari, which were hailed by the children with shouts of joy. Ebony had wisely positioned himself to one side, as had the little green monkey.

The statues were set down before the entrance to the great temple, and the villagers made offerings of flowers and fruit.

'In the time of the ancestors,' said the Wise Woman, 'abundance and righteousness reigned upon the earth; the thorn did not prick, the serpent did not bite and the crocodile did not devour its prey. Walls were solid and did not crumble. May our founder and our royal mother give us the strength to build as in the time of the primordial gods: may we be enlivened with the breath of the golden age.'

Like his fellow craftsmen, the traitor was taking part in the festivities and he tried to look cheerful despite his worries. If

* The word *kemet*, 'Egypt', is formed from the root '*kem*', 'black', an allusion to the rich black silt deposited by the Nile flood.

Egypt was about to go to war, what fate lay in store for the Place of Truth? The authorities would see that both it and the Valley of Kings were closely guarded, and he'd be unable to have any contact at all with the outside world.

The day when he could at last enjoy his accumulated wealth seemed to be getting further away. Besides, his protectors might be swept away in the turmoil, in which case all his efforts to change his life and grow rich would come to nothing.

But perhaps he was being too pessimistic. General Mehy was a highly resourceful man and would know how to profit from the situation – whatever it was.

The traitor must not lose hope. He must go on working in the shadows, trying to uncover the Brotherhood's hidden secrets; the more he knew, the stronger his position would be.

From his terrace, Nefer the Silent contemplated the village. Forgetting their cares, its inhabitants were celebrating their holy patron and the black queen with great enthusiasm. Pai was thundering out songs, which were echoed by the throng, and delicious food kept appearing from the open-air kitchens; Ebony and the other dogs gazed longingly at the dishes.

Uabet's pastries were very popular, and Paneb filled everyone's cup with a fine red wine which induced Unesh and Casa to tell stories salacious enough to make the priestesses of Hathor blush.

Ubekhet took her husband's hand.

'They're all so happy,' he murmured, 'but I can't forget that an evildoer is prowling the village. Can you identify him by reading his thoughts?'

'Unfortunately not, for he is protected by a thick shell which he has forged through the years.'

Nefer stroked his wife's hair. 'Only your love enables me to endure the trials and to carry out the duties I'm charged with. Without you, I'd be nothing but a wanderer, lost on darkened pathways.'

'And without you, I couldn't have taken on the inheritance of all the Wise Women who preceded me.'

'All the villagers are your children, Ubekhet, and they expect their mother to care for them and comfort them, whatever the circumstances. It's a large and very demanding family, but its work is so important that we must think of its good qualities rather than its faults.'

'We've devoted our lives to it,' she said.

'And yet, a member of our family has broken his word.'

'Did he really swear the oath with all his heart? The words his lips spoke were only a deception, as much of himself as of others. The Place of Truth has given him everything, but he has sought nothing but lies.'

'If I fail or if I die,' said Nefer, 'don't let the flame of the Place of Truth go out. In the name of our love, Ubekhet, promise me to continue.'

She kissed him with such ardour that Nefer forgot his worries under the protection of the starry night.

55

'I need blocks of top-quality sandstone in order to continue building the temple according to your plan,' Hay told the Master. 'At this stage in the work, it's also necessary that Hathor illuminates the innermost shrine and the materials we're using.'

'Your request is legitimate,' said Nefer, 'and there's even an urgent aspect to it.'

'What do you suggest?' asked Kenhir. He was having his hair cut by Renupe, who had an undeniable talent for it.

'If you, Kenhir, will oversee the work in the Valley of the Kings, Hay can take charge of the temple and I'll go to the quarry at Gebel el-Silsila.'

'We'll need the government's agreement, and soldiers to protect your expedition.'

'Ask General Mehy.'

The Scribe of the Tomb sighed. Instead of busying himself with his literary work, he'd have to drag himself once again to Mehy's office.

'I also intend to visit the Two Infernos,' said Nefer.

'There are other shrines to Hathor which are easier to get to.'

'The energy this one contains is particularly powerful, as you know very well, Kenhir.'

'Well, you may be right. Are you taking the Wise Woman with you?'

'Yes. You're perfectly capable of watching over the village in our absence.'

Kenhir did not even try to argue. The Master never raised his voice, but he was even more stubborn than himself. And when it was a matter of the Work, he never gave an inch.

'It's no problem at all, my dear Kenhir,' said Mehy warmly. 'How many soldiers would you like?'

'Everything's quiet. Ten will be enough.'

'I'll give you forty, for the Master's safety must be absolutely guaranteed. Where is the expedition going?'

'To the sandstone quarry at Gebel el-Silsila.'

'That's the best in the country, isn't it?'

'Yes, it is. Please tell the soldiers that they'll be helping to transport the blocks.'

'I'll make a note of it.' He did so, then straightened up again. 'Now, please permit me to thank you for the extremely kind note you sent to the king about me. Meneptah himself read your message in front of me, and I was very flattered, I must confess. There's no need to tell you that I'm ambitious and that I hope to achieve great things, in the army as well as the government, not merely for my personal satisfaction but above all to serve my country. I love my work and I want to make myself useful: that's the key to my success. I'll no doubt be accused of vanity, but what counts is results.'

Mehy's frankness astonished Kenhir and strengthened his conviction that Thebes would soon be too small for the general. But he felt reassured, too: to achieve his aims, Mehy would have to carry out his duties faultlessly – and that meant he'd ensure the wellbeing of the Place of Truth.

'Are you allowed to tell me if you're satisfied with the way the work's progressing?' asked Mehy.

'The sandstone blocks from Gebel el-Silsila are destined for King Meneptah's Temple of a Million Years. Work is about to start on building the walls, and the craftsmen of the

Place of Truth are carrying out their duties conscientiously.'

'I am happy to hear that.'

'But, naturally, they're concerned about all these rumours. You've just been to the capital. Is there any truth in the rumours of war?'

Mehy shook his head. 'I'd like to know that myself. Our troops on the borders have been reinforced, but that doesn't necessarily mean war is imminent. In fact, I believe the reinforcements have been sent as a precaution, to prevent war. There's one thing I can assure you of: the king holds your Brotherhood in high esteem and it can do its work in peace and safety.'

Even as he spoke those reassuring words, Mehy was formulating a plan which might enable him to rid himself of the inconvenient Master without suspicion falling upon him.

The hot season of the second year of Meneptah's reign was coming to a close when the craftsmen reached the great sandstone quarry of Gebel el-Silsila, several days' voyage to the south of Thebes. Here, the cliffs bordering the Nile were close together and the current ran fast. Paneb was full of admiration for the captain's delicate skill as he brought the craft gently to the eastern bank. Close to the riverbank there were several shrines, which indicated the sacred nature of the place.

The soldiers disembarked first, and took up positions around the entrance to the quarry, whose vast dimensions impressed the young man.

'To work,' commanded Nakht. 'We aren't here to stand around talking.'

Nefer and Fened chose the layer of rock that seemed the most mature,* and issued instructions to the quarrymen.

* For the ancient Egyptians, stone was born, grew and came to maturity.

Under Nakht and Paneb's guidance, the layer was worn down in places, and shallow crevices were dug out round the future blocks, whose sides were thus clearly marked. Then wooden wedges were inserted into deep, evenly spaced slots and soaked with water; as they swelled, they split the rock and detached it from the face. The blocks could then be extracted row by row and layer by layer.

While the craftsmen and quarrymen worked on the blocks, Nefer engraved two stelae in honour of the royal family.

When the first blocks had been freed, Paneb called him to check them.

Nefer inspected them carefully. 'They're of excellent quality,' he said, and he marked them with the sign of the port crew's stone-cutters.

Paneb helped the quarrymen settle the blocks on wooden sledges. Ever on his guard, Paneb checked the sledges' ropes and brakes; he found nothing untoward.

Before they left the quarry to haul the sledges to the waiting boats, the Wise Woman spoke the appropriate ritual words to the craftsmen. 'God took form when the earth lay in the primordial ocean, and he created minerals in the belly of the mountains. May the stones which have been brought to light today be given back to the gods, and may they serve to build the dwelling that will house them. The quarry has just given birth; let us take care of her children and may they remain eternally young by becoming living stones in the temple.'

At the end of the last day's work, a fire was lit at the entrance to the quarry, and Nefer gave dried meat to the quarrymen, who were delighted by this unexpected feast.

Even when night had fallen, the atmosphere was stifling, as if the sandstone walls were giving back the heat they had accumulated during the day. Only Paneb was unaffected.

'What material were you carved from?' one of the quarrymen asked him. 'Anyone would think you were born in an oven.'

'I'm lucky enough not to have a frozen tongue and bottom like you and your colleagues.'

All the quarrymen got to their feet.

Paneb went on eating. 'No foolishness, friends. Don't you know I'm indestructible?'

One of the quarrymen burst out laughing, and the others followed suit. 'Then let's drink a toast to your good health.'

As Paneb passed round the jar of beer, he said to the head quarryman, 'Tell me, friend, I have the impression that you're not up to full strength. One of the Nubians who pulled the sledges is missing.'

'We've only just taken him on, that fellow. I don't know where he's got to, but that needn't stop us drinking.'

While the little celebration was in full swing, the Master took a loaf of bread and headed for the heart of the quarry. A torch in his hand, Paneb joined him.

'I must lay an offering before the stelae to feed them,' explained Nefer.

They went deeper into the quarry, at whose heart the vertical rockfaces loomed high above them.

Paneb became jumpy. 'I can sense danger.'

'Probably snakes. Don't worry, your torch will scare them away.'

'Let's go back.'

'I can't. Without this offering, the stelae won't be brought to life.'

For the Nubian archer positioned at the very top of the sandstone cliff, the plan was unfolding exactly as he'd been told to expect. The Master was coming to make his offering, accompanied by a craftsman who carried a torch. The flames lit not only the path before them but also the archer's target: he was delighted to have such an accomplice, albeit an unwitting one.

The two men halted for a few moments. If they turned

back, he might not be able to see his prey clearly. But they carried on again, and the archer drew his bow. A few more steps, and he would be certain his arrow would not miss the Master's head.

Still on edge, Paneb fingered his eye-amulet.

A vision came to him: a flame darting out of the rockface, a flame which joined the flame of the torch, becoming one with it and consuming Nefer.

He pushed the Master violently aside, just as the Nubian's arrow whistled through the air. It parted Nefer's hair and broke on a stone.

Paneb rushed to the rockface and tried furiously, but in vain, to scale it and pursue the archer.

The Nubian scrambled at top speed down the slope and headed for the riverbank, where the woman who'd instigated the attack was waiting for him.

She was standing in the shadow of a tamarisk; further down the river, tied up to the bank, was a fast boat, ready to set sail.

'Did you succeed?' she asked.

'No, I just missed him. We must get away quickly. People will be looking for me.'

'Yes, you're right. You go first.'

As he turned towards the river, Serketa sank her dagger into his neck. Arms flailing, tongue protruding, the man staggered, then collapsed.

Serketa retrieved her dagger, wiped the blade on the trunk of the tamarisk tree and spat on the Nubian's body: he'd been incompetent.

Then she walked serenely to the boat that would take her back to Thebes.

56

In the light of his torch, Paneb saw the archer's corpse, which he had been looking for for a good part of the night. He called to Nefer and Ubekhet.

'He's been dead for some hours,' said Ubekhet. 'He was stabbed from behind.'

'It seems,' said Paneb, 'that he made the mistake of trusting the person who hired him.' He went down to the riverbank and started searching along it, though without much hope of success.

'There are some footprints, but that's all,' he said to Nefer. 'The killer fled in a boat, which is long gone.'

'You saved my life again.'

'The trap was carefully laid, Nefer. We must be still more careful.'

'But why should anyone want to kill me?'

'Because you're becoming more and more of an obstacle to their plans,' said Paneb. 'They think your death will be fatal to the Place of Truth.'

'But that makes no sense. A new Master would soon succeed me.'

'Of course, but he might not be as good as you. If there is one thing I've learnt about our Brotherhood, it's that everyone's irreplaceable, particularly the Master. Someone doesn't like the way you are steering our ship, and hopes to get rid of you and make it sink. Someone cruel and determined enough to commit a crime like this.'

Nefer and Ubekhet were impressed by Paneb's impassioned words.

'We must take this man's body back to Thebes,' said Nefer.

'Why not bury it here?'

'Because he was Nubian. That means we must expect the worst.'

The captain of the escort troops was deeply uneasy. 'I was ordered to protect you and I can't—'

'Go back to Thebes,' repeated Nefer, 'and hand over the body to General Mehy.'

'But what about you? When are you planning to return to Thebes?'

'Soon. Have a good voyage, Captain.'

While Nakht and Fened were overseeing the stowing of the stone blocks on the boats, the Master rejoined Ubekhet and Paneb, who had hired a fishing-boat. Paneb rowed strongly, making light of the current, until they reached the Two Infernos, a small shrine on the eastern bank, built at the foot of an imposing rock which jutted out of the mountain.

Falcons soared over the silent place. Paneb had the impression that no human being had set foot on this sacred soil for a long time.

'Do you remember the first time you saw the Stone of Light?' asked the Wise Woman.

'Of course. It was in our Brotherhood's meeting-place, and everyone tried to tell me I was simple-minded.'

'In this shrine, Hathor has created an environment favourable to the birth of the Stone of Light, and it was here that the Master was initiated into its handling. Before you begin to paint the walls of a house of eternity, you must become better able to perceive the importance of our most precious treasure.'

Followed by Paneb, she crossed a small courtyard with two pillars and opened the single door of the shrine. On the walls were paintings depicting Osiris and the pharaoh, who was offering sistra to Hathor. At the far end of the shrine, which was five paces long and three wide, was a strange statue of the goddess, from which a soft light radiated.

'Hathor is the gold of the gods and the silver of the goddesses,' said the Wise Woman. 'This statue is made of all the metals whose brightness she reveals. Touch her foot, Paneb, and your hand will be illuminated. When the time comes, it may be called upon to complete the work that is done in the House of Gold.'

'Come with me,' ordered Paneb.

Sobek stiffened. 'We've made our peace, but that doesn't mean you can give me orders.'

'The Master wants to see you.'

'Where is he?'

'In General Mehy's office, with the Wise Woman.'

'What's going on, Paneb?'

'Are you coming with me or not?'

'If you are disturbing me for nothing, you'll regret it,' warned Sobek.

'Have I ever disappointed you?'

Nefer, Ubekhet and Mehy all looked very serious.

'What's all this about?' asked Sobek, sounding less confident than usual.

'Follow us,' said Mehy.

They went to the central infirmary. There, on a stone bench, lay the body of the Nubian archer.

'Do you know this man?' asked Mehy.

'No.'

'He isn't one of your men?'

'Certainly not.'

'Are you sure you're telling the whole truth, Sobek?'

'What does that mean?'

'You are a Nubian, and so is this would-be murderer.'

'Are you accusing me of complicity?' demanded Sobek angrily. 'For your information, merely being Nubian isn't enough to gain my friendship. The men who serve under me belong to my own tribe, and their loyalty is absolute. I've never seen this man before in my life.'

'I hope so, for your sake,' said Mehy drily.

'Am I to understand that I'm being dismissed?'

'No,' cut in Nefer. 'We had to ask you about this man, but we believe what you've said. You remain in charge of the village's security.'

'If you have even the slightest suspicion about me, I'd rather resign.'

'We haven't,' said Ubekhet.

Sobek bowed before the Wise Woman and withdrew.

'This affair is very worrying,' said Mehy. 'Although it won't be pleasant, I must thoroughly investigate every man under Sobek's command. I'll be as discreet as I can, and I'll let you know the results as soon as I have them.'

The Wise Woman's beauty and innate nobility enthralled Mehy. The undying bonds between her and Nefer filled him with jealousy and with a fierce longing to destroy their harmony, which was blocking his way. It was because of these two that the secrets of the Place of Truth were still out of reach. But he knew the bonds uniting them were more powerful than those of mere human love. Breaking them would not be easy, and he must expect ferocious resistance.

'I'll also make inquiries about the quarrymen,' he said. 'Did they hire this Nubian in all innocence, or were they part of the plot?'

'We must also find out who he was,' said Paneb.

'Yes, of course. You can count on me.'

Mehy congratulated himself on Serketa's skill. She had

carried out his instructions to the letter. She'd have murdered the Nubian even if he'd succeeded in killing the Master, and used him to cast suspicion on Sobek and his men. From now on, the Master's trust in the guards would be less than complete, and the breach would grow wider . . .

'I can't stand that man,' announced Paneb. 'He's so pleased with himself that he'll end up choking on his own smugness.'

'The important thing is that he isn't hostile like his predecessor,' said Nefer. 'What do you think of him, Ubekhet?'

'Much the same as Paneb does.'

'According to Kenhir,' Nefer went on, 'ambition is his main driving-force, and all he thinks of is being appointed to a high position in Pi-Ramses.'

'The sooner the better,' said Paneb shortly, 'and good riddance.'

'But his successor might be worse. At least Mehy's eagerness for promotion means he has to ensure the village's wellbeing, so as not to displease the king.'

'All the same, we should keep our distance as much as possible,' advised Ubekhet.

The trio walked briskly along the road to the village. At the first fort, Sobek was waiting for them. He looked haggard.

'I've never been so humiliated,' he told Nefer. 'If you have the faintest shadow of a suspicion, tell me honestly, and I'll leave at once.'

'Not even a shadow of a shadow,' Ubekhet assured him. 'I tell you again: we trust you completely and absolutely.'

Her eyes were filled with the light of truth. Sobek was convinced. He took a deep, healing breath.

'There's a lot of fuss this morning,' he said 'Twenty "women of the city" have come to grind grain – for a high fee.'

Ubekhet and Nefer looked at each other in astonishment. 'An inspection by the tjaty?'

'Not that I've been informed of,' said Sobek.

In the lay workers' area, people were washing, cleaning and tidying with great enthusiasm. And it was the same in the village, which looked as smart as on the most beautiful of days.

'Here you are at last!' exclaimed Kenhir, who was stumping up and down the main street, leaning on his cane. 'I was beginning to wonder if you'd gone back to the quarry.'

'We had a few problems,' replied Nefer.

'Well, forget them. When will the sandstone blocks be delivered to the port crew?'

'They're being unloaded now. But why all this to-ing and fro-ing?'

'Meneptah has just announced that he is coming here again. He wants to check the progress of the work.'

57

'Watch out!' yelled Paneb. 'It's moving too fast!'

Nakht grabbed the brake and managed to slow the sledge, which was laden with six huge sandstone blocks.

There were only six of them to haul this enormous load, which they were moving on a ramp made of silt, moistened constantly by Renupe and Pai.

'You're making the ramp too wet, you idiots,' said Paneb.

'Don't try to teach us our job,' snapped Pai.

'Go on like that, and the sledge will overturn.'

'We've never had an accident before.'

'Then don't start now.'

Renupe and Pai were annoyed, but they heeded Paneb's advice and started work again, watched anxiously by Hay, whose crew could do no more work until they had the sandstone.

'Just a moment,' said Casa. 'Something's wrong.'

'I thought so,' said Paneb. 'What idiot tied on this rope? It has to be attached as low as possible on the front of the sledge, to give the best angle for pulling. I've told you so a hundred times – it isn't difficult to understand.'

Casa re-attached the rope in the right place, and the six men set off again, singing couplets whose rhythm helped them coordinate their movements.

That very morning, the two crews had put in place a

colossus fifteen cubits high. It represented King Meneptah seated, with his hands laid flat on his kilt and his serious face enlivened by a faint smile. The crews had used the same method, a muddy ramp kept permanently moist, for moving the vast weight. Paneb had helped by climbing on to the knees of the colossus and beating time.

As the sun began to set, Paneb once again scaled the monumental effigy to untie the many ropes round it and reveal it in all its splendour. He sang at the top of his voice while he worked, and didn't notice that a heavy silence was falling over the site. Eventually, he did notice, and turned to see what was up. His colleagues were standing stock still, their eyes fixed on the plinth of the colossus. Paneb followed their gaze, and the song died on his lips.

There before the colossus stood Meneptah, wearing the Blue Crown; around him were 'pure priests' with shaven heads and wearing white robes.

All Paneb could do was jump down to the ground and hurry away, hoping against hope that the king wouldn't be angry.

'Come here,' ordered Pharaoh.

Paneb was almost paralysed, but somehow his legs carried him forward.

'When offerings descend to the earth,' said Meneptah, 'the gods' hearts are filled with joy and the faces of men are filled with light. Making offerings is an act of light which must be carried out each day, so long as the offerings are beautiful and pure. They alone can give life to this colossus, which embodies the supernatural power of royalty.'

Paneb took some lotus-flowers from a priest and handed them to the king, who laid them at the feet of the giant statue. Then he set down a round loaf, a basket of fruit, some incense and a jar of wine.

'May the energy hidden within the veins of the stone begin to circulate,' said Meneptah.

Priests and artisans withdrew to leave the king alone with his colossal, superhuman image. Paneb was the last to leave the site; he was enthralled by this mysterious communion between the master of the country and his embodiment in stone.

Meneptah had given statues to the Temple of Amon and led a procession from Karnak to Luxor; and he had spent a lot of time with Nefer in the Valley of the Kings, examining the work on his tomb.

Everyone said his visit proved there was no longer a risk of war. In addition, by staying on the western bank and again showing his regard for the Place of Truth, the king had silenced all criticism of it. He had even attended a banquet there, held to mark his position as supreme leader of the Brotherhood and to underline the importance of its work.

The traitor fretted, resentful of the Brotherhood's good fortune, which they attributed to the Wise Woman and the Master. He had to take part in the general rejoicing and make them all believe he was wholeheartedly with them.

However, in this gloomy landscape, there were bright spots: his deception was still undiscovered, and his wife had honoured their pact. A good housewife, she carried out her daily tasks without complaint, and waited patiently to become a rich woman.

After the king's departure, the Scribe of the Tomb granted the craftsmen another day's holiday. At last the traitor had an opportunity to leave the village and go to the eastern bank to meet his accomplices.

He walked out of the great gate early in the morning and set off along the path that led along the side of Ramses' Temple of a Million Years. Just before turning right, on to the main track to the Nile, he spotted a Nubian sitting in the shade of a tamarisk tree. He couldn't see the man's face, and couldn't get close enough to find out if this was one of

Sobek's men. The traitor felt uneasy, and decided not to take any risks.

He walked on until he reached a little travelling market, bought some beans, then retraced his steps.

On his return to the village, he bumped into Uabet, who was drawing water from one of the big jars in the street.

'Aren't you going into Thebes?' she asked.

'I'd have nothing to do there, so I'd rather rest at home.'

'With the government's new restrictions, that's a sensible decision.'

'What do you mean?'

'Kenhir used to be content to note down in the Journal of the Tomb the reason why someone was absent. But now he's started registering everybody's movements as well. He can't really afford the time, but he's watching over our safety. And besides, scribes like to write, and nobody will change them.'

'Quite so, Uabet. Good day.'

So Sobek's men were working closely with the Scribe of the Tomb. A worrying question came to him: how long had Kenhir been making those notes?

The Master and the Scribe of the Tomb were, once again, sitting in the tranquil half-light of Mehy's big office.

'My men have been working flat out,' said Mehy. 'I asked you to come and see me so that you'd be the first to know the results of my inquiries.'

Kenhir and Nefer were all ears.

'As regards the quarrymen of Gebel el-Silsila, there's no evidence that they knew anything. None of them had any links with the Nubian, and they engaged him as a labourer for a few days, because they needed someone strong. He behaved completely normally right up to the time of the crime.'

'Have you found out who he was?' asked Kenhir.

'Yes, we had a stroke of luck. There's a Nubian village near the quarry. My soldiers questioned the villagers, and one of them confessed. The archer was a fugitive from justice. He'd escaped from the prison at Aswan, to which he'd been sentenced for assaulting a fisherman. He'd hidden in the village for a few weeks, and then looked for work.'

'Did he tell anyone about his plans?'

'No, but he always operated the same way. He'd spot an interesting place, make friends there and then rob the richest people. Moreover, he's suspected of several assaults, some of them fatal.'

'Is there anything else?' asked Kenhir.

'I don't think I've left anything out.'

'So it looks as though the murderer hadn't set his sights on the Master of the Place of Truth as such, but simply attacked what seemed the most interesting prey?'

'That's certainly one theory, but we can't prove that it's right.'

Mehy hoped that, by showing his reservations on this point, he'd convince his visitors that he wasn't trying to influence them. He waited for a reaction from Nefer, but the Master remained silent.

'What about your investigation of Commander Sobek's men?' asked Kenhir.

'I have assembled as much information as possible, and I have excellent news for you: there's no reason whatsoever to suspect them. Their service records are impeccable; none of them has committed even a minor infraction of the regulations.'

'Are you as full of praise for Sobek himself?'

'I haven't a word to say against him. His file contains nothing but praise for his thoroughness and probity. The king told me himself that he was satisfied with the measures the commander has taken to ensure the village's safety. Personally, I find it inconceivable that he could have done anything wrong or caused someone to do so.'

Mehy knew these forceful words would not completely

dispel his visitors' suspicions, but he hoped they would both be reassured as to his objectivity.

'What do you conclude from all this?' asked Kenhir.

'A dangerous criminal is dead, killed by an accomplice, probably another Nubian. The killer has got away, and unless someone denounces him we may never find out who he is. Let's hope that this was simply an isolated incident; but we ought, nevertheless, to act as though the danger remains. Go on watching inside the village, Kenhir, while Sobek continues to oversee his area and I take care of the west bank.'

'The pharaoh's visit reassured us a lot,' said Kenhir.

'It is true that the rumours of war have quietened down and peace is being more firmly established. Will you need my soldiers again to transport sandstone?'

'We'll have to make another trip soon, because the port crew is working more quickly than expected. Meneptah will soon be able to benefit from the magic energy of his Temple of a Million Years.'

58

All the craftsmen of the starboard crew were asleep in their huts at the pass.

Only the Master was awake. As he did every evening, before going to sleep Nefer thought about his men, about their cares, and about how to solve the problems each had encountered that day, so as to maintain the crew's unity and efficiency.

One of them was so evil that his heart lied as foully as his lips, while he tried to eat away at the Brotherhood from the inside. Nefer was finding the burden of this knowledge harder and harder to bear. His world was that of the fraternity between the craftsmen and the light-filled stone, not that between hypocrisy and this sly evil which he did not know how to fight. He felt that each day he lost ground in the struggle against his masked opponent; and he was beginning to doubt that he'd be able to carry the Great Work to its conclusion in such difficult conditions.

A light, sweet-scented breeze came from the Peak of the West, which showed clearly in the light of the half-moon. Nefer gazed at it for a long time. His turmoil abated, and he remembered the words spoken by the former Scribe of the Tomb, Ramose, at his initiation into office: 'The Hidden God comes in the wind, but we do not see him, though the night is filled with his presence. That which is above is like that which is below, and it is he who accomplishes it. How good it is to be in the hand of Amon, the protector of the Silent one, who gives the breath of life to those he loves.'

Neither god nor man knew the true form of Amon, the only doctor capable of curing a blind man; but would a man not fall down dead with the shock of seeing him? Although invisible, he revealed himself by swelling the sails of boats. Never born, he would never die.

At that moment, Nefer understood the magic power of the Peak of the West, which had answered his call and lightened his burden by permitting him to commune with Amon, source of the energy he needed.

'So you can't sleep, either,' whispered Paneb. 'Spending the night at the pass is the supreme reward. Life is stronger here than anywhere else.'

Nefer said nothing. Paneb sensed that this man, whom he thought he knew, was not only his friend and his superior but above all an exceptional person invested with a mission which came from beyond time, a mission which filled his spirit and his hand like a consuming fire. He might be calm and self-controlled but, like Paneb, he was also an ardent man with an unquenchable flame.

Paneb shared the silence with Nefer, and he felt the breath of Amon in the breeze.

'You are indeed ill,' said Ubekhet.

Karo shivered. 'I caught a chill in my hut at the pass. To think that some people actually enjoy spending nights up there! When the winter wind blows, it freezes your bones. I shall have to take to my bed and miss the next work period.'

'I hope not.'

The Wise Woman had a vast store of remedies with which to fight infection. Onion juice and the deposit that formed at the bottom of beer-pitchers were among the treatments for stomach pains and chills, and would rapidly give Karo relief;

but the most effective remedy would be a curative substance which formed in and impregnated the lower layers of grain stored in a particular way in the silos.

'You're a strong man, so I'm very optimistic.'

'And if I still have a fever in two days' time?'

'I'll examine you again.'

Karo went home, and Ubekhet began labelling phials of a liquid exuded through the pores of a frog from the Great South. It soothed pain and cured infection, and she'd used it the previous day to treat Nakht's wife, who had a kidney infection.

Often, even while seeing patients, the Wise Woman thought of Ched the Saviour. She had read and re-read the scrolls on diseases of the eye, and was preparing new ointments and lotions; but without any great hope of success.

During the rituals celebrated in the Temple of Hathor, the High Priestess directed the female community's magic towards the painter, for human science would not be enough to combat his blindness. The starboard crew needed Ched's genius. Without it, despite Paneb's ardour and the artists' talent, the painted decoration of Meneptah's tomb would not be properly executed.

'A week's holiday? Are you out of your senses?' Kenhir had exclaimed.

'That is the minimum you must give me,' Niut had said calmly. 'I could demand more, but I don't want to cause you problems.'

'But the cleaning, the cooking . . .'

'I'll leave the house sparkling clean, and there'll be plenty of cold food. Have yourself invited to lunch two or three times, and eat as little as possible in the evening – I shan't be here to stop you overeating and I don't want to find you ill when I get back.'

'Surely you aren't leaving straight away?'

'Next week.'

That had been last week, and now she was gone. To Kenhir the house suddenly felt very empty. True, the girl was an absolute pest, but he missed her. He even had to admit that she was not unuseful – except when she took it upon herself to cause chaos in his office.

He pushed away thoughts of Niut and took out the scroll on which he was writing his *Key of Dreams*; he intended to get several more pages done.

But before he had time to draw a single word on the papyrus, his assistant interrupted him.

'What's wrong, Imuni?'

'Paneb has asked me for more cakes of colour.'

'What's unusual about that?'

'I have worked out exactly how many a painter ought to use each day, and Paneb is using far, far more. If the other craftsmen behaved like him, the running of this village would become impossible!'

'Yes, yes,' said Kenhir irritably, 'I'm sure—'

'There's more. Not only does Paneb refuse to obey the rules, but he threatened me again.'

'What did you do?'

'I thought it best simply to walk away. But he should be officially reprimanded.'

'I'll deal with it,' promised Kenhir.

'So I can tell him that he will no longer be permitted to use so much colour?'

'I've just told you, I'll deal with it.'

Imuni would never understand that rules must be applied intelligently, and Kenhir didn't feel up to explaining it to him. Ched had told him that Paneb needed large quantities of colours, in addition to those he made himself; brushes, too, because he wore them out at an impressively remarkable rate. The young man was ruthless towards even the tiniest flaw in his technique and made anything up to a hundred sketches before painting the finished figure. The result was so dazzling that even Ched made only a few small modifications. In these circumstances it mattered little if Paneb needed extra colours and brushes. But try getting Imuni to see that!

The traitor and his wife were sitting on his terrace, enjoying the cool evening air, when the Scribe of the Tomb passed by, thumping his walking-stick down on the ground to give his steps an energetic rhythm.

'I wonder where he's going,' said the traitor.

'Probably to have dinner at the Master's house, like yesterday. Since Niut went away, he's been out almost every evening. When you're used to having servants, you often can't manage on your own.'

'When's she coming back?'

'At the end of the week.'

'As soon as it's dark, I'm going out.'

'Where are you going?'

'To remove a threat. If anyone comes to see us, tell them I'm not feeling too well and have already gone to sleep.'

Nervously, the traitor slunk barefoot along the housefronts, hoping he wouldn't meet anyone. If he did, he'd justify being out at such an hour walk by saying he had a bad headache.

As luck would have it, he reached Kenhir's house without incident. If the front door was locked, he'd give up . . . but it opened soundlessly, and he slipped inside.

How much time did he have? Ubekhet cooked well, Kenhir was a good guest. But all the same, he must hurry. If he was caught he'd be accused of theft – or worse – expelled from the village and imprisoned, and all his dreams would come crashing down.

All he had to do was find the place where Kenhir kept the Journal of the Tomb. And then carry out one particular task.

*

Cheered up by an excellent dinner, Kenhir wanted to do a little more work and consult the Journal of the Tomb so that he could begin drawing up a list of the craftsmen who had most frequently gone to the western bank over the last ten months. Then, before going to sleep, he'd read one of the old classical texts, which would help him forget the troubles of the day. But first, the list . . .

At first he thought he must be mistaken, but eventually he had to face the facts: the papyrus on which he had made his notes had disappeared.

59

The fourth year of Meneptah's reign was drawing to a close. No war had broken out on the borders, and work on the pharaoh's tomb was going very well. The first three 'passages of the god' were finished; these punctuated the first part of the corridor that ended in the well from which rose the energy of the *Nun*, the cosmic ocean, with which the royal sarcophagus would be impregnated when it was lowered into its last resting-place. Also finished were the first pillared chamber, designed to drive back rebels and malign forces; a new corridor where the reborn pharaoh's soul would rise to the zenith; the chamber of Ma'at, who maintained it eternally in righteousness; and the beginning of the last corridor, which led to the chamber of gold where Meneptah's mummy would lie.

The artists had drawn the hieroglyphs that made up the *Invocation to Ra*, certain extracts from the *Book of Doors* and the *Book of the Hidden Chamber*. This last would provide the pharaoh with the words he must speak to overcome the gatekeepers of the afterworld, so that he might enter freely into the paradise where just souls dwelt.

Meneptah offering unguents and incense to Osiris, and wine to Ptah; Ra and Anubis giving life to the king; a winged representation of Ma'at; and numerous dialogues between the pharaoh and the gods: such were the figures that Ched and

Paneb had painted while their colleagues drove deeper into the entrails of the rock.

The many lamps gave a clear light, undimmed by smoke. The two painters prepared their colours outside and rivalled each other in the virtuosity with which they superimposed layers of varying thicknesses and created subtle nuances, notably of reds and blues. These were made to shine by applying a layer of varnish, the secret of making which Ched had taught his pupil.

Paneb's energy was so infectious that Ched never felt tired when working beside him; it even seemed to him that his sight improved while his hand was bringing to life the golden ship in which the gods sailed during the hours of the night.

'This time, it's too much,' exclaimed Unesh. 'Ched, you must do something.'

Ched went over to him. His two colleagues, Pai and Gau, stood on either side of him, gazing at a fine figure dressed in a blue wig and a gold kilt, standing in the prow of the ship of the sun. Written above the figure's head was his name, Sia, 'creative intuition', which, alone, steered the course.

'What's "too much"?' asked Ched.

'I drew the grid with precise indications,' said Unesh, 'and Paneb has ignored them.'

'That's right,' agreed Gau.

Pai said nothing; he looked embarrassed.

'Look at the painting as a whole,' said Ched, 'at the boat, at Sia, and at the celestial beings holding the tow-rope.'

Unesh frowned. 'I don't see . . .'

'That's why you aren't a painter. You drew up a rigid plan on the wall, respecting the rules, and Paneb has made them live by bending them a little. The plan has disappeared; beauty has been born.'

'So Paneb can do what he likes, can he?' said Unesh angrily.

'Of course not. If we go slowly, it's because he must study

the grid in such minute detail that it ends up being incorporated into his hand. And sometimes his hand goes beyond formal constraints to bring forth that which did not exist before.'

'All the same,' objected Gau, 'he's taking unacceptable liberties.'

'You're wrong,' said Ched. 'He creates the proportions without which a painting is condemned to fade away. Do you really think I'd permit him to stray from the path, especially in a royal tomb? Look more closely, and tell me what's wrong with this scene.'

The three artists tried to put their criticisms into words but failed.

'Well, then,' said Pai, 'we'd better get on and prepare the next grid.'

Ubekhet had gone to call on Kenhir.

'How is he this morning?' she asked Niut.

'Much better. He's got his appetite back at last, and he grumbles all the time about everything and nothing. I think your treatment has completely cured him.'

The Scribe of the Tomb came out of his bedroom, looking sulky. 'I'm behindhand with my work. Ah, Ubekhet. May the gods smile upon you. Must I take those fortifying pills for much longer?'

'No, because you've got your energy back.'

'After the theft of the papyrus, I thought I'd die. A theft from my house, from my office! What could anyone hope to gain from such a crime?'

He had indeed been very ill, and had suffered for weeks from deep depression. Fortunately Imuni had proved of invaluable help by taking on many of Kenhir's daily tasks, while the Wise Woman, using both magic and medicine, had restored his health.

'I feel strong enough to return to the Valley of the Kings,' he announced.

'That's for the Wise Woman to decide,' said Niut, 'not you.'

Ubekhet smiled. 'That remedy will complete the work mine began, and the crew will be happy to see you again.'

The Scribe of the Tomb was overwhelmed.

'You have created a masterpiece,' he told Nefer. 'Even the tomb of Ramses is not more beautiful than this.'

'The most difficult work is yet to be done,' cautioned the Master. 'So long as the sarcophagus chamber remains unfinished, I shall worry.'

Kenhir went back and forth along the corridors of the house of eternity, not knowing which detail to marvel at in the riot of colours.

'The artists and painters have surpassed themselves,' he said. 'Death shall never reign in this place.'

'The whole crew has put its soul into this work,' agreed Nefer.

Outside the tomb, the men were eating their midday meal of dried fish, salad, onions and bread; only very light beer was permitted. Kenhir had taken his place on his seat hollowed out of the rock; despite his sour nature, everyone was happy to see him back.

At the end of the break, the crew went back into the tomb.

'I can't stop thinking about that stolen papyrus,' Kenhir confided to Nefer when they were alone. 'Every time I knew a craftsman was leaving the village I'd noted it down, and I meant to check, man by man, and see how often each one had gone outside the walls. The one we're searching for must have foreseen that, and stolen the document.'

'Don't you remember it at all?'

'I don't clutter my mind with such details; I prefer to write them down. Without those notes, I can't establish the facts.'

'Our man must be getting more and more suspicious. He

probably noticed that Sobek has put new security measures in place.'

'His situation is becoming difficult. If he doesn't dare leave the village, how will he communicate with his accomplices?'

'Sobek's right,' said Nefer. 'At some point he'll make a mistake. It is up to us to remain alert.'

'When are you planning to use the Stone of Light again?'

'When the sarcophagus chamber has been excavated and roofed. Its walls will be impregnated with energy before the artists and painters set to work on it.'

'To be honest, it's becoming almost impossible to tell Paneb's work from Ched's. The pupil is the equal of the teacher. The colours in this tomb are even more alive than those in Ramses' last dwelling.'

'According to Ched, Paneb has perfected new tints by experimenting with shades of red. And that, apparently, is only the beginning.'

'Isn't Ched a bit jealous?' asked Kenhir.

'No – in fact, quite the opposite. Seeing his pupil's progress has given him back youth and enthusiasm. Ched is a man of great works, and nothing embitters him more than routine. For a long time, he despaired of finding a worthy successor.'

'And then Paneb arrived. Another wonder of the Place of Truth! But we must be careful that pride doesn't destroy his heart and his hand.'

Nefer nodded. 'That's the danger we are all watching out for. For the moment, Paneb is faced by so many difficulties that he has constantly to surpass himself. So long as he struggles with and against himself for a work greater than himself, his fire will be a creative one. And we can count on Ched to push back his pupil's limits a little more each day. Now, if you will forgive me, I must go and see how the crew are getting on.'

As he was about to cross the threshold of the tomb, the answer came to him: 'Uputy!'

'What about him?' asked Kenhir.

'The traitor is communicating with the outside world by letter.'

Uputy was scandalized by Kenhir's request. 'I have sworn to preserve the secrecy of the messages I carry. If I break my oath, the Staff of Thoth will strike me and I'll lose my job. People have often tried to bribe me, but no one has ever succeeded.'

'I'm glad to hear it, Uputy, but I'm not trying to bribe you.'

'Yet you want to know the contents of the letters written by the craftsmen and the names of their recipients. My answer is no, Kenhir, and that is final.'

'I understand your position, but you can be assured that my probity is no less than your own and that I am acting in the best interests of the Brotherhood.'

'I don't doubt your word, but my decision is irrevocable and in accordance with the solemn promises I made when I entered my profession.'

Within the framework of a criminal investigation, the Scribe of the Tomb could no doubt have obtained authorization to consult the correspondence carried by Uputy; but he must preserve the honour of the Brotherhood and not bring this dark business into the light of day, especially not while the two crews were in the middle of such important work.

'At least tell me one thing, Uputy,' said Kenhir. 'Over the last three months, who has entrusted you with the most messages?'

'Why do you want to know?'

'To note it down in the Journal of the Tomb, make comparisons with previous years and prepare a file on our volume of correspondence – the tjaty is bound to ask me.'

This pious lie satisfied Uputy. 'In that case,' he said, 'the one who writes the most is Pai. But that's all I'm going to tell you.'

60

'Don't you want another slice of lamb, Pai?' asked his astonished wife.

'No, not this evening.'

'No tripe, either?'

'No. I'm full.'

'But you've eaten hardly anything, and I prepared a special meal to celebrate our wedding anniversary.'

'And delicious it is, too.'

'You must be sickening for something.'

Seeing Pai's big belly, his plump cheeks and his beaming expression, no one would have thought him underfed.

'I'm going for a walk,' he said.

'Don't be too late back, or you'll wake the children.'

'Don't worry.'

Resisting the smell of the food was torture; it was better to take the air and try to forget it. His stomach rumbling, Pai set off down the main street.

'Ah good!' exclaimed Paneb. 'I was hoping to see you.'

'Me? Why?'

'The Master and the Scribe of the Tomb would like to speak to you.'

'Right now?'

'Right now.'

'I was going to bed and—'

'Really? But you've just come out of doors.'

'No . . . well, yes . . . but I was going back.'

'They sent me to fetch you, and I'm fetching you. Understood?'

'Yes, yes, understood.'

Paneb's politeness was even more alarming than his anger. Pai followed him obediently to Nefer's house and nervously went inside. Nefer and Kenhir were both there, and so was Ubekhet; for once, her gaze seemed more penetrating than friendly.

'You look worried,' she said. 'Have you got indigestion?'

'No, I'm well, very well.'

Standing there, his hands resting on his walking-stick, Kenhir was brusque. 'You've been writing a lot of letters recently.'

'I may have. But that's my business.'

'It is also the business of the Place of Truth. Whom do you write to?'

'You don't need to know that.'

'Oh yes I do!' barked Kenhir. 'And if you refuse to tell me, I shall convene the court.'

Pai looked stunned. 'But . . . but that's insane.'

'If you're at peace with yourself,' said Nefer, 'answer us. Your refusal implies that you are concealing behaviour unworthy of a Servant of the Place of Truth.'

Pai hung his head. 'You know everything, don't you?'

The only answer was a heavy silence.

'It all began about a year ago, when I celebrated my mother's eightieth birthday. She lives on the eastern bank, near the fish market. I ate too much tripe and lamb, I admit it, and she flung in my face that famous bit from *Teachings for Kagemni*: "Gluttony is contemptible; we must point the finger at it. A cup of water is enough to satisfy thirst and a mouthful of vegetables to fortify the heart. Unhappy is he whose belly is greedy when the mealtime has passed." She is pitiless, and has refused to see me until I've lost weight. I've sent her more than twenty letters telling her how hard I'm trying, but she wants me slim, and much, much lighter. This evening, I tried again just to pick at my food . . . and I'm absolutely starving.'

'Pai is innocent,' said Nefer.

'What if he's an excellent actor?' said Kenhir dubiously. 'If he knew he was in danger of being unmasked, he'd have had an explanation ready, and no one would dream of doubting such an absurd one.'

'That would suggest he doesn't know you very well,' commented Ubekhet with a smile.

Paneb spoke up. 'I believe Pai, but I think we should check his story. Tomorrow morning I'll go and see his mother, and then we can be sure.'

'Pai's mother? She lives in the third alleyway on your left.'

Paneb thanked the fishmonger, who went on setting out his stall, and followed his directions. But instead of turning into the third alleyway he went straight past it and broke into a run.

Behind him came the sound of someone running. He'd been followed ever since taking the ferry, perhaps for even longer.

So Pai hadn't told the truth. His explanation was nothing but a tissue of lies and, as he feared it would be checked, he'd told an accomplice on the outside to kill the checker.

Paneb was delighted: his follower would certainly have plenty to tell him. He hid in the angle of a wall and peeked out. He saw a Nubian halt and look round in every direction.

Paneb stepped out of concealment. 'Are you looking for me, friend?'

The Nubian's fist shot out. Paneb parried the blow with his forearm, and kicked his adversary in the stomach. The man staggered back several paces, but stayed on his feet.

'You can fight, and you're tough,' said Paneb. 'I'll have to hit you harder, unless you'd rather tell me who you're working for.'

The man took a deep breath and rushed at Paneb, head first.

At the last moment, Paneb leapt aside and brought his clasped fists down on the back of his opponent's neck. The man ended his run against a wall.

His forehead dripping blood, he staggered but still didn't fall.

'You really are a tough one,' said Paneb admiringly.

The Nubian fought for breath. 'If you kill me . . . you won't escape . . . There's no escape from . . . Sobek's men.' His eyes swam out of focus and he fainted.

Housewives looked cautiously out into the street.

'Bring me some water,' ordered Paneb.

It took a whole jar to bring the Nubian round.

'Are you really one of Sobek's guards?' asked Paneb.

The unfortunate man groaned. 'Do you want to fight again?'

'Not if you tell me the truth, no. Why did you follow me?'

'Those are my orders. I have follow any craftsmen who go to the east bank, to find out where they go.'

'I'm following orders, too.'

'Commander Sobek didn't say anything to me about it.'

Of course! No one had thought to warn the commander. Paneb helped the Nubian to his feet and took him to a seller of medicinal plants, who applied a healing balm to the wound on his head.

'I'll have to make a report,' said the guard. 'What am I going to tell Sobek?'

'Tell him to talk to the Scribe of the Tomb – he'll explain everything.'

Paneb peered doubtfully at the old woman standing in the

doorway of her house. She was small and wrinkled, and looked far from pleased to see him.

'Are you Pai's mother?' he asked.

'What do you want with me?'

'I'm a friend of your son.'

'Is he any thinner?'

'Yes, a bit, but—'

'Tell him to stop writing to me and get on with it! That glutton is the shame of my family. He's not to come and see me again until he's made himself presentable.'

'I assure you he's trying very hard and—'

'Trying isn't good enough. Tell him to succeed.' She slammed the door in Paneb's face.

General Mehy drew his bow, took aim at the centre of the wooden target and fired. The arrow sank into the very centre.

'Good shot,' said Daktair.

Mehy pulled out the arrow and checked that its point was almost intact.

'That's good, Daktair. Your new metal is exceptionally hard. With arrowheads like this, the Theban archers will outmatch any enemy's. What about the swords?'

'I'm making good progress.'

'But you seem disappointed and discontented.'

'I'm reduced to something little better than a senior workman. Our dreams of greatness seem so far off.'

'You're wrong about that,' said Mehy.

'Meneptah reigns unchallenged, you still have to protect the Place of Truth, and we haven't learnt any of its secrets. The walls of that village really are impenetrable.'

'Do you think I've given up?'

'I think that you're pursuing a brilliant career and that mine will end in this workshop.'

'We shall win in the end, because we know how to take the measure of our opponents,' Mehy assured him. 'But they're much more formidable than we thought. The Master and the Wise Woman give the Brotherhood a unity like that which binds the stones of a temple together, and it won't be easy to destroy it. The small victories we've won so far aren't enough, I admit, and we've had some serious setbacks, but we've learnt from them. The main thing is to deprive Nefer of support. We know from our spy that the Scribe of the Tomb has been ill. In view of his age, he shouldn't bother us much longer. But Nefer has a most annoying guard-dog, young Paneb. I tried to get him to enlist in the army, but he refused. So much the worse for him.'

61

Paneb and Turquoise had just made love with all their usual passion. Paneb looked down at her as she lay beside him, triumphant in her nakedness, and he stroked her long red hair.

'Only Hathor can inspire you to such loving games, Turquoise. If you go any further, will I be able to follow you?'

'Surely your strength isn't fading?'

'Try me.'

They threw themselves into a new joust, neither caring who would emerge the victor or the vanquished. They were surprised and delighted by their desire each time they embraced.

Afterwards, when they were calm again, Turquoise asked, 'Are you happy with Uabet?'

'She's decided to be happy with me; it would be cruel to upset her. And then there's my son. I'm going to make a real warrior of that little chap, and no one will ever beat him.'

'Ah, but he's also Uabet's child. Perhaps she has other plans for him.'

'For Aapehti? Impossible! He already wants to fight.' Paneb caressed Turquoise. 'Shall we stop talking? Night will fall soon, and you'll show me the door.'

'If I weren't a free woman, would you still love me?'

With all gentleness, the painter's hands answered her, following the curves of her body.

Suddenly she rolled away from him. 'There's someone at the door.'

Clear-headed now, Paneb listened: someone was knocking insistently.

Turquoise wrapped herself in a shawl and went to open the door. It was Gau.

'Is Paneb with you?' he asked.

'Why do you ask?'

'I'm afraid he may be in trouble. According to Unesh, who overheard them talking, the stone-cutters are going to lodge a complaint against him. They're arguing with the Scribe of the Tomb right now.'

Paneb appeared behind Turquoise, looking furious. 'What did you say?'

'That's all I know, but the two other artists and I have the impression that people are plotting behind your back.'

'I'm going to see Kenhir.'

Nakht and Casa glared at Paneb, Karo turned his back on him and Fened pointed an accusing finger. 'You're the thief, and you'd better confess.'

'Take back your insults this minute, or I will—'

'This seems serious,' cut in Kenhir.

Paneb turned to him. 'What's happened?'

'The large pickaxe used for breaking up the rock has disappeared.'

'And Paneb stole it,' said Fened. 'Who else could have? He's the one who carried it to the store.'

'That's true,' agreed Paneb.

'Then how do you explain the fact that it's no longer there?' asked Kenhir.

'I don't have to explain. I left the pick with the other tools in front of the door of the store. It was the stone-cutters who put them inside, not me.'

'Don't try to get out of it,' protested Nakht. 'We all agree that you were the last person seen with that pick.'

'Stealing a tool is a serious offence, Paneb,' said Kenhir. 'If you've been using it for your own personal work, it would be better to admit it straight away.'

'But I haven't.'

'We're bringing a complaint against Paneb,' said Casa, 'and we demand an immediate inquiry.'

'What does that mean?' asked Paneb.

'That I am obliged to search your house in the presence of the Master and two witnesses,' replied Kenhir.

'Search my house? Never!'

Casa sneered. 'That's just how a guilty man would react.'

'If you're innocent,' added Nakht, 'why not just let the search go ahead?'

'You all know I've done nothing wrong.'

'In that case,' said Nakht, 'let Kenhir prove your innocence.'

Paneb threw a fiery look at the stone-cutters. 'I'm going home to wait for you.'

'Out of the question!' snapped Casa. 'You'd hide the pickaxe. You'll stay here. Kenhir will appoint the two witnesses, someone will go and fetch them, and the full commission of inquiry will go to your house.'

By the time the Scribe of the Tomb, the Master, Pai the Good Bread's wife and Thuty the Learned crossed the threshold of Paneb's house, the whole village knew of the accusation levelled at him.

The traitor had carried out the plan his accomplices had suggested in their last letter, hoping to get Paneb expelled from the Brotherhood. Taking advantage of Kenhir's illness and a moment's inattention on Imuni's part, he had stolen the pick. It was now hidden in Paneb's house, in a part which he was preparing to alter so that he could enlarge the kitchen, and which was currently open to the outside. And the rumour, started by a friend of his wife who had exaggerated the original facts, had worked very well.

Uabet stared in wide-eyed astonishment at the members of the commission. 'What do you want?'

'Your husband has been accused of theft,' explained Kenhir. 'We must search the house from top to bottom.'

'Well you can't. I won't allow it.'

'Be reasonable, Uabet. That is our law, and we must apply it, by reason or force.'

Paneb took his wife by the shoulders. 'Let's go outside and sit down, and let them get on with it. The man who's trying to destroy me thinks he's succeeded, but I shall find out who it is and break his bones.'

The search seemed never-ending. Paneb spent the time teaching Aapehti the different ways of clenching a fist and training him to hit the palm of his enormous hand. Laughing merrily, the little child demanded to play the game over and over again.

Kenhir was first to leave the house. He wiped his brow with a square of linen. 'We didn't find the pick, Paneb. You are cleared of the offence.'

Paneb got to his feet and drew himself up to his full size, more impressive than ever. 'That changes nothing, since neither you nor the others believed my word.'

'If you want an apology you'll get it.'

'That isn't enough.'

'What more do you want?'

'I want nothing more to do with this village, Kenhir. You can strike my name from the starboard crew.'

'I don't want to leave,' protested Uabet. 'I was born here and I'll die here.'

'You're free to stay. But as for me, my decision is irrevocable.'

Uabet's tone hardened. 'Why? Because you're guilty?'

'What do you mean by that?'

'Did you steal that pickaxe?'

'You too? Even you accuse me?'

'Did you steal it, yes or no?'

'On my son's head, I swear I didn't.'

'You can thank your son. He's the one who saved you.'

'What? How?'

'He went to play, without permission, in the part of the house you want to alter. I found him scratching the ground and unearthing a wooden handle – the handle of a large pickaxe. I thought of telling you, but you were having fun with Turquoise. So I warned the Master.'

'Nefer! What did he do?'

'He took it away.'

Paneb ran immediately to the Master's house, and found him making an amulet in the form of a set-square.

'Where did you hide the pickaxe, Nefer?'

'What pickaxe?'

'The one that had been hidden in my house.'

'My memory must be going . . . Anyway, it's been proved that you weren't involved in that unfortunate episode.'

'If you saved me, it is because you believe I am innocent.'

'You aren't without your faults,' said Nefer, 'but you're not a thief. Besides, you know about the difficulties we're facing and you've been appointed to protect me. If our enemies had eliminated you, they'd have destroyed a large part of our defences.'

'Kenhir and the stone-cutters have dragged me through the mud, and everyone knows it. The whole village thinks I'm a thief, and everyone will look at me with different eyes. I know I no longer have a place in this Brotherhood.'

'Forget this humiliation, and don't let your pride rule you.'

'Your action was in vain,' said Paneb mournfully. 'The evil is done, the break cannot be healed.'

'You're behaving like a beaten man.'

The two men stared at each other for a long time.

'Thank you for saving me from an unjust judgment, Master. But I no longer wish to live among men who hate me and whom I despise.'

'You will lose everything, Paneb, and your life will once again be like a twisted staff.'

'At least I can use it to break the head of anyone who stands in my way. I feel sorry for you, chained up in this village, forced to serve second-rate people. I am going to win back my freedom.'

62

'Will you come with me, Turquoise?'

'No.'

'With me you will lead a wonderful life, such as you can't even imagine.'

'I'm not interested in that.'

'This village is ruled by injustice and jealousy. If you moulder away here, you'll regret it.'

'That's just anger and wounded pride speaking.'

'Oh no, not you too!' He took her in his arms. 'I'm going to take you away, Turquoise.'

'Have you forgotten that I am a free woman and that no man can impose his will upon me?'

'But what can you expect from this Brotherhood?'

'Each day, here, truly is a new day. And as a priestess of Hathor, I have sworn an oath of fidelity to the goddess.'

Paneb drew back from her. 'Are you accusing me of breaking my oath?'

'That's for you to judge.'

'I'll miss you, Turquoise.'

'I couldn't persuade Paneb to stay,' Nefer told his wife. 'The humiliation was too deep, and he no longer trusts his fellow craftsmen.'

'Not even you?'

'He knows I believe in his innocence and that I dealt with the pickaxe, but his revolt against this injustice is too violent.'

'You need him, don't you?' said Ubekhet.

'He's already become an exceptional painter, and I'm not sure Ched will have the energy to finish the decorations of Meneptah's tomb on his own. But Paneb's free to leave the Place of Truth, and there is no one left but you to convince him to serve the Work he has begun.'

'The Wise Woman who initiated me told me, "When I have rejoined the West, may the goddess of the peak, She Who Loves Silence, become your guide and your eyes." Tonight, I shall go and consult her.'

The enormous female cobra came out of its shrine at the summit of the Peak of the West and reared up at the Wise Woman, who bowed before it. The moonlight glimmered on the band of gold she wore across her brow.

Lit by the silvery glow of the night sun, the reptile swayed gently from left to right and right to left, not taking its eyes off Ubekhet. If it attacked, she would have no chance of escape.

Beyond fear, the Wise Woman began a silent dialogue, her eyes speaking to those of the cobra, the incarnation of the goddess of silence. Ubekhet spoke of Paneb, and of Meneptah's house of eternity, and begged the goddess to show her which path she should follow to preserve the harmony of the Brotherhood.

One by one, the stars disappeared as if a black veil was covering them. As the night drew to an end, a drop of water fell on to Ubekhet's hair.

The Wise Woman realized that the goddess's answer would be terrifying, but that Paneb was strong enough to bear it.

Uabet could hold back her tears no longer. 'You can't leave, Paneb.'

'Follow me if you want, but I shan't change my mind.' He rolled up his travelling-mat.

'And what about Aapehti? Have you no regrets about leaving him?'

'You'll bring him up very well, and I'm sure he'll know how to handle himself, like his father.'

'Your painting, all the work you've done, all you've achieved: does none of that mean anything any more?'

'Don't go on, Uabet.'

'Why won't you admit that the only reason you're being so stubborn – more stubborn than a mule – is because your pride's been wounded? Even if you don't get on with the stone-cutters any more, what does that matter? The Master is your most faithful friend, and – just in case you've forgotten – in this village there are at least two women and a child who love you.'

Paneb tied the mat to a travelling-bag containing a loaf of bread, a goatskin of water, sandals and a new kilt, and left his house without looking back at his weeping wife or kissing his son.

Dawn was breaking, but it was no ordinary dawn. On this twenty-seventh day of the first month of the summer season, in the fourth year of Meneptah's reign, large black clouds obscured the east and blocked out the sun. The air was heavy, almost unbreathable, and charged with a tension which made Paneb's bones ache.

A flash of lightning streaked across the sky, and struck Obed's forge. Woken with a start, he called for help from the few lay workers sleeping on the site, and started a flurry of panic.

With unheard-of violence, a rainstorm came thundering down on the Place of Truth. The rain was so hard that Paneb felt as if he were being stabbed by thousands of needles.

The monstrous storm battered the western bank of Thebes; a succession of lightning-flashes striped the threatening clouds, and the rain grew still heavier. In the main street of the village, a flash-flood began, and, near where Paneb stood, a small, half-finished wall crumbled and fell. Several housewives came out on to their doorsteps and watched incredulously as the flood rose.

'Climb up on to the terraces!' yelled Paneb.

Children began to cry. Outside Pai's house, a small boy standing up to his knees in water lost his balance and the flood began to sweep him away. Paneb grabbed him by the feet, plucked him clear of the water and handed him to Nakht, who had just splashed his way up the street.

For a moment, the two men glared at each other with hatred.

'Take that child home,' said Paneb urgently, 'and check that no others are wandering about outside. And pass on the word, quickly: everyone on to the terraces.'

At the rate the water was rising, all ground-floor rooms would soon be awash. In the lay workers' area, the walls of dried mud would collapse.

Paneb turned pale.

The power of the storm could mean only one thing: another, even more serious, danger threatened. Forcing his way through the water, he went as quickly as he could to the Master's house.

'We must go to the Valley of the Kings at once,' he said. 'Meneptah's tomb is in danger.'

Ignoring the turmoil in the village, the two men passed through the main gate and hurried up to the pass. Without their perfect knowledge of the path, on which stones clashed together and rolled under their feet, they could not have got through the curtain of rain and would have lost their way on the mountain, where the thunder's roar was deafening.

But neither of them had time to be afraid or to think about their cut and bruised feet. At breakneck speed, they scrambled down the slope to the entrance to the Valley of the Kings.

Soaked but stoical, Penbu was at his post.

'Come with us, Penbu, quickly!' shouted Paneb above the roar of the wind.

The three men hurried to Meneptah's tomb, where Tusa was frantically piling up limestone debris to form a protective wall in front of the entrance. A torrent of mud and scree was hurling itself against the fragile barrier.

'It's no good, it won't hold,' yelled Tusa. 'Let's get out of here before we're washed away.'

The stream of mud would flood into Meneptah's tomb and cause irreparable damage.

'You go,' Paneb yelled back. 'I'm staying here.'

The two Nubians hesitated for a few seconds, then made for safety.

'Go with them, Nefer. You're exhausted.'

'No good captain abandons his boat when it's in danger of sinking. Let's act, not talk.'

The only solution was to build a wall made out of shards of rock and thick enough to divert the stream. Ignoring his tiredness, Nefer worked harder than ever, though he kept losing his footing and at times the rain blinded him. In front of him, the young giant heaved rubble into a rampart in front of the tomb.

From time to time, Paneb let out cries of revolt against the heavens' onslaught, but he never slowed his pace, and the Master found it more and more difficult to keep up. Using up his last reserves of energy, Nefer nevertheless managed to help his friend. Knee-deep in the mud, he pulled out large stones which Paneb heaped on top of one another.

A vicious bolt of lightning ripped through the clouds and struck the Peak of the West.

'Ubekhet!' screamed Nefer.

'She's up there?'

'She went to consult the goddess, and she hadn't come down again when you came to find me.'

The rain calmed suddenly, and a corner of blue sky appeared.

'Meneptah's tomb is safe,' said Paneb. He was covered in mud, but his smile was joyous.

'Ubekhet . . .'

Paneb pulled Nefer out of the muddy tide, whose last waves were breaking against the wall.

'I must climb to the summit,' said Nefer, 'and find out if she's safe.'

'You can't take another step. Rest here. I'll go.'

The sun burst through, and the two men drank the last drops of rain that washed their faces.

'Look, Nefer, look! There she is!'

Her head circled with gold, the Wise Woman was walking down from the peak, holding the great pickaxe.

63

The Wise Woman held up the pickaxe, and showed it to all the assembled villagers.

'Here is the tool you thought Paneb had stolen. I exposed it at the summit to conjure the anger of the god Set, whose storm almost destroyed the pharaoh's tomb and our homes. Lightning struck the pickaxe, and its terrifying light has traced signs upon it.'

Thuty the Learned approached and was able to make out the head of the beast of Set, its long muzzle and large ears traced by the sky's fire.

'Paneb saved Pharaoh's house of eternity,' said Nefer. 'Had it not been for his courage, the crews' work would have been reduced to nothing and the Place of Truth would have been accused of negligence. In the name of Set, son of the sky and master of the storm, may this pickaxe belong to him for ever.'

'This unusual gift must be noted in the Journal of the Tomb,' observed Imuni, 'otherwise, Paneb will have difficulties with the government.'

Nakht grabbed him by the collar of his pleated shirt. 'Why don't you keep your mouth shut, you little runt?'

'Actually,' said Paneb, 'I agree with him. These events ought to be noted down so that no one can argue about my ownership of this tool.' Roaring with laughter, he raised the pickaxe to the dazzlingly blue sky.

'Does that mean you won't be leaving just yet?' inquired Nefer.

'Who said anything about leaving?'

'You invited me to Thebes, General Mehy, and here I am,' declared Prince Amenmessu confidently.

Mehy bowed. 'It's a great honour, for Thebes and for myself.'

'I'm eager to ride the stallion you promised me.'

'It is at your disposal.'

'Will you leave your office and your scrolls, and come and show me the best rides in the desert?'

'With pleasure.'

As happy as a child who had just been given a longed-for toy, Amenmessu leapt on to the back of a magnificent black charger which was led up to him by the general's groom. Mehy had chosen for himself an animal which was less spirited but a stayer, and the two horsemen set off at a flying gallop westwards, towards a dried-up riverbed.

When Amenmessu stopped, he was drunk with pleasure. 'What a wonderful place Thebes is – I like it far better than the Delta. You're very lucky to live here, General.'

The two men dismounted and sat down on some nearby rocks to slake their thirst with water from a goatskin bag.

'Does your visit, Prince, mean that Pharaoh has indeed consolidated the peace?'

'No, General, it means just the opposite. The king has just sent huge quantities of wheat to the Hittites, because they're worried that the rulers of some of the neighbouring states may be considering invading. Egypt must feed her allies so that they'll stay loyal and form the first line of defence against an invasion from the north.'

'Is that usual?'

'Fairly usual,' said the prince. 'But I think there's another and more serious threat: the Libyans.'

'But surely they're too weak and too divided to be a serious threat?'

'That's what many people say. But my father doesn't agree. His informants in the region think the Libyan tribes might start banding together, and if they did they'd become extremely dangerous.'

'Has the pharaoh been told about this?'

Amenmessu looked uncomfortable. 'Some of it.'

'Is he as worried as your father?'

'Yes and no. He's more concerned about the eastern states than about Libya.'

'I'm going to show you something remarkable, Prince.' Mehy took an arrow from his quiver and passed it to Amenmessu. 'Look closely at the arrowhead.'

The prince examined it for a long time, and fingered it. 'It's incredibly hard.'

'Even harder than you think. It was made at the workshop on the west bank, and it will soon be used by the Theban troops. And there are other new weapons to come.'

'Impressive, very impressive.'

'You're the first person to see this little marvel.'

'You mean . . . before even Pharaoh?'

Mehy didn't answer.

'Do you think, General, it would be better if no one else knew about it?'

'That might be useful if you accede to the throne.'

Amenmessu suddenly saw a vast horizon opening up before him. 'Would the Theban troops be loyal to me if I asked for their support in . . . what shall I say? . . . exceptional circumstances?'

'I firmly believe, Prince, that you have all the qualities of a great leader, and that you will show them in the service of Egypt.'

Amenmessu was overwhelmed. Mehy had put into words his secret ambition, which he had not yet dared to admit so clearly, even to himself. Meneptah was old, Seti too authoritarian and too unpopular at court; whereas he, Amenmessu, was young, dashing and charming . . .

'I'll take you all round Thebes, and introduce you to all the most useful people,' promised Mehy. 'And we'll visit the main barracks, where you can see my elite troops on exercise.'

Paneb had feasted on perfectly roasted sucking-pig flavoured with sage, cooked by Ubekhet, and drunk a celebration wine worthy of a royal banquet. Ubekhet and Nefer watched him, smiling.

'Thank you for that wonderful meal,' he said, when at last he could eat no more. 'I really didn't deserve it. I behaved like a complete idiot, and I have to admit I'm still not sure I've overcome my pride and could bear injustice without fighting back.'

'We've taken a serious decision about you,' said Nefer.

'My punishment?'

'I hope you won't think of it that way. But we have to summon you before the court.'

Paneb's face fell. 'Will I at least be able to defend myself and explain why I wanted to leave?'

'That won't be necessary. All you'll have to do is answer yes or no.'

'The stone-cutters accused me falsely, and they—'

'It isn't about that.'

'It isn't? Well, then, what is it?'

'In accordance with a common custom, Ubekhet and I want to adopt you. If you're officially our son, you'll be entitled to our protection; anyone who attacks you will be attacking us as well. In addition, you'll become our heir – but don't expect to get rich!'

'But the decision is yours,' stressed the Wise Woman with a smile which would have calmed the most savage of demons.

Paneb emptied his wine-cup in a single gulp. 'Can't you tell what it is?'

Mehy was furious and worried.

Furious, because his plan to get rid of Paneb had failed. Not only that but, according to his spy's latest letter, Paneb had been adopted by the Master and the Wise Woman, which meant an attack on him was now virtually impossible unless he committed a serious crime, and he seemed to be growing more and more wary.

Worried, because he was about to go to the landing-stage on the west bank to greet Prince Seti, who was paying an unexpected official visit to Thebes. Mehy would much have preferred to maintain the initiative by going to Pi-Ramses to meet the prince, and indeed was in the middle of planning such a trip. Seti's visit might be dangerous.

It was only a few weeks since the visit of Seti's son, Amenmessu. He had thoroughly enjoyed his stay, and Mehy and Serketa had done all in their power to foster his ambition to become pharaoh, and to convince him he had the ability to rule – with their support, of course. Nor had they neglected other aspects of his character. During a drink-fuelled banquet, Serketa introduced him to a young Nubian dancing-girl whose amorous skills had entranced him. Amenmessu would not hear a word against the general or his wife.

Mehy had warned Amenmessu to guard his tongue, not to let slip anything about his ambitions, and to keep their friendship secret so that it would be all the more useful when the time came. But perhaps Amenmessu had been indiscreet? Perhaps he had said too much, or even boasted too loudly, and had stirred his father into action? Mehy had an appalling vision of his career in tatters, and even Serketa's sensual wiles could not calm him as they usually did.

He paced anxiously up and down the landing-stage, waiting for the prince to disembark.

Seti was a powerful man, in the full flower of maturity; he had a handsome but stern face and a confident step.

Mehy bowed deferentially before him.

'I am glad to see you again, General, after our brief conversation at Pi-Ramses. I have heard so much praise of your troops that I decided to come and see them for myself, and see whether the praise is justified. No doubt I'm merely being sceptical – but then, some of the sages do advocate constructive doubt. Let us lose no time: yours and mine are both valuable. Show me your barracks.'

'Am I to understand, my lord . . . Do you wish me to order a general mobilization?'

'No, no, General, nothing like that. Thanks to Meneptah's firm hand, our potential enemies are quiet, and the situation is calm. Nevertheless, I take the greatest interest in the Theban garrisons, for who can predict the future? One thing alone is certain: all men grow old. My beloved father bears the weight of the years, as do we all; on the day when I must succeed him, I hope to be able to count on the loyalty of all officials and senior officers. Do I make myself clear?'

'Thebes is devoted to you, my lord, and will remain so.'

'Did my son enjoy his visit?'

'Yes, my lord, I believe so. He liked Thebes and its surroundings; most of all, he liked the horse I had the pleasure of offering him, and he took it back to the capital.'

'He is a good horseman and a dreamer who likes enjoying himself. So long as he is content to look no higher, he will lead an agreeable, carefree life. And that's the best thing for him, don't you agree, General?'

64

Presided over by the Scribe of the Tomb, the court of the Place of Truth ratified Paneb's adoption by Ubekhet and Nefer. From now on, he would be referred to in all official documents as Paneb, son of Ubekhet and Nefer; he was his adoptive parents' heir, and he would serve their *ka* after their death.

Of course, this joyful event was accompanied by a celebration and several days' extra holiday, which were greatly appreciated after the long, intense work on Meneptah's tomb and temple.

The stone-cutters came to see Paneb, heads hanging low.

Fened acted as spokesman. 'We're not much good at apologies,' he said gruffly, 'but we blundered and we wanted you to know that we know it. So maybe it would be best if we made peace. After all, the main thing is to form a crew, and you could say that today we've adopted you, too.'

'You really have a gift for words,' said Paneb, embracing him.

'Paneb, do you remember the promise I made you, several years ago?' asked the Master.

'You've made several, and you've kept them all.'

'Not this one, not yet. To be honest, I was waiting until you were fully ready to receive what will be given to you.'

Then Paneb remembered. 'You mean . . . a journey to the pyramids at Giza?'

'You have a good memory.'

'But the tomb . . . my paintings . . .'

'The walls of the burial chamber will have to be polished and prepared for the grid before you can begin work on them, so you won't lose any time. Ched will lead the crew while we're away.'

Paneb hugged his adoptive father so hard that he almost suffocated him.

'Until my return,' Nefer told his wife, 'you will act as Master of the Brotherhood as well as Wise Woman. I'm sorry to burden you with these extra responsibilities, but it's necessary to show Paneb the message of the pyramids. There shouldn't be any major difficulties at either the tomb or the temple.'

'Is the North really as calm as people say?' asked Ubekhet anxiously.

'Seti's visit suggests that there's no imminent danger of war. In any case, even if the situation suddenly deteriorated, Memphis wouldn't be involved.'

'All the same, be very careful.'

'With Paneb beside me, I'm not afraid of anything. You and Kenhir are the only people who know where we're going and how long we'll be away. Kenhir has hired a boat in the name of one of the lay workers, and we shall leave tomorrow, before dawn.'

Ubekhet was still uneasy. 'It's strange: I sense this journey sometimes as a gentle setting sun, sometimes as an unpredictable storm. Promise me you won't take any risks, Nefer.'

The Master kissed his wife tenderly.

Paneb took in the landscapes as if he were drinking a great vintage wine from the Delta, and he enjoyed the mounting

April heat, as yet still tempered by the north wind. He always stood in the prow of the boat, and he felt as though he was taking possession of a new land, each aspect of which he was engraving in his memory.

He saw small villages with white houses, built on mounds beyond the reach of the Nile flood, palm groves and a peaceful countryside dotted with little shrines and imposing temples, which were served by landing-stages.

But all these were as nothing compared to the wonder he saw early one morning, bathed in the eastern light: the plateau of Giza and, rising above it, the pyramids of Khufu, Khafra and Menkaura,* guarded by a gigantic sphinx with the face of a pharaoh and the body of a lion. Awed by such beauty and grandeur, he stood for a long time contemplating the stone giants, whose limestone covering glinted in the sunshine.

'The builders of the Old Kingdom,' Nefer told him, 'created the origins of life by transforming the primordial unity into three hillocks, which rose up out of the primordial ocean.'

'Is that why the tomb of a Servant of the Place of Truth always has a little pyramid on top?'

'Yes. Even in a modest form, this symbol links us to our predecessors of the golden age. The pyramid is a ray of petrified light which comes from the world beyond, where death does not exist.'

Nefer led Paneb to the former map room where the giant pyramids had been designed; there stone-cutters were working, charged with the upkeep of the tombs of nobles who had faithfully served the builder kings.

* Khufu, 'May He [God] Protect Me', is sometimes known by the Greek name of Cheops; Khafra derives from Kha-ef-Ra, 'Like Ra, He Rises in Glory'; Menkaura's name means 'Ra's Creative Power is Eternal' ('Men-kau-Ra'); he is sometimes known as Mykerinos.

A bald, thickset man, who was obviously in charge of the workshop, greeted the visitors and asked who they were.

'My name is Nefer the Silent, and this is my adopted son, Paneb the Ardent.'

The overseer took a step back. 'Do you mean . . .? Are you the Master of the Place of Truth?'

Nefer showed him his seal.

The man's face lit up. 'There isn't a stone-cutter in the land who hasn't heard of you. It's a great joy to welcome you here.'

'Will you help me? I'd like you to teach Paneb the sacred geometry of the pyramids. We could have taught him at the village, but it's better that he should learn about it here, where he can see the monuments themselves.'

The overseer was only too delighted, and the lesson began at once. Paneb learnt the essence of the triangle whose sides were in a ratio of 3–4–5; the 3 corresponded to Osiris, the 4 to Isis and the 5 to Horus. The divine triad lived at the heart of the stone and was made active by the golden proportion, the key to the principle of harmony inscribed in natural forms and to the unity of a structure. He learnt the laws of the dynamic balance of architecture, where symmetry had no place, and he succeeded in reproducing complex calculations such as the volume of a shaft of a pyramid.

Enthusiastically, Paneb showed Nefer that he had learnt his lessons well.

'Don't get mired in theory,' advised the Master. 'Trust only the truth of the material and the experience of your hands; consider each monument, whether it is a small stele or an immense temple, as a living, unique being.'

'But I'm a painter, not a stone-cutter.'

'We're here to enlarge your vision, Paneb. A craftsman of the Place of Truth must know how to do everything, for no one can predict what work he may be called upon to do for the good of the Brotherhood.'

Each evening, father and son watched the sun go down over the pyramids of Giza, and for Paneb the experience was unforgettable.

King Meneptah was leaving the Temple of Amon, where he had celebrated the morning ritual, when he was stopped by the head of his personal bodyguard.

'A messenger from Syria has just arrived at the palace, Majesty, and is asking to see you urgently.'

The king received him in the audience chamber.

'The situation is very grave, Majesty. An enormous enemy alliance has been formed and is preparing to cross our north-eastern border and attack.'

'Who are the members of this alliance?'

'According to our scouts, there are Achaeans, Anatolians, Etruscans, Canaanites, Israelites, Minoans and Sards, and perhaps some Libyans and Bedouins. They make up a force of several thousand men who are determined to invade us and destroy everything in their path.'

'Why was I not warned sooner?' asked the king angrily.

'Majesty, the messengers had great difficulty getting through, and when they did they found it hard to convince some of the officials serving in the region. Many of the officials believed that the memory of Ramses was sufficiently alive to prevent such an alliance being formed.'

Meneptah immediately convened his council of war, to whom the messenger gave as many details as possible of the enemy's position and weapons.

'What do you propose?' asked the king.

'There is only one effective strategy, Majesty,' said the oldest of the generals. 'We must mass our troops on the border and make it impossible for the enemy to cross.'

His colleagues nodded in agreement.

'If we do that,' said Meneptah, 'on their march to the border the enemy will raze many villages to the ground and massacre thousands of civilians who thought they enjoyed our protection.'

'Alas, Majesty, such are the misfortunes of war.'

'If we wait for the enemy to reach our borders, General, we risk defeat. We shall adopt quite another strategy: we shall attack the enemy while he is on the move, in the heart of Syria.'

'That would be a very bold move, Majesty, and—'

'That is my decision, General. All our forces are to take part in the attack, so that we can strike hard and quickly.'

The head of military security on the north-western border was asked to report on how things stood there.

'I am extremely anxious, Majesty. The Libyan tribes are banding together, and I believe they're preparing to attack us.'

'How long do you think it will be before the Libyans are ready to attack?'

'About a month, Majesty. That is realistic if their objective is Memphis, as our spies believe.'

The members of the council of war were appalled. The Delta threatened from both east and west, Lower Egypt caught in a vice-like grip from which it would not emerge intact, a thousand-year-old civilization under threat of destruction . . .

'Majesty, we could use Theban troops as reinforcements to protect the city,' suggested one of the generals.

'Out of the question,' snapped the king. 'If the Nubians took advantage of the disturbances to rebel, Thebes would be defenceless.'

'But in that case, Majesty—'

'Our course of action is clear: we have one month in which to destroy the alliance and then return and save Memphis from the Libyan attack. Egypt's survival depends on it.'

65

When Paneb's training in geometry was over, the Memphis stone-cutters invited him and Nefer to visit the ancient city, Egypt's first capital. With them, Paneb explored the ancient citadel with its white walls, temples to Ptah, Hathor and Neith, the royal palaces and the craftsmen's quarter, before ending the day in a tavern where delicious cool beer was served.

The group had a splendid time swapping funny stories about their work and customers; Paneb was in the middle of one when an officer followed by a dozen soldiers entered the tavern.

'Silence!' he ordered. 'Listen carefully, all of you.'

Anxious eyes were fixed on him.

'The troops quartered in Memphis are on full alert, for there may be a Libyan attack at any moment. The situation is so grave that we need as many volunteers as possible to defend the city; if it falls into enemy hands, the whole population will be slaughtered. I hope you'll show how brave you are, and stand up now.'

Nefer wanted to get to his feet like the others, but Paneb prevented him, laying a hand firmly on his shoulder.

'Not you, Father. You're the Master of the Place of Truth, and you mustn't risk your life.'

'And you're a painter, and—'

'If I'm killed, Ched will finish the work.'

One of the stone-cutters spoke up on behalf of his comrades. 'Paneb's right, Nefer, and the officer will agree. Everyone knows how important the Place of Truth is to the king. Your place is there, not on the battlefield.'

'But Paneb's a member of my crew, and—'

'Exactly,' interrupted Paneb. 'It is up to me to defend the honour of our Brotherhood. Don't worry, the Libyans won't be disappointed.'

Meneptah struck quickly and hard, throwing almost all his troops into a decisive attack, at a moment when the alliance's leaders were quarrelling about who should be in command of whom, and how they were going to share out the prodigious booty they considered already won.

The first Egyptian army attacked from the east, the second from the south and the third from the west. The fourth acted merely as reinforcements, when the battle was already won. Disorganized and confused by contradictory orders, the alliance burst apart like an overripe fig. Some fugitives took refuge in the towns of Gezer and Ashkelon, which the Egyptians also captured; others escaped and joined the main body of the Libyan forces, which were massed near Fayum, south-west of Memphis.

The king gave his armies hardly enough time to catch their breath: as soon as the last pockets of resistance had been eliminated and Syria and Canaan were once again under control, he headed for Memphis at a forced march.

Prince Seti was waiting for him at the entrance to the white-walled citadel. 'Memphis will fight to the death against attack, Majesty.'

'We must not wait for the attack,' said the king. 'We must use the strategy that gave us victory in Syria. We shall engage all our forces.'

'But, Majesty, that would mean leaving Memphis utterly defenceless.'

'Last night, Ptah appeared to me in a dream and gave me a sword which drove doubt and fear from me. Send men to find out the Libyans' exact position. We shall crush them before they can attack.'

The Libyans had held several meetings to work out their plan of attack. Eventually, it was decided that a tribal chief named Merieh was to lead ten thousand warriors to conquer Memphis.

The defeat of the Syrians and their allies had not in the least shaken his resolve. That battle had been a tough one, and the Egyptian troops would be weary. Moreover, Memphis had few defences. When its defenders saw bearing down on them a yelling horde of tattooed, bearded warriors, each man's plaited hair garnished with two large feathers, they would be terrified and would not hold out for long.

After seizing Memphis, Merieh would sack the sacred city of Iunu, whose destruction would demoralize the enemy. Victory would follow upon victory, until the entire Delta had been conquered; then the Nubians would complete Egypt's downfall by invading from the south.

The alliance's defeat had not surprised Merieh. In any case, their major role had been to weaken the enemy by luring the troops far from Memphis, thus leaving the way clear for the Libyans to attack.

Merieh was determined to wipe out centuries of humiliation. Libya would, for the first time, defeat Egypt and seize its treasures. He himself would kill Meneptah, running him through with his spear, and he would not spare a single member of his family: the dynasty must be wiped out.

The new king of Egypt would be called Merieh.

The third day of the third month of the third season was torrid, as the end of May so often was. His wrists circled by bracelets, Merieh had donned a richly coloured robe decorated with floral motifs, and slung a belt across his chest. At his waist hung his dagger and short sword. His barber had trimmed his beard into a point and divided his thick hair into three sections, so as to create a long central braid, coiled up at the bottom; he had then decorated it with two ostrich feathers, one on either side.

After a copious lunch, which had reinforced their already high morale, the Libyan soldiers were simply waiting for the signal to leave.

Just as Merieh was leaving his tent, a horseman galloped into the camp and wrenched his horse to a halt in front of his leader. 'The Egyptians – over there!'

'Scouts?'

'No, an army, an enormous army with the pharaoh at its head!'

'It can't be. He can't possibly be back from Syria already.'

'We're surrounded!'

The first volley of arrows claimed only a few victims, but they caused panic in the Libyan camp. Merieh had the greatest difficulty in gathering his men together, for they were running about in all directions. The first Egyptian foot-soldiers were already breaking through the makeshift palisades, supported by archers who fired relentlessly.

'Quickly!' shouted Merieh. 'To the canal!'

Trying to defend the camp would be suicide: they must get to the boats and beat a retreat.

Leaping flames rooted Merieh to the spot: the Egyptians had attacked from all sides and set fire to the boats. Around him his men were falling to an implacable foe who was making lightning progress.

The battle was entering its sixth hour and would soon be over. After the initial rout, the Libyans had recovered and had fought hand to hand, knowing the enemy would give no quarter. Merieh had regrouped his last forces to attempt a counter-attack, in the hope of breaking out of the circle.

Paneb was having a wonderful time. He'd seen the Libyans scatter like mice and he'd caught a good fifty of them on the run. Swords and daggers held no fears for him; he joyfully broke each opponent's forearm and then knocked him out with one blow. He reaped prisoners everywhere he fought, watched in disbelief by the other soldiers.

The Libyans' camp was in flames, and the smoke covered their flight. Paneb knocked out a dozen who made the mistake of fleeing in his direction.

He spotted one tall man, dressed in a multicoloured robe and the finest-quality sandals, who was trying to climb aboard a chariot drawn by a horse which was too terrified to move. The animal reared, whinnying, and the Libyan gave up.

'You, over there!' roared Paneb. 'Surrender or I'll break your bones!'

Merieh threw his javelin, but his aim was uncertain and it whistled past Paneb's shoulder. Annoyed by the attempt, Paneb rushed at him.

A Libyan attempted to protect his leader's escape, but Paneb smashed his nose with his elbow. Terrified, Merieh took off his sandals to run faster; the feathers from his head-dress fell to the ground and were trampled by his pursuer. They soon became soiled with the blood of the Libyans.

In a single bound, Paneb leapt on to Merieh's back.

Although the victory had only just been won, a host of scribes had already started making notes so that they could present Pharaoh with a detailed report.

The most senior scribe approached the king, who was contemplating the battlefield where his men had saved Egypt, and presented him with the first estimates of the goods taken from the enemy: 44 horses, 11,594 oxen, donkeys and rams, 9,268 swords, 128,660 arrows, 6,860 bows, 3,174 bronze vases, 531 items of gold and silver jewellery and 34 lengths of fabric. Of the Libyan forces, 9,376 had been killed and 800 taken prisoner; the rest had fled.

'Majesty, there's one more prisoner to add to the list,' said a strong voice. 'Their leader.'

He came nearer, pushing Merieh in front of him. Trembling, the Libyan threw himself at Meneptah's feet to beg for his forgiveness.

The king ignored him and looked closely at his captor. 'I know you,' he said. 'Are you not a craftsman from the Place of Truth?'

Paneb bowed low. 'Majesty, I am Paneb, son of Nefer the Silent, Master of the Place of Truth, and Ubekhet, the Wise Woman.'

'Why are you here?'

'Nefer wanted me to see the pyramids and Memphis. The gods in their generosity permitted me to take part in this battle and bring you back this coward, who was trying to run away.'

Paneb hoped his exploits would soon be celebrated throughout the whole country, and people would know that the Place of Truth's craftsmen would not hesitate to fight alongside Pharaoh's soldiers.

'I shall entrust you with an important mission, Paneb. A scribe will give you a papyrus containing the account of my victory over the Libyans and the victory of light over darkness. You are to go to Karnak, where you are to engrave this text on the inside wall of the eastern side of the innermost courtyard of the Temple of Amon. Let all those present worship Amon for guiding our hearts and giving strength to our arms.'

A silent prayer rose to the blue sky of a hot May evening. The Two Lands would savour their safeguarded peace.

66

The letter from the governor of Aswan was alarming: according to trustworthy informants, rebellion was brewing in Nubia. Several tribes considered it a good time to invade Egypt from the south and attempt to join forces with the northern conquerors. It would then be time to begin negotiations and to share out the spoils of the shattered country.

Mehy could not act without orders from Pharaoh, who might need the Theban troops in the Delta, where the outcome of the war was uncertain. He therefore restricted himself to putting his garrisons on full alert and sending a messenger to Pi-Ramses to ask for precise instructions.

The arrival of Prince Amenmessu dispelled all doubts.

'Total victory, General. The Libyans and their allies have been destroyed. The king's strategy worked wonders; attacking the enemy before they could attack him.'

This news did not cheer Mehy.

'You seem annoyed, General. Aren't you pleased about Meneptah's victory?'

'It gives me the greatest joy, but the danger isn't over: there's a rebellion in Nubia.'

'The pharaoh foresaw it, and I have indeed returned here to give you his orders: attack immediately, leaving as few soldiers in Thebes as possible. We shall share command.'

If Meneptah had sent only Prince Amenmessu, it was

because he counted on Mehy's authority and the power of the Theban army to crush the Nubians, who were brave but badly organized. The prospect pleased Mehy because it meant he could try out, in a real battle, Daktair's new arrowheads and short swords.

'My men are ready to leave, Prince.'

'This will be my first victory, General.'

Cheered by the lay workers who had already heard of his exploits, which kept on growing as they passed from mouth to mouth, Paneb was greeted warmly by the two crews of the Place of Truth.

'Did you really kill more than a hundred Libyans?' asked Nakht.

'I didn't kill anyone, but I took a few prisoners, including their leader.'

'Did you see the king?' asked Pai.

'He ordered me to engrave the account of his victory on a wall at Karnak.'

The craftsmen parted to allow their Master through.

'I was forced on to a boat for Thebes,' he explained, 'though I wanted to stay in Memphis.'

'And quite right too,' said Paneb. 'As I promised you, I really had nothing to fear. And through me the pharaoh has decided to reward the Brotherhood.'

'Is he giving us choice foods and great wines?' asked Renupe.

'They'll be delivered tomorrow, and we shall also receive a huge quantity of precious metals, part of which is for making tools.'

'And the rest?' asked Fened anxiously.

'It will be shared among us.'

'So,' said Didia, 'we are going to be rich!'

'Well,' declared Karo, 'I'm going to buy myself a milk-cow.'

While everyone was talking loudly about what they were going to do when they were rich, Uabet brought Aapehti to see his father; she was very proud of her husband's exploits.

'I was afraid,' she confessed, 'but I knew you'd come back.'

'Even a little scrap of a woman like you could have beaten the Libyans. All they can do is run – the only frightening thing about them is their tattoos. I brought back the chief's two feathers for Aapehti; they'll remind him that you must never run away.'

'You've become a hero,' commented Ched, not without irony.

'Do you know what I was thinking about before I knocked out those Libyans? The paintings we've still got to create in the royal tomb.'

'I didn't make much progress while you were away.'

'Ipuy and Renupe will help me engrave the hieroglyphs at Karnak, and I'll be back here as soon as possible. If you could see the colours I have in my head . . .'

Paneb thought he could see a kind of relief in Ched's eyes, as if the teacher had been waiting impatiently for his pupil. But no, he must be mistaken.

The celebrations lasted long into the night. Everyone realized that Paneb, whatever his faults, was an indispensable part of the Brotherhood. And even his strongest opponents knew it was his boldness and bravery that had enriched them.

Eventually, arm in arm, Ubekhet and Nefer left the revels and made for home. When they got there, Nefer went into the bedroom. He was about to lie down on the bed when Ubekhet's voice froze him to the spot.

'Don't go any further, I beg of you!'

She lit a lamp and came up to her husband. By the light of the flame, they made out an enormous black scorpion on the pillow, its tail raised, ready to strike. If the Master had lain down, he would have been stung on the back of the neck and would have had little chance of survival.

'Step back slowly,' she told him.

'I'll go and fetch a stick.'

'No, don't try to fight it. There's an evil energy within it – that's what I detected.'

The Wise Woman advanced, and so did the scorpion. She recited an ancient incantation revealed by Isis: 'Do not move: I shall close your mouth. May your poison become frozen, or I shall cut off the hand of Horus and blind the eye of Seth. Remain calm, like Set the vindictive before Ptah, the master of artisans! Turn your poison against yourself; go back into the darkness from whence you came.'

The creature turned round and seemed to grow smaller. Suddenly, with a violence which took the Wise Woman by surprise, it stung itself and died in front of them.

Ubekhet burned the body.

'Someone put this killer in our bedroom,' she said, 'and put a spell on it. It's a spell all the craftsmen use to avoid being stung when they are in the mountains, but this time the magic words were reversed, to make the scorpion grow and become more aggressive.'

'The shadow-eater again,' said Nefer. 'When will he stop doing harm?'

'He's gone too far to give up. From now on, you shall wear an amulet representing the knot of Isis; inside it, I shall place a tiny papyrus on which words of protection are written.'

Thanks to a steady wind, the Egyptian fleet sailed rapidly towards the Great South. Mehy had brought a large supply of foodstuffs, in case the campaign was a long, harsh one. And Prince Amenmessu was very impressed by the number of arrows, bows, javelins and swords loaded on to the cargo vessel.

'We've made great strides,' Mehy told him. 'The

spearheads are now as hard and solid as the arrowheads, and they can pierce armour. As for the cutting edge of the swords, it will surprise you.'

'So many new weapons – it's remarkable.'

'They'll certainly help us defeat the Nubians. But don't you think that, for the time being, only the Theban troops should use them?'

'A wise suggestion, General.'

Amenmessu's regard for Mehy was greater than ever, because the general had shared with him a military secret of the utmost importance. As soon as Meneptah died, a ruthless struggle for the throne would begin between Seti and his son; and Amenmessu now had an advantage which would prove all the more significant because his father was unaware of it. Mehy had chosen his camp, that of youthful ambition, and Amenmessu would remember that well when he ascended the throne.

'This countryside is magnificent, but it worries me,' said the prince. 'Archers could well be lying in wait among the palm trees.'

'I've sent out several mounted scouts. Some have taken the track that runs along the side of the Nile, the others have ridden into the desert. As soon as they spot the enemy, they'll turn back to warn us.'

'Your men seem very confident.'

'They're well trained and ready to react to the first sign of danger. That is the result of the reforms I've carried out over the last few years to shake up the garrisons.'

Amenmessu admired the general. His court would be composed solely of battle-hardened men like him.

In the distance, he made out a cloud of dust. A scout was galloping towards them.

The horseman's detailed report enabled the Theban troops to launch a surprise attack on the Nubian camp. The new weapons proved terrifyingly effective: the arrows and spears easily pierced the Nubians' shields, while the swords sliced through their daggers and javelins.

Despite their courage, the black warriors could not hold out for long and soon found themselves reduced to a last square of men who, despite the victor's orders, stubbornly refused to surrender.

Mehy ordered his archers to back off, and the Nubians thought that he was going to spare their lives. But in fact he wanted to know the greatest distance from which new arrowheads would kill, after piercing shields and breastplates. The experiment pleased him, for not one of the Nubians survived the volley, even though it was fired from so far away that with ordinary weapons it would have been virtually harmless.

When they heard of the massacre, the second rebel tribe laid down their arms, and their chief begged General Mehy to grant him pardon. Mehy deferred to Prince Amenmessu, who felt it necessary to prove his firmness by condemning the rebels to slavery in the gold mines.

'My lord,' said Mehy deferentially, 'you can now write and inform the king that you have put down the Nubian revolt and that Egypt has no more to fear from the South. My men and I congratulate you on this magnificent success, which will undoubtedly be greeted by great celebrations both in Pi-Ramses and Thebes.'

The first victory of a future pharaoh . . . Amenmessu listened delightedly to Mehy's words; the general had been clever enough to discern his true nature.

67

Following the Master, Paneb walked along the series of straight passageways leading to King Meneptah's funerary chamber, which was lit by lamps with smokeless wicks.

The two men halted on the threshold of the great vaulted chamber with its two lines of columns, to the east and the west. To the north and south, four small rooms had been excavated, and in them the royal treasure would be placed. Sixteen small niches hollowed out of the eastern and western walls would receive statuettes designed to watch over the sarcophagus where, night after night and day after day, the mystery of resurrection would take place, away from human sight.

Beyond the vast chamber was a sort of vault made up of three shrines, the middle and smallest of which went deep into the rock.

'The stone-cutters' work is finished,' declared Nefer. 'It is now up to the artists and painters to bring these walls to life, with the exception of the last small room.'

'Is the tomb to remain unfinished?'

'Only apparently, like all those in the Valley. It is fitting that the Invisible and the mother rock, not man, should lay the last glance upon a house of eternity.'

The area to be decorated was considerable, and Paneb felt an immense longing well up within him, a longing to bring these as-yet-dumb walls to life.

'How much time are you allowing the painters?' he asked.

'The symbolic figures Ched has chosen will be particularly difficult to execute, but they're in accordance with the dimensions of the place. We are in the heavens here, and time no longer counts; all that matters is the quality of the work.'

At the age of six, Aapehti was already the size of a ten-year-old; and he had a ferocious appetite. He was beginning to put his father's teachings into practice, and used his fists freely to force his companions into games he wanted to play.

But his father, who had firm ideas on children's upbringing, was not content with these first successes. Like all children born in the Place of Truth, once he could read and write Aapehti would be free to leave the village to work at the profession of his choice. Some chose to carry on their studies at the school for scribes in Karnak, others became managers of nobles' estates or set themselves up in town as craftsmen. The girls who decided to leave usually found good husbands, who were glad to marry an educated woman, and some went into business.

Paneb was unbending when it came to Aapehti's performance at school, and he made him do any failed exercises all over again. He also taught him to decorate pots, to make sandals, to help his mother do the cooking and to help any artisan who needed a hand.

When she saw Aapehti carrying a heavy jug of fresh water, Uabet felt it was time to intervene. 'You demand too much of him, Paneb.'

'When you're young, you mustn't under-use your strength. That little lad has energy to spare, and by making himself useful he'll learn how to live. Soft hands and tired feet produce nothing but useless individuals.'

'But he's only six!'

'Yes, he's already six. Luckily, Gau and Pai have agreed to teach him the rudiments of arithmetic. Aapehti often has his head in the clouds, so he'll get a few raps on the knuckles, and a few strokes of the stick, which will open up the ear on his back.'

The boy heard that, as he came out the kitchen, and punched his father on the leg.

'Not hard enough, boy. You need more training. Come on, we'll box.'

The walls and ceilings of the funerary chamber were ready to receive their complex decorations. Ched had invested all his knowledge and skill in this project, whose sheer extent had astonished Paneb.

To prepare himself for this work, which might be beyond his abilities, Paneb had decided to spend the evening alone, beside a water-channel which ran alongside the fields. The sun was going down, the peasants were bringing their flocks back from the fields, and music played on flutes wove patterns in the warm twilight air.

When a woman came out of the water, Paneb at first thought she was the dangerous goddess the stories talked of, the one who seduced men, turned them away from the path of righteousness and drew them towards a death so sweet that they fell asleep in her arms, listening to her song.

But then he recognized her long red hair, which tumbled down over her naked body. Turquoise moved with sensual grace, so excitingly that Paneb rushed towards her. But just as he was about to touch her, his mistress escaped him and dived into the canal.

She swam less strongly than he, but was more agile; several times, she escaped him when he thought he had caught her. Then she let herself be caught and, mad with desire, they rose to the surface, limbs entwined. Their faces bathed by the last rays of the setting sun, they made passionate love.

Afterwards, as they lay stretched out on the bank, Turquoise said, 'Don't you know that dangerous creatures live in these waters and that you have to conjure them with magic words?'

'What words would you like to hear?'

'Those of a painter who does more than merely doze in the cosy comfort of his little family. Few people are privileged to decorate a pharaoh's chamber of resurrection, and you're wasting your good fortune by squandering your energy on humdrum activities. Anyone can love his wife and be a good father. But you, you've been chosen by Ched to bring symbols of eternity to life in the heart of the Valley of the Kings.'

Paneb closed his eyes. 'If I confess that I'm afraid of what awaits me, will you believe me? I never stop thinking about the chamber the Master showed me, and the scenes sketched by Ched. I have realized my dream: I can draw and paint; but that tomb demands more from me. Perhaps I shan't come out of it alive. That's why I am bequeathing to my son as much as possible of what I've learnt. Do you understand that?'

There was no reply, so he opened his eyes. Turquoise had disappeared.

For a moment, he wondered if he had fallen victim to the formidable seductress who lived between two waters; but neither Turquoise's deeds nor her words had led him towards oblivion.

In the great audience chamber in the palace at Pi-Ramses, General Mehy appeared before King Meneptah to report on the pacification measures he had taken in Nubia, and on his running of the Theban province; in both cases, the results were good.

The king, who listened rather distractedly, made no comment and withdrew into his private apartments the moment Mehy had finished.

Disappointed and anxious, Mehy was walking slowly away from the palace when Seti stopped him.

'You look worried, General. And yet people say nothing but good of you, in Pi-Ramses.'

'To be honest, I have the feeling that my report did not please His Majesty.'

'Did he make any criticisms?'

'No, none.'

'Then there's nothing to worry about. My father has no taste for diplomacy. When he's dissatisfied, his words are as sharp as a sword.' Seti lowered his voice. 'Confidentially, he has been a little unwell these past few days. He has reduced his audiences to a minimum, and the simple fact of his having received you proves that he holds you in high esteem. Many dignitaries have not had your good fortune.'

'I hope Pharaoh's health will soon improve.'

'Our doctors are skilful, and his constitution is robust; but each of our destinies is in the hands of the gods. But tell me, General, your troops performed remarkably well in Nubia, did they not?'

'Their courage was indeed exemplary.'

'Did my son Amenmessu really prove himself worthy of the task?'

'He fought with great skill and courage, and you can be proud of him.'

'Would you do me a great service, General?'

Mehy bowed. 'If my modest abilities permit.'

'I fear he may react badly because of his youth and inexperience. I think it important to send him away from the capital for a while, until the future becomes clearer. And I think a man of your quality could help him to mature and understand his responsibilities. He will enjoy himself at Thebes, I'm sure. Who would not, living in that fine city under Amon's protection?'

'So I'm condemned to exile!' raged Amenmessu.

'Your father did not give me the impression your stay in Thebes is a punishment,' replied Mehy.

'He takes me for a fool, and he wants to get me away from

the court, where all the crucial events are going take place. You may not know it, General, but the king is ill and his doctors don't hold out much hope. Seti and Tausert consider themselves already crowned.'

'Possibly, Prince, but don't lose hope. If your father wants you away from Pi-Ramses, it's because he considers you a dangerous rival. Thebes is a long way from the capital, but it dominates the whole of Upper Egypt, and Pharaoh could not do without its wealth and Amon's protection. After all, the balance of the country rests on the union between South and North.'

'Are you hinting that Thebes might show its loyalty to me by daring to oppose my father?'

Mehy said solemnly, 'As long as Meneptah reigns, I shall carry out his orders faithfully.'

Amenmessu smiled. 'I shall go to Thebes with a joyful heart, General. With an ally of your calibre, my future looks brighter. And I shall retain sufficient support in Pi-Ramses to uphold my cause.'

Mehy wondered who, the father or the son, would win the war of succession. Seti seemed the favourite, but young Amenmessu's ambition was growing every day. It would, Mehy realized, take all his skill to ensure that he emerged a winner from this confrontation, whatever the outcome.

68

By the time Ched had finished the portrait of Meneptah wearing the ancient wig with stripes of blue and gold, and had put the last touches to the golden cobra rearing up on the monarch's brow, his eyes were very tired. He went down to the burial chamber, where Paneb was completing the essential scene representing the three states of Light, corresponding to the three stages of resurrection: a bright-red naked child, a black scarab and a red disc lighting up the name of Meneptah. Underneath was the hardest figure to execute: a ram with immense wings, evoking at once the creative power of the first sun and the capacity of the king's reborn soul to take flight.

Ched inspected the work. 'You've taken good care over the smallest details, Paneb, both simplifying the line and making the colours brilliant.'

The compliment astonished his pupil. 'Does anything need correcting?'

'No, nothing. Today, I can admit to you that the Master's plan terrified me: a tomb vaster than Ramses', larger chambers, a single central hub and a scheme of sculpture and painting the like of which has never been seen before. Nefer wasn't content to copy what his predecessors did; he has created a house of eternity in a new style, which will serve as a model for those who come after us. And I myself have had to change my way of painting while teaching you the intangible foundations of our craft. You were born with this tomb, Paneb. Your hand has been formed here, and you have no further need of me.'

'You're wrong, Ched, I need you badly. Without your eyes to guide me, I'd lose my way.'

'I alone know that you sometimes need reassurance when you have to go forward into the unknown. But you've never hesitated, and that's why I've given you everything that was given to me. You're no longer my pupil, Paneb. You're my equal.'

'I'm sorry to bother you,' apologized Imuni, 'but there have been some irregularities which I must warn you about.'

'I'm listening,' said Kenhir, but he went on writing his chapter on the temples built or restored during the reign of Amenhotep III.

'Gau has used much more papyrus than he was allocated.'

'No, Imuni. I gave him an extra supply so that he could draw detailed sketches for Hay.'

'A note to that effect must be made in the Journal of the Tomb.'

Kenhir threw his assistant a sidelong glance. 'Are you trying to teach me my job?'

Imuni turned pink. 'No, of course not.'

'Have you finished?'

'I must also point out that Userhat has received a block of alabaster whose destination was not stated on the delivery document.'

'That is quite normal, since it is destined for the preparation of the royal coffin.'

'No one told me,' complained Imuni.

'That is also normal. You are neither the Scribe of the Tomb nor the head sculptor, unless I'm very much mistaken.'

Imuni swallowed, but went on. 'Paneb's behaviour is also

unacceptable. He refuses to tell me how many cakes of colour he makes, he uses more wicks than necessary, and he wears out an incredible number of brushes. If the rest of the crew broke the rules the way he does, there'd be chaos.'

'Let us take these problems in order,' said Kenhir. 'Has there been any unrest on the site?'

'No, no, not yet.'

'And may I write in the Journal of the Tomb that Paneb has been present every single day?'

'Yes, that is true, but—'

'Do you agree that the work is going well, and that I can write a report to Pharaoh, giving this good news?'

'Indeed, but—'

'If you could tell the difference between important and trivial things, Imuni, you wouldn't make so many mistakes.'

'But measures must be taken to punish Paneb.'

'Don't worry, I shall take them.'

'May I know what they will be?'

'I shall speak to him and give him a warning, and tell him to make no changes whatsoever in his working methods.'

Her consultations over, Ubekhet continued her efforts to find a remedy which would prevent Ched from going blind. She had succeeded in slowing down the degeneration of his eyes, but that was all.

When Nefer entered her workshop, she was consulting a papyrus from the age of the pyramids, which described treatments of the disease-causing agents that could destroy sight.

'You work too hard, Ubekhet, and you're wearing yourself out.'

She smiled as he embraced her tenderly. 'I must try everything I can to save Ched's sight.'

'You never give up, do you? And have you found a possible cure?'

'His eyes are dying slowly because dangerous parasites

have entered them and little by little are destroying the blood and other liquids. To get rid of the darkness that threatens to invade the eye, I've used a solution made from frankincense, resin, white oil, bone marrow and balm-tree sap. The results haven't been satisfactory, though, and I think I now know why. There's an ingredient missing, one which will bring the whole thing to life and destroy the parasites without harming the eye.'

'What is this ingredient?'

'A mineral which the ancients called "wisdom".'

'In other words, the Stone of Light.'

'That's right. I have tried many, many other minerals, but they haven't worked.'

'So you'd like us to take a piece from the Stone, include it in your remedy and try to cure Ched.'

'I know what you'll say: the Stone must remain intact to give life to the sarcophagus, and the pharaoh's house of eternity should take precedence.'

'That's true,' said Nefer. 'But there's another consideration we can't ignore, even though it's terrifying. Suppose Ched is the shadow-eater?'

'No, Nefer, he isn't.'

'How can you be sure?'

'His manner might make him a suspect, I agree, and he has little regard for some members of the crew, but I hope to cure him.'

'Is this a demand from the Wise Woman?'

'That is for the Master to decide.'

The Scribe of the Tomb listened to the Wise Woman's explanation; the Master stood silently beside her.

'I do not at all like the idea of moving the Stone before taking it to Meneptah's tomb,' said Kenhir, frowning. 'In the present circumstances, it would be extremely dangerous. Can we not wait until the tomb is completed?'

'Between now and then, Ched will go blind,' said Ubekhet. 'If we act at once, there is still a chance of saving his sight.'

'A chance . . . but not a certainty.'

'We need your agreement,' said Nefer.

'Shouldn't the success of the Great Work take precedence over the wellbeing of one person?'

'Ched is an exceptional painter,' said Nefer, 'and he's the person who'll put the finishing touches to the major scenes in the tomb. Besides, he hasn't yet finished training Paneb, even if he does consider him an equal. If Ched is cured, both the Work and the Brotherhood will reap the benefits of his genius.'

'Now that is certainly a Master's reasoning.'

'Does it find favour with the Scribe of the Tomb?'

'Yes, I suppose so. But how will you take the piece?'

'In view of the Stone's hiding-place,' replied the Wise Woman, 'I shall use a copper chisel to chip off a small piece at sunrise, when the Stone is being re-charged with light. At that time of day, the craftsmen and their wives will be celebrating the cult of the ancestors, and no one will notice.'

'We should also arrange a decoy,' suggested Nefer. 'If the shadow-eater is indeed trying to find the Stone, he might well make a fatal mistake.'

Nefer assembled the starboard crew at the Brotherhood's meeting-place, and announced that work on Meneptah's tomb would soon be finished. Painters and artists were putting the finishing touches to their work, while the sculptors were finishing statues and sarcophagi. And Thuty was making the last items of jewellery that would accompany the royal soul into the afterlife.

Everyone knew that only the Stone of Light could bring to life the statues created in the village workshop. And no one was surprised to see the place locked and guarded by Paneb the night before they were to go to the Valley of the Kings.

As the next day would be a hard one, everyone went to bed early.

The traitor waited until the village was asleep, then he went out to watch the workshop where, he was sure, the Stone must be. Outwitting Paneb would be impossible, but he could not resist his desire to come as close as possible to the treasure.

To his immense surprise, the traitor saw that Paneb was not at his post. To gain access to the Stone, all he had to do was break a wooden lock. His hands moist, he crept forward, almost far enough to be seen, then panic stopped him in his tracks. What if this was a trap?

Yes, of course: they had set a trap for him. The treasure wasn't hidden here, but Paneb would be watching from concealment in case someone tried to steal it.

With catlike tread, the traitor crept silently away.

69

Userhat's chest swelled as he looked at the gilded statue of Hathor. Her body would be eternally young and slender, and her celestial smile would light up the darkness of the tomb.

'Polish the left heel a little more,' he told Renupe.

Renupe did so, using a round pebble wrapped in leather, while Userhat checked the other statues. They were made of gilded wood, and their eyes were set with cornelian, shining limestone and alabaster. Osiris, Isis and other deities would watch over Meneptah's treasures and take part in his resurrection each day.

Ipuy rushed into the workshop. 'I hope everything's ready. Tomorrow, the king's specialists arrive, and they'll be present when the statues are moved.'

'Is the Master missing me already?' asked Userhat. 'Instead of rushing around all over the place, help us finish.'

'I'm worried about the sarcophagi.'

'But the instructions I gave the stone-cutters were absolutely precise.'

'Karo's having breathing problems, and Fened's hurt his foot.'

'Tell them to see the Wise Woman and then get back to work.'

'They already have,' said Ipuy, 'but I'm still worried they may be late.'

'Take care of the statues. I'll go and see.'

In the workshop where the royal sarcophagi had been carved, Userhat found Nefer helping Nakht, Karo, Fened and Casa.

Userhat checked the sarcophagi carefully, and was completely reassured: they were masterpieces. 'There are just a few tiny details to sort out,' he said.

'Lifting them and lowering them into the tomb may well cause us problems,' said Nefer.

'Problems are my speciality,' said Casa. 'I shall check each rope myself and I promise we'll have no trouble.'

'What about the painters and colourists?' asked Userhat worriedly.

'They'll have finished by this evening,' replied Nefer.

Each man had the same thought. Up till now, the gods had been favourable; would they be at this final stage?

As he placed each drop of the Wise Woman's new remedy in his eyes, Ched the Saviour felt a slight burning sensation, which quickly faded. But there had been no noticeable improvement. Since the previous day, colours had a tendency to blur, and the deterioration of his eyes was becoming more apparent.

In the lamplit tomb, Ched looked at the paintings with their glowing colours. Paneb had succeeded beyond all Ched's hopes. He had made each shade of colour vibrate with an intensity only he could feel and bring to life.

Suddenly, the detail of a royal crown seemed more precise, and the contours of the royal eye, like that of a falcon, suprisingly clear. The colours shone more brightly, as if more lamps had been lit.

Ched swayed, but he did not dare lean against a wall or a column

Paneb's arm came round him and kept him from falling. 'Are you ill?'

'No, no, just the opposite.'

'Shouldn't you consult the Wise Woman?'

Ched smiled broadly. 'What a good idea, Paneb, what a marvellous idea! She's the very first person I shall go and see when we get back to the village.'

From his stone seat, Kenhir watched people coming and going. Fortunately, none of the starboard crew was missing from the call. Ubekhet had tended the sick during the two rest days and had pronounced them all fit for work.

Nefer brought Kenhir a cup of water.

'It's fortunate that someone in this Brotherhood thinks about me. The others would cheerfully leave me to die of thirst. If they think it's fun overseeing everything, so that nothing goes missing and no one can accuse us of anything . . . Ah well, each of us has his burden to bear. If the court of the afterlife judges us on what we have endured, I have nothing to fear.'

'I wish our trap had worked,' said Nefer regretfully.

'I've been thinking about it,' said Kenhir, 'and I find our failure rather reassuring.'

'But surely it means the shadow-eater is as suspicious as he is cunning?'

'Perhaps, but I have the feeling he's realized he hasn't the power to harm us.'

The Master considered Kenhir's words. One of the crew had taken the wrong path, forgetting Ma'at and her call. But was that error irreversible or had the man, because of his contact with his spiritual brothers, realized that it would lead only to his ruin? Had he decided to stay loyal to the village?

'But we cannot afford to relax our vigilance,' said Kenhir, 'especially now the Great Work is drawing to a close.'

'Do you know which dignitaries will be present when the statues are transported?'

'A band of pretentious little scribes, obsessed with their

petty privileges and prerogatives, who'd be delighted to be able to hand the tjaty a venomous report showing that the Brotherhood have no special talent.'

'That isn't exactly reassuring.'

Kenhir's expression became confident. 'Have you given the best of yourself, Nefer? And does the work conform to the plan adopted by Pharaoh and by yourself?'

'The answer to both questions is yes.'

'In that case, you can sleep soundly.'

'This gesture may seem irreverent, and I ask forgiveness in advance,' said Ched to the Wise Woman, 'but may I kiss you on both cheeks while your husband is not here?'

The patient and his healer shared an intense surge of emotion, and both shed a few tears.

'You must put two drops in each eye, morning and evening, until the end of your days,' Ubekhet reminded him.

'What a simple thing to do, and yet it enables me to see again, the way I used to. I've learnt a great deal during this period preparing myself to leave the world of colours. Without them, my life had no meaning and I was truly ready to die.'

'You're in excellent health,' said Ubekhet, 'and you seem to me a serious candidate for extreme old age.'

Ched said, a little awkwardly, 'I have little regard for the human race, Ubekhet, which seems to me thoroughly second-rate compared to the sky, to the light of day and of night, to animals, to plants and to all this prodigious creation where the gods make their voices heard. I even wonder if the celestial artist lost control of his brush when he drew us, myself as well as everyone else. But I have met one person who almost makes me believe a human being is worthy of admiration. I shall never speak of this to Nefer; but the Wise Woman, whom I admire unreservedly, will keep my secret.'

*

The Nile flood had been perfect, neither too strong nor too weak, and the harvest would be good. As governor of the west bank, Mehy had had to oversee the preparation of the water-channels and reservoirs. Nothing had gone wrong: he could be pleased with himself.

Serketa had just received a coded letter from the traitor. She read it quickly and said furiously, 'The Master has succeeded, and the king's tomb is almost finished – and still no trace of the Stone of Light! Our spy is a useless idiot.'

'I'm more hopeful than you,' said Mehy. 'He has to be very cautious, don't forget, but his help hasn't been worthless. Because of him, we know a great deal about the village and the Brotherhood. For example, we know that Meneptah and the tjaty have ordered senior officials from the Treasury to be present when the statues and sarcophagi are installed.'

'Will that be a problem for the craftsmen?'

'Not unless Nefer has made serious mistakes, which he almost certainly hasn't.'

'Couldn't you put pressure on the scribes so that they do find some faults?'

'No, it wouldn't be wise, not when the situation's so tense. Meneptah's health is deteriorating, and many people at court would oppose Seti's accession because they think him rigid, unintelligent and incapable of governing. Support for Amenmessu is growing stronger, and he himself believes more in his lucky star each day. So it's important that I'm not seen to side with either faction, and that I keep up my stance as the protector of the Place of Truth, whose role appears more vital than ever.'

'Amenmessu hasn't the bearing of a true king,' commented Serketa.

'You are undoubtedly right, my sweet, but that may be something we can profit from. A monarch like Ramses, or even Meneptah, would block our path to power. With Amenmessu, wide horizons beckon.'

'All the same, we should be wary of him, because he's both violent and unpredictable. And we mustn't neglect Seti, either, because he has many staunch followers.'

'The ideal solution would be a civil war, which would weaken both of them and enable us to emerge as the victors.'

Serketa ran her finger slowly over her greedy lips. 'What we must do is ask our spy in the Place of Truth to do something which will weaken the Master's position.'

She told her husband what she had in mind, and, although sceptical, he agreed.

70

On the eleventh day of the third month of the flood season in the seventh year of Meneptah's reign, an official delegation appointed by the pharaoh arrived at the main gate of the Place of Truth, where it was greeted by the Scribe of the Tomb.

The delegation was headed by a senior scribe from the Treasury, whose sole pleasure in life was the assiduous adding up of figures. Born in Thebes, he rarely left the city and this was the first time he had ventured into the desert; he hoped this onerous task would not take long.

He asked Kenhir, in a self-satisfied tone, 'Is everything ready?'

'What do you expect me to say?'

Taken aback, the scribe turned to his colleagues. 'Is there a special procedure which I have not been informed about?'

One of the tjaty's assistants said in his ear, 'Kenhir has a very bad temper. It's as well not to cross him.'

The scribe tried to smile.

'Why are you grimacing like that?' asked Kenhir. 'If you have criticisms to make, out with them. I shall examine them one by one.'

'But I haven't any! I've simply come to register that a certain number of statues have been moved, and to bring you some jars of good oil and some sweet pastries from the tjaty, to reward you for your work.'

'I'm glad tradition is being respected. Well, let's get on with it.' Leaning on his walking-stick, Kenhir stumped off, bumping into several officials who did not get out of his way quickly enough.

'Won't we be staying in the village?' asked the Treasury scribe.

'You are not authorized to enter, and the pharaoh's tomb has not been excavated here. We are going, under armed escort, to the Valley of the Kings.'

The scribe was dismayed. 'Do we really have to climb that mountain in this heat and dust?'

'When you check, check properly. That way, you can report accurately on the state of our equipment.'

Kenhir's old legs carried him along at a good pace, and his companions, though younger and stronger, had difficulty keeping up. It did not displease him to see them struggling along, constantly fighting for breath, their expensive clothes soaked in sweat; too many hours in the office had cut these scribes off from nature, and this little trial would make them less arrogant.

'Whatever you do,' he advised them, 'do not stray off the path. Around here, there are a lot of deadly scorpions; not to mention the horned vipers.'

To exhaustion was added fear, and the inspection of the settlement at the pass took only a few minutes. The Treasury scribe would have certified that almost anything was in perfect order, just to end this abominable walk as quickly as possible.

'Now,' warned Kenhir, 'we climb down to the Valley of the Kings. Tread carefully, because it's slippery and you could easily fall down the hill and break a few bones.'

As agile as a goat, old Kenhir had to wait several minutes at the entrance to the Valley for the delegation to catch up.

'Will we have to go back the same way?' asked the Treasury scribe anxiously.

'No, chariots will take you back by the road that ends near Ramses' Temple of a Million Years. Now for the search.'

'This is pointless!' protested the scribe.

'The rule must be followed to the letter,' said Kenhir emphatically. 'And I shall authorize only two people to enter the Valley: you and the tjaty's representative. The others will remain outside.'

A chorus of protests arose, but Kenhir refused to budge; the Nubian guards proceeded with the search.

Once the two officials had passed through the stone gateway, they were met by the Master. Without a word, he guided them to the monumental entrance to Meneptah's tomb, beside which the starboard crew were standing in a line, bearing offerings. At their head was Userhat, who held the 'worshipful staff' of gilded wood. With it, he would bring the statues to life so that they would open their eyes and light up Pharaoh, master of the land of Light, when he departed towards the sky.

The Treasury scribe and the tjaty's representative were breathless again, but this time it was because of the splendours they saw.

'The gods and goddesses have travelled from the House of Gold of the Place of Truth to that of the Valley of the Kings,' declared the Master. 'They are about to take the place reserved for them in this house of eternity, where they will watch over Pharaoh.'

Marvelling, the two scribes stood open-mouthed, watching the principal figures of the Egyptian pantheon pass by, all covered with gold; it took the craftsmen several trips to carry all the statues down into the tomb. The Treasury scribe wondered how so few men could have created so many masterpieces.

Kenhir had read the report of the tjaty's representative, and had told Nefer it was full of praise. The scribe and his

Treasury colleague had witnessed the statues being carried into the tomb, and the report stressed the excellence of the work accomplished under Nefer's direction. All that remained was the final stage: carrying the sarcophagi into the tomb.

That night Nefer was so tired that he hardly had the energy to wash his face.

'Until the last statue,' he confessed to Ubekhet as she prepared their beds, 'I was afraid something bad would happen. I begin to think our shadow-eater is losing his taste for destruction.'

'I fear the opposite is true.'

'Why?'

'Because your head-rest has disappeared.'

Nefer checked, and she was right: the wooden head-rest on which his pillow was laid was not in its usual place. 'Perhaps I put it in the sycamore chest by mistake,' he suggested.

Ubekhet lifted the lid. 'No, it's not here.'

They searched the whole house, but did not find it.

'Why would someone steal that humble object and nothing else?' said Nefer. 'It doesn't make sense.'

'I'm afraid it does, if the head-rest is indeed what the thief was looking for. And if I'm right, he'll try to use it against you.'

'How?'

'Your dreams and secret thoughts are imprinted in the wood. Anyone who knows how to decipher them would have power over you and could influence your decisions in future.'

'Is there any way of countering his power?' he asked.

'Yes, another head-rest on which are written incantations protecting sleep and driving away the thieves of dreams.'

'I'll make it tomorrow.'

'You must also inscribe incantations on your bed. Tonight, you cannot sleep there.'

'Will you let me share yours?'

*

Along with other craftsmen's wives, the traitor's wife went to the market held close to Ramses' Temple of a Million Years, on the edge of the farmed area. Delicious lettuces and a wide variety of spices were sold there.

As usual, each sale was preceded by long haggling. A peasant woman jostled the traitor's wife, who immediately set her basket down on the ground. Inside was the head-rest her husband had stolen from the Master's house. She picked up the empty basket the peasant woman had put down next to hers, and filled it with provisions.

'Here it is, my love,' said Serketa. 'I really enjoyed myself in that market, dressed as a peasant woman! Our ally does have his uses.'

'What are you going to do with it?' asked Mehy.

'I shall ask a magician to extract the dreams it contains and take possession of Nefer's thoughts. Then we'll be able to manipulate him like one of those jointed dolls children play with, and we'll know where he's hidden the Stone of Light.'

Mehy shrugged. 'Where are we to find this magician?'

'Tran-Bel knows a Syrian one who gets remarkable results.'

'Isn't dark magic illegal?'

'It is, and those who use it are severely punished. But the only one who'll be running any risks is the Syrian. We, my love, will be safe.'

'Are the sarcophagi finished?' asked Kenhir.

'Unfortunately not,' replied Nefer dejectedly. 'On closer examination, I found some small flaws which I couldn't permit. I've repaired them, of course.'

'Who was responsible?'

'I was. I should have noticed them sooner.'

'Hmm. You are taking someone else's error on yourself.'

'That's a crew-leader's duty.'

'You're lucky,' said Kenhir. 'The tjaty has been delayed at Pi-Ramses, and has informed me that the descent of the sarcophagi into the tomb will have to be postponed.'

'What's the new date?'

'It hasn't been fixed yet.'

'Does that mean there's trouble in Pi-Ramses?'

'I fear so,' replied Kenhir gravely.

71

The Syrian magician worked in a small house which Tran-Bel rented to him at an extortionate price – he also took a large cut from all the Syrian's fees. In the cellar, the Syrian had laid out the things he needed for his sinister art, from wax dolls, in which he stuck needles, to ivory batons covered with evil signs designed to harm the enemy from a distance.

The magician's head was too large for his body, and his thick lips and a pointed chin made him look grotesque. He liked to inspire fear by dressing in a black robe striped with red. But the woman standing before him seemed unimpressed.

'You are to make this head-rest speak,' ordered Serketa. 'I want to know the thoughts of the man who used it.'

'What is his name?'

'You don't need to know that.'

'On the contrary, it's vital that I do.'

'Do you swear never to repeat a word of our conversation?'

'Absolute discretion is one of the keys to my success.'

With Tran-Bel's agreement, the magician betrayed to the authorities the occasional client whom he considered too dangerous. In this way, everyone benefited, and the authorities left him in peace. He could tell that, beneath her girlish exterior, this woman was formidable. She was of high rank, without a doubt. He decided to denounce her, in exchange for a sizeable fee.

'His name is Nefer the Silent,' she said.

'Where does he live and what does he do?'

'Can't you work that out for yourself?'

'Yes, but it'll take time. If you're in a hurry, why not go straight to the essentials?'

'Are you a charlatan, then, not a real magician?'

The magician closed his eyes. Then, in a monotone, he described Serketa's bedchamber with incredible accuracy, leaving out not a single piece of furniture.

'Are you satisfied?' he asked. 'If not, I can describe everything you did yesterday evening, in detail. It's easy, because you're here with me: all I have to do is read your mind. But if you want me to extract thoughts from the head-rest, I need to know more about it and its owner.'

'Nefer the Silent is the Master of the Place of Truth.'

The magician licked his lips greedily. 'He is a very important person indeed. Perhaps we should first come to an understanding about the price of my services.'

'One gold ingot.'

'Add a house in the centre of the city. To someone with a fortune the size of yours, that's a mere trifle.'

'What do you know of my fortune?'

'Your clothes and your wig are only a disguise. Don't forget that the more I look at you the more I learn.'

'Make this head-rest speak, and you shall have whatever you want.'

Wealth . . . At last, the magician was reaching his goal! As soon as he had been paid, he would immediately alert the authorities, who would be delighted to capture such a prize and would not quibble about his fee.

The Syrian smeared the head-rest with a yellowish oil, then plunged it into a big alabaster basin of water in which poppies were floating. He murmured a series of incantations in an incomprehensible language, and laid his hands on the ends of the head-rest.

'What do you want to know?' he asked.

'Where is Nefer the Silent hiding the Brotherhood's most valuable treasure?'

'You must be more precise. Is it gold, documents or something else?'

Serketa hesitated for only a moment. 'It's a Stone of Light.'

The magician was intrigued: such a marvel would be very useful to him. But first he must make the head-rest speak, and he concentrated his thoughts on it.

'Where is the Stone hidden?' asked Serketa impatiently.

'I don't understand. I can't . . .'

'What's the matter?'

'There's a barrier, a barrier I can't cross. Someone has made this head-rest dumb. Someone has used magic stronger than mine.'

'Try again.'

Large drops of sweat stood out on the Syrian's brow. 'I am exhausting myself for nothing, and it's becoming dangerous. The head-rest is completely inert; it will tell me nothing.'

'You're nothing but a charlatan – and a charlatan who knows too much.'

Seizing the magician's hair, Serketa forced his head down into the basin of water. Worn out by his failure, the Syrian could resist only feebly. He breathed in water when he tried to call for help, and died of suffocation.

While waiting for the royal order concerning the descent of the sarcophagi into the tomb, Nefer, Ched and Paneb had checked each detail of the house of eternity.

The gilded cedar-wood door had been installed and locked, and two Nubian guards kept permanent watch over the site.

As he did every morning, the Master went to see Kenhir.

'Is there any news?' asked Nefer.

'Still nothing,' replied Kenhir. 'If there were serious

disturbances in the capital, rumours would be spreading. I don't know what to think any more.'

'Should we consult General Mehy and see if he's had any information?'

'I'll go and see him this afternoon.'

'Since the tomb's protection is assured, I shall take the starboard crew to Meneptah's Temple of a Million Years. The rites have already been celebrated there, and it, too, is almost finished.'

Although much smaller than Ramses', Meneptah's Temple of a Million Years was in no way inferior in terms of the quality of the materials or the splendour of the gateways, the porticoes and the columns.

What mattered was not the temple's size but its symbolic function, which was ensured by three shrines dedicated to Amon, 'the Hidden One', to his wife Mut, 'the Mother', and to their son Khonsu, 'He Who Crosses the Sky', and by the Osiran chambers where the royal soul was reborn. The temple was linked by magic to the tomb in the Valley of the Kings, and the two structures combined to maintain the pharaoh's immortality, thanks to the power of the hieroglyphs and paintings.

Amon and Osiris did not reign alone in this temple; to them was added the god of the Light, Ra, whose presence completed the process of transmutation. As he walked across the open-air courtyard devoted to Ra, Nefer sensed that the subterranean kingdom of Osiris and the celestial empire of Ra were the two faces of a single and identical reality, whose synthesis was created by the Stone of Light.

He would gladly have meditated for days on end in these peaceful chambers, far from the tribulations of daily life, but the craftsmen called him quickly back to the demands of his office. He must oversee the completion of the palace beside the first courtyard, the sacred lake and the brick-built warehouses. Soon priests, scribes and groups of people from different trades would live here, making this temple, like all the others, both a generator of spiritual energy and a centre of economic regulation.

'There soon won't be enough work for two crews,' commented Fened. 'The lads in the port crew haven't dragged their feet, and I haven't spotted any defects in the construction.'

Nefer entrusted the stone-cutters with the sacred lake's facing, the sculptors with positioning the statues, and the artists with drawing astronomical and astrological figures on the ceiling of the room leading to the innermost shrine.

Paneb looked critically at the colours. 'They aren't intense enough,' he said. 'The tomb is more alive than this. I shall go over everything again, to give it more impact.'

'The gods present on the walls will take charge of that,' predicted Nefer.

Paneb was silent for a few moments, then he said, 'The crew are worried.'

'Why?'

'If we aren't taking the sarcophagi into the tomb, it must be because Pharaoh is no longer capable of giving orders.'

'We mustn't jump to conclusions.'

'Can you think of any other reason for the delay?'

'We'll know when Kenhir has spoken to Mehy.'

'I'm needed in the courtyard, to pull blocks of stone. There's no better pastime when I want a rest from painting.'

Suddenly, Nefer realized that he hadn't seen Hay, so he retraced his steps. He found all the members of the port crew except their leader. He asked them where Hay was, but no one knew. Hay had certainly come with them to the temple in the early morning, but then he had vanished.

He knew he must tell Sobek at once. To his relief, as he was leaving the temple precinct he saw the commander coming towards him.

'I'm worried, Sobek. Hay has left the site without telling anyone where he was going. He may be in danger.'

'I don't think so.'

'Why do you say that?'

'I've waited a long time for the shadow-eater to make a mistake. And Hay has at last done just that.'

72

Nefer was stunned. 'You must be mistaken. Hay's the overseer of the port crew. He can't possibly be a traitor.'

'I don't make the accusation lightly,' said Sobek.

'But what proof is there?'

'During the last two months, Hay has gone five times to the east bank. He took care no one from the village saw him, and he succeeded in throwing my men off his tail. And now, today, he's even left his post, probably because he has urgent information to pass on.'

The Master was seriously alarmed. As crew-leader, Hay knew where the Stone of Light was hidden. Had he gone to warn his accomplices, so that they could try to seize it by force?

'I have put a lot more security measures in place,' Sobek said reassuringly, as though he'd read Nefer's thoughts. 'If Hay doesn't return to the village, there'll be no room for doubt about his guilt.'

'I do sympathize, my dear Kenhir, but you're asking a great deal.' Mehy paced to and fro across his office, hands clasped behind his back.

'Surely the Brotherhood should be told what's happening in the capital,' insisted Kenhir.

'Why is it so urgent?'

'Because King Meneptah's tomb and temple are finished. We're awaiting the inauguration of the temple and the order to take the sarcophagi down into the tomb.'

'I understand, I understand.'

'Is the king still at the helm of the ship of state?'

'According to my latest information, yes; but I don't know anything like all the labyrinthine goings-on at court. The tjaty is staying down in Pi-Ramses, and he'll enlighten us as soon as he returns to Thebes. By the way, Prince Amenmessu, one of the serious candidates to succeed Meneptah, is living here at the moment.'

'Will it be an open succession?'

'I don't know,' said Mehy. 'For my part, I shall obey orders only if they come from the palace and are duly authenticated. In the meantime, I shall continue to protect the Place of Truth; and anyone who tries to attack the Theban region will come up against my troops.'

Reassured, Kenhir set off back to the village. At the first fort he found Sobek and the Master waiting for him, grim-faced.

'Our suspicions have fallen on Hay,' said Sobek, and he repeated the reasons why.

'Hay?' cried Kenhir. 'That's impossible! Have you questioned him?'

'He hasn't come back yet. In my opinion, he won't dare to.'

'There are two full hours until sunset.'

The three men sat down on craftsmen's stools and watched the track, which remained cruelly empty. All were thinking about Hay's character, his behaviour, the attitudes that led them to think that he might have betrayed the Brotherhood.

At last Hay appeared. He was striding along, but when he saw the three men, he froze.

'If he tries to run away,' announced Sobek, 'I shall seize him.'

Hay seemed to hesitate, then he came on towards them. 'What are you all doing here?'

'Where have you been?' demanded Kenhir.

'That isn't important.'

'You left the temple site without an explanation, and that is a serious dereliction of duty.'

'I gave my orders this morning, and the work can't have suffered during my brief absence.'

'Nevertheless, it is not the correct procedure,' said Kenhir. 'You should have informed me, so that I could register the reason for your absence in the Journal of the Tomb.'

'Yes I should; so you'd better punish me.'

'Whom did you go to meet?' demanded Sobek.

'I told you: that isn't important.'

'In that case, why did you evade my men?'

No trace of emotion showed on Hay's stern face; his brow was furrowed with deep lines. The man seemed to have aged suddenly under the effects of a painful trial.

'I don't like being followed,' he said.

'Not good enough,' said Sobek. 'What are you trying to hide?'

'It's nothing to do with the Place of Truth.'

'If you refuse to talk, I shall arrest you.'

'You can't, not without authorization from the Scribe of the Tomb and the Master.'

'I have that authorization.'

Hay looked from Nefer to Kenhir. 'So you're all against me.'

'I'm sure you have nothing to be ashamed of,' said Nefer, 'and you have my complete trust. If you'll tell me what's going on, perhaps I can help you.'

'Do you mean that?'

'On Pharaoh's life, I swear it.'

'I'll tell you, then. But only you.'

Sobek was about to protest, but he was silenced by a

gesture from Kenhir. Nefer and Hay walked off towards the village.

Hay said, 'You may find it hard to believe, but before becoming a Servant of the Place of Truth I was a rather disreputable youth. Among the girls I knew before I came here, there was one I never forgot. A little while ago she wrote to tell me she was suffering from a serious illness, so I decided to go and see her; for obvious reasons, I had to do so in the greatest secrecy. Today, I was present at her last moments.' His voice was unsteady; he cleared his throat and went on, 'I can understand your suspecting me, because behaviour like that doesn't fit with what you know of me; and yet it is the truth. There must be no shadow of doubt between us, so I insist that you check what I've said.'

'Hay is innocent,' Nefer told Kenhir and Sobek.

'How can we be sure?' asked Sobek.

'By going to the east bank.'

'I shall come with you.'

'I promised Hay that I'd go alone to the place he told me about. His explanation was more than enough to make me sure of his innocence.'

'It could be a trap,' warned Sobek.

'Hay told the truth. I have nothing to fear.'

'As Master, you do not have the right to run such risks,' said Kenhir.

'If I don't, you'll go on suspecting of Hay and we won't feel confident about working with him. Since I know how to prove him innocent, I shall not change my mind.'

'You're forgetting one important detail,' Sobek reminded him. 'Who insisted that I did not tell anyone about the shadow-eater's presence within the Brotherhood? Hay. Him again!'

'Let us go and consult the Wise Woman,' suggested Kenhir.

*

Hay was ordered to stay in his house, and the craftsmen were told that he was ill and that Nefer would therefore direct the final work on Meneptah's temple.

As soon as the crews had a rest day, the Master left the village after the dawn rites, followed at a good distance by Paneb, whom the Wise Woman had asked to protect her husband.

If Hay had lied, Nefer would fall into a trap which had been set for a long time. Thus, even unmasked, the traitor would have his revenge.

As he'd promised, Nefer had refused to reveal where he was going; despite Sobek's repeated accusations, he remained convinced of Hay's innocence. In all the years they'd known each other, they'd never quarrelled; Hay had never shown jealousy of Nefer's rise, and he had both carried out the Master's plans and shared his views. Hay was austere and authoritarian, it was true, but no member of the port crew had any cause to complain about him, for he followed the path of righteousness.

On the ferry, Nefer found himself in the middle of a flock of goats. The herdsman explained that he hoped to sell them, for a good price, to the head of the herds at Karnak, for animals of this quality should serve none but Amon.

Paneb judged such company preferable to that of a crowd in which the Master might have been lost. Enlivened by a quarrel between two housewives about an inheritance, the crossing took place without problems, and Nefer disembarked with the goats.

Following him was not easy, for there was a swarm of people on the riverbank; a cargo boat laden with fresh fruit had just docked, and the citizens were having a heated discussion about the prices. Nefer forced his way through, though not without difficulty, and Paneb had to make vigorous use of his elbows so as not to lose sight of him.

'You might at least say "Excuse me",' protested a water-carrier. 'You almost knocked me over!'

'That's true. I saw it all,' chimed in an onion-seller; and he was instantly backed up by several idlers who hadn't even been there.

Paneb could have knocked them down, but that might have unleashed a general riot and attracted the intervention of the security guards. Fists tightly clenched, he apologized, and the tension eased.

But Nefer had disappeared.

73

Paneb had questioned dozens of people, but in vain. Not sure what to do next, he paced up and down the riverbank, which was now deserted. Should he return to the village to warn Kenhir and set a search in motion, or should he explore the winding streets himself? But he had no idea which direction to take.

He was furious with himself. He had failed lamentably in his duty. If anything happened to Nefer, he'd be entirely to blame, and he'd banish himself from the Brotherhood to lead the most miserable of lives.

No, there was something better he could do: avenge his friend and adoptive father. He would rip out of Hay the names of his accomplices; not one would escape. Paneb's sole ambition would be to make them pay for their crime, in this life and without delay. And neither the security guards nor the judges would stop him.

The soft light of the sunset made the Nile sparkle. Overhead soared hundreds of swallows. Suddenly, Paneb made out the figure of a man coming out of an alleyway. The sun was in his eyes, and he couldn't see clearly, but it looked like Nefer. He couldn't believe it: it was a miracle. He ran towards the figure.

'It's you, it's really you!' he exclaimed joyfully.

'Have I changed so much since this morning?'

'I lost you, do you realize? I don't deserve to belong to the Brotherhood any more.'

'What a peculiar idea! In my opinion you protected me perfectly, and I can't see anyone daring to claim otherwise.'

'Why were you so long?'

'A few problems to sort out, to give a family in distress a little comfort. I had to approach a government department, and that's always complicated; but the result should be satisfactory.'

'Does that mean Hay's innocent?'

'Did you ever doubt it?'

With his habitual care for others, Nefer had obtained an allowance for the aged parents of the dead woman; she had been faithful to her memories of Hay. The two crew-leaders now shared a secret which strengthened their bonds yet further. Sobek had apologized to Hay, and Hay, far from gloating at the commander's humiliation, had assured him that he understood his attitude and bore no resentment.

Ubekhet cooked a special dinner to celebrate the happy ending of the affair, and all the main players attended and joined in the jollity – or almost all. Kenhir looked doleful.

'Is the beef not to your liking?' asked Ubekhet.

'It's perfect, but nothing has been resolved. Of course, I rejoice greatly that Hay's innocence has been proved, but the real criminal has managed to stay hidden in the shadows. And why are we still waiting for the king's orders about the sarcophagi?'

'Worry about those things tomorrow, Kenhir. Like you, I'm very aware of the dangers that threaten us; but this evening we're celebrating our rediscovered harmony.'

Kenhir could never resist Ubekhet's charm, and he grumbled for a only few minutes longer before putting aside his cares and allowing himself to share in the joy of the occasion.

*

Panting, Fened rushed into the Scribe of the Tomb's office. 'A message . . . from the palace! Uputy's just brought . . . a message from the palace!'

A few minutes later Uputy arrived and handed Kenhir a scroll sealed with the royal seal. Kenhir broke the seal and quickly read the text.

'Good news?' asked Fened anxiously.

'Excellent!'

Forgetting his walking-stick, Kenhir hurried as fast as he could go to the Master's house. 'Nefer, you must assemble all the craftsmen. Meneptah's order has arrived. See, here it is.'

Nefer read the scroll, whose message was clear: the moment had come to take the sarcophagi down into the tomb.

So they could be sure no one would overhear them, Mehy and Serketa had taken a boat out on the small lake in the grounds of their house. Reclining languidly in her seat, Serketa watched Mehy admiringly as he rowed.

'The crisis seems to be over,' he said. 'Meneptah has recovered from his illness, the quarrels over the succession have calmed down, Seti has been appointed head of the armed forces, and Amenmessu is continuing his gilded exile in Thebes. I've been confirmed in my two positions, with the tjaty's congratulations. In other words, we have peace and stability.'

'Don't be downhearted, my sweet: that's only the official version. The king is still getting old and he won't regain the vigour of a young man. As to the plots, they'll soon begin again. Young Amenmessu is pawing the ground with impatience, and Seti must be kicking his heels and hoping Meneptah will die before long.'

'You always know how to give me hope, my little quail.'

'You are promised to a great destiny, Mehy, and trifling obstacles will not prevent you from realizing it. Let us keep to our plan, sowing trouble and reaping profit from the situation. Day after day, we must turn Amenmessu more strongly against his father, without losing the trust of either. Isn't that the lesson you taught me?'

'You are my best pupil.'

'The best – and the only one.'

Serketa took off her dress and lay down on her back, caressing her breasts. Mehy let go of the oars and flung himself on her, eager to accept her invitation to pleasure.

Three sarcophagi in pink granite: that was how the 'masters of life' were presented, the stone boats in which would rest King Meneptah's mummy, his Osiran body which would serve as a basis for the process of resurrection.

The sarcophagi were covered with texts and pictures of protective deities. At the bottom of the smallest one, which would be in direct contact with the royal mummy, sticks, weapons, pieces of fabric and other ritual objects had been engraved; inside the lid was the sky-goddess, Nut, whose robe was covered with stars, and who would bring the pharaoh to rebirth among the constellations.

The outer sarcophagus, which was some eight cubits long, showed Meneptah lying inside the oval of the universe, his arms crossed and holding the symbols of his office, the good shepherd's crook and the flagellum made in three stylized parts, evoking the threefold birth: subterranean, solar and celestial. Around all was an immense snake, the expression of sacred time and of the vital cycles whose harmony would remain perceptible as long as a pharaoh enabled Ma'at to reign on earth.

Paneb took the greatest care to check the sledges and the ropes.

'Don't you trust me?' asked Casa indignantly.

'Two pairs of eyes are better than one.'

'You seem to be getting involved in things that don't concern you . . . My work has been done well, and it doesn't need checking.'

'All the same, add another rope – you can never tell.'

Casa's big eyes were stormy, but Paneb was wise enough to get out of his way. The stone-cutter checked the ropes on the first sarcophagus and, all the time softly cursing the young giant, added another one.

At the entrance to the tomb stood the Wise Woman, who spoke the hieroglyphic incantations written in the stone, and so brought them to life for all eternity.

The sledge was ready to begin its descent into the depths. It was itself a hieroglyph which served to spell out the name of the creator, Atum, He Who Is and he Who Is Not; and when a stone was placed on the sledge, a new hieroglyph was formed: 'miracle, marvel'. In fact, by the magic of the creator, the miracle happened once again; the sarcophagus destined to receive Meneptah's body was transformed both into a matrix capable of restoring life and into a boat which would convey the reborn pharaoh through the landscapes of the otherworld. As it passed along the 'passageways of the god', pace by pace, the sarcophagus would become impregnated with all the symbols and incantations present in the house of eternity.

The Wise Woman spoke the words of protection so that the voyage would be a happy one, and the Master gave the signal to begin.

Thick ropes, checked by Casa, had been coiled round a small stone pillar, the other ends enwrapping the sarcophagus on its sledge. Casa, Nakht, Karo and Fened began to let the ropes out slowly, and the sarcophagus began its descent.

Suddenly, the pace quickened.

'Too fast!' yelled Nefer.

The four stone-cutters had done nothing wrong, but they could not control the enormous weight, which continued to gather speed. Paneb rushed into the tomb, almost slipping as he reached the sledge, grabbed the extra rope Casa had tied to the back and pulled on it with all his strength to slow it down.

His muscles bulged until he thought they would burst, and the sledge came to a halt.

'Blocks, quickly!' he gasped.

The stone-cutter ran to get wedges and slipped them under the sledge's runners, and Paneb was able to let go of the rope.

'You prevented a disaster,' Nefer told him.

As he walked back up towards the tomb entrance, Paneb ran his finger over the ground.

'Sabotage,' he whispered in the Master's ear. 'Someone spread colourless grease on the ground.'

Nefer was devastated. Not only had the shadow-eater not given up doing harm, but he was even prepared to ruin the Great Work.

74

'A new tjaty has just been appointed,' the Scribe of the Tomb told the Master.

'Do you know him?'

'No, he's a man of the North, who will probably delegate most of his powers to Mehy, as governor of the west bank. In any case, he seems friendly to us; he has congratulated me on the completion of Meneptah's tomb and temple. And he isn't content with fine words: to celebrate both our success and his appointment, he is sending us a hundred and fifty donkeys laden with food! Yet more work for me, to register all these provisions . . . But if we bestir ourselves, we'll organize a celebration the village will not forget in a hurry. You don't look very happy about it.'

'I can't forget the shadow-eater.'

'You've succeeded, Nefer, and he has failed. Meneptah's temple has been consecrated, and is working, and his house of eternity is a marvel. Your reputation as Master is firmly established, the two crews admire and like you, and everyone knows the Wise Woman's magic is protecting the village. So let's forget the shadow-eater, at least for a little while, and rejoice in our happiness.'

'I wonder what our next mission will be?' mused Nefer.

'We'll speak of it when the time comes. Now it's time for you to rest and celebrate.'

*

The information spread through the province of Thebes, then rapidly reached the entire country; once again, the Place of Truth had completed its Great Work without a hitch. The monuments vital for the validity of a reign had been completed and, even if only a handful of Egyptians would be allowed to see them, everyone knew that their presence was maintaining the link between the gods and men, between celestial harmony and social unity.

Paneb would always remember Meneptah's sarcophagus, placed upon a bed of gilded stone, in the secrecy of the chamber of resurrection. Like his brothers, he had the feeling that he had taken part in the royal eternity; returning to daily life, at once so close to and so far from the Valley where the pharaohs lived another life, had been a real shock.

But he had to prepare for the celebration, restore some housefronts and play with his son, who was learning arithmetic with Pai and Gau, but showed no taste at all for reading or for the tales in which his mother tried to interest him. He was quite fond of drawing, and he could already defend himself in wrestling-bouts against considerably older friends.

Uabet continued to be happy in her own way and asked nothing more from life than what it gave her. But when she saw Paneb smashing her bed apart, she became afraid. Was her cosy little world breaking apart for some reason she could not understand?

'Stop, I beg you!' she cried.

'Too late, Uabet. My decision is final.'

She had dreaded hearing those words one day; neither her love nor even his son could hold Paneb back if he had chosen to leave his home.

'You . . . you're really going to leave?'

'Leave? Who said anything about leaving?'

'Then . . . why . . .?'

'You can't go on sleeping on a bed like this – it is very bad for your back. Use this second-rate wood for heating the house. I'm going to make a bed worthy of my wife.'

She smiled through tears.

'What's the matter?' asked Paneb. 'Are you ill?'

'On the contrary, I feel very well . . . and touched.'

'Look what Didia gave me.' Paneb showed her a hand-drill for use on wood. It was worked by means of a bow whose curvature varied according to the craftsman's movements. 'Didia told me the curvature isn't just found by chance. A good carpenter obtains it by making the branch of a tree grow the right way. Now, to work.'

When she saw the result, Uabet was delighted: her new bed would have made a Theban noblewoman woman green with envy. At first she scarcely dared even sit on the new mattress, but she soon lost her nervousness. She slid the straps of her dress off her shoulders and lay down.

'Would you like to try it out with me?' she asked gently.

It was a perfect day, with a gentle sun, a light wind, and no sick people to care for; and Nefer had at last agreed to take some rest.

After celebrating the morning rites, Ubekhet had dozed off on the terrace, dreaming of her happy years in the village and the radiant love she had the good fortune to experience. Not for a single moment had she regretted setting off on this remarkable adventure, even if the daily work was more demanding than anywhere else.

Footsteps and loud laughter awoke her. They seemed to be coming towards her house. Ubekhet went down the stairs, and was surprised to find that her husband was not there. Curious, she opened the door and found herself face to face with him, at the head of a procession of all the villagers.

The laughter stopped when he presented her with a jewellery-box with four feet and a sliding lid. Decorated with tiny gold tiles, it was an enchanting little work of art.

'Permit the village to offer you this gift,' said Nefer. 'We wish to honour the Wise Woman, who takes care of everyone, day after day. May this box be the expression of our respect and our love.'

Ubekhet was moved to tears. There was such a lump in her throat that she couldn't utter a single word.

'Long life to the Wise Woman!' shouted Paneb in his warm, deep voice. And all the villagers joined in.

'I won't do it,' said Nefer.

'I must insist,' said Kenhir.

'You go in my place. You know how much I hate official ceremonies.'

'Mehy wishes to congratulate you in the presence of all the leading citizens of Thebes, and I can't replace you.'

'Tell him I'm too busy,'

'You must go, Nefer, if we want to know what the future holds for us. This won't be an ordinary handing-out of decorations, I feel sure. Mehy will use the occasion to talk to us about confidential matters, so we may find out some of our future tasks.'

'And what if it proves to be nothing but a society fancy-dress party?'

'He wouldn't have invited you. What's more, through you, the Place of Truth will be honoured and strengthened. Shouldn't you sacrifice yourself for the general good?'

'You're a formidable debater, Kenhir,' grumbled Nefer.

'Just an old scribe who loves his village and wants to keep it safe. In spite of yourself, Nefer, you've become a very important person, and this official recognition will give us extra protection.'

Ubekhet agreed with Kenhir, so Nefer reluctantly attended the ceremony, which was held in the open-air courtyard of

Meneptah's temple. Nefer had to dress elegantly, as had Kenhir, whose wide-sleeved festival robe was most striking.

Not one leading citizen of the rich city of Thebes was missing from the audience. Completely at ease, Mehy first recalled the early career of the Scribe of the Tomb, then congratulated him on his excellent management of the Brotherhood, and voiced the hope that he would continue in office for as long as possible.

Then he called upon Nefer, who was deeply embarrassed to become the centre of interest.

'The Master of the Place of Truth had a particularly difficult mission to accomplish,' said Mehy. 'Everyone knows that he dislikes leaving the village, but his reputation has spread beyond its walls. It therefore seemed necessary that, through me, Thebes should honour the man who has made it still more beautiful and more prestigious by creating His Majesty's house of eternity and the temple where we are standing. Nefer the Silent is at once a leader of men and an architect of genius. With the approval of the pharaoh, I present him with the Golden Collar and, in the name of you all, I embrace him.'

Nefer stood rooted to the spot, and did not allow himself even the ghost of a smile.

That night Mehy gave a sumptuous banquet at his house. It was very late when the guests eventually left. The general asked Nefer and Kenhir to come to his office, where artfully arranged lamps gave off an intimate glow.

'Peace at last, my friends! I share your dislike of this kind of worldly event, but unfortunately they're essential.'

'Why wasn't the tjaty here?' asked Kenhir.

'Officially he is detained in Pi-Ramses, but he gave me instructions concerning you. I am not to give them to you in writing, and they will not feature in any official document. This trust has honoured me greatly, I confess, and I am extremely proud to share, even in a small way, in the secret of your new work.'

'Go on,' said Kenhir.

'King Meneptah commands you, as in the past, to prepare the tombs of the inhabitants of the village and to maintain them. As soon as possible, you are to go to the Valley of the Queens and the Valley of the Nobles to begin work on the houses of eternity listed here.'

Mehy handed Kenhir a rolled papyrus, bearing several royal seals, together with the seal of the tjaty, along with a date.

Kenhir slid it into his left sleeve. 'Is there anything else?'

'My work is done, and I am sure that you'll do yours to perfection.'

Kenhir and Nefer withdrew; Nefer had said not a word.

Mehy found it difficult to bear the silence of this Master, whose honest, penetrating gaze made him uncomfortable. Exploiting whatever weaknesses he had would not be easy.

75

As the tenth year of Meneptah's reign began, the Place of Truth's tranquil happiness was tarnished by a sad loss: the death of Ebony, who died quietly in Ubekhet's arms. As upset as his wife, Nefer embalmed the dog and made him an acacia-wood coffin. The faithful witness to their love would wait on the other bank and guide them along the pathways of the afterworld. As luck would have it, Ebony's spitting image had been born in a litter of three pups, and Ubekhet adopted him straight away.

The port crew were working in the Valley of the Queens, the starboard crew in the Valley of the Nobles; and Paneb was finishing a picture of an offertory table in dazzling colours which had won him general admiration. Sides of beef, bunches of grapes, a trussed goose, lettuce, strings of onions and round loaves were assembled into a harmonious composition which delighted the eye.

'Your brush is more alive than mine,' said Ched, who was more than happy with his pupil's progress. He had given Paneb no respite in several months, so that he could master the secrets of the craft.

'Is that a criticism?'

'Sometimes, as with this offertory table, it is a compliment; it is good that the food destined for the soul of the deceased, which will be ceaselessly renewed thanks to this painting, should burst with gaiety and luxuriance. But you still lack gravity of spirit – no doubt the trials of life will instil it in you, if your pride doesn't destroy you first.'

Ched went back to his own work, ignoring Paneb's indignant glare.

'What stage have you reached, Daktair?' asked Mehy.

Daktair tugged the red hairs of his beard, his little black eyes shining with satisfaction. 'I've succeeded,' he said smugly, 'and you were right to trust in me. We have at our disposal a large quantity of arrowheads whose piercing-power is twice that of the ones we have been using up to now.'

'You should do better.'

'But I'm still making progress. If I tell you I've succeeded, it is not a boast. I've lightened the points of the spears and increased their efficiency at the moment of impact. They'll reach targets much further away, and still with remarkable precision. But I'm proudest of all of the short swords with the double cutting-edge. I have used foreign blacksmiths' methods and improved on them. The soldier who wields this sword will tire less quickly than his opponents and, even if he only wounds them, they will be unable to fight on. You cannot even imagine the power of this weapon.'

'I am going to check it myself,' said Mehy, 'and then I shall train my best men to form an elite regiment.'

'Will you tell Prince Amenmessu?

'He already knows enough. On my advice, he is showing himself a great deal in Theban high society, which is beginning to take him to its heart. But the right timing depends more than ever on caution.'

'We seem to be getting less and less news from the capital,' complained Daktair.

'According to my spies, peace is firmly maintained in Syria and Canaan, and Seti will shortly be inspecting the region with a large number of troops to discourage any wish to rebel. The best news is that the king will soon be seventy-five.'

'His father lived to be much older than that.'

'Indeed, but Meneptah seldom shows himself any more, even at official ceremonies where his presence is desirable. His health must be failing.'

Daktair took pleasure in puncturing the general's hopes. 'Since you strengthened the reputation of the Place of Truth, it seems unassailable.'

'That's what the Brotherhood believes, not realizing that this period of calm precedes a storm whose ferocity I can sense. Amenmessu will rise up against Seti, and father and son will tear each other apart.'

Daktair looked bored. 'I'm not interested in those disputes. All I want is to remain in charge of this workshop.'

'You try to deceive yourself, but your ambitions are as alive as mine. Contrary to what you think, I was right to show patience and strengthen my position. No pharaoh can do without Thebes; and when Meneptah dies he will take with him the last shreds of Ramses' greatness. That's when we shall act. And none of the secrets of the Place of Truth will escape me.'

Casa's wife had decided she wanted no more children, so Ubekhet began preparing a preventative based on crushed acacia-thorns. Suddenly, her head started to spin. She thought at first that it was a passing malaise, but a painful sensation of fatigue forced her to lie down on the bed where, ordinarily, her patients stretched out.

When Nefer came to look for her, worried that she had not come home, he found her asleep and gently woke her by stroking her hair.

'I'm exhausted,' she confessed.

'Do you want me to call a doctor from outside?'

'No, there's no need. I have lost too much magnetism these last weeks, and the Wise Woman taught me how to cure myself. I must climb to the summit of the Peak of the West.'

'Wouldn't a good night's sleep be better?'

'Help me, will you?'

Nefer had known for a long time that it was pointless to struggle against this smiling will, which had seduced him from the very first moment.

'If you find you can't manage the climb,' he said, 'will you let me bring you home?'

'If you'll help me, I shall succeed.'

Under the starry vault they climbed arm in arm, step by step. Ubekhet did not take her eyes off the peak, as if she was absorbing the mysterious energy emanating from it as it loomed over the west bank. Neither of them gave a thought to the effort needed to reconquer the sacred mountain, whose call must be answered.

Reaching the shrine at the summit, they gazed at the pole star, around which the ever-living stars formed a celestial court.

'Grant me a favour,' begged Nefer. 'Whatever happens, don't leave this earth before me. Without you, I couldn't do even the smallest tasks.'

'That is for destiny to decide. But I do know that nothing, and certainly not death, will separate us. The love that unites us for ever, and the adventure we're experiencing, will overcome it.'

When dawn broke, Ubekhet collected the dew of the sky-goddess, with which she had washed the face of the reborn sun, and moistened her lips with it. In this way she would regain the energy necessary to care for the villagers.

After talking with the leader of the lay workers, Kenhir judged that the incident was serious enough for the two crew-leaders and the Wise Woman to be told of it.

'The price of pork has just risen sharply, and that's a worrying sign of economic instability,' he explained. 'The prices of other foodstuffs will go up, too, and the rations allocated to us by the tjaty will be reduced accordingly.'

'Shouldn't we consult him as soon as possible?' said Hay.

'The tjaty is staying in Pi-Ramses. I'll write to him there to let him know of the situation. I suggest that we should react by raising the price of every object, from statuettes to sarcophagi, which we make for the outside world.'

'But then won't the farmers and traders have to put their prices up again?'

'There's a risk of that, yes, but we can't let ourselves be faced with a crisis. And I shan't hide from you the fact that this situation worries me. Let us hope it's only a temporary disturbance, not the prelude to a grave economic crisis in which the village won't be spared.'

'Are our granaries well-stocked?' asked Ubekhet anxiously.

'I've always been cautious,' said Kenhir, 'and I felt it was as well to build up big reserves in case bad times came. Considering the guarantees we've been given by the state, I shouldn't have had even to think of doing so. Today, I'm glad I did.'

'Shouldn't the government of the west bank take steps to deal with the situation?' asked Nefer.

'Mehy will surely not remain idle, but we need to know why the pork-sellers are behaving like this.'

'Because of fear,' suggested the Wise Woman.

'What are they afraid of?'

'For the last few days, a wind of fear has been blowing across the valley and it's troubling people.'

'Does that concern us?' asked Hay.

'No one will escape it,' replied Ubekhet.

The sandstorm had raged through the night, forcing the villagers to block all the openings in their houses. The sun could not break through the heavy yellow clouds, and the morning rites had been delayed. It was impossible to see more than five paces ahead, and the trip to fetch water was an onerous one.

Many people had sore eyes, so the Wise Woman prepared several phials of eye-drops, with different dosages according to the seriousness of the inflamation.

'I shall ask Kenhir to shorten the working day while the storm lasts,' Nefer told his wife, 'and we'll restrict ourselves to the village tombs.'

Little Ebony had settled himself on the Master's knee, making it very clear to him that he was not permitted to move. The puppy was so well-behaved that he did not even chew the legs of the furniture, and he happily wolfed down the mixture of meat, cheese, vegetables and bread that Ubekhet prepared for him. He had the same hazel eyes and lively intelligence as his predecessor.

'You are very worried, aren't you?' said Nefer.

'The wind is abnormally strong. Its flurries contain a kind of madness, the bearer of destruction.'

There was a knock at the door, and Kenhir's voice called, 'Open up quickly.' Nefer hurried to obey.

The old man was leaning heavily on his walking-stick, and his head was covered by a hood.

'What's happened?' asked Nefer.

'Uputy braved this damned storm to bring us tragic news. King Meneptah has just died.'

76

Standing before all the villagers, the Master spoke the ritual words contained in the official message sent by the palace to the Place of Truth.

'The pharaoh's soul has taken flight towards the sky to be united with the solar disc, to meld with its divine master and rejoin the creator. Henceforth, Meneptah, of just voice, will dwell in the realm of Light. May the sun shine once more, while the whole land waits for the new Horus who will ascend the throne of the living.'

Faces were grave; no one dared ask the question on everyone's mind. No one, that is, except Paneb.

'What fate lies in store for us?'

'The Place of Truth answers to no one but the pharaoh,' Kenhir reminded him.

'Who will succeed Meneptah?'

'Probably his son, Seti.'

Everyone wondered whether, with such a formidable name, the new king would manage to master the power of Set, the god of storms, lord of the thunder.

'If he reigns,' predicted Karo, 'this will be a terrible period and we must fear the worst.'

'Why are you so pessimistic?' inquired Gau.

'Because no one can take on the name of Seti, the father of Ramses. No king dared bear it before him, and no other should have imitated him.'

'I've heard it whispered that Prince Amenmessu covets supreme power,' ventured Nakht.

'Stop tormenting yourselves,' advised Pai. 'Whatever happens, a pharaoh will reign, and he will order us to build his temple of a million years and dig his tomb in the Valley of the Kings.'

'Unless civil war breaks out,' suggested Paneb, and his words made everyone shiver.

Civil war . . . At last, the traitor felt hope rise again. Because of Meneptah, he had had to lurk in the background, he who hoped to benefit as quickly as possible from the fortune he had accumulated outside the village. Everyone had said Meneptah was weak, but he had saved Egypt from invasion and supported the Place of Truth without showing a sign of weakness. Would Seti II follow the same path, or would he give way beneath the weight of an office too heavy for him, especially if his own son, Amenmessu, rose up against him?

In the event of civil war, the Place of Truth would necessarily be weakened and would lose some of its magnificence. Its safety would be less and less well assured, and the traitor could act more effectively. To discover the Stone of Light's hiding-place, he would systematically search the village, taking precautions to ensure he was not spotted. A period of lawlessness would leave his hands free.

'Until the new order is established,' said the Master, 'we are under the protection of Commander Sobek and his guards, and you have nothing to fear. The Scribe of the Tomb and I will consult Mehy to learn as much as we can about what is happening. While you await our return, do not leave the village.'

'And what if you don't come back?' demanded Paneb.

Fened said angrily, 'How dare you envisage such a tragedy?'

'If rival factions clash, even the surroundings of the Place of Truth will not be very safe.'

'If we don't come back,' said Nefer, 'the Wise Woman will rule the village.'

The wind was beginning to drop, visibility was improving, and the west bank of Thebes seemed calm. Little by little, the peasants were returning to the fields, and the animals were being taken out of their stables. Housewives were energetically sweeping out sand which, despite their precautions, had got into every nook and cranny.

Many soldiers were cleaning the great courtyard, which was surrounded by the central government buildings.

An officer stopped the two visitors. 'Where are you going?'

'To see General Mehy,' replied Kenhir.

'By what right?'

'The right of the Scribe of the Tomb.'

'Please forgive me. But I'm afraid the general isn't here.'

'Where is he?'

'I'm sorry,' said the officer, 'but I'm not permitted to disclose that to civilians.'

'Have you had any instructions concerning the Place of Truth?'

'No, none.'

'When will the general be back?'

'I don't know.'

Kenhir and Nefer set off back to the village; they were far from reassured.

Prince Amenmessu was drunk with rage. 'If I understand you correctly, General Mehy, you are keeping me prisoner in this apartment.'

'Of course not, Prince. My only concern is your safety.'

'But I'm not free to come and go.'

'During this period of uncertainty, it is necessary to keep you safe, under the protection of the Theban army.'

'I want to take command of that army, and leave to attack the capital.'

'Think, Prince, I beg of you. A war between North and South would result in thousands of deaths and would weaken Egypt so gravely that she would become easy prey for her enemies.'

'As soon as my father is proclaimed pharaoh, I shall be reduced to no more than a cipher!'

'We've had no news from Pi-Ramses. Perhaps Seti will recall you there,' suggested Mehy.

'If he did, it would be to kill me!'

'Why do you assume he has such dark designs?'

'Because supreme power is in the balance. Certain dreams will be realized, others will be broken for ever: and I will never relinquish mine. Whether you like it or not, confrontation between Seti and myself is inevitable. Either my father gives up the throne, or I shall refuse to recognize his authority and have myself crowned here, at Thebes. And everyone will have to take sides.'

'I bow to your authority, Prince, but I beg you to stay here in the barracks until Seti's official decisions are known.'

'Very well, General, but keep the troops on alert.'

Mehy withdrew, very satisfied with the turn events were taking. He had feared that the young prince would bow the knee too quickly before his father; but it seemed that, on the contrary, Meneptah's death had doubled Amenmessu's ambition. Mehy must calm him down. It would require skill and intelligence to set the two men against each other, while at the same time making each believe Mehy was his staunchest ally.

That very evening, Mehy would send a highly confidential letter to Pi-Ramses, indicating to Seti that his son's behaviour threatened to become dangerous. A faithful servant of the state, the general would say that his only goal was the country's peace and prosperity.

Whatever the outcome of the struggle, he, Mehy, would emerge the victor, thanks to the many weapons at his disposal. And one of the first victims he would strip without pity was the Place of Truth.

'What, no dried fish?' Nakht was astonished. 'Are you really sure?'

'If you don't believe me,' replied his wife, 'go and see for yourself.'

The stone-cutter strode up to the main gate, where several housewives had gathered.

'Haven't the fishmongers delivered?' he asked.

'Neither the fishmongers nor the butchers,' replied Fened's ex-wife.

Nakht went at once to Kenhir's house, where the Master, Paneb and other craftsmen had assembled and were complaining loudly.

'That's enough,' growled Kenhir. 'These complaints are pointless.'

'Tell us the truth,' demanded Paneb.

'Our food deliveries have been stopped,' said Kenhir in an ominous voice. 'But we have several weeks' provisions stored up.'

'You must do something,' insisted Casa. 'You must tell the tjaty and the king.'

'Which king?' asked Thuty ironically. 'The truth is that we've been abandoned. The soldiers will soon expel us and occupy the village.'

'No one is authorized to enter,' Paneb reminded him.

'You surely don't think we could resist?'

'Why so pessimistic?' asked Didia. 'The government's in disarray, certainly, but why should the new pharaoh be hostile to us?'

'We shouldn't speculate like this,' said Nefer. 'There is a great deal of delayed work to be done.'

He shared out the tasks between the shrines, the tombs and the houses. Improving their homes reassured the craftsmen and made them forget their worries for a time. Traditional songs were even heard, giving a rhythm to the work of peaceful days, as if the danger was receding.

The Master gazed at the place where the Stone of Light was hidden. For many generations of craftsmen, it had been passed on faithfully, to allow the work to be accomplished; but it seemed that this miracle was on the point of ending.

Ubekhet came up to him and, like him, marvelled at this priceless treasure.

'I need to talk to the Wise Woman,' said Nefer.

'You want to resign your office, don't you?'

'Not because of cowardice, or fear of facing the storm, but because my work is done. Hay has all the qualities needed to succeed me.'

'All except one: he isn't a leader of men, so he wouldn't make a good Master. There are dark times ahead, and it will take more than an excellent craftsman to defend the village and save what must be saved. Neither the gods nor the Brotherhood leave you any choice, Nefer. Forget yourself and continue fulfilling the office for which you were chosen.'

Ubekhet raised her eyes to the Peak of the West. 'Can't you hear it calling, with ever-greater intensity? Its voice fills the sky, and its generosity knows no limits. Hear its words, and put them into practice.'

Nefer took his wife in his arms and held her close. With her love, he might perhaps manage to overcome the darkness and save the Stone of Light.